LINDSEY N. RHODEN

A TETHER THROUGH THE RIFT

BOOK 1

For more information on Lindsey N. Rhoden's work, visit www.lindseynrhoden.com

Cover design: Etheric Tales

Interior illustrations: Mithlista

Map Design: Azura Arts

To my husband who's always been there to help me find my way out of the darkness. And to anyone who's ever had to do the same.

Content Warnings

A Tether Through The Rift is an adult fantasy novel that contains strong language, mention of suicide, strong themes of anxiety and depression throughout, brief mention of sexual assault (not on page), descriptions of torture, death on page. Some of this content may be triggering to individuals and should be taken into account before reading. If you are struggling with anxiety, depression, or suicidal ideation, please don't hesitate to reach out to one of these national mental health agencies, or find an agency local to you for those not in the US. Your mental health matters and you don't have to suffer alone.

988 Suicide & Crisis Lifeline – free and confidential 24/7 emotional support to people in suicidal crisis or emotional distress
Call or text 988 or chat 988lifeline.org

MHA Crisis Text Line – free, text based support 24/7
Text MHA to 741741

The Trevor Project – national 24 hour, toll free confidential suicide hotline for LGBTQ youth
Call 1-866-488-7386 or text START to 678678

Town
The
The Cottage
The
The Rift

TALAMH OF TIR NADAAR
Meadow
Crystal Spring
House
Gate
The Lake
Dark Woods
Daravaana, Kahlis' Lands
N
W
E
S

Playlist

- **LOSE CONTROL**
  TEDDY SWIMS

- **DARLING DIVINE**
  WILD CHILD

- **SALT AND THE SEA**
  THE LUMINEERS

- **BANKS**
  NEEDTOBREATHE

- **STORY**
  KINGS KALEIDOSCOPE

- **I CAN'T GO ON WITHOUT YOU**
  KALEO

- **YOU'RE GONNA BE OK**
  JENN JOHNSON

- **WORK SONG**
  HOZIER

- **SIMPLY THE BEST**
  NOAH REID

Pronunciation

TIR NADAAR	TEER NAH–DAHR
TALAMH	TALAV
SGÀIL	SGAːL
STRATOS	STRAH–TOHS
VATR	VAH–TER
SCALDOR	SKAHL–DOR
AURIS	AWR–IHS
KAHLIS	KAH–LEES
HAZLENN	HAZ–LIN
AERMIDH	AIR–MIHD
KIRWAN	KEER–WINN
MIRREN	MEER–EHN
CAILLEACH	KALʲəx
DAEOMI	DAY–OH–MY
COTHROM	KɔRəM

*SOME WORDS HAVE BEEN *INSPIRED* BY THE GAELIC LANGUAGE AND CELTIC FOLKLORE/MYTHOLOGY. PRONUNCIATIONS HAVE BEEN PULLED FROM LEARNGAELIC.SCOT/INDEX.JSP FOR APPLICABLE WORDS, HOWEVER THIS IS A WORK OF FICTION AND NOT ALL PRONUNCIATIONS WILL BE THE SAME AS THEIR CELTIC INSPIRED COUNTERPART. IF YOU HAVE ANY QUESTIONS ABOUT FURTHER PRONUNCIATION, PLEASE FEEL FREE TO REACH OUT TO ME VIA EMAIL OR ON INSTAGRAM.

CHAPTER 1
HAZEL

The wind was a bitter rush against my face, jolting me awake and pulling me back into the clutches of pain and terror vibrating through my body. I was flying. Long, leathery appendages dug into my body; claws ripped into my skin. I didn't need to open my eyes to know where I was, or at least to know what was happening to me.

It was a dream. That dream.

Slowly I forced my eyes open and peered down to the land looming below. I would have been more scared if it wasn't for that sight. I let loose a shaky breath, taking in every inch of that beautiful world flying past—like somehow I knew it was the last time I would see it. Breathtaking wasn't even good enough to describe it. Yet my breath hitched. It did every time I dreamt of it. My eyes pored over every extraordinary detail, desperate to hold on to any part of it, to find a way down into it. It was unlike anything I had ever seen in real life. I couldn't think of a single thing to compare it to. But here in my dreams, it lived.

Forests made of the deepest green I'd ever seen, endless seas of velvet grass flowing with the occasional wave of wildflowers, small cottages and vast estates made of stone and wood, so like the forests and meadows surrounding them. It was impossible to tell where nature ended and civilization began. Instead, it just merged together in a beautiful, fantastical cascade. I wanted to live here, to know here. But I couldn't stop flying. It was not my own strength that propelled me forward, but rather some dark force that held me, moved me against my will. I wanted to linger in the beautiful peace of that world below.

I didn't want to press on. I knew what came next.

And as quickly as it appeared, that world of deep greens and warm sunlight disappeared and I was plunged into darkness. It surrounded me—consumed me—as I plummeted down. My arms flailed for anything to grab onto, trying to save myself. I found nothing, just as I did every time this dream reared its ugly head. Next would come the screaming, like that of some dark creature desperately hungry and out for blood. Out for my blood. Even though I could barely see my hands through the darkness, I knew they were covered in the sticky, red liquid. I could smell the metallic tinge of its scent heavy in the air—could feel it dripping, heavy and slow down my arms. Whether it belonged to me or to someone—something else—I did not know.

I hit the ground with a sickening crunch that promised no less than one broken bone, trying desperately to get my feet underneath me and start running—running and tripping and falling over myself in a chaotic attempt to escape those screams. I knew my life depended on it. I didn't dare stop, despite the fact that my legs felt heavy as stone. A wave of terror hit me as I wondered if I was even moving at all. It seemed entirely possible that I was merely treading water, so to speak. My eyes squinted, trying to adjust to the emptiness around me. It was useless. There was no adjusting to pure darkness. That's what I had fallen into. Pure, relentless black. I kept running though, hands thrown out in front of me to keep from crashing. The screams were getting closer. The vibrations of its powerful stride rattled my bones as it tore through the space separating us. Those long, piercing claws I'd felt around me earlier were now nipping at my heels, my back. There was nothing I could do to get away, no hero coming to save me. I could feel my body relenting to the exhaustion pulling it under, could feel it slowing down and willing my mind to give up. Just as those cruel, taunting claws dug into my skin, I awoke.

I lay there for a few minutes, waiting for my mind to return to my body. It was like I was drifting between two worlds: not wholly in this one yet, still retreating from another. My mind was lost to whatever lived there. I'd had this dream for as long as I could remember. Which, if I was being honest, wasn't long. I couldn't remember anything prior to one year ago, when Arlo had found me out in the woods on his journey between towns. Anything prior to that was a complete mystery to me. When I felt my awareness return and was confident that I could stand up without fainting or puking, I swung my legs off the side of the bed and sat up, pressing my clammy palms into the hollows of my eyes. My head was pounding from the fear rushing through me.

I reminded myself I was safe. I was here. Just like Arlo taught me. I looked over to where he was lying in the bed, fast asleep and looking more perfect than ever. The lines of his face were more relaxed than when he was awake, his concern for me taking a momentary reprieve while he slept. I didn't know what I'd do without him. I wouldn't have survived long in this world if it weren't for him. I debated waking him, telling him

I had the dream again, but I thought twice and decided to go wash up instead. He had enough to deal with; he didn't need me running to him every time I had this nightmare.

I tiptoed over to the bathing room and eased the door closed, trying to soften the click of the latch. A bath was often my remedy for a night full of bad dreams and restless sleep, the comfort of water causing both my body and my mind to feel weightless. I turned the faucet handle all the way on and sat with my head in my hands while I waited for the tub to fill with the tepid water. Thoughts of pain and blood flooded my mind as soon as I closed my eyes. I fought back the tears as I took three deep breaths.

How could that pain feel so real? It was just a dream.

I blinked back the tears threatening to spill as I peeled off my sweat-soaked clothes and climbed in. The endless list of questions circled in my mind as the water coiled around my body. *Why does this nightmare haunt me? What does it mean? Who was I before I showed up here? Why do I feel like I don't belong, can't belong here?* I could feel the water reaching up to pull me under, and I welcomed it gladly. Despite the sweat that still clung to my skin, I found myself longing for warmth, wishing I had taken the extra time to heat a kettle and pour in the boiling water before I'd climbed in.

I sat there like that for a long time, long enough to let the feel of the water drown out the endless thoughts. When I felt like my mind had settled somewhat, I pulled the stopper for the drain and stepped out of the comfort of the bath and into the chilled air of the bathroom, wrapping a towel around my body to trap as much warmth as I could against my skin. I stared at myself in the stand up mirror situated in the corner of the room, the reflection disrupted somewhat by the speckled fogginess of the glass. My green eyes stared back at the pathetic image in unkind judgment. My auburn hair hung around me in wet, dripping clumps, circling my shoulders and falling down my back in deep red contrast to my skin which looked too light – too tired. The dark circles under my eyes reminded me of how little sleep I was getting these days. I breathed out a disheartened sigh, letting my gaze fall away from the mirror and down to the floor. I heard a soft knock and looked up to find Arlo leaning against the doorframe. His beautiful, slender form was backlit by the sunlight pouring in from our bedroom. I found myself incapable of focusing on anything other than the way he stood there, looking at me.

"Was it the dream again?" Arlo asked, concern etched on his face.

I nodded. I might be broken and dysfunctional, but with him standing there, the morning sunlight glowing around him like some sort of god, I didn't care about any of it. He was my silver lining, my light in the storm. He had an uncanny ability to pull me back from the edge of my darkness. And I hoped one day I could return the favor, although I doubted he would ever need it.

He pushed off the frame and took a few steps into the bathing room, wrapping a hand around the back of my head and kissing my brow.

"It's okay, Hazel. I've got you." He paused before adding, "You know it's not real, right?"

I nodded again. Although I didn't know how convinced I was that he was right, or how convincing I was to him with that nod.

"I know, it just *feels* so real. I don't know how to shake it when I wake up."

"This right here? This is real," he said. He hooked a finger under my chin, lifting it toward him, and kissed me. Soft at first, as if to make sure I'd allow it. Then deeper to remind me how real this was.

I smiled against his lips and kissed him back.

"Always the chivalrous knight," I said. "What would I do without you?"

"Be hopelessly bored, I'm sure. And not nearly as satisfied." He pulled back with a wink and placed his hands on my shoulders. "You are okay, though?"

His concern was more than genuine; I could see it on every inch of his sun-kissed face. It had been bad before... This wasn't like then. In my worst moments I'd struggled to understand what was real and what was just part of my dreams. I'd kicked and screamed at invisible threats and cowered in the darkness of our bedroom for fear of anything lying in wait beyond. He couldn't tell when I was okay or when I was getting bad again because the battle was in my mind. I constantly had to remind myself that he couldn't feel those emotions or hear those thoughts. That was my curse, not his.

"I'm fine, I promise. Just a rough night."

He eyed me for a minute, trying to decide whether to accept what I said or push me a little further.

"Good," he finally said, with one more kiss on my forehead. "I'll go make us some tea."

He turned to leave and I watched as his elegant form disappeared around the corner, into the kitchen. I inhaled a deep breath and sighed a little as I let it out. He was another question I hadn't figured out.

What had I ever done to deserve a man like him?

Something told me I'd never get the answer.

I emerged from the bedroom, dressed in my favorite cozy wool tunic and a pair of leggings. Arlo was measuring out tea leaves as I strode over to the bread and jam waiting on the middle counter and tossed a couple pieces of the loaf on to the stove eye to toast.

I took a minute to just watch him. His golden brown hair fell slightly on his forehead as he bent over our mugs, his amber eyes focused on the water he was pouring into them.

The memory of the day he found me slowly crept back into my mind. He'd had that same concentrated look in his eyes as he sized me up and tried to figure out what exactly he believed about me. He had found me, out of my mind and wandering in the middle of nowhere. I'd told him that I had no idea where I was, no idea *who* I was. I was trembling, covered in dirt and blood. I remembered that gleam in his eye, the recognition of utter terror, and what I felt was a wave of empathy washing over him. I was hysterical—completely inconsolable. Yet he helped me, believed me.

It was complete luck that he had found me at all; we were so far from any of the local towns. He walked me to the nearest village and got me seen by the healers. He insisted I get checked out to make sure I was okay. He stayed by my side the entire time, even as the Guard was brought in to question me, and even when I realized I had nowhere to go once the healers cleared me to leave. I never understood how someone could do that for a stranger. I asked him about that at one point, and he told me he just knew. He took one look at me and knew that he was meant to protect me, love me. That he had been put on my path that day, not by some coincidence but by some higher power that knew I needed him. I thought it sounded crazy at first, but he continued to prove how true that was on a daily basis.

I had needed him then, and I needed him now. The nightmares that haunted me constantly were like shredded remnants of that day refusing to let me move on.

He turned, two steaming mugs of tea in his hands, and cocked his head to the side.

"What?" he asked.

I shook the reverie from my mind and realized I was standing there like a fool with a jar of jam in one hand and a butter dish in the other, totally lost in the memory of that day.

"Nothing," I lied. "You just never cease to amaze me."

"Because I made us tea?" he asked with a little chuckle. "I mean, I know I make a good brew, but I promise my magical abilities stop there."

He glided over to our kitchen table and set down our mugs. I jumped a little as the smell of burning bread wafted through the kitchen, remembering what I was supposed to be doing. Grabbing the bread off the cast iron stove, I threw it down on our plates and juggled everything over to the table to sit down across from him.

"So, any plans today?" he asked.

I handed him a plate and started coating my toast in the creamy butter.

"Not much. I was thinking I may head down to the library, do some more digging."

I had become obsessed with digging for answers about my past, searching the town's records and archives for anything that was remotely similar to my situation. I devoured it with a desperate sort of hunger. If and when I couldn't find any more content to look over, or the weight of it all became too heavy, I'd wander the library's other sections and look for a good book to get lost in. Yet another one of my coping mechanisms, it would seem. I firmly believed there was nothing a bath, a good book, or a soothing cup of tea couldn't solve—aside from my memory loss, obviously.

Arlo paused mid-sip and gave me a quick, concerned glance. I knew what he was thinking. That I shouldn't spend so much time cooped up in the library. But I honestly didn't know what else to do with my time. Feeling at home in this town was hard enough, let alone trying to find a purpose along with it. I knew no one—had no family, no friends. All I had was my crusade to find answers about my past.

"Hazel, maybe it would be beneficial for you to find something better to fill your time with. Something healthier, I mean. I know you want answers, but there's only so much good poring over those archives is going to do."

I knew he was right, but I couldn't help rolling my eyes at yet another argument about it. He thought half the information I came home with was complete nonsense—just lore the locals came up with because they were bored and looking for extraordinary meaning in the ordinary, everyday events of our world. I wasn't sure if the stuff I had found was true or not, but I figured I'd take a look at anything that might give me even a clue about my past or what had happened to me.

"If it will make you happy, I'll limit my time there today. And I'll make sure to take a walk through the town on my way home." I knew this wasn't an argument he was going to win. He was always concerned about me digging, but he knew how much I needed answers. And he'd never stop me from doing something if my mind was set to it. He loved me too much to stand in the way like that.

"Alright, you drive a hard bargain," he said and gave me a little smirk. He took one last sip from his mug and stood up. "I need to get going. Be careful, and just come home if it gets to be too much out there."

He planted a kiss on the top of my head and walked out the front door.

I smiled, looking where he'd just been moments ago. Then, as my eyes trailed around the house, the silence crept in. I was alone. As the weight of that loneliness hung in the air, the smile faded from my lips.

CHAPTER 2
HAZEL

The library loomed over me, my eyes squinting in the bright sun. I pulled the hood of my cloak a little tighter over my face, shrinking into its dark folds as the rest of the town bustled around me. I took one more deep breath, pausing for only a moment longer before heading through the big wooden doors, their weight a familiar comfort against my hand. There were two places that felt like home to me: Arlo's house and here. I spent the first few weeks after Arlo found me held up in the house, petrified of any loud sound or sudden movement and convinced I was still living in the nightmares that frequently found me. When I realized that being cooped up was just making things worse, I asked Arlo to start taking me out.

Slowly but surely, I became familiar with the town's sounds and movements. I still struggled not to jump when things happened unexpectedly, like a cart clambering by too fast or merchants shouting too close for comfort. I'd gotten a lot better at hiding it, though. Even Arlo couldn't always tell when something set my teeth on edge or caused an uproar of panic in my mind. Once I felt comfortable enough being outside, I started going on daily walks through the town, trying to get my footing and acclimate myself back into society. I discovered the town's library pretty early in those days, often swooping in for a much needed relief from the overwhelming world outside its doors.

Everything here was gray and hard, from the walkways to the tall buildings that shot up throughout the landscape like some obscene intrusion. I despised it. It seemed to me that whatever powers that be in this town looked out at their land and thought, *What would make this town boring and dull and hard? Let's remove every shred of nature and replace it with cold, hard stone.* I could never understand why people preferred this over the beauty in nature. When I stood in the soft grass or got lost listening to the sound of a nearby bird, I could feel the rumble of my mind ease. Like a weight was slightly lifted—not totally gone but lighter than before.

That's why the library was an easy haven for me. It was made up of floor-to-ceiling windows and laid out like a square. The center was a hollowed-out courtyard full of beautiful plants, lush green grass, and sitting areas for anyone who wanted to take a book or two outside for the afternoon. Inside, it was blissfully quiet. No loud cafes or bartering between merchants. Just the peaceful flip of pages turning, the occasional cough or whisper, and enough faces around to make me feel like I wasn't totally alone.

I made my way to the section of the library that was meant for archives and records. As I walked amidst the tall shelves, I ran my fingers over the old spines. Despite wanting to bury myself in here all day, I knew Arlo was right about limiting my time. Some of my worst days occurred after spending endless hours here, digging and reading until I was cross-eyed.

Those days felt so similar to my constant dreams—the defining lines of reality blurring and my mind feeling utterly lost to another world.

Something was weighing on me today, too. There had been gentle reminders lately: the sun shining a bit stronger than days past, the chill of the air slipping away as the little bits of ice that remained pooled in wet puddles during my walks, the birds coming out from their long winter reprieve. They were signs that spring had come, and if spring had come then that meant it was almost the one-year mark of when Arlo found me, when I'd lost my memories.

My eyes drifted across the courtyard as I watched several people enjoying the first of spring's warmth. A young couple strolled through the newly blooming flowers, swept up in their own private world. Others sprinkled the soft grass, lounging on blankets and excitedly discussing whatever secret treasure they'd discovered in the library. Arlo and I had yet to talk about the fact that it had almost been a year since the incident—the day he found me in the woods. Since neither of us knew exactly what had happened, it was hard to refer to it as anything else. I wondered if he'd say anything, had been waiting to see if he'd bring it up. Somewhere inside, I could feel a gentle pull to do something, to acknowledge it somehow. I shook my head, returning to the delicate records stacked within the shelves. I didn't want to risk what those thoughts would do to me, so exposed out here in the public's view. Instead, I let my eyes focus on the faded titles beneath my fingers, and dove into the world of possibilities they offered.

Several hours later, I'd given up my research and perused the small section of tales and quests that the library offered. It was a true testament to how desperate I was getting, that most of my research consisted of folklore from town drunks and village wives' tales. It had been over six months since I started digging through the library's records and I wasn't any closer to finding answers. Not only that, but I was running out of resources to pull from. The library only had so many books on such topics as these.

I let out a frustrated breath as I turned my attention back to the stack of books in front of me. It only took me a matter of minutes to pick out one that looked promising, some fantasy story about love and a heroic journey. I took it to the records keeper at the front of the library, throwing a quick smile at her as she made note of the book in her archives.

"Oh, this is a good one," she said.

She turned the book over in her hand, looking at it like it was an old friend she hadn't seen in a long time and nodded in approval. I envied her in that moment, the ease with which she blended in here. The way she played her role as librarian. It was an ease that I couldn't remember ever feeling.

"It's been a while since I read it, but it sure was good. You'll enjoy it!" She handed me back the book with a reassuring tap against the hardcover. I took it quickly, mumbling in agreement before flashing her a forced smile. I could feel her eyes on me as I walked away.

I still hadn't mastered the art of small talk. Lingering too long in the presence of anyone seemed like too much of a chore. I paused and took a deep breath before pushing through the doors, back out into the loud, beige world beyond.

I veered to the right, head covered with my hood and tucked down low, and made my way to the small path by the woods on the outskirts of town. It was always less crowded there—quieter, and so much more peaceful. It was also a shortcut to get back to our house, so I often found myself choosing this path. I'd promised Arlo I'd go the long way, through town. He was always encouraging me to put some effort into meeting the townspeople, joining the bustle of the busy streets rather than isolating myself on the road by the woods. Some days it just felt impossible to be around others, and I found myself longing to be by the forest. I found more comfort there than I ever did in town.

As I made my way past the towering trees, I thought about the year I'd spent in this town—a year spent failing to find answers about what had happened to me. The idea of getting better—moving forward—should have excited me. A whole year had passed between me and that painful day full of terror and confusion. I should feel reassured to be putting that kind of space between me and that gut-wrenching memory. Yet it somehow haunted me without any relief. I may have gotten better at hiding its hold on me, but I wasn't healing.

Not truly.

Maybe I would bring it up to Arlo, see if he remembered or if he thought we should do anything. I didn't even know what someone did for such a date as that, but it felt wrong to not even acknowledge it. Anytime I tried to bring up details of that day, of any information that may have come out of the short amount of time we spent in that town before coming back to Arlo's home, he always shut down. I wondered if things would be different this time, if we'd be able to discuss it and finally get somewhere.

I slowed my pace and let myself enjoy the first of the season's blooms popping up along the path—bright white bundles of flowers swaying slightly in the crisp spring breeze. They were my favorite of the blooms I'd found in this area. They always seemed to be along my path or around our house and I'd grown to look at them as a sort of good luck charm. The shades of green sprinkled throughout the woods were starting to appear a tad deeper too, as if they'd been waiting for the refreshing burst of sunlight that comes with the end of winter. The air was still brisk, but there was no denying that spring was here.

As I slowed to a stop, I fixed my gaze on a clearing in the canopy just ahead. The way the sunlight broke through it left a buttery haze in the air. It reminded me of Arlo leaning against the door this morning, his bare skin bathing in that sunlit glow. It reminded me of something else, too, something distant and warm that I couldn't quite put my finger on. It felt like true happiness, so I let myself linger there a little while longer, memorizing everything about those rays falling across the foliage of the woods—illuminating the fluffy white cloud-like flowers growing there. I felt myself longing for what felt like the millionth time to just go, to run. I didn't know where, or why, but somewhere inside of me I could feel a pull, something calling me to anywhere but here. I'd been here for a year, and still nothing made sense.

Perhaps it was time to look elsewhere. I'd ignored it for months now, but after another day of pointless research and the same monotonous routine in this dreadful town, I wanted to follow that call and see where it took me.

I spent my afternoon lounging by the fire, legs draped over the armchair, head buried deep in the book I'd picked up from the library. I'd lost track of time and jumped slightly at the sound of Arlo opening the front door. *Was it evening already?* I finished the paragraph I had been reading as the sound of Arlo's voice, along with the delicious smell of herbs, wrapped around me. As I marked my place for later and put the book on the table beside me, Arlo leaned over my head from behind. He smiled gingerly and planted a short, sweet kiss on my lips.

"I brought your favorite," he said, holding up a large jar of stew from the local tavern to show that my nose had indeed been correct.

"Hi to you, too," I said with a sarcastic grin. I pushed off the chair and grabbed for the sacks of food, heading toward the kitchen to unload them. I hadn't realized how famished I was. I hadn't thought to grab lunch on my walk home, nor had anything to eat after coming home and settling in with my book. Along with my recurring and vivid nightmares, forgetting to eat was one of those pesky little habits that the constant worry of my mind caused. Arlo knew it too, and was always checking in and pushing plates of food and little snacks in front of me. I explained to him once that it wasn't that I didn't like to eat or was trying to avoid food. It was just that sometimes the endless thoughts in my head consumed me, distracting me from the feeling of hunger. They distracted me from a lot of things, really. I didn't know how to silence those thoughts, or how to ignore them when they relentlessly circled, and it often led to me skipping meals or pausing to determine when I'd last eaten.

The corner of Arlo's lips curled upwards as he looked me over.

"Did you really not hear me say hi when I came in?" He laughed and shook his head. "You and those books, Hazel. I swear nothing could come between that love affair."

I rolled my eyes at him as we made quick work of dishing out the thick stew, still warm from when Arlo picked it up on his way home. I dug in and almost melted as the savory, warm taste filled my mouth. Arlo knew me almost too well. The brothy mixture of stewed meat and potatoes was pretty much my favorite meal. It was one of the first things I ate after the incident. I had no idea how long it had been since I'd eaten before that, but judging by how quickly and fully I devoured that meal, I'd say it had been a while.

Ever since then, Arlo was scarily skilled at sensing when I was having a rough day or my body needed sustenance and would show up with a bowl full of the deliciously stewed meat. I blamed it on the fact that he knew I couldn't turn it down, assuming it was always a safe bet. Sometimes, though, he really had me wondering if he could somehow read my mind or sense my emotions because of how good he was at detecting that need.

Between spoonfuls of broth, I could see him watching me, grinning as if he knew he'd hit the mark.

"Hungry, are we?" he said as he gestured toward my half-empty bowl.

"Okay, so maybe I forgot to eat lunch today," I said, rolling my eyes again. He might have been right, but I wasn't going to let him be cocky too. "But it doesn't take a genius to know this is my weakness." I waved a hand over the food.

He chuckled a little as he turned back to his own bowl. "So what did you do today, besides forgetting to eat lunch?"

"Did we not already discuss that love affair?" I gestured toward the chair by the hearth where I had been utterly lost in my book moments ago.

"Yes, yes, but that's old news. I know you're too wild for me to be the only man in your life."

My eyes shot up to him and I gave him a sarcastic, hurt damsel look. "Me? I would never."

"Whatever you say, dear, but my only request is we keep it to fictional men, okay? I think that's where I draw the line."

A slow grin crept over my face. "You *think*?" I asked, winking at him.

I loved the way his eyes looked at mine when we were together and playful, not bogged down with the darkness that lulled in the corner, even now. It would emerge again. It always did, but this was perfect. This felt like home.

The thought of that ever-present darkness, and the realization that it wasn't as overbearing in this moment, had me turning my thoughts in a much more solemn direction.

"Oh, by the way," I said, trying to sound casual, "I wanted to talk to you about something."

I didn't fool him. He immediately perked up, set down his fork, and gave me that concerned look he always did when things turned more serious between us.

"I'm all ears."

He waited, face unwaveringly patient; those caramel eyes focused on me with unrelenting care and love.

It took me a minute to work up the courage to say what I had thought about earlier that day.

"Today, I—" I loosed a breath and tried to calm my mind. "I realized recently that it's almost the anniversary of the incident, of when you found me."

I could see Arlo stiffen. His face remained unreadable, but I could have sworn I saw the smallest amount of dread dance across his eyes.

I continued on. "I didn't know if you remembered or—"

"Of course I remembered, Hazel. I didn't want to bring it up in case it upset you. But how could I not remember the day you came into my life?"

A small smile pulled on my lips.

How could so much bad be wrapped up in so much good?

Sometimes it was hard to remember that such a traumatic moment in my life was also such a blessing in his. He'd do anything to get me answers, figure out what happened to me, or help me heal, but he also hadn't hesitated to make sure I knew coming into his life was the best thing to ever happen to him.

As if he read my mind, he said, "I know that time holds so many bad memories for you, but, Hazel, I thank whatever powers that be that I stumbled upon you that day. I know you think I saved you, but it's you who saved me. You've given me love and trust unlike anything I've ever known. How could I not be grateful for that?"

Color rose into my cheeks; it was impossible to keep it away. I could feel the burn of the tears pooling in my eyes, but I wouldn't let them come. I needed to talk to him about this, and if I let myself cry, I didn't know when I'd stop. This man was too sweet, too good. I didn't deserve him. My eyes flitted down to my bowl at the thought, but he took my hand as if to gently urge me to keep talking.

"I'm grateful for you too, Arlo. More than you could ever understand, probably." I paused, letting the acknowledgment of our love hang in the air a little longer.

"Um, anyway," I said, not really sure how to move on. "I was thinking about that today and the idea hit me. What if—" I tentatively looked back up to him, gauging how I thought he'd respond to this idea. This ridiculously stupid idea that I couldn't let go of. "What if we went back? Visited the area you found me? You know, to commemorate the year together?"

Confusion and shock washed over his features. I could tell he didn't like this, not one bit.

"What?" he asked, as if he didn't believe—*couldn't* believe—he'd heard me properly.

"Well, it's just that, it feels odd to not acknowledge the day at all. And I'm getting nowhere with my research here, so I thought maybe going back—digging around the area a little—might give us more information to go through."

"You want to go back? After all the progress you've made this year, the life we are building here? Why on earth would you want to go *back*?"

I knew this was going to come as a shock to him. Talking about that time in our lives always proved to be difficult. It had always been silently understood that we'd look here for answers, dig as much as we could, but there was never a discussion of actually returning to that spot—of going back to the place he'd found me or talking with the people in the town he took me to after. I wasn't going to let this go, though. I'd been fighting this feeling for long enough. It was time to act on it, trust my instinct.

"I know it seems counterproductive, but Arlo, I need answers. And I'm not getting any here. And I just think—"

"Am I not enough?"

The answer cut through the air like a knife. It stopped me dead in my tracks.

"What?" I said.

"Am I not *enough*?" he repeated, quieter this time.

"Arlo, how could you even ask that? Of course you're enough, you are all I have!" I felt hot tears starting to run down my cheeks. I hated the weakness they were revealing.

"If I'm enough, then why can't we just stay here, move forward? Why are you so obsessed with finding answers, Hazel? It's only going to bring you heartache. Who you were doesn't matter. What matters is who you want to be, what kind of life you want to build for yourself. I want you to heal, to find a life to settle into and to move forward."

I didn't understand. Arlo had always been so supportive of me, so encouraging. The bluntness of his words stung. Maybe I had been healing, but I wasn't building a life. I was stuck in the same monotonous loop. It was like his composure was failing—a mask I hadn't noticed before slipping ever so slightly to show how desperate he was to keep me here, keep me safe.

"I just think that going back, asking questions—it may give me a better idea of what happened. I can't move on until I have that."

That was a reality I hadn't voiced before. That's what had kept me digging this past year, why I couldn't just *move forward* like Arlo said, and he knew it. I saw the pain on his face as I said it. I told him that he was enough, but maybe it hadn't been entirely true. As good as he'd been to me, it wasn't enough for me to give up and build a life here with him. At least, not without trying everything I could first to find out what happened to me.

The silence between us was a palpable thing. It hung there thick and heavy as I watched him. More tears ran down my face, but I would not give myself over to them. Arlo hung his head low, pushing his hands through his hair as he battled internally for what to say next.

"You know I would do anything for you, Hazel." His voice was forced and shaky. "If this is what you think you need, then I will be by your side every step of the way. I just wish..." He trailed off, searching for the right words to say. "I just wish we could figure out how to move past this. Without answers, without going back. Because I think it's only going to hurt you—hurt us—more."

He didn't say it to manipulate or wound me. He said it because he honestly believed it. He was worried about losing me. Either to the past that I'd come from if I found those answers or the pain that would amount from not finding them or not liking what I found. I knew that he was right on some level. If we went digging, really digging, it would put an end to this little bubble we'd built around us. If we stayed here, focused on each other, on moving forward... that bubble would remain intact. We'd have nothing but time and our future to live for. We'd have each other.

The thrum of that monotonous loop played over and over in my head, the endless misery of being trapped in this dull town that I hated so much. I knew that was the life I would be stuck in if I chose to just stay here and not look back: here, but not fully living. I knew that was something that I couldn't do anymore, not even for Arlo.

"I'm sorry, but I have to at least try," I said.

"I know," was his only answer.

CHAPTER 3
HAZEL

Several days passed without any kind of consensus being made. I loved Arlo deeply, but I wouldn't let him keep me from this. My mind was constantly replaying my dreams, thinking of the world I always saw from a distance but could never quite touch. I wanted to find something like that here, a tangible version of what my mind had conjured up in those dreams that haunted me practically every night. Maybe even find out if that world existed somewhere, if it truly was some broken memory from my past. I could feel Arlo's hesitation though, could tell it wasn't going to be an easy fight to win.

I was digging through the wardrobe in our bedroom, trying to find some nightclothes to change into. Arlo had been sulking for days and I was annoyed by his sullen movements across the room as I dressed for bed.

"Why are you so against this idea?" My voice cracked slightly as it cut through the silence.

He held my gaze for what felt like an eternity. Finally, he dipped his head low and said, "I don't want to lose you, Hazel."

He dropped down onto the foot of the bed, shoulders sunken and face trained on his hands fiddling in his lap.

"How does going on this trip equate to you losing me?" I shot back.

I was tired of his wallowing. I knew deep down this was where his hesitation stemmed from, but he hadn't admitted it yet. Hearing him say it now, it was like he thought I was some caged bird, trapped and ready to take off the moment we stepped foot out of this town. He had to know that I would never do that to him, that he was everything to me.

"Hazel, we don't know what going back is going to bring. You may actually find a life previous to the one we've started building together. What if you find a family, maybe even a partner waiting for you? How could I ask you to stay with me after that? That's not fair to you."

I started to object, but he cut in before I could. "And I would never ask that of you. I don't want to keep you from those who love you, from those you once loved and were taken from."

He paused, his breath shaking as he inhaled deeply then let it out. He still sat with his back to me, purposefully refusing to meet my gaze. "But that's not even my main concern, because it's something I've always expected to happen at some point. I'm not naive enough to believe we will never find the life you belonged to before we met. But what am I supposed to do if we go and find nothing and that's the last straw for you? The last pebble on the pile and you can't take it anymore.

"I don't want to lose you to yourself, to that darkness. I know how much this stuff weighs on you and I'm worried if you keep digging, it's going to actually break you. I don't know how to keep you safe from that. I helped you heal physically after the incident. I took care of you, helped you learn things that you couldn't remember, and made sure you stayed safe in our little town. That's why I brought you here, because it's safe and calm. None of that is the same as helping protect you from your own mind. I don't know how to do that for you."

For the first time I saw the weight of the last year heavy on his shoulders. I knew it hadn't been easy dealing with me, the constant nightmares and fits of terror. I hated that he had to put up with that from me, had to figure out how to navigate our relationship around that always present darkness. I had never truly known how much it had weighed him down. He didn't deserve this. This shouldn't be his burden to bear.

I closed the doors to the wardrobe and walked over to where he sat on the bed. He parted his knees far enough to let me step between them. I took his hands in mine and dipped my head to meet those amber pools in his eyes.

"You are not going to lose me. Ever."

He let out a short breath, almost like a laugh, as he said, "You can't guarantee anything, Hazel. And I won't be the reason you don't find your family, your past. I couldn't ever do that to you. I know what this journey means to you, how much you need it. That doesn't make it any easier, though. It won't make me worry any less."

He wanted so badly to protect me, but we had finally come to the point where he would have to choose between that protection or supporting me on this journey. And I truly believed he loved me too much to keep me caged for his sake. I cupped his face in my hands and pulled him into me. The weight of my body leaned into him. Even sitting down, his tall form reached my mouth easily. His lips met mine and I kissed him, a long and deep kiss that I hoped conveyed the depth of my need for him, now and forever. I let go, only backing away far enough that I could speak. My forehead rested on his brows as I wrapped my arms around his neck and whispered what he'd said to me so many times before, "Remember. This right here? This is real."

I could sense the edges of his smile, his features moving ever so slightly against my skin.

"I don't think it's fair when you use my own words against me," he whispered back. Before I could reply, he pulled me onto the bed and wrapped his body around mine as he nuzzled his face against the crook of my neck. "It's us against the world, okay? We go together, we fight together. I'm here beside you every step of the way. I'm yours, Hazel."

Whether it was his words or the feel of his warm breath against my ear, a chill crept down my spine. He ended his statement with a smattering of kisses down my neck and worked his way up my jawline back to my mouth. He was right. It was us against the world and the idea of that, the safety I felt here in his arms, was nothing like I'd known anywhere else. I felt my mind drift in and out of consciousness as he held me. I could think of nothing else but this moment, how he made me feel and those words he'd whispered with fierce absoluteness. We lay there, entwined together as if we were one body, one soul. I was so thankful for this man and all he'd done for me. Sleep found me fast and hard.

And so did the nightmares, glimpses of that all-too-familiar dream. It was like an endless loop playing over and over again in my mind. Pieces here, another part there, but nothing cohesive and nothing that made sense to me. I woke with a start, breath heavy, and eased my way off the bed and out from under Arlo's arm. He barely moved at the disruption, lost entirely to his own exhaustion.

I began my usual ritual of filling the tub and climbing in, letting the tepid water sink into my skin and wash away the visions of the nightmare. I cupped the water in my hands and let it run down my shivering body, letting each and every horrible memory fall away with it. The darkness of the bathing room was suffocating in the midnight haze, forcing me to wonder if there would ever be an escape from the fear that found me in the dark shadows of my nightmares. I let that thought linger, overtaking my mind and blotting out any light left within me, until I heard the creak of the floorboards.

Arlo found me there and climbed into the tub, wrapping me in his embrace. He held me for a long time against his bare chest, trying to calm the shaking that had begun to ravage my body. Silent tears ran down my face as I pressed into his solid form, and I knew. I knew he understood why I had awoken—that these horrific dreams I was desperate to scrub from my skin were penetrating every part of me. Maybe he even understood why this journey was so necessary for me, even if it terrified him. I needed to find out what they were, why they refused to leave me alone. If there was somewhere out there that I belonged. His hand moved in small, reassuring circles across my back, as if in answer to my own thoughts. He finally understood, and he held me until I stopped crying.

CHAPTER 4
HAZEL

The road leading out of town was eerily quiet due to the early hour in which we'd decided to leave. Arlo had somehow acquired a horse for us so we didn't have to walk the whole way. Several times I found myself starting to spiral mentally, so I buried myself against Arlo's back, welcoming the warmth he provided. I was pleasantly surprised to realize how well his presence distracted me from the worry of what lay ahead. I couldn't believe we were actually doing this. The longer we traveled, the more I caught myself staring off the path and losing track of time. Watching the landscape transform from our overcrowded town full of busy walkways and obtrusive buildings to winding roads cutting through towering rock formations and vast meadows had my heart leaping out of my chest. I knew things like this existed outside of our town, but it was one thing to know it and an entirely other thing to be in it—be a part of it. If this was just the road to get there, then I couldn't wait to see what we experienced when we arrived.

Arlo kept glancing over his shoulder at me and smiling, or even outright laughing. After about the fourth time, I smacked him on the arm.

"What is your deal?" I said, letting out a breathy laugh.

"You're just a sight to behold. You look like a child who's been given a piece of candy."

I rolled my eyes. "I do not."

"Whatever you say. Just be careful not to lean over too far or you might fall off the horse. That would be embarrassing." He gave me a wink before I let out a huff of air and turned back to look out across a particularly colorful meadow we were passing.

"Just keep your eyes on the road and leave me to my gawking, okay?"

"Yes, dear," he agreed. However, I could still see him out of the corner of my eye, stealing the occasional glance, the corner of his lips tilting up each time.

His amusement brought a smile to my own lips.

"I've just never seen anything like it," I found myself saying after a few moments passed, quiet enough that I wasn't sure if I meant that for him or me. The smile fell from his lips then. A long stretch of silence passed before he reached back and ran his fingers over my leg.

"I'm glad we're doing this, Hazel. I know I wasn't at first, but you deserve to see this. You deserve to see the whole damn world for that matter, as long as it makes you smile that way."

I wrapped my arms around his waist again, not letting his hand fall from mine as I squeezed. I didn't know how else to answer his sweet words, but I let my mind drift to all the places I'd read about this past year. I wondered how much of it I would get to see in my lifetime. Or what places I might have already seen and just couldn't remember.

By the time we got to the next town, the sun had set. We found a small, quiet tavern to grab a quick dinner before inquiring about the rooms for rent upstairs. Arlo led us through a dark hallway above the nightly commotion of the tavern and stopped in front of a wooden door, aged with the constant use from previous tenants. With each step we took down the hallway, I felt a sort of finality. We were here—truly, honestly here. I didn't know whether that fact terrified me or exhilarated me more. I held my breath as he jiggled the key the landlord had given him until the lock turned and led the way inside.

As Arlo made his way around the room, lighting the candles, the small space was flooded with warm light. I let my eyes adjust from the contrasting dim of the hallway. The room was a sea of neutral colors. Various shades of brown and gray spilled over the walls and floor, reaching every corner. A large bed sat against one wall, its sheets a dull beige with a display of somewhat worn decorative pillows fanning out across the top. On the other side of the room was a small table for two overlooking a pair of glass doors and a balcony beyond them. While I wasn't a huge fan of the color scheme, I could definitely get used to that view for the next two weeks. I dropped my rucksack on the floor by a wardrobe cabinet and took in the rest of the room. We had a small setup to make coffee or tea and a little chaise next to a small hearth opposite the bed. Overall, it wasn't a bad room. It seemed a little dated and well-loved, but welcoming, and I felt the tightening in my chest ease just the slightest amount.

It had been late by the time we got into the tavern, so we hadn't done much with our evening and found ourselves ready for bed almost right away. As we lay in the enveloping darkness of our room, thoughts of unease started to creep in. I hated sleeping in a place that was unfamiliar. I wondered if I'd get any rest tonight, if my thoughts would still long enough for me to feel safe. We hadn't discussed what tomorrow would bring and my mind raced with all the possibilities. Would we find anything useful? Maybe even someone who remembered me, knew of my life from before? My stomach twisted in knots as I thought about what it would be like to finally have some tangible answers.

"You've been quiet since we got here."

Arlo's voice startled me, his low tone reverberating through the room. I turned on my side and realized he was already on his, watching me. Trying to assess how I was doing. The darkness of the room made his features hard to distinguish, but it was impossible to miss the concern laced through his words as he searched my face for any hint of unease.

"I've just been thinking about what we should do tomorrow," I said. It was the truth, or at least part of it. I hadn't been able to silence my mind since we'd got here; really, since we'd left home. I had been so confident that this was the right decision. Now, I wasn't so sure. I felt the waves of uncertainty and fear wash over me for what felt like the thousandth time today.

"Well," Arlo said with a deep breath in.

I wondered if it was a breath of relief or a confirmation of concern.

"Did you want to start with getting a feel for the town? Walking around the shops and speaking with some of the locals may prove to be useful."

I nodded into the darkness, realizing he probably couldn't see the movement. I waited a minute before I spoke next.

"I was thinking I'd like to speak with the Guard first, let them know I'm in town and hoping to do a little research into my past here."

The tension radiating off Arlo was hard to miss.

After a beat, he simply said, "Okay. We'll go there first. And whenever you're ready for a break or want to leave, then we can check out the shops. Sound like a plan?"

A knot formed in the back of my throat as tears threatened to spill over my eyes. I swallowed hard and nodded again. My gaze met his and I almost fell apart at the way his gold-flecked eyes glowed in the darkness. I found myself burying my head into his chest before I even realized I was moving.

"Thank you," I managed to choke out against his skin.

He let out a little laugh and kissed my forehead. Wrapping his arms tighter around my waist, he pulled me into him and closed the small gap between our bodies.

"Just promise me you will talk to me. Let me know what's going on in that head of yours. I know this is hard for you, Hazel. I just want to help you through this. But I can't do that unless you talk to me."

I squeezed my arms around him. "I will," I promised.

I could feel the small uptilt of his lips against my forehead.

"Good," he said, and I swore I heard a small sigh of relief escape him. "Now get some sleep, we've got a big day tomorrow."

With that, I found myself drifting off, still safely wrapped in his arms. My last thought as I succumbed to the exhaustion pulling me under was that I hoped somehow the nightmares wouldn't find me tonight.

CHAPTER 5
HAZEL

The small building that the Guard used as their base was not a comforting sight. We sat in an overly cramped alcove amid several other people. The wooden chairs that were scattered throughout the small space were practically kindling. I was scared to put my full weight on mine for fear of it collapsing beneath me, and several others seemed to be in the same or even worse condition. A woman two chairs over kept rocking back and forth due to the wobbly nature of the particular seat she'd chosen. The incessant clunk of her chair leg hitting the floor over and over again had set my teeth on edge. People chattered endlessly in the background. Practically every desk had a concerned citizen seated at it, here to voice some immediate concern.

The hum of voices was a steady nagging on my mind, constant chatter only disrupted by barks of laughter or the occasional booming yell of someone overly excited or upset. Each time an outburst was made, I flinched slightly in my seat. This level of concentrated noise was unbearable. I didn't know how anyone else was able to stand it. We'd been sitting here for far too long and I felt like I was losing my mind. I clenched my fists, digging my nails into my palms and trying to get ahold of myself. It took everything in me not to jump up and run out into the fresh air just outside. The ringing in my ears had started and I knew a full hysteric episode wasn't far behind. Just as I braced myself to launch out of the chair and through the front doors, I heard my name.

"Hazel?"

I looked up and my eyes met those of a middle-aged man with a balding head and an unconcerned drag to his face. He held some papers in his hand—my records, I presumed. He didn't strike me as an overly ambitious type of man and my stomach curled with dread at the way he looked me over.

Arlo stood up next to me.

"That's us!" he called out, taking my hand and guiding me to my feet. I wasn't entirely sure I would have been able to get up on my own.

"Hi there, Miss Hazel. I'm Holt. What can I do for you?"

The guard's voice was thick and slow, like his thoughts were churning through water just to make it out of his mouth. He looked at me with a slight smile on his face, one that I didn't find comforting or endearing.

"I was hoping I could talk to the member of the Guard who handled my incident last year." My gaze shot down to the record in his hand.

He noticed me eyeing the papers and tucked them annoyingly behind his back as he said, "Sure thing, sweetheart. Follow me."

He turned to walk and weaved us through rows of desks toward a sitting area just off the room, where that ridiculous amount of noise continued to grow, showing us two beat-up chairs and a faded green couch that reminded me exactly of how my stomach was feeling right now. We were right out in the open, with no sense of privacy or calm to discuss the more intimate details of my record.

I knotted my hands together nervously as I glanced around the over-crowded room. Swallowing hard, I pushed myself forward toward the seat the guard had offered me. I felt his hand reach for the small of my back, guiding me into the chair closest to him. I stiffened at the abrupt touch and moved quickly to get out from under his grasp. Arlo cleared the way for me to sit on the couch while the guard—Holt—took a seat in the better-looking of the two chairs.

The three of us sat there awkwardly for several moments. Finally, I found my voice and asked, "Are any other members of the Guard joining us?"

I didn't remember seeing him during my brief time here or in the heal-ers' quarters last year. I thought I'd remember that way he was looking at me. I couldn't decide if it was pity or desire I saw in his eyes, or maybe a mixture of both. I didn't like it, though.

"No, ma'am, I'm your best option right now. I can answer any ques-tions you may have."

I seriously doubted that, but I didn't come all this way just to leave without answers because the members of the Guard were too busy or too careless to attend to my questions. He must have seen the unease in my eyes because he followed up by saying, "It's okay, you're safe with me, sweetheart."

He reached to pat me on the knee and I jumped. Arlo moved fast, faster than I realized he could, and grabbed the guard's hand before it could reach its intended destination. "We appreciate your willingness to speak with us, but we'd both feel a lot more comfortable if you could find a way to keep your hands to yourself."

The guard recoiled slightly in shock as heat rushed to my cheeks. Clearly, he was a man not used to others questioning his authority. The whole day was starting to feel like a mistake. I doubted very seriously this incompetent, handsy guard was going to give us any useful details and every minute in this building had my stomach twisting in on itself. My breathing had turned ragged and I momentarily forgot what we were even trying to accomplish.

Arlo took my hand tenderly as he said, "Hazel, did you have anywhere specifically you wanted to start?"

He knew that I was struggling, I could tell by the way his fingers swirled little patterns against my palm as a gentle reminder of his presence. It was a tether to reality that I latched onto and followed all the way back until my mind was clear and I knew what I needed to ask.

"I wanted to know if you had any conclusion about my incident—what exactly it was you thought happened to me last year, or if anyone had been in contact to ask about me."

The guard leaned back, sucking a sharp breath through his yellowing teeth before he spoke. "Your record is closed, I'm afraid. No movement has been made with it in quite some time. It has been closed for the better part of a year, if I remember correctly."

A mixture of hope and irritation rose in me. *How had my record been closed? Did they actually figure out what happened to me?* Before I could even voice my questions, Arlo was speaking.

"How the fuck could you close her record? Shouldn't she be notified of something like that? This is absolutely ridiculous. Isn't there some sort of protocol in place to prevent shit like this from happening?" Okay, he wasn't speaking. He was borderline yelling, but he was right.

How could they not have told me that my record was closed?

Arlo continued with his stream of not-so-subtle insults, while the guard tried—and failed—to explain himself.

"What did you find?" I cut in before Arlo could continue. Closed could be good—closed could mean they had information to give me, a past to point me toward, or somewhere for me to return to.

The guard turned his attention from Arlo to me. He held my gaze for several moments before he let out an irritated sigh and reached for the record he'd brought with him.

He opened it and started reading:

"After a thorough investigation of the area, the victim's wounds, and any and all evidence collected, we have determined that the victim is suffering from memory loss resulting from exposure to the elements and a possible animal attack. It is our belief that the victim was traveling alone, inadequately prepared for the harsh conditions, and became lost and disoriented. We suspect that she was wandering for several days before being found. It is clear that at some point the victim was attacked by some sort of animal commonly associated with the area, most likely a type of wolf or wild dog, causing some of her more severe wounds. The victim is suffering from memory loss and unable to verify any of these details. It appears the victim has no next of kin to contact. We are closing the record due to a lack of evidence to further investigate and notes from the town healers that indicate our findings to be accurate."

The silence that hung as he finished reading the statement was thick. None of those annoying noises from our surroundings penetrated it. I stared at him in utter disbelief. This wasn't just another dead end, it couldn't be. We'd come so far, I'd been so sure that this was the right move. I'd convinced myself that if we could just get back here—back to where it all happened—that I'd find *something*. Moments passed before I found the courage to speak.

"It was not *just* an animal attack."

"I understand your confusion, sweetheart. I'm sure you had quite the scare out there in the woods for those few days. It's a prime example of why we recommend those of your delicate nature not travel the roads in between towns alone. But all the evidence points to this. And we can't just keep records open because a victim with memory issues and poor decision-making skills tells us we got it wrong."

I wanted to hit him. For one, because he kept calling me sweetheart like I was some five-year-old girl. Secondly, because my words held no weight for him. In his eyes I was just a helpless victim who was of no use because I couldn't provide any account of what happened. It triggered memories of my stay with the healers, of how frustrated the guard had been that I couldn't remember anything. They kept reworking their questions. When they weren't hounding me for hours trying to jog some sort of memories that just weren't there, they were laying into me about how stupid I'd been for traveling alone *in my fragile state*; in other words, while being female. Eventually, one of the healers had kicked them out and told them they were interfering with my recovery.

But that's what I was, wasn't I? A victim—fragile, worthless to them. To anyone, really. Tears welled in my eyes as I tried my hardest not to let that pain break through. I swallowed once, then twice.

"Do you have any records or information about who I am?"

He looked at me, confused, so I added, "Who I was, before all of this."

Realization hit him then. "You mean, you still don't remember any-thing?"

I shook my head as my gaze dropped to my lap.

"I'm sorry, sweetheart, but no, we have no information about you. The man who brought you to the healers was the one to give us your name. Aside from that, no one ever came around to say they knew you or even to ask about a missing woman fitting your description."

Arlo squeezed my hand, holding tighter than he had before. He spoke this time:

"Isn't there any way you can reopen her record? Keep searching for her family or something?"

"I'm sorry, but we can't reopen a record without new evidence coming to light or suspicion that something was mishandled the first time around."

"So reopen it! Obviously things were mishandled the first time around. For fuck's sake, she didn't even know you had closed it!"

The guard flinched slightly at Arlo's words. "If that is something you would like to pursue, you are more than welcome. But you'd have to go before the town council to get the record reopened. I know it's not what you folks want to hear, but the incident is pretty cut and dry."

Arlo was spewing anger. I could see the regret fighting with the rage across his features. If we had come sooner, perhaps we would have been able to convince them to keep the record open. Perhaps if Arlo hadn't insisted on keeping me sheltered and safe, far away from whatever nightmare took place here, we would have played a more active part of the process and found answers.

But there wasn't much left to say. Suddenly, I found myself standing.

"Thank you for your time," I said, nodding toward the guard.

With that, I turned and made my way through the busy office area and out the front doors. The sun was bright and blinding as I pushed through them, out onto the path through town. Arlo was fast on his feet behind me.

"Hey." He grabbed my hand and turned me to face him.

Tears were streaming down my cheeks. He pulled me into his arms. My silent tears turned into actual sobs as he stroked my hair and whispered in my ear, "It's okay, Hazel. We'll figure this out."

He never hesitated, never relented his hold on me, until I signaled that I was ready.

I pulled back, wiping my face and trying to gain composure.

"I'm sorry, I just—"

"Why are you apologizing?" Arlo asked. "There's nothing to be sorry for, Hazel. This is a lot for anyone to take on."

He was right. I went into today with the hope that I'd find some missing piece, some part of the puzzle that would hopefully bring us closer to the bigger picture, if not reveal it completely. What I got was a dead end, a handsy waste of time who couldn't take me seriously if his life depended on it, and a whole bunch of lies.

My eyes met Arlo. All sense of fear and dread was gone. Tears no longer stung my eyes or ran down my cheeks. I was stone-faced as I told him the two words that kept running through my mind since the guard had read their official statement.

"They're wrong."

CHAPTER 6
HAZEL

Arlo took a deep breath in.

"Arlo, I know it. They are wrong. There's no way that's all this was."

"I know you want to believe that. And I'm not saying they are right, Hazel, but you came here for answers, so maybe it would be best to chase down this lead too, before completely dismissing it."

Anger rose in me again, this time directed at Arlo instead of the guard inside. His hands had landed around my waist, leaving a small gap between us. I stepped backward, forcing the space between us to grow.

"How could you honestly believe that's the answer? You saw me—my wounds back then. What about my life before, my family? The fact that I have no idea who I am or where I came from and no one is even so much as inquiring about me. *None* of that says animal attack to me."

Arlo took a step closer as I backed away again. I didn't want to be distracted by the warm feeling of his hands on my skin or by his calming presence so close to my body. I wanted him to tell me what he really thought and not what he thought I needed to hear.

"Tell me, Arlo. Tell me how any of this makes sense. Tell me what you really believe happened."

He dropped his hands and lowered his head. I was desperate to know the thoughts wrestling in his mind. There was something there, something he was reluctant to tell me. He finally looked up at me and opened his mouth to answer when I saw a figure out of the corner of my eye approaching us.

"I'm sorry, I didn't mean to interrupt. I just—I heard you speaking inside with Holt and I was hoping I'd catch you before you left."

I blinked, trying to understand who this woman was or what she wanted with me. Her voice was barely more than a whisper. Her dull brown hair hung loose around her shoulders. A look of caution and hesitation rested across her face. I wondered if it was the argument she'd interrupted that caused that look or if it was just a default characteristic for her.

"I'm sorry, who are you?" I blurted out, noticing how much anger was still coursing through my voice as she flinched at my words.

"Oh," she gasped timidly. "I'm Willow M..." she stuttered, her eyes locked with mine briefly before dropping her gaze to the ground. "...M eyers. Willow Meyers. I'm a scribe for the Guard. But I just happened to overhear some of your conversation... with H-Holt. And I was hoping to give you a little more information."

She seemed nervous about speaking with us. She could barely hold my gaze and I was getting dizzy watching her eyes dart from me to Arlo, to the path around us. It was not lost on me that she hesitated when saying the guard's name. The feeling of his harsh, sweaty hands on my back and reaching for my leg fluttered through my mind. I couldn't help but wonder if this woman had been at the receiving end of those hands before. Given the way she shied away from even the sound of his name on her lips, I assumed she probably had.

I shook the thought from my mind and stepped toward her. Mustering as much composure as I could manage, I stuck my hand out to greet her.

"I'm Hazel, you're not interrupting anything. I'm sorry, it's just been an emotional day. I'd be more than grateful for any information you have."

She tentatively took my hand, glancing between me and Arlo once more.

"It's nothing huge. I probably should have kept my mouth shut."

This time Arlo stepped forward too, sliding his arm around my waist.

"I'm sure that's not true," he said calmly.

I was worried his presence would scare her away, seeing how hesitant she already was. But it seemed he had the opposite effect. She took in a deep breath and closed her eyes, nodding to herself before she continued.

"Well, I heard him tell you that they think you were involved in an animal attack. That you were found out in the woods?"

I nodded to confirm, still feeling the residual anger from the ridiculous theory.

She took in a shallow breath as she looked me straight in the eyes and said, "I don't think that's what happened to you."

It felt like the world had fallen away as I clung to her words.

"I'm sorry, what did you just say?"

"I don't want to make this any more confusing for you than it already is, but I just wanted to make sure you knew that their word isn't final. They have their explanation for what happened, but that doesn't make it true. I've heard the state you were in when they found you. Your wounds..." She paused and clutched her hand to her chest. "Well, it was all quite messy back then. You were so frenzied and scared. I'm not a member of the Guard, so I can't speak to the evidence, but I know they considered it pretty open and shut given your wounds. But details get around here. Things that don't make it into the records. I heard the things you mentioned back then, the details you gave and could still remember at the time. You were frightened far past the point of a wild animal attack. You believed you were being followed, intentionally hunted. I just don't want you to give up your search based on the inferior work of a couple guards who've probably never seen something like this before. "

"Something like what?" The question left my lips before I'd even finished forming the thought. She spoke like she knew exactly what had happened and was frustrated at how idiotic the Guard was being for not seeing what was right in front of them.

"What do you think happened?" I asked in an even quieter voice.

Something passed over Willow's expression, too quick for me to interpret what it was, before she quickly brushed off the tension in her body and said, "Oh, I'm not sure—I'm so sorry if I gave you that impression. I don't know many of the details, but I felt like you should know the amount of effort that went into your record, or lack thereof. And some of the details that may have been left out. Holt can be... difficult at times. And I could tell you both were rather upset by what he said."

"We appreciate your help," I heard Arlo say from over my shoulder.

"Is there anything you remember?" I quickly added. "From back then?"

She shook her head slightly. "I'm sorry I can't be of more help. I'm not really involved in much of the investigative work. Like I said, I'm just a scribe and really only hear things through the office gossip."

My heart sank a little. It wasn't much, but it was more than we had before. It was confirmation that the Guard could be wrong, and I needed to focus on that.

I forced a small smile and thanked her for her time.

She hesitated for a moment longer then pulled a bundle of papers from behind her and shoved them quickly into my hand.

"Here." Her voice had dropped to nothing more than a whisper. "Just in case you wanted to go look for yourself." Her eyes finding mine, she gave my hand a tight squeeze before letting go. Her gaze lingered, searching almost. She looked like she might say more but finally stepped back, breaking eye contact.

"I really need to be getting back now."

Her head swiveled down the path, landing at last on the front door as she turned and shuffled back into the building behind us.

My gaze followed her path until she was once again inside the decrepit building. Once she had disappeared, I turned my attention to the papers she'd handed me. Confusion washed over me as I felt Arlo's presence against my back.

"What did she give you?"

I flipped through the papers, trying to decipher what exactly was in my hands. Crisp, clean handwriting lined the pages with sparse details. Bits and pieces stuck out to me, sparking memories from somewhere deep in my mind. As I pored over the pages, the realization hit me. In my hands was my record from the Guard.

We walked briskly back through town. I wanted to get out of there before anyone else showed up to question what she had been saying or what she had given us. I couldn't believe she'd been willing to risk this for me, a total stranger. I didn't know much about the Guard's protocols, but I was sure this had to be a huge violation.

"I don't understand why she would have given this to me."

I couldn't stop flipping through the pages as Arlo led us back to our room.

"Maybe she remembered you from before," Arlo offered.

"She did seem kind of familiar, didn't she?"

Arlo didn't answer as we walked into the tavern. It was practically empty in the midday lull, but he made us stop to order a couple sandwiches from the barkeep then headed up to our room. Once inside, I sat down and spread the papers out over our table.

"Alright," I said, stepping back.

"There's not much here, but I think it does give us more to go off of than we had before."

Arlo came up beside me, his sandwich in hand and already missing a bite.

I glared at him.

"What?" he said with a mouthful of food. "I'm sorry, I was hungry."

I rolled my eyes and gave an exaggerated sigh.

"It's okay," I said. "It's not like it's my entire life on the line."

"Rather dramatic today, aren't we?" Arlo said, eyeing me.

That bought him an elbow to the ribs. Ignoring his feigned grunt of pain, I turned my attention back to the table.

"So from what I can make out, it doesn't seem like there was really much of an investigation. But we do have a general map of the area, the ridiculous statement they read us today about closing my record, and details from when they interviewed me after you brought me to the healers."

I paused on the last part, the whole situation feeling so surreal. I had been with the healers when they'd come to ask me questions. I could barely remember what I'd said because I had been delirious at the time. I took a couple steps toward the table and picked up the papers.

"Were you there for this?" I asked Arlo.

"I don't think so. Any time a guard came in, they asked me to step outside. Or at least made me feel like I shouldn't be there, so I typically found some excuse to go do something else."

He looked over my shoulder at the paper. "Why, what's it say?"

I took a deep breath in then read the statement out loud:

"Victim is a female, most likely in young adulthood. Victim claims her name is Hazel. Dark red hair, green eyes. Victim is suffering from memory loss, only able to recall her name. Appears severely disoriented and hysterical. Victim suffers from a deep, three-pronged cut down her abdomen and another on her left leg, along with several abrasions that indicate an attack. According to the healers, she also experienced some sort of trauma to the head which could account for the memory loss. Upon arrival, it was determined that the victim was suffering from exposure to the elements, indicating that she was lost or abandoned somewhere in the area in which she was found. Most likely traveling the road between towns and lost her way. Victim's statement is included below, and she will be referred to by her name from here on out.

"Hazel could not provide much information about what happened to her. She is in a disoriented state but continuously murmuring nonsensical things. She appears afraid and is unwilling or unable to give details about what happened. After questioning her extensively, it is our belief that she was attacked by some sort of animal, survived, and wandered through the wilderness until she was able to find help. Several days in the woods mixed with the trauma of the attack most likely sent her into a crazed state."

Memories flooded my mind, things I hadn't thought about since the day I left the healers and Arlo took me home. The pain had been unbearable, my body feeling like it was burning with unyielding fire or a deadly venom coursing through my veins. I remembered the panic and the confusion—the feeling of being totally and hopelessly lost. It was a terror only matched by the fear I felt in my recurring nightmares. My room became a nonstop flow of people with official-sounding titles and important questions to ask. I didn't even know who half of them were or why they were there, but I could remember that fear. The fear of being in an unfamiliar place, the fear for my life and the constant looking over my shoulder like I thought I'd find something just behind me, poised for the attack.

I had been overwhelmed with the incessant need to go back—but back to what, I couldn't remember. It was right there, right on the edge of my mind. If I could only concentrate hard enough to remember what important thing I was forgetting, what I felt so desperate to get back to. It never came, and the longer I stayed in that room with the healers, the more distant that memory became. Standing here now, though, reading the record from last year and with constant memories flooding my mind, that incessant need to go back had returned with a vengeance. A wave of desperation crashed over my body. I could feel the paper shaking in my unsteady hands.

Arlo squeezed my shoulder, pulling me out of my reverie.

"Hazel," he whispered softly into the air. "Talk to me. What are you thinking?"

"I just—" I hesitated. "I was thinking about those days with the healers. Really thinking about them, probably for the first time since we left it. It's like I had totally forgotten I'd even been there until right now."

"What did you remember?" he asked.

"That's the thing," I said, throwing the paper back on the table. I walked away and ran my hands through my hair. I could feel the frustration rising in me again—the feeling that I couldn't quite recall what important thing was tugging at me, begging me to remember.

"I can't. I can't remember anything useful. I just know that *something* happened. It's like my body knows and is crying out for my mind to remember, but I just can't."

I sat down in a frustrated huff and started flexing my hands to get them to stop shaking.

Arlo watched me for a minute then turned his attention back to the papers.

"So we keep digging."

I stared at him, leaning over the table and taking in all the information that lay there.

"You mean that?" I finally asked.

He pulled his attention away from whichever paper he had been reading and held my gaze. "Of course, Hazel."

"I know this wasn't exactly where you wanted to be or what you wanted to be doing but—"

"I didn't want to come," he interrupted, "because I was worried you'd get hurt. Not because I didn't want you to find answers. But seeing you here now, how close we are to it all... I can see that it's the not knowing that's really hurting you. I think I just got used to our rhythm at home. I got used to taking on that role of protector and healer, trying to make sure you were really ready to get back out into the world."

He let out a breath and stalked over to where I sat. Taking my hands, he dropped to his knees before me.

"You asked me at the Guard's office what I really thought of their statement, what I really thought happened to you. The truth is I don't know. I think their story is an easy one to accept. I hate to admit it, but it's one I found myself almost hoping to be true. Because if it is, then it's done. Case closed, day done, and we can go home and move on. But that nagging feeling you have? That one telling you it's not possible? I'd be a fool to not admit I feel it too. Not as strong as you do, clearly." He gestured down to my shaking hands. "But it's there. I know their story doesn't add up. And I know there's something here for us to find. I'm scared to death, Hazel—fuck, am I scared. I don't want to see you get hurt. I don't want to lose you. But we can't come this close to answers and just walk away. So I'm here. However you need me, I'm here."

The sight of him there, completely vulnerable and surrendered to me, had me coming undone.

The steady, clear focus of his warm, caramel eyes convinced me that he meant it. Every word dripped with sincerity. I took a breath, then another, never breaking that penetrating stare. It was like he was seeing me, truly seeing me for the first time in our relationship. It reminded me of how he looked at me that day he found me out in the woods, fully understanding just what he was getting himself into. He'd loved me the whole time, but this was different. This was him admitting that he wasn't the one calling the shots, that I didn't need him to take care of me anymore. This was him accepting that shift in our comfortable and familiar roles and rhythms, and acknowledging the strength that I had somehow found along the way, and I loved him even more for that.

I leaned in hard and fast to kiss him. It wasn't gentle like it usually was between us. It was a reflection that something different had crept into our relationship without either of us realizing it. Before I knew it, he was lifting me out of the chair and carrying me to the bed. His lips never left mine. His hands grasped firmly on my thighs. He paused in front of the bed, my feet dangling above just enough that I could feel the soft linens brushing against my toes. He pulled back long enough to look me over, taking in the sight of me. My breath was heavy as my arms wrapped tighter around his neck, desperate for more of him. He shifted one arm under me and the other around my back and up to my neck. Gently, he lowered me to the bed below us, kneeling on the edge as he looked down at me lying before him.

"I never want to forget the look of you wanting me," he breathed out. He stayed there a minute longer, taking in every piece of me.

It felt like torture, not having him on me. The taste of him still heavy on my lips, I wanted nothing more than for him to devour me fully. Nothing else mattered at that moment. Not the Guard or the papers on the table. Not the place where we were or the unanswered questions hanging in the air. This was all that mattered.

"You know," he said suddenly, "I've been thinking about that guard all day, how he couldn't seem to keep his hands off you." I shuddered slightly at the thought of him, my body involuntarily reacting to the feel of his uninvited hands on me.

"That right there, I should have ripped him apart for making you feel like that." The sheer violence in his words shocked me. He had a tendency to be protective, but I'd never heard him talk like that before.

"It's okay, he didn't do anything really," I said quietly.

"No, it's not okay. No one should make you feel like that and get to walk away unscathed." He lowered himself to me, painfully slow. "But we aren't there anymore to teach him a lesson. So I guess all that's left for me to do is to help you remember how your body should be worshiped as you see fit, not pawed at without consent."

I let out a small noise resembling a gasp as he hooked his fingers around the top of my leggings and tugged them down in one smooth motion.

"Remind you," he continued, his lips tipping up along the edges as he unfastened the button of his own pants, "what your body is deserving of, and what your mind should spend time thinking about. And his sorry excuse of an existence isn't it."

"What should I be thinking about then?" I asked, my voice sounding breathy and faint.

"That you are divine, and any being worthy of touching you should do so with a sense of awe and wonder. And that's exactly what I plan to do."

I didn't even have time to process his words before he took control. His lips danced along my body, trailing behind his hands as he yanked my tunic over my head and kissed every intimate part. His tongue flicked against my skin in the most sensitive places. He worked his way down my neck to my breasts and even lower before coming back to my lips. I kissed him relentlessly, clawing at his back, desperate to get closer to him. To have him inside me. He could feel that desperation, had tasted it when he'd kissed me at my center. He ran a hand up the side of my body, cupping my breast. He closed his hands around its peak as he thrust himself inside me. The impressive rhythm of his body had me crashing over the edge fast. He didn't slow, that relentless rhythm making my body come undone over and over again.

When we were both finally spent, he collapsed on the bed beside me. Our heavy breathing was the only noise filling the room. Minutes passed like this, his fingers grazing my skin every so often. I turned to kiss him and whispered, "I couldn't imagine anywhere else I'd rather be than right here."

He brushed the hair away from my face and kissed the top of my head, pulling me in tighter.

CHAPTER 7
HAZEL

I was standing on the edge of a clearing. Thick, overgrown forest loomed behind me. Forcing me forward. I could hear the rageful shouts of fighting ahead of me. My eyes swept across the clearing, trying to make sense of what the forms were. Angry, dark clouds hung low above me, around the trees that stood like giants, stretching toward the sky. A streak of light ignited the sky just as some sort of creature took flight. Its leathery wings were vast, causing the air to ripple as it flew. The shock of watching it take off momentarily distracted me from the rest of the scene unfolding before me.

A deep, powerful thunderclap tore my eyes away from the sky and back to the field in front of me as an explosion of light erupted in the clearing. It rattled every bone in my body, rattled something deeper. I realized it wasn't thunder at all. That dark, powerful surge had come from the one figure left standing in the clearing, surrounded by unmoving bodies scattered across the forest floor. I didn't understand how an individual could make such an unearthly sound, how it moved from just a sound reaching my ears and became a powerful entity I could feel in my skin. The vibration faded as moments passed. The leathery-winged creature had disappeared from my view. Our view, I realized, as the figure's attention lingered in the sky with mine. It fell to its knees, its breath ragged, skin bleeding. I took a step forward, unsure what I intended to do.

A twig snapped beneath my foot and the figure's head jerked to discover I was there. Its eyes locked on mine, pure agony and rage radiating from them. Rage turned to shock and then hesitation as it opened its mouth to speak. It was too far away for me to make out any features aside from those glowing eyes. Too far for me to be able to hear what it said. Yet somehow, I did.

"Hazlenn?"

The word echoed around me, whispering over my skin. I wanted to go to it, understand what it spoke and why. But as soon as I took a step forward, I lurched back and was consumed by the never-ending darkness I always found in my nightmares. Tumbling and plummeting through a void of nothingness, my feet desperately trying to find solid ground.

Then, I was running. The familiar screams filled my ears as the metallic scent of blood hit my nose. I looked down at my hands and saw the dark red liquid covering them. There was so much blood. And I couldn't tell whose it was, where it came from. But the blinding pain radiating throughout my body as I ran didn't bode well. I couldn't see what was chasing me. It was right there at the edge of my vision, a shadow I couldn't quite grasp. But I knew it was getting closer and I needed to get away. My vision swayed. I wondered if I would pass out, but just as those familiar claws curled around my leg, I felt my body lunge forward. Sweet relief filled my mind as I somehow believed I'd gotten away, but it was short-lived. What came next was chaos and heat, ripping me apart and surrounding every piece of me.

The feel of the silent scream was still radiating through my body as I woke with a sharp inhale. I scanned the room, taking in my surroundings. Disoriented, it took me a minute to remember we were in our rented room above the tavern, instead of the familiar feel of Arlo's home. Arlo's even breathing was the sound that brought me back to reality. Relief rushed my body as I realized I was safe and not in fact running for my life as I had been in my dream. But with the grounding that those thoughts brought, came the reminder of all we had found out yesterday. I knew that today would be long, that we had things to hunt down, answers to find. I was already exhausted by it.

I rolled out of bed, stretching my arms behind my back. I hadn't realized how stiff I was lately, the stress of everything going on affecting me both in my body and my mind. As I worked to loosen the pain in my neck, I padded along the rough floor of our room. Coffee seemed like a smart choice, so I began working at the small, wood-burning stove on the opposite side of the room. As I fumbled with the beans, my mind wandered to our escapades of yesterday evening. A smile spread over my lips as I thought of all the ways Arlo had made love to me. He'd told me he wanted to worship my body, and that he did.

It was funny, being here had brought out a side of him I'd never seen before. He'd begun to let that incessant need to protect me above all else slip just a little bit. Everything seemed less serious between us these last few days. It wasn't weak, damaged Hazel, and strong, overprotective Arlo. We were just... *us*.

I heard the rustle of the sheets as I waited for the coffee to finish brewing. Within a heartbeat, I felt Arlo's chest against my back and his arms wrapping around my waist. I leaned my head back against him and let out a deep, contented sigh.

"Good morning, my darling divine," he said, his voice still dripping with the promise of things he wanted to do to me.

My eyes rolled, despite the smile creeping across my lips.

"Good morning, Arlo," I threw back in a sarcastic tone. "Quite a little nickname you've come up with there."

"Well, when you're in the presence of perfection such as yourself, a simple title like *beautiful* or *princess* just doesn't seem good enough."

I gave him a little shove with my arm and turned around to hand him his coffee.

I took a long sip before meeting his gaze, the question lingering in the air between us.

"So, you ready for today?" he asked.

I nodded, although I wasn't sure I was.

There was a heavy weight I could feel settling on my shoulders. By the look of Arlo's stance, he felt it too. I couldn't help but wonder if yesterday's endeavors were his way of being with me, one last time, before all of this unfolded—like some sort of unknowing goodbye. The thought sent a shiver through my body and I quickly shook it off before I dwelled longer on what that could mean for us moving forward. Arlo might have been worried about losing me, but I was determined to make sure that didn't happen. I didn't care what answers we found: he was mine and I was his. I wasn't going anywhere.

I walked back to the table where we'd left the papers the stranger from the Guard's office had given me. Thumbing through them, I found the map I was looking for and laid it out.

"So I was thinking we could go search the area today," I said, focused on the papers in front of us.

I heard Arlo's wary sigh behind me, but he made no other moves to protest. Slowly, he joined me beside the table.

"That area is pretty unsettled," he offered. "We need to grab some supplies if we're going to travel through it. And we need to get a move on if you're wanting to go today. We can't be stuck out there once it starts getting dark, or it will be impossible to find our way back and we'll have to make camp out there."

"How long do you think it will take to search the area?" I asked, my eyes dancing over the map in an attempt to soak up as much information as possible.

Arlo paused, doing the same before answering, "It's hard to say. I'm not sure how tricky the terrain will be." He brought the map closer to his face, his eyes tracing the details. "Probably a couple days. Maybe longer if we have to make our way back through the area we've already searched each time we go out there."

I nodded, silently contemplating what to say next.

"I know what you're getting at, Hazel. I don't think camping out there is a good idea."

"Why not? It would save us a lot of time. We wouldn't have to travel back and forth each day and we'd be able to track our progress along the way."

Arlo sighed. "Because you've barely left the house in the last year, let alone spent any kind of time in the woods. Besides, we don't know what going out there is going to do to you. What if it triggers memories of what happened and you can't handle it?"

What he was saying made sense, but it didn't make it hurt any less. I had zero experience, at least from what I remembered, doing something like this. Setting up camp in the woods, under the starlight and with nothing else around, should scare me. But it just didn't. Images of Arlo holding me after some of my worst episodes flooded my head. I knew why he was saying this. I've been a fractured shell more times than I could count, helpless and depending on him to piece me back together. But regardless of what memories it might stir up for me, I knew I needed to go. I knew I could handle whatever happened out there.

"Arlo, I know you're just trying to protect me." My voice was quiet but resolute. "But you have to let me decide what I can handle. This is my past, my problems to deal with. You can't save me from everything. You can't save me from this. It's the whole reason we're here."

"I know, and I promise I'm here for whatever you think we should do. But I want you to take a minute and think about this. Is this really such a wise decision? Do you really think that, without a doubt, you can handle whatever we may come across out there?"

I turned away from the table, forcing myself to meet his eyes—forcing every ounce of strength and determination into mine. The golden flecks that always appeared in his eyes when he was at his most focused were shimmering in the yellow hum of the room's morning light. I took his hands in mine and took a deep breath.

"I'm ready, Arlo."

He stared at me for a minute, his jaw clenched. I wondered if he was going to fight me, insist that we stay here, or worse yet, go home. Everything with Arlo up to this point had been a fight. Only in the last couple days had he let his guard down, but I wasn't foolish enough to think that meant he had given up the fight to protect me from what we might find. I braced myself for his words, expecting the worst, expecting that we'd both be putting up a fight for what would come next. Finally, he closed his eyes and squeezed my hands.

"Okay," he said. "Then we better get moving."

After we got dressed and loaded up the few items we brought with us that would actually be useful, we grabbed a quick breakfast at the tavern downstairs and made our way to the shops in town. I would be lying if I said I wasn't nervous. No matter how badly I wanted to do this, to get out there and hit the ground running until I found something, I also had this small feeling in my gut that something bad was going to happen. Maybe it was the safety information Arlo was grilling into me, or the dagger that he'd thrust upon me at the blacksmith's shop and refused to return when I told him he was being ridiculous, but I had a pit in my stomach that I couldn't seem to get rid of.

Arlo continued pelting me with protocols for the woods as he guided our horse down the road, out of town, and toward the direction the map indicated. I was wearing a pair of thicker leggings for riding and a linen chemise with a heavier wool tunic layered over it. I pulled at the thick wool, ensuring my arms were covered, as the chilled wind whipped around us. At the inn, I'd donned myself in a pair of boots and a lightweight rucksack with various items tucked inside, including an extra pair of clothes, a canteen for water, and a little food for our journey. Since leaving the shops in town, Arlo had added his own emergency supplies, and more food and water to the bags strapped to the horse's sides. Not to mention the items he'd attached to me like he was outfitting a pack mule. Strapped to my leg now hung my very own personal dagger. The stiffness took some getting used to but not as much as the shock I felt every time I glanced down and remembered the gaudy knife was attached to me and on display for all to see. He'd insisted on carrying the bulk of our equipment, but he'd helped me attach a bedroll to my pack before we'd made our way out of town.

I leaned around Arlo, taking in the open land laid out before us. Deep green and brown trees lined the road on either side of us, before thinning out and making room for the walls of rock jutting up around them off in the distance. It was the first real look I'd taken in since we'd left the town's borders. A couple groups of travelers made their way to and from nearby towns on the long stretch of road ahead of us. As we pushed further into the wilderness, the annoying grit of the other travelers' voices fell away. I found myself closing my eyes to breathe in the peaceful midday air. It was practically buzzing with energy, and a feeling of peace built inside of me as my lungs greedily sucked in the crisp feeling.

The sunlight was refreshing against the chill of the spring air. It felt different out here. I couldn't understand how this beautiful piece of land that I knew nothing about felt more like home than any of the places back in our town, felt more alive than anything I'd ever remembered experiencing. It was like my lungs were desperate for the air, lapping it up with every eager inhale. I was terrified that I'd miss something if my eyes didn't move fast enough, even more scared that this might all in fact be a dream and disappear with the next blink of an eye. I was all too familiar with that ever-flowing nature that made a recurring appearance in my dreams, and this seemed eerily close to that. Perhaps it felt so similar because it was all just one relentless dream that I'd found myself trapped inside.

I couldn't explain why my heart jumped with electric excitement as Arlo eventually led the horse off the main road and toward the foliage of the woods. I couldn't explain why a ringing echoed through my ears so strong it felt like it was vibrating my whole body. All I knew was that everything else melted away and it was only me and the earth left to greet each other once again like old friends.

We would be fine. Things would be okay. I repeated those words like a mantra with every stride we made into the woods, away from civilization. I'd be safe. Because Arlo was with me and he was always there to protect me. But no matter how many times I repeated that mantra as we made our way deeper into the rock formations, something within me couldn't let go of my all-too-familiar nightmares. In my dreams, the darkness always swooped in just after the inherent beauty of nature.

This wasn't like that, though. There was a difference between my dreams and reality. I wasn't alone like I always was in my dreams. Arlo was here, and he'd be able to keep me safe, no matter what came. Despite the comfort that his presence should have brought me, there was a small voice somewhere inside me saying it wouldn't be enough.

CHAPTER 8
HAZEL

Massive formations of red rock shot up around us. It didn't take long for the thick green of the woods to fall away and be replaced with solid walls of caramel and crimson. Arlo helped the horse navigate some of the trickier terrain, but eventually we fell into an easy stride on flatter land. The map hung loosely in his hand and he would drop his gaze every few minutes to compare what lay ahead with what he saw on the map.

There was an awkward quiet that fell over us as we ventured deeper into the wilderness, our only source of conversation being the things surrounding us: the shape of that rock formation, the color or look of a specific tree root, a unique looking bug as it flew by. It was idle talk, half-hearted and absent-minded. We both knew we didn't want to address what we were really doing out here, so the quiet hung in the air like a storm cloud, heavy and swollen with apprehension. My eyes darted at every movement; my body jumped at any abrupt sound. I needed to get a grip on myself before I totally lost it. I gritted my teeth and hoped

Arlo hadn't noticed how unsettled I was. I wanted to show him that I could do this, that I was okay. The steady trembling in my hands wasn't helping get my point across, though, and I tucked them behind me in hopes that he wouldn't notice.

Instead, I focused on the land around us. It was hard not to get lost in it. The roll of the red rock cutting through the foliage of the forest was unlike anything I had ever seen. Its inherent beauty distracted me as time passed and we traveled further and further away from civilization. The buzz of energy remained in my chest, propelling me forward, calling me to go deeper still.

Out of the corner of my eye, I vaguely registered Arlo talking to me. The movement pulled me from the daze. I tilted my head toward Arlo, my face a blank slate. After a moment, I realized he was waiting for me to reply to something I hadn't heard him say.

"What?" I asked. My eyes blinked a few frantic times as I tried to clear my head. Arlo seemed practically unphased by the beauty around us.

Had I really been that sheltered this past year that I felt this shaken at the first sign of honest, untouched nature?

"We should stop here for the night." The volume in his voice startled me after spending the last several hours in practically total silence.

"Here?" I asked. "Do you think this is a good spot?" I looked around, shocked that we'd traveled so far already.

"It's as good as any. I'll look around a little, find the best spot to make camp. Maybe there's a more shaded area up ahead that would provide more coverage."

He folded up the map and dismounted before offering me his hand and helping me down. He tied the reins around a nearby tree and made off in the direction he'd gestured toward setting up camp, calling over his shoulder that he'd be back in a minute. I sat down on a nearby boulder and peeled off my heavy tunic, the lightweight fabric underneath sticking to my skin. The morning had started off with a crisp breeze, but by now I was burning up and deeply regretting my choice in riding attire. I laid it out on the rocks beside me, hoping the sun would help dry it out a little before I had to shove it in my rucksack tomorrow. I rummaged around in my bag for some of the food we had packed and settled on a small jar of nuts.

Leaning back on the rock, I inhaled deeply. Even after riding most of the afternoon, my lungs still hadn't gotten used to this air. I almost didn't want them to. I closed my eyes and continued taking deep, glorious breaths. I hadn't realized just how tired I was while we were traveling, but now that my body had a chance to rest, I could feel the exhaustion rolling over me. Muscles I hadn't used in ages were sore from the ride and the slight breeze felt good against my clammy cheeks.

Hazel.

My eyes shot open as I sat up straight. I could have sworn I heard my name whispered through the air with that last breeze that hit me. My arms and legs were covered in gooseflesh. I called out to Arlo, wondering if it had been him calling for me. No answer came. The humming vibration I felt when we first veered into the woods began to spread over me again. The few noises left around me, the soft birdsong and hum of unseen insects, fell away as the gentle lull of vibration took over my ears. I couldn't escape it. I didn't want to. It was calling me and carrying me. I was useless against it.

Just as I felt myself falling fully under its call, a strong hand clamped down on my shoulder, shaking me.

"Hazel!" the voice yelled.

It took a painstakingly long time to come out of the trance, to realize it was Arlo who had a hold on me, who was still shaking me.

Slowly, my brain was able to form thoughts, to push words out to him in an attempt to calm him—maybe in an attempt to calm myself, too.

"Sorry, I just got distracted, daydreaming." I waved my hand to gesture toward my head.

"Daydreaming, my ass, Hazel. I've been calling you for almost two minutes. You were walking into the woods! Alone! What is going on with you?"

Wouldn't we both have loved to know the answer to that.

"I think," I trailed off, trying to understand what exactly it was I thought. "I think I just need some water. I'm not feeling well, or I wasn't." I shook my head, trying to make sense of my thoughts. "I'm fine now, though."

Arlo stared me down, his breath ragged and his face strung tight with fear. He didn't believe me. I didn't even believe me. But I didn't know how else to describe what just happened. It had to be from lack of water, right? That caused things like tingling and numbness, dizzy spells and fainting. Or maybe something like hunger was at fault. It had to be something like that because I didn't know what else it could have been. The problem was, I felt that back on the road before we'd even ventured out, before any kind of exhaustion from our journey would have set in.

After several more rounds of assessments, he'd decided to accept my theory. He'd made me sit down and drink a whole canteen of water. I didn't complain, mostly because I was exhausted from the day, but also because the drink was a sweet relief against the rugged dryness the weird buzzing had left on my tongue and it had me chugging what was left of the water. Maybe I really did need something to drink.

I sat in a daze while I watched Arlo finish setting up our campsite. It struck me how natural this came to him, like he'd done it a thousand times before. I briefly wondered if he had done this in a previous life, a life before I came into the picture and became the only thing he ever focused on. As I watched him so carefully focused on his work, my heart broke for who he could have been before the chaos that was my life knocked down his door.

We settled in with a small fire and an assortment of food pulled from our pack for dinner. It wasn't much, but it was enough to restore the strength I'd lost during the day. We could only bring so much, and I wanted to make it last as long as possible so we didn't have to head back into town to restock before we were done with our search.

If we'd ever be done searching, that is. We'd spent a day out here already and hadn't found anything. I didn't even know what I thought we'd find, but I just felt like maybe one of us would recognize the area, remember where I'd wandered all those months ago, lost and scared in the woods. Maybe we'd even find some sign that I'd actually been out here.

I took a slow breath and tried to remind myself that we hadn't been out here that long. That it was going to take time to search such a large area, especially without knowing exactly where to start. I glanced at Arlo through the glow of our little fire. The smoke curled around us, its bitter scent filling my nose. He had been distracted this evening, fumbling around and muttering to himself. I could tell he was worried. He'd kept his eye on me since the incident earlier while somehow simultaneously managing to avoid my gaze. I wondered if he was starting to regret coming out here. He didn't even want to bring me here to begin with, but I needed to reassure him that I could do this.

After all, the symptoms from earlier had all but corrected themselves. I was no longer dizzy. I thought I'd been going crazy when I'd heard my name through the wind, but if things like ear ringing and loss of awareness could be caused by a lack of water, I'm sure hearing things in general could be too. Besides, I hadn't heard anything since that initial whisper. The gooseflesh had long since disappeared from my skin, and that vibration I'd felt had slowed, settling into a steady hum in my head. I chalked that up to the clean air I wasn't used to and the pure exhaustion I felt after what seemed like the longest day of my life.

I pushed myself off the hard ground and made my way over to Arlo's side of the fire. As much as I wanted to reassure him I was okay, I also just felt safer with him next to me. His presence was calming, his touch grounding. Well, it was usually. Tonight though, he felt stiff and uncomfortable. I wiggled in close to him, leaving the smallest amount of distance. Just enough for him to close in, if he chose to.

The more distance we put between us and that little room at the inn, the more distant he was becoming. Maybe this wasn't worth it. Maybe I was doing more harm than good and was just pushing him away. Would it be worth it to get answers about my past if it meant losing him? That's what he'd been afraid of, why he didn't want to pursue this path. *What if we keep pushing and don't find anything and I still lose him in the process? Could I live with that?*

This whole thing was starting to feel like a huge mistake.

As if he sensed my unease, my rambling thoughts, he finally dropped his arm around me and pulled me into his body, closing the distance between us. We leaned back on the boulder behind us and stared up into the night. Stars sprinkled the onyx sky, glowing and dancing to the music of the cosmos. They looked truly happy, and I wondered what it would be like to know that kind of joy. To dance to the music of the earth and live carefree enough to not be bothered by the pain that lay waiting to take me down or the darkness waiting to consume me. It seemed like the kind of thing I'd only be able to appreciate from the outside looking in, not something I'd ever be able to experience for myself.

We spoke softly to each other, admiring the beauty around us and making plans for the rest of our time here. Every time Arlo brought up something from home, I veered the conversation away. It felt wrong to talk about that here; the dreary monotony of our home life wasn't even comparable to the space that we now invaded. I didn't want to think of that life when it felt so distant from where we were now.

Before I knew it, I was dozing on Arlo's chest and he was gently trying to wake me and move us to the tent. The exhaustion pulled me, barely letting me hit the blankets before taking me under again. As sleep crowded my brain, I could vaguely feel Arlo's lips against my forehead, hear his words hanging in the air:

"I love you, Hazel."

CHAPTER 9
HAZEL

*H*azel.

My eyes shot open. What time was it? Arlo was still fast asleep beside me. Daylight hadn't yet invaded the night sky. I paused and listened, trying to make sense of what I'd just heard. My name. The same way it had whispered through the breeze earlier today. There was nothing now, though. Maybe my mind was playing tricks on me. Maybe the symptoms from earlier had lingered well into the night. Maybe the memory of my name on Arlo's lips as he'd kissed me goodnight had permeated my dreams. Maybe that's all this was.

I was about to close my eyes and chalk the whole thing up to my affinity for vivid dreams and Arlo's sweet gesture as I had fallen asleep, but there it was again:

Hazel.

Barely a whisper. It couldn't even truly be my name because it wasn't a fully formed word. Just the sound of the breeze lazily breathing against the tent. I sat straight up this time. What in the world was going on? This was definitely not from lack of water. The hum that had lingered in my head ever since this evening, ever since we left town really, was growing. It made my hands shake as I pulled on my boots.

When had I gotten up? When had I decided to put my boots on?

The temperature had dropped in the night. The air was chilled and I found myself grabbing for my wool tunic before ducking out of the tent and into the open air. I glanced back at Arlo, still dead to the world. I debated waking him, asking him to come with me. But I didn't even know what I was doing. Convincing myself I was just going to take a quick look around and didn't need to bother him, I dropped the fabric of the tent entrance.

With each step I told myself I was acting crazy. There hadn't been anyone calling to me, no whisper of my name on the wind. That sounded truly insane. That wasn't real. That was the kind of thing that happened in fairy tales and folklore. Suddenly, I was kicking myself for not looking more into the folklore of this area. For a girl who lived to research local records and lore, I'd had a huge oversight in prepping for this journey into the wilderness. What if I was walking right into a faerie ring or some dark pit of a big monstrous creature that called to weak girls in the middle of the night? No, this was all insane. I was just going to take a look around the area before I'd tuck myself back into our little tent and reassure myself that it had all been some vivid dream, my mind playing tricks on me.

If that was true, where was I going now?

I'd intended to circle the campsite, pausing often to quiet my movements and listen for anything that wasn't supposed to be there. I'd grabbed my dagger, but nothing else because I didn't *need* anything else to just circle the tent. My first few steps were true to my plan, strapping the sheathed knife against my thigh as Arlo had done earlier. The further I walked away from the tent the more I realized I wasn't actually circling anything, though. I was letting my feet lead me, following that all-too-familiar pull in my chest. I was walking directly away from the campsite.

Step after step, minute after minute, I fought myself to turn around and go back. This wasn't safe. I needed Arlo. But my body wasn't listening. My feet moved as if propelled forward by some invisible force. I knew Arlo wouldn't want me to go searching in the dark. If I went back and got him, he'd tuck me in the tent with the knife he bought me and tell me to stay put until he had a look around. The realization didn't have me turning around. It had me pushing further into the night.

Almost absent-mindedly, I reached down to ensure the dagger was still attached to my thigh. I didn't know what good it would do since I had zero idea how to use it. I gave it a reassuring pat, relieved to find I'd secured it properly and it was staying put. So far, I'd found nothing out of the ordinary. The night was quiet, much different than the atmosphere I was used to back home. I was keenly aware of the lack of noise, no late-night townspeople stumbling home or neighbors talking. No dogs barking relentlessly, being ignored by their owners. But the silence didn't bother me. It gave me the strength to press on, allowing my mind the space it needed to quiet, to rest—maybe even to move without the feeling of overthinking what I was doing.

That's exactly what I was doing. I wasn't thinking. I had no idea where I was going or why I was still walking. The distance from the tent was too far. A large rock formation jutted up in front of me, causing me to veer to the right. Once around it, I'd lose sight of our camp altogether. Turning back didn't even cross my mind this time. I rounded the rocks and paused only long enough to verify that the tent was indeed out of sight. It should have scared me, should have caused me to want to turn around and go back. Instead, I found myself breaking into a sprint, running toward the pull.

I didn't think I'd ever felt such a drive as I was feeling now. It was impossible to ignore, even harder to fight. I wasn't just moving toward something absent-mindedly anymore. I was actively choosing to run toward it with all my might. All sense of caution and suspicion was gone. The pull was so strong, I felt like I'd split in two if I didn't get there, didn't satisfy that longing. A wave of grief and despair washed over me, the sense of loss and hopelessness a tangible entity all around me—feelings that weren't my own and that I didn't understand. It pushed me to run faster, begged me to move quicker. It would only be satisfied once I answered the call, once I found the source pulling me ever deeper into the wilderness.

I lost all sense of where I was, how long I'd been running. The sky was still darkened with the deep blue of night, but the first strip of day's light was starting to break through the darkness. Crimson rock formations and plants the color of death rushed past my vision as I ran. The world around me fell away as I connected with one thing and one thing only: that call that I've carried with me practically every day since I lost my memory. It had never left me, not really. Now that I was here, now that I could feel its pull ringing through every inch of my body, nothing else mattered.

Just as the vibration humming inside me reached an all-time high, just as I thought my head would explode from the intensity of it all, it stopped. I stopped. I doubled over in pain, trying to keep myself from losing the contents of my stomach. My feet ached. My sides were screaming. My breath was ragged, impossibly uneven as I tried to recover from running that far, that fast.

How far had I gone? Given the periwinkle haze growing on the horizon, I knew it was almost sunrise by now. It was impossible. I thought of Arlo back at the tent, how worried he'd be when he woke up to find me gone.

I straightened, wiping my sweat-slicked palms on my thighs as I stood. Trying to get my bearings, I turned slowly. There was no one in sight. Nothing here to indicate I'd been running toward anything intentional. I had no idea what direction I'd even come from, no idea how to get back to Arlo. As I turned in circles, panic took hold of me. If there was nothing here, then maybe there had been nothing calling to me. There would be no answers, no signs to say I'd been here before or to tell me what had happened to me. The hold on my chest tightened, forcing breath from my lungs. Just then, something caught in the corner of my vision. I closed my eyes and took in a shaky breath. I didn't know what I was looking for, but I hoped there was something—anything—to make me feel like I wasn't losing my mind.

I spun quickly, turning to face whatever it was head-on. Ahead of me stood a towering wall of red rock. The moon hung brightly above it, like a beacon calling me. The ground around it was covered in varying types of twisting roots—and of course small bunches of those familiar cloudlike flowers that always seemed to find me. Bits of rock and gravel came together along the banks of a quiet river, forming a makeshift path up to the mountain. Any kind of civilization was at least a day's ride away; it would be a terrible decision to follow the river up the mountain. My eyes lingered on the path the water made, following it up to the wall of stone just ahead. A small gasp escaped my lips as my eyes met a large archway in the stone.

That hadn't been there a second ago, had it? It didn't seem like something I'd miss. It was breathtaking and expansive. I felt my boot sink into the soft crimson sand and realized that I was moving up the path and closer to that gap in the rock. I couldn't make out what was on the other side; all I could see was the dark night sky, now glowing with the haze of early morning light. If I could just get closer, see what about it intrigued me so. The pull that I had felt was less intense now, but still there: a constant coaxing to keep going, a small promise that everything would be okay.

Before I knew it, I'd climbed to the top of the path and was now crawling over boulders to get up into the middle of the arch. The closer I got to it, the bigger it felt, like it was a constantly growing entity, showing off for me just how powerful it was. My hands ached as the solid rock dug into my palms. Sweat dripped down my neck and it felt almost impossible to get to the top. The more I climbed, the further away it felt, like I was stuck in some endlessly looping dream.

Finally, I climbed over the last boulder and looked up. I'd made the ascent and now stood directly in the middle of the archway. The humming was back to an overwhelming high, but its weight felt a little more bearable. Less like a desperate call and more like a reassuring nudge.

I'd done it. I was here. I didn't know what it meant, I knew even less what I was supposed to do now, but I couldn't help the smile that spread across my lips at the feeling of accomplishment that settled over me. I peered through the archway, trying to make sense of what I saw on the other side. It was like I couldn't quite get my eyes to focus on the sheer depth of the darkness there.

Maybe I just needed to get a little closer to see what it was.

I'd be damned if I was going to climb all this way and not be able to actually see what I was climbing for. I planted my boot on the next rock, tested my weight, and took another step. The stones up here were much more unstable and I needed to be careful I didn't slip and fall. The last thing I wanted was to be trapped out here with a broken leg and no way to find help. As I took another step, I quickly wondered how long it would take Arlo to find me. I wondered if he was already awake and searching for me, panicking as he realized I was gone.

Hazel.

I paused midstep. My name carried through the air once again. This time it sounded like it was coming from every direction. It was all around me, inside of me, rushing through me. It was carrying me those last few steps to the top and over the edge.

Hazel.

It was becoming much more real, more personal. No, that one had sounded different entirely. I turned back and heard my name ring out again. My heart sank as I realized it was Arlo, shouting my name somewhere in the distance.

What was I doing? Guilt overcame me as I realized how scared he had to be, how much of an idiot I'd been running out into the wilderness in the middle of the night with nothing more than a dagger and a whim.

Hazel.

This time I couldn't differentiate between the calls. Arlo's voice cried out as the air whispered my name all around me. Both pulsed with desperation. I was frozen to the spot with fear and confusion, tears welling in my eyes. In my mind, I was walking back down the path, back to Arlo. He'd meet me at the bottom and we'd both laugh at how silly I'd been as we walked lazily, hand in hand, back to camp. But my feet weren't moving. My body was still facing the vast openness on the other side of the archway.

I willed my body to turn back, to run to Arlo. I didn't want to be here anymore. I'd made a mistake. I told my feet to turn and go before whatever was calling me pushed me over the edge. I was caught in a doorway between two worlds and frozen in time. I was hit again with the feeling of being pulled apart, split in two from the inside out. Tears streamed down my face. Even as I begged my body to stop, screamed at it to turn around, it took a step forward. Then another. I turned back one last time.

"Arlo." His name, nothing more than a whisper on my lips. There one minute, then gone the next. I begged my body one last time to relinquish control, to listen to me, but it was useless. With my next step I was through the archway and the rocks below my feet gave way. I was falling and there was nothing there to catch me, no one there to save me from my fall. Darkness closed in as the air was pulled from my lungs and I folded in on myself. The last thing I heard was one final cry, one final plea to come back.

"HAZEL!"

CHAPTER 10
VANDER

*H*azlenn.

I jerked awake, eyes wide and breath heavy. I felt her. For the first time in years I felt her, saw her in my dreams. I'd long since given up hope. Long since abandoned any idea of seeing her again, sensing her presence. So much so that I wrote off the little pulls I've felt here and there over the past few weeks. I chalked it up to my stupid heart, unwilling to let her go. Even in my dreams, I had stopped looking for her. This, though? This was clear as day. Hazlenn had been there, silently observing quite possibly the worst memory I had. That day has consumed every part of me for the past ten years. Seeing Hazlenn ripped away, feeling her fear grow to an unbearable pitch. And then not feeling anything at all.

The memories from that day flooded my nightmares endlessly. Just as they did tonight. Perhaps that was why I preferred spending my nights out there, hunting. Out there, I was well aware of the nightmares that lurked. I could seek them out before they overtook me. And I was in control. I could end them, watch their breath sputter out as their blood flowed freely from their bodies like a trapped torrent, finally breaking free.

A cold sweat broke out over my body. I paused only long enough to gather my thoughts, to decide what the next course of action should be. Sweeping my legs out from the bed, I rushed across the room. I began to form a plan as I walked toward the front door. Shifting would be the fastest way to reach her, if she was indeed back. I hesitated, trying to decide if I should let Bastian know I was going. I didn't want to admit what I'd felt. I didn't want to lend anyone false hope.

What if I had been wrong? What if what I'd felt was just lingering emotion? What if the dream was just that—a dream?

But it was never just a dream with Hazlenn.

I closed my eyes and took a steadying breath. I needed to get my shit together or I'd end up getting myself killed out in those woods before I ever even found her.

If I ever found her. *If* she's even back.

I shook my head. I couldn't let myself think that way. Not until I hunted down this lead. This was the closest I'd felt to her since she disappeared ten years ago, and I wasn't going to let it go by without doing everything in my power to find her.

Which meant taking Bastian with me. My brother was a lot of things, but he was the only person I could count on to have my back. He'd done so much for me in those early years after we'd lost her. He still did so much for me now. And I hated him for it. He was a better male than I, and his constant presence in my life was just one huge reminder of how much I'd failed. That wasn't his fault, though. I would be a fool to let my petty resentment get in the way of utilizing his skill set right now. I stormed through the house and right up to Bastian's door. Banging loudly, I called out to him. He'd better get his ass up, I didn't have time to sit here waiting for him to get his beauty sleep.

His groggy eyes peered out from behind the door.

"Vander? What are you doing?" He opened the door a smidge wider, letting his eyes pore over me. "Did you go hunting? Are you hurt?"

I rolled my eyes. Like I wasn't able to take care of myself. Even if I had been hurt, I wouldn't be standing here in the middle of the night, begging him to nurse me back to health.

"No. Bastian, I need your help with something."

I was tempted to push through the door and stalk into the room. He was still lazily rubbing his eyes, not sensing the urgency in my voice. I braced my hand on the door, ready to blow through, but stopped short. I peered behind him to see Aermidh draped across their bed, fast asleep. The picture of divine peace. The sight calmed me somewhat. At least one of us had found that sort of comfort and happiness. It made sense that Bastian was the one who ended up with it. It wasn't like I really deserved it, anyway.

I turned my attention back to Bastian. He was eyeing me, wary of my tone and my hand hovering over the door.

"Let's take this out to the sitting room. I don't want to wake Aerie."

I gave a curt nod and turned to leave, then paused for a moment, looking back at him over my shoulder.

"Be quick, Bastian. It's about Hazlenn."

The look on my brother's face was one of utter exhaustion. I noticed the deep grooves around his face, the dark circles that hung like sand bags under his eyes.

When had he started to look so tired all of the time?

Yet another reminder of my failure. The weight on his shoulders should have been my burden to bear. I was the firstborn, after all. It wasn't always a guarantee for firstborns to take over as chieftain for the tribe, but it was typically tradition. Occasionally, usually in bigger families, siblings could challenge each other for the title. Our tribe prided itself on valuing skill and ability over things like bloodlines and hierarchies.

Still, it burned somewhere deep inside of me that it had been my job to lead our tribe and I hadn't been able to follow through. Not after losing Hazlenn. That was a crushing weight that I hadn't been able to survive. The tribe knew it. Bastian knew it. And mercifully, he stepped in before I led our tribe into the grave. Now you'd think he was the older brother with the years of wisdom and worry etched into his face.

"So you're telling me"—Bastian's booming voice broke me from my thoughts—"that you think Hazlenn dreamwalked to you?"

I gave a tight nod.

"And that you can sense her again?"

I paused, considering. "I have sensed her. I don't all the time. I couldn't even tell you when I started to realize I was. I thought I was imagining things at first."

Bastian leveled an icy stare at me. "Brother." His voice was a low rumble and I knew he was furious with what I'd just admitted. "You mean to say that you have sensed her, been sensing her, for Fates know how long? And you didn't think to *mention* that to someone?"

I rolled my eyes. "You're missing the point, Bastian, I think she's—" My voice trembled over the word. "I think she's back."

With that, the anger disappeared from his face.

"What do you need me to do?"

"Well, I'm not exactly sure what to do. It's not like this is a drawn out map I'm able to follow. And only picking up things here and there severely limits my ability to find her." I ran a hand over my face, the worry becoming almost too much to bear. "If this were any other time, I'd go out on my own. I have before, you know that. But this feels so much more real than any time before. And if it is real, you know Kahlis will be there. If not because he has her, then because he's searching for her too. He already has his creatures stationed throughout the Dark Woods."

Bastian sat listening silently, nodding in agreement. He knew all too well the constant presence of Kahlis' hand at our borders.

"So we leave by dawn's first light," he said, finally. "That gives us a couple hours to prepare. I'll go pack the essentials and tell Aerie the news. Perhaps she has something to send us with that could help. You ready the horses."

I shook my head in defiance. "No, it will be faster if I shift. I can track her better that way too. You take a horse and our supplies. I'll stay with you unless I get a lead on her. Then I can run it down and you can catch up."

The look on Bastian's face told me he didn't like the plan, but he knew better than to argue with me.

"If you insist, brother. But I don't like it. This feels off. We need to prepare for things to get bloody. We don't know if she's escaped Kahlis or if he ever had her at all, but regardless of the answer, there's no doubt he will be after her as well."

A shudder ran through my body thinking of Hazlenn in the hands of the Dark One. Kahlis had been snaking his way into Tir Nadaar ever since his banishment, just waiting for the perfect time to strike and wreak havoc on the tribes with his creatures. I suppressed the urge to shift at the mere mention of his name as I forced myself to hold Bastian's gaze.

"Brother, when am I not prepared for things to get bloody?"

As the first of dawn's golden glow crept up over the horizon, I could make out Bastian's broad form stalking toward the stables. I had his horse watered, fed, and ready to ride. The chestnut mare was one of the sweeter spirits in the stable but also one of the fiercest. She nuzzled lazily at my side as we waited for him.

"You ready, girl?" I whispered softly. "It's going to be a tough ride, but if anyone can make it, you can."

Brigid had a fierce strength that was something otherworldly. She was a horse deserving of a chieftain, and it was the only reason I'd agreed to Bastian taking a horse with us at all.

A broad, steady hand clamped down on my shoulder.

"Ready, brother?"

Bastian was dressed in a pair of black riding leathers and a dressed down version of his battle armor was strapped to his arms and chest. A leather sheath trailed across him, concealing what I'm sure were some of his well-loved daggers. His long brown hair was pulled up halfway in a series of braids, mirroring the ones tied through his beard, until it came together in a bun at the crown of his head. Peeking over his shoulders were the tops of twin silver blades, my brother's weapon of choice. The battle axes were emblazoned with an intricate design, swirls of black that ebbed and flowed over the bright silver. He'd told me at one point it was some protection ward that Aermidh had insisted on etching into the metal. I didn't buy into it much at first, but I'd also seen him use them against enemies in battle and I wasn't one to doubt their capabilities. He looked every bit the picture of the Chieftain of the Tribe of Talamh.

Taking the reins from me, he began strapping a few packs to Brigid, full of supplies I'm sure we wouldn't need. But I appreciated the lengths he was willing to go to in order to make sure we were prepared. I looked down at my plain clothing, nothing more than a simple black tunic and matching pants. Once I shifted, the clothes would be useless anyway, and Bastian had clearly packed enough weapons for the both of us. This was why he was the chieftain and I was the shadow in the night, relying mostly on my primal form to get the job done.

Bastian mounted his horse with ease and turned her around, ready to start.

"Lead the way, brother."

With that, I took off in a run. Within five strides, I called to that primal part of me and let the beast come to the surface. I felt my bones shift in the familiar way, watched my tanned skin transform into the thick black fur of my primal form. My stride shifted slightly as my body adjusted to running on four limbs instead of two. I debated sending up a prayer to the Fates, begging them to let me find her. But they hadn't done anything to help me thus far, so what was the point?

Finding my rhythm, I let loose one deep snarl. The ground reverberated beneath my paws, as if to echo my call, and I let that power seep into my bones as I took off.

Hold on, Hazlenn.

I'm coming to find you.

CHAPTER II
HAZEL

My eyes lazily fluttered open despite being heavy with sleep. The distant sound of thunder had pulled me from unconsciousness. Vaguely, I wondered when a storm had rolled in. I reached over absent-mindedly to nudge Arlo awake. Instead of his warm, solid body, my hand found a mixture of damp earth and decaying leaves. Confusion washed over me as I jolted up and looked around.

Instead of finding myself nestled safely beside Arlo in our tent, I was alone on the damp forest floor. Muck covered my legs and hands, as if I had stumbled through the woods before landing here. The trees were dark and looming, a sentient being watching my every move. I pried my eyes away from my surroundings and back to my hands, now trembling in my lap. Slowly, it came back to me.

Arlo's voice had called out through the blackness, growing more faint with each passing second. I had fought desperately to get back to him, thrashing and clawing at nothing but empty space. Thick, unrelenting darkness surrounded me, rendering me utterly helpless. When I realized

I was falling, my fear suddenly shifted from what I was leaving behind to what I was heading toward. My fingers no longer grasped for Arlo's but for anything I could hold on to. Still, I found nothing.

I'd kept falling and falling until finally, my body connected with earth in a sickening thud. The pain in my right shoulder and my head was a reminder of that. Thankfully, my legs seemed to be in working order. I'd found the strength to stand, or rather stumble, the short distance I'd been able to travel before collapsing completely and losing consciousness.

An all-too-familiar heat rolled through my body. Panic gripped me, coating my throat dry and heavy. I tried to calm my mind, to jump into action and piece together what I needed to do. I could tell by the track marks in the earth what direction I had come from. That seemed like a good place to start, so I made my way, painfully slow, back toward the arch.

Except the archway wasn't there. It was like the terrain had changed completely. I was no longer in the calm, quiet wilderness with the magnificent red rock and sandy earth. I was in a dark woods, surrounded by unfamiliar shadows that had me jumping at every small noise or movement. Instead of a beautiful stone archway, I found a grotesque hole—a crack hung in midair leeching the color and life of the things surrounding it. The smell of death and decay wafted from it. I was keenly aware of the horrible feeling in my gut that cut and twisted like a knife the closer I walked toward it. How was that even possible? My panic grew as I started calling out for Arlo, quietly at first. I didn't want to draw unnecessary attention from whatever creatures might call this place home. But my voice quickly rose to a frantic scream as I went unanswered. There was no Arlo here. There was no one.

The low rumble of thunder sounded again. I looked to the sky to gauge how long I had until the storm hit. Maybe I'd be able to find some sort of shelter in the forest to wait out the storm. I needed time to think through my options anyway. Only, I realized that the low rumble hadn't come from the sky at all. It was getting dark by now, or maybe it was still dark from the night. The skies looked clear enough and the sound echoed lower, like it was coming from inside the trees. I spun slowly, trying to figure out where that noise was coming from. It sounded again, only this time much closer.

Then I felt the shadow emerge. I had been here before. I knew that low, bone-rattling rumble. It had permeated too many of my nightmares to count.

I attempted to track the shadow dancing between the trees, but it appeared and disappeared too quickly. I crouched low, readying my body to run just as the shadow took form and a dark creature prowled out of the thick forest. It stalked toward me on four legs, like a predator sizing up its prey. Its features were distinctly canine-like, but the low growls reverberating with every step it took warned me it was something much darker. It had to be as tall as my chest, at least. Long, obsidian claws dug into the decaying earth as it made its way closer. Muscles bulged from its legs and neck as if it was straining, holding back until just the right moment to strike. It stilled on the edge of the tree line, cocking its head ever so slightly as it watched... and waited.

My stomach turned on itself, threatening to bring up what little food I'd had for dinner. Had that only been last night?

Focus.

None of this made sense. My timeline was warped and confusion prickled through my mind, but I couldn't spend time thinking about that right now. I needed to deal with the threat right in front of me. The beast began circling me then, and I desperately looked for an escape route while trying to keep one eye on it.

In the light of the little clearing, I could see the more horrifying details of the animal. Its long, razor-sharp teeth were bared and waiting. Its eyes glowed a deep, haunting red that matched the color of its breath huffing out with each growl, like endless pits of fire lay within. Elongated ears curled up around its head in a horn-like manner and in place of the fur that any other canine might have, this creature's skin stretched over its skeletal frame in a gnarled, leathery mutation.

A voice cut through the still woods, tearing my eyes away from the immediate threat.

"Hello there, sweetheart. We've been waiting for you."

A silhouette stood behind the beast, casually leaning against one of the trees and picking at his nails. His voice was velvet smooth, dripping with elegance in an accent I couldn't quite place.

I squinted, trying to make out his features, but he was enveloped in the darkness.

Slowly, he stepped forward into the clearing.

"I don't think that little toothpick strapped to your thigh is going to do much good against this one here."

Shit. I'd completely forgotten I had a weapon on me. *Totally useless,* I told myself again. I wasn't quite sure if I was referring to the knife or myself. As if compelled by his words, my hand fell to my side, palming the knife.

"Who are you? What do you want from me?" I hated the way my voice shook as it called out through the clearing.

"Oh, Hazlenn." His head shook as he laughed. "I'd say you're in more trouble than you realize."

He stopped next to the beast and patted its head. The gesture seemed obscene given the size of the beast and the capabilities I assumed it had to rip us both to shreds without a second thought.

The man was dressed head to toe in impeccably clean, silky black. Under different circumstances, I would have thought he was viciously handsome. His features were sharp and striking in a way that almost drew me to him, inviting me in. If it weren't for the beast beside him, I might have actually gone. Another growl echoed through the woods and I was instantly pulled back to the reality of the situation, whatever spell he had on me broken.

His lips crooked up in a wicked grin as his gaze met mine. His eyelids flicked and a penetrating ebony took over what had been the whites of his eyes seconds earlier. Every ounce of warmth left my body as he sized me up with those black pools of emptiness and said, "This is the part where you run, sweetheart."

Before I could process what he'd said, the beast next to him let out a bone-crushing roar and I knew I needed to start moving. I stumbled backward, my mind trying to catch up with my body and understand what was happening. I turned, running with any strength I had left. My body ached in protest, already exhausted from whatever journey it had made. My legs felt like sandbags as I coaxed them into moving faster. I was running deeper into the forest. Not exactly ideal, but I was unfamiliar with the terrain and what mattered most right now was finding coverage. I knew I couldn't outrun the beast, but maybe I could find a place to hide and wait it out. Maybe he'd get frustrated with the chase and find some other helpless being to have for dinner.

Another snarl ripped through the air and I veered to the left to change my direction. The trees were taller here and there was no chance I'd be able to climb them. I needed to find a cave or some sort of thick underbrush to hide in.

"Come now, Hazlenn, let's not play this game. I appreciate your effort, but it's futile."

The man's voice echoed through the woods, somehow seeming right next to me and simultaneously miles away. No, not a man. He was a creature too, with those liquid black eyes. Nothing with those eyes could be human.

Did he call me Hazlenn?

I darted to the left again, hoping to disorient the beast. He'd been right though, I knew this was futile. I wouldn't make it much longer if I didn't find a spot to hide.

I slowed slightly so I could get my bearings and decide which direction to go. Up ahead I saw a cluster of rocks and small caves. It would be an obvious hiding spot but a spot nonetheless. As I got closer, I realized the rocks stacked tall enough that I'd be able to climb up to some of the surrounding trees, if I could just get up there. My shoulder was pulsing with pain and I didn't know if my hands had the strength to make the climb. But the alternative was certain death, so I had to try.

"Kahlis grows tired, Hazlenn, which means I'm growing tired. And I'm much less prone to being nice when I grow tired, so let's just get this over with. Be a good little plaything and just come out."

His voice spurred me into action. I clambered up the rocks, gritting my teeth as each grip nearly knocked me out from the pain. Just as I was reaching the top, a slow, steady laugh broke out below me. I risked a look back. I had to know how close they were.

"You never cease to amaze me, you know. No matter how hopeless it is, you never give up. Just look at you, struggling to scramble up a couple of pebbles like even that would make a difference in this fight." He clicked his tongue as he looked up at me and cocked his head to the side. "It's cute."

I stifled a whimper as I tried to heave myself on top of the rocks and away from the voice below. Blinding pain exploded as a set of claws tore into my leg, pulling me down. I screamed in agony as I hit the ground. My hands flew to grasp my leg as hot, sticky blood coated me. The metallic scent stung my nose as I looked down and saw it. So much blood. Sudden realization penetrated the cloud of pain. I'd been here before, lived this nightmare time and time again, or at least some version of it. This wasn't the first time I'd been chased through these woods. The memories—the running, the blood, the screams and roars and claws—crashed into me in wave after wave of familiarity and terror.

The beast circled me now, waiting for the command to strike. The creature next to it was the epitome of calm, cool, and collected. The look on his face was almost one of annoyance at a task that was beneath him. I was beneath him, I realized. I was the one with whom he was annoyed. He crouched down and grabbed my chin.

"Valiant attempt, sweetheart, really. Full marks for effort and all that, but if you don't mind, I think we better get you back to Kahlis before Daddy has a hissy fit." His eyes slid over my torn clothes, the blood still pouring from the wound in my leg. Something evil danced in his eyes and he licked his lips. "However, Daddy didn't say anything about not having a little fun of my own first."

I threw out my good leg and kicked him as hard as I could in the chest. Caught off guard, he fell backward with a frustrated huff. I tried to get up, but standing was impossible with my leg in this condition, let alone running. The beast pounced all at once, not striking to kill but applying just enough force to knock me on my ass once again. One of its huge paws landed firmly on my chest, pinning me to the ground.

"That," the creature said, righting himself and picking the muck off his ruffled clothing, "was uncalled for." In an instant, he burst into an explosion of black, transforming into a towering, skeletal creature. His clothes were gone, replaced with oily, pitch-black skin. Massive wings unfolded behind him, as leathery and mutated as the beast holding me down. From both hands jutted out three long claws, each easily the length of my dagger.

Fear like I'd never felt took hold of me.

"If you thought the hound was bad, just wait until you see what I have planned for you."

CHAPTER 12
HAZEL

A deep, guttural growl broke out through the trees, shaking the branches and the ground along with them. This time, though, it hadn't come from the beast pinning me down. I wondered if this is what dying felt like, if the confusion was so strong because I was no longer connected to my body but rather watching all of this as some silent observer.

A wave of pain rolled through me as the beast shifted his weight onto my chest. Both the beast and his nightmarish master turned toward the sound. They seemed caught off guard. To be honest, so was I. None of this made sense and I was barely holding it together. I wanted answers to questions I was too frightened, or maybe too incoherent, to ask.

"Now, who could that be?" The creature with the oil-slicked skin sauntered a few steps away, closer to the thick woods that lay in front of us.

"Seems like we've got company. You wouldn't know anything about that, would you?" He shot back a glare as he crouched into a fighting stance. "Looks like our plans are going to have to wait, little plaything."

I tried to ignore the shiver that ran down my spine, tried not to focus on the thought of what his *plans* entailed. I wanted to be prepared for whatever was about to break through those woods. If my first two encounters here had been as bad as the beast and its master, I didn't even want to think about how terrible the next thing to come out of these woods would be.

The growl had quieted to a dull rumble. Everything else in the forest had gone eerily still; no birds chirped, no insects buzzed. My breathing was the only sound lifting into the woods around us. The beast still stood firm above me, intent on keeping its prey cornered and pinned. I wiggled helplessly beneath it, trying to grab for my knife and keep my eyes on the trees. Each movement sent searing pain up my body, but I stifled my whimper as I waited for the next nightmare to emerge. It felt like an eternity of watching and listening, but nothing came.

Just as the oily creature turned to make his way back to me, a flash of black fur and white teeth shot out of the trees. It tackled the creature to the ground, biting and swiping as it went. A scream of pure rage and pain crackled through the air, a scream I once again realized I'd heard before in my dreams. It didn't slow the animal with the black fur though. Without any hesitation, the animal rolled off of its first attack and ran toward the beast, toward me. A scream escaped my lips as I struggled to get away. The beast must have been scared too, because its paw no longer held me down.

I scrambled against the forest floor, decaying leaves and mud sticking to me as I crawled backward. The beast was backing away in the opposite direction, eyes darting between the animal in front of it and its master, crumbled and bleeding to the side. The animal had placed itself between me and the beast. A wolf, I slowly realized. Or, at least, something related to a wolf. It was even larger than the beast it was cornering. Its midnight fur was just as dark as the beast and its master but different in a comforting way. The way its body moved as it prowled in front of me—protecting me, I realized—had the tension in my shoulders easing slightly. I immediately had the urge to bury my hand in that fur, to cuddle up to it right here on the forest floor and not let it leave until all my pains were gone.

Get yourself together, Hazel.

I could feel all semblance of sanity slipping away. This had easily been the most confusing and terrifying situation of my life. Well, of the life I could remember, anyway. I drew my attention back to the fight in front of me and palmed my knife, just in case. The beast didn't seem interested in fighting, though. It ducked past the wolf, darted to its master, and in an implosion of inky black smoke, they were both gone.

An eerie kind of quiet fell over the clearing. I was alone with the wolf. The idea should have terrified me, but I couldn't feel anything other than curiosity at the creature standing gloriously tall, watching my every move. It cocked its head to the side, studying me. I tried to swallow, but my throat was too dry. This was all too much. The pain, the creatures, the exhaustion pulsing through my body after how far I'd run. I'd seen extraordinary, unbelievable things in a matter of minutes and my brain was fighting to process it all. I was amazed and terrified and confused all at once.

The wolf didn't move, just stood there watching. With several grunts, I hoisted myself to my feet. A new wave of pain tore through me as I attempted to walk. I felt more and more lightheaded with each step.

How much blood had I lost, was I still losing?

I stopped short just in front of the massive wolf, its golden eyes glowing like something otherwise.

Because it is something otherworldly.

An edge of courage, or maybe stupidity, overcame me as I raised my hand to touch its neck. Before my hand could find purchase in that deep midnight fur, the world went hazy and then turned black altogether. A ringing pierced through my head and I felt reality slip away as my body went limp. Somewhere in the recesses of my mind, I waited to hear my body hit the ground, to feel the pain overcome me once again.

But it never came. I faded in and out of consciousness as I tried to understand what was happening. Briefly, I came to and saw those golden eyes staring down at me yet again. This time, though, instead of being surrounded by that beautiful black fur, I found the face of a man instead.

Arlo? How had he gotten here? I became aware of my weight in his arms, my head against his chest. The rich scent of clove and citrus swirled around me and I found myself burying my face deeper against him, breathing in the warm aroma. I clung greedily to his warmth, realizing how cold I'd suddenly become.

Where had the wolf gone? I tried to form words, to ask if he had killed the wolf, if I was safe with him. But nothing came. I heard him speak in a clipped, warning tone; felt the warm vibrations of it in his chest. Too soon, too quick, I realized he was handing me off to someone else.

"There now, Hazlenn, we've got you. Just hold on for us now, okay? We will get you patched up as soon as we can." I wondered if this was the voice of the golden-eyed man or someone else. My eyes allowed the smallest glimpse as we began to move. I was draped across what I believed to be a horse, looking up into the deep brown eyes of a broad-shouldered man. His features were strong and stoic, but I felt oddly comforted by his presence. When he saw me peeking up at him, a warm smile spread across his face.

"Welcome home, Hazlenn."

And with that, I found myself struggling to hold on to consciousness. I knew I should stay awake. I knew it would be safer to fight, to question what any of this meant. But the exhaustion pulled at me and it felt impossible to not give in and go under. Questions could come later. I felt safe for now. The gentle saunter of the horse lulled me to sleep and I gave in, desperately.

CHAPTER 13
VANDER

Bastian didn't question me when I handed Hazlenn over to him—but I could feel his eyes on me the whole journey home. I'd shifted again, in hopes that he wouldn't pry as we traveled. I didn't have the heart to tell him what I felt when we found her. I didn't even want to admit it to myself.

It was impossible to ignore, though. I'd expected Hazlenn—*my* Hazlenn—to be in those woods. The girl we found might look like Hazlenn, but she was altogether different. My heart lurched at the idea that this might not really be her. After all this time, all that searching. It might truly break me to finally get her back, only to realize she was something else entirely.

Like you're not wholly broken already.

I shook off the thought, the dark magic still crawling beneath my skin. This deception wreaked of Kahlis' magic.

And what had she called me? Arlo? I didn't know who she thought I was, but given the way she stared up at me with those round, hopeful eyes—twin jade stones every bit as crippling as I remembered them being—I'd assume she would be pretty disappointed to find out I'm not him.

Nothing about this felt right.

As we came up to the gate, Aermidh greeted Bastian and ushered them to the greenhouse to begin the mending on Hazlenn's leg. I was sure there'd be other injuries. She'd lost a lot of blood from the look of that clearing and her face had been covered in bruises. My body trembled with anger at the thought of that Daeomi putting his hands on her. I swore at myself for not finishing him off when I had the chance.

I'd felt Hazlenn's pain traveling through the Dark Woods. I'd felt her cry out as those claws ripped into her leg. That had been enough to trigger my anger, to push me into the hunt. It hadn't been the cleanest attack, and I knew Bastian was furious that I took off without telling him what was going on, but I'd be lying if I said I hadn't enjoyed the way the Daeomi's skin felt, ripping beneath my teeth.

I watched from a distance as Bastian and Aermidh got Hazlenn settled in the little greenhouse. Bastian had built it for Aermidh as a wedding gift, a place for her to grow her herbs year-round and it doubled as an infirmary when it needed to. The mid-afternoon sun gleamed off the glass panes, giving the plants inside an ethereal glow. Aermidh was a mystery indeed. She was deserving of such a structure. I wasn't quite sure if it was the magic surrounding it or the magic within that gave it such an air of divinity.

Before long, Bastian made his way out of the greenhouse and across the grounds to where I paced, still in my wolven form. He stopped a few feet away, waiting. He'd be waiting there all day if he thought I was going to break the silence.

"What the fuck happened back there, Vander?"

Ignoring him, I prowled the grassy area and kept my eyes on the greenhouse in the distance. Inside, I could see Aermidh hastily running her magic over Hazlenn. I wondered what manners of injury she was finding, what her prognosis was for recovery.

"*Vander.*" Bastian's voice was low, clipped. He wasn't going to let me sulk my way out of this one. "Either shift right now and talk to me or I will come over there and beat your wolven ass until it shifts purely by my will."

I let out a huff. Funny how he thought he'd be able to make me shift. Clearly he hadn't been around to see just how badly I'd been beaten before. Not once has anyone forced me to shift back. I knew I needed to talk to him, though. I owed him that much for coming with me.

With another sigh, I willed my body back into my mortal form and walked over to where Bastian now stood. He handed me a change of clothes he must have grabbed while he was at the greenhouse.

"What do you want to talk about so badly, brother?" I said in a casual way as I pulled on the pants and tunic.

"Don't start that shit with me, Vander. What in the Depths is going on?"

I put my hands up, easing him back. "Alright, okay, I'll talk."

He gave me a stern look, planting himself firmly in front of me, and waited.

"When we got to the edge of the forest, I felt Hazlenn. I knew she was in pain, that she was scared. So I took off because I needed to get to her fast and I didn't think you'd be able to keep up."

"Did it ever cross your mind to share that information with me before just running off like a bloodthirsty lunatic into the Dark Woods?"

"No," I deadpanned.

Rage rolled over Bastian's expression, but he held his tongue and waited for me to continue.

"I got to the clearing, took out the Daeomi and his little pup. No issues at all, but when I turned to Hazlenn..." I trailed off, struggling to find words to explain what I felt. "She didn't even recognize me. She actually screamed when I came up to her."

At that, Bastian let out a small chuckle. "Well, I hate to be the one to break it to you, brother, but you're not exactly a comforting sight when you've come back from a hunt, all blood-soaked and smelling like death. She's allowed to be scared of that."

"It's not just that," I said, gritting my teeth. "When I saw her... It wasn't the same as before. It's like that connection isn't there, the tether isn't intact."

"That's ridiculous, Vander. You just said you felt her in the forest. How could that be if the tether was broken?"

"I know." My tone was too forced, too angry. It wasn't Bastian's fault that any of this happened. He was just trying to talk me through it, help me work it out. But I couldn't help the anger that I was feeling toward him. He didn't understand what this felt like, didn't have to deal with losing... losing someone like Hazlenn. "It's just different."

"Is that why you gave her to me instead of carrying her home yourself?"

I clenched my jaw, turning back to the greenhouse and waiting for Aermidh.

Bastian sighed, rubbing his face. "Don't do this, Vander. Don't distance yourself. She needs you now more than ever. Let's get her healed up and have a little talk. We can work out the rest later."

"It took me too long to get her the first time. I don't know if I'll be able to do it again."

We stood in silence, watching the greenhouse and waiting for news. The minutes ticked by at a painful pace and I found myself reaching out to that tether several times, searching for any hint of how she was doing. I found nothing each time. I wondered if it was because of her condition or because the tether was breaking.

Eventually, Aermidh emerged from the greenhouse and made her way over to us. I walked briskly to meet her halfway.

"How is she?" I asked, too eager.

"She's sleeping now. She was in and out of it for a while. I mended her leg and gave her something to help recover from the blood loss. Those were her main injuries, thankfully."

I nodded as a wave of relief settled over me. I pushed passed Aermidh and started to make my way to the greenhouse. I had to see her. Aermidh grabbed my wrist before I could make it too far.

"Wait, Vander," she ordered, Bastian by her side now. "When I was searching her for injuries, I found something else."

She hesitated, chewing on her bottom lip.

"What?" I pressed her.

"I think... I don't think she remembers anything."

Anger rose as my face bunched, trying to understand what she was saying.

"What do you mean?"

"Well, I don't know the details. My magic doesn't work that way; it just allows me to find the injuries. I could just tell that something was wrong, that her mind wasn't how it should be. It's like there's a void, a darkness. And when she saw me healing her leg, I had to put her under because she wouldn't calm down. She's in shock, but the magic should have helped her, not scared her like that."

I swallowed hard, remembering the fear in her eyes as I walked toward her in the forest. I wanted to hurt something, wanted to run deep into those woods and find the first available thing to kill.

This wasn't right. Ten years I'd worked to get her back and now she was here but not here. Now, she was an entirely different person and the tether was withering away. Worst of all, there was nothing I could do about any of it.

"Let's just talk to her, okay? We won't know anything until she wakes up. Give her some time to bathe and eat and then I'll bring her into the main house and we can discuss everything."

I gave one slight nod before turning to walk away.

"Vander," Bastian called to me. "Don't do anything reckless. Just give her time."

I paused but didn't respond to his warning. I tightened my fist and continued toward the house. I was going to need a stiff drink to get through the rest of this night.

The scent of herbs and tea filled my nose. I was kneeling beside a sofa, staring at an older woman. Her skin was practically gray; it hung loosely from her bones as if she hadn't eaten in weeks. A mixture of bottles and loose herbs lay beside us on a table, seemingly abandoned some time ago. A warm and frail hand touched my cheek. My skin was wet, though I couldn't remember when I'd started crying. Nor did I understand why I'd be crying for this woman who was a stranger to me. Her eyes were milky, on the brink of leaving this world. She continued to stroke my cheek as her lips parted and I heard my name, at least some version of it.

"Hazlenn. My Hazlenn."

Her hand slowed then fell to her side. A burst of pain bloomed in my chest before our surroundings faded to black.

The earthy aroma of sage and a spice I couldn't place pulled me from unconsciousness. For a moment, I thought I was still in my dream, still beside that dying woman, the smell of the herbs holding me between those worlds. A small room took shape around me as I blinked my eyes, trying to focus my vision. A patchwork blanket was draped over my lap and I was sprawled across a small bed in the corner. So much of this room was similar to the dream I'd just found myself in. Yet both were wholly unfamiliar to me and I pushed myself up in a panic as I took in the entirely real room around me.

Herbs hung from every inch of the dark wood beams above. On the far side of the room was an alcove lined with mismatched glass, forming some makeshift version of a greenhouse. In the windows sat every kind of plant imaginable. Some were a true deep green, reminding me of life and earth and the smell of the air after it rained. Others were variations of hues I'd never seen in plants before. Flashes of purple, swirls of black, and beautiful, bright-colored blooms danced from every surface and in every corner. The shelves were lined with clear glass jars, dark amber bottles, and ancient-looking books I was immediately weary of ever touching, for fear they'd turn to dust in my hands. In the middle of the room stood a rough wooden worktable covered in a variety of plant matter and tools.

I jumped as the door on the other side of the room creaked open, the panic reaching new heights as unfamiliar forms took shape within the doorway.

"Oh good, you're awake."

A soft, singsong voice drifted to me, making me question if I was still in a dream. Its owner, gliding gracefully across the room to my side, was easily the most beautiful woman I had ever seen. Her presence instantly put me at ease in a way I couldn't describe. Her hair fell in long pale locs down her back and around her sides. It was light, like fresh-fallen snow, but pieces of it glowed golden when the light hit it through the greenhouse windows. She wore a simple sage green linen gown, its skirts sashaying with each step she took toward me. Her beige apron was bunched in her hand as she lifted it to walk, revealing her bare feet, which softly pattered on the wooden floorboards.

She kneeled gracefully beside me as she tucked one of her locs behind her ear—her very pointed ear. My eyes went wide, lingering on it shamelessly. I'd read about faeries and elves before, but that was a thing of folklore and fairytales. That wasn't real. I forced my gaze back to her face, suddenly aware that her piercing blue eyes were waiting for mine. Her face was soft and kind, despite noticing my stare, and something about it told me that I could trust her.

She took my shaking hand gently in hers.

"How are you feeling?"

There was sincerity in her voice, a reassurance that I was safe and that she would take care of me, but as I opened my mouth to answer, I became aware of the two shadows behind her.

The broader one, closest to us, I'd remembered from the woods. He was who I'd spoken to—or rather, who spoke to me—before I'd lost consciousness. The same kind of sincerity was in his eyes, although they were laced with something else. Anger? Worry? I couldn't tell. The other one stood further back, in the shadows of the far end of the room. I couldn't make out much about him, just his tall, slender form and those deep golden glowing eyes watching me.

Had he been the one carrying me in the forest? The memory flooded my brain and I sat up straighter.

"Arlo," I said in a hopeful whisper.

The woman kneeling next to me tilted her head to one side, brows knitted together in confusion. "Who?" she asked softly.

I had seen him, felt him in the forest. Hadn't I? It suddenly felt impossible to remember Arlo's face. I'd been so sure in that moment that Arlo had carried me away from that nightmare. The eyes watching me from the corner, though, told me otherwise. Those had been the eyes of the wolf that saved me in the forest. Not Arlo's. I rubbed my aching head with my free hand, putting every ounce of energy I had left into remembering Arlo's face. His eyes were lighter, kinder. They swirled like honey and a summer sunset. The eyes watching me now glowed with a darkness I didn't think I'd ever want to understand. They were tense and rough—a warning to stay away and a demand to not look too closely. The gold was still there, but it was overpowered with rings of onyx and the brown of an ancient, haunted woods.

How had I thought those eyes belonged to Arlo? The differences were strikingly obvious to me now. I wanted nothing more than to get far away from that watchful gaze penetrating me from the corner of the room. I turned my attention back to the woman in front of me and forced a small, tight grin.

"Sorry, I thought Arlo was here. He's my..." I trailed off, trying to decide how to describe him. *Protector? Lover? The only person in the world that I actually know?* "He was with me before. I just thought he'd be here now. I don't know where he is."

The beautiful being in front of me briefly looked back at the two others behind her in some sort of unspoken conversation before turning her attention back to me.

"There was no one with you in the woods, aside from the Daeomi and his hound."

I tried to push my way off the bed, my fear finally reaching a tipping point. "I need to go back. I need to find him. What if he's lost out there? What if he's hurt?"

She listened patiently but held firm on my hand as she settled me back onto the bed. "It's okay, Hazlenn, it's okay. Just slow down for a minute so we can talk."

My breath was ragged as I let her calm me. Her touch was reassuring and warm. Tears pricked my eyes, but I nodded, giving in. My body felt weak and my head was spinning from the rush of movement.

"I need to get back to him," I repeated, my voice shaking. She paused before answering, concern etched into her eyes.

"We can discuss all of that later. My first concern is your health. It looks like you've healed up nicely, but your body still needs time to recover. You may be sore for a few days, and with the amount of blood you lost, I think it would be best to take it easy for now."

I glanced down at my leg. Images of that savage beast tearing into my flesh flashed across my mind, reminding me of the blood that coated my body, my hands. Nothing was there, though. My leggings were still ripped and blood-stained, but my leg was whole, my skin a rosy pink. I was unscathed.

"How?" It was the only thing I could think to say, less of a question and more of a statement. I didn't understand how it was possible, how any of this was possible. A lump formed in my throat as I tried to swallow back the tears threatening to spill from my eyes yet again.

"Come now, it's alright." I knew it wasn't, but the lull of her voice had me almost believing that it was, had me wanting to believe anything she said. "Let's get you cleaned up and maybe a little food in your belly. Then we can talk. You've been through a lot today and I'm sure it's all been overwhelming. Let's take things slow for now."

With that, she was up and rushing the others out of the room. They lingered by the door for a minute, tense and whispering amongst themselves. Those dark golden eyes were still watching me and I had to suppress a shiver as I turned my attention to anything else. After a few minutes of hushed conversation, they left and the white-haired lady turned back to the room. She busied herself, cleaning up and fussing over me. From a cabinet next to the bed, she pulled out a clean pair of clothes before making her way back over to me.

She helped me to a little bathing room. The space was small, so tucked away within the greenhouse that I hadn't realized it was there. It mimicked the rugged elements that the rest of the greenhouse boasted. The consistent feel of the rough wood floors guided me into the small space. Next to a basin for handwashing stood a narrow cupboard full of fresh linens. The woman grabbed an assortment of different-sized towels and set them on a hand-carved chair off to one side, along with the clean change of clothes. To my surprise, nestled in the corner of the small space, a bath was waiting. Tendrils of steam danced off the still water in an oversized copper tub and the calming scents of lavender and peppermint filled the air. My muscles ached to be in that warm water and I was suddenly aware of how much exhaustion still riddled my body.

"You can clean up in here, take as long as you need. When you're done, I'll make sure a plate of hot food is waiting for you." She gave me a genuine smile as she added, "I promise you're safe here."

Then she turned to leave and pulled the door closed.

It took me far longer than I expected to scrub my skin clean of the dried blood and caked dirt from the forest; even longer to scrub away the memory of the beast or its oily black master's touch. The wonderfully warm water had gone cold by the time I stepped out and dried off. I hadn't seen her fill the tub, but I was curious how she'd heated the water to the perfect, soothing temperature.

I was trying to focus on the tasks at hand: scrub off any remaining blood, put on those clothes, comb the tangles out of my hair. It was the only thing grounding my mind and keeping me from spiraling into full blown hysteria. If I paused too long, if I let my mind wander, the panic would take hold and squeeze my chest until it popped. I couldn't let that happen, especially without Arlo here to help me pick up the pieces. I had to hold it together until I found him, then I'd let myself unravel.

Slowly, I cracked open the door and peeked out into the main room. No one was there, but a tray sat on the bed, waiting for me. The scent had my mouth watering and I was at the bed in two strides, staring down at a bowl of thick, creamy stew. I hesitated, wondering if I should really trust this. It seemed idiotic to accept food from strangers, especially strangers who were nowhere to be seen, but I remembered that sense of calm and safety that had come over me as I'd looked into the blonde woman's eyes. I scooped up a tentative bite, testing the contents against the tip of my tongue first. I melted at the delicious taste as the stew slid down my throat and warmed every inch of my body. I hastily took another bite, then another, until the stew was gone and I was scraping the sides of the ceramic bowl with my spoon just to get every last bit.

The click of the door drew my attention to the far side of the room. The blonde woman was back, looking just as elegant and graceful as she had before.

"So I see you liked my stew," she said with a twinkle in her eye.

I tried to look less eager with my bowl, but there was no point. "Yes, thank you. It was delicious."

I quietly set my bowl back on the tray before picking up the mug next to it and taking a sip. My eyes lit up as the sweet liquid coated my tongue.

"A little treat of my own concoction. I find it helps to perk my patients up after they've experienced a trauma like you had today."

I brought the mug to my lips again, this time taking a long, greedy gulp. It was like the nectar of some forbidden fruit I'd never had the opportunity of trying before. The sweetness was strong but not over-bearing as I drank and I noticed the smallest hint of sea salt as I finished off the mug. As if my body was answering in agreement, I could have sworn some of that exhaustion and panic eased away. I set the mug back on the tray and fumbled with my fingers for a minute, not sure what to do. I wondered if she could feel the awkwardness hanging in the air, radiating off me. When I looked up, though, all that met me were kind, starlit eyes.

"The others are in the sitting room of the main house. They'd love the chance to talk with you about what happened in the forest. That is, if you're feeling up to it."

I didn't want to leave the warmth and safety of this little green-house, with its rich scents and soothing ambiance. The idea of facing the strangers, of facing those piercing onyx eyes with the golden swirls, had my body begging to retreat further into the bed. I paused, remembering the way the bigger one had carried me to safety, how he'd looked at me with kindness.

I needed to face them. I needed answers and hiding in here wasn't going to get me anything. Arlo was out there somewhere, and I needed to find my way back to him. I needed to figure out what in the world was going on.

CHAPTER 15
HAZEL

The woman, who'd told me her name was Aermidh, but insisted I call her Aerie, led me across a covered path to a much larger house than the small greenhouse we had been in. It was grand and beautiful and my eyes couldn't move fast enough to take it all in before we were crossing into the side entrance. Aermidh led me through a large kitchen with a stonework hearth that matched the backdrop for the ovens. I found myself getting dizzy trying to get a look at everything as we walked, so I briefly closed my eyes and then refocused on Aermidh's graceful movements through the house.

We made our way into a cozy little sitting area. A fire blazed to the side, surrounded by rich leather sofas and expensive-looking rugs. The only light was coming from the fire; the sun had gone down some time ago. It created a warm and welcoming environment that I almost would have believed, if it weren't for the two brutes waiting for us to join them.

The broader one hovered in the corner, talking in stern, hushed words with a disheveled-looking guard. When he saw us enter, he ushered the guard out quickly, replacing the worried lines of his face with a forced smile. Aermidh took her seat and slid her arm around the man as he joined her. The one with the glowing eyes sat to the side, separate from everyone, and carefully watched as I picked a seat. I wasn't sure what to say, so I stared at my clammy hands, wringing them in my lap. Finally, Aermidh broke the silence.

"Hazlenn," she offered in a quiet, reassuring voice. "Do you remember anything? About this place, about them?" She gestured to the other two figures sitting eerily still and tense.

I recoiled slightly as I looked up at her in confusion and slowly shook my head. *Remember them? Why would I remember them?*

The one sitting closest to her dropped his gaze and let out the slightest sigh. I could feel the other one's eyes burning into me, but I refused to look in his direction.

"That's alright," said Aermidh. "You've been through a lot. It's common for someone who's experienced trauma to lose their memories or block certain things out." She paused, assessing my body language, gauging how I was responding. "Let's start with the basics. As I told you earlier, my name is Aerie. This is my husband, Bastian Darroch. And that is his brother, Vander. Does any of that sound familiar?"

I shook my head slowly. My eyes fell to Bastian, taking in his appearance, because there was no way I would let my eyes move to the other brother. He was large, intimidatingly so, but his face was kind and watchful, just as it had been earlier. His long hair was a beautiful shade of brown. A beard the same color as his hair covered the lower half of his face and part of his chest. Despite the look of kindness on his face, I couldn't help but notice how tense his body was. He was reading me, analyzing each moment, ready for whatever might happen. His hands were strong and flexed as they sat clasped between his knees. I couldn't help but notice a band of black ink on his forearm, peeking out from under his tunic.

"Why do you call me Hazlenn?" I asked, suddenly realizing they all had referred to me by that name. Even the creature in the forest had.

The room stilled. All eyes were on me.

This time, it was Bastian who spoke. "Because that's your name, Hazlenn. What else would we call you?"

My eyes darted back to him, defiance rising in my blood. "No, my name is Hazel. I've never heard Hazlenn before today in the forest." That wasn't entirely true. I'd heard it before. In my dreams every now and then. I hadn't understood it then either, and I didn't want to give them any more reason to use it.

Bastian started to respond, but Aermidh cut him off before he could.

"Alright—Hazel, it is. I'm sure you're overwhelmed. And seeing as how it appears you're missing memories, maybe it would be best if we started with any questions *you* may have. I think that would be easier."

Questions I may have? My mind hadn't stopped racing with questions since I'd left Arlo in the tent. I didn't even know where to start. Frustration rose as my ears reddened. I hated how they were all looking at me, like I was some cornered, wounded animal they were trying to coax to come home with them. I let my eyes fall to my lap and stared at the leg that had been mauled and mangled earlier that day.

"How did you heal me?" My voice was shaky, my throat dry. This felt like probably the least important question to ask, but it felt safe, easy. Maybe I wasn't willing to admit I'd realized, on some level, that these people acted like they knew me. I wasn't ready to ask those questions or to admit that pull inside me was satisfied the moment they'd saved me in the forest.

"A little bit of magic, a little bit of herbal medicine. I was a healer in another life. My magic works to find ailments and injuries then works to heal what's broken." She watched as my brows rose at the mention of magic.

"So you're a faerie?" I asked tentatively, eyeing the point of her ears peeking through the locks of her golden-white hair.

"I've been called many things, but yes, fae or faerie would be a good way to describe me."

I nodded slowly, trying to wrap my mind around that idea. My eyes shot over to where the two others sat. "And you two?" I asked.

"Fuck no." The curse broke through the air fast and hard. Vander, still hiding in the shadows, cleared his throat as he shot a look between Bastian and Aermidh. "I, uh—sorry, Aerie. I didn't mean it like that."

A sarcastic smile spread over her face as she shot him a look through raised eyebrows. Bastian's face held less sarcasm and more irritation as a muscle in his jaw ticked. It would have been hard not to let a grin slip over my lips if it hadn't been for the confusion and fear that gripped a firm hold on my chest.

"What my eloquent brother meant to say," said Bastian, grimacing, "was that no, we are shifters. We come from the Tribe of Talamh, earth magic. The fae are very rare, practically extinct. We are lucky that Aerie is with us."

He took her hand and squeezed it softly. For a moment, I saw a look of grief flash over Aermidh's features, but it was gone as fast as it had come.

"The fae haven't always had the best reputation, especially amongst the tribes. I took no offense, Vander." Though Aermidh looked pointedly at him.

"So you really don't remember anything? At all?" Bastian's tone was desperate, searching.

I didn't know what they were so hopeful I'd remember. It wasn't like I'd ever been here before, a place with magic and fae and shifters. Whatever that was. I wasn't entirely sure that I wasn't just asleep, trapped in some never-ending dream. I stared at him for a long moment, trying to understand what he wanted from me.

"Look, I don't know what you're trying so hard to get me to remember, but no, I don't. None of this makes any sense to me. Two days ago I was sitting at home with Arlo, fully believing that magic wasn't real and only existed in my books. Now I'm here, being chased by giant black dogs and shapeshifting creatures and having my leg healed by some beautiful faerie woman."

Aermidh grinned at the blunt confession of my words. "Well, I don't know about *woman*. I'd have to be mortal to be considered a woman. But I appreciate the sentiment."

My breathing was heavy with my little outburst. The longer I sat here, the more my frustration grew and I could sense that rising panic once again taking hold in my chest. I closed my eyes and dug my fingernails into my palms, imprinting tiny crescent moons on them. I needed to calm down.

"Why don't you start by telling us what happened to you. When did you lose your memories?" Aermidh leaned over and put a reassuring hand on my knee.

I wasn't sure if it was her magic or just her presence in general, but I could feel some of the panic settle. I took a deep breath. That, I could do. I'd been reliving those memories, trying to figure out what had happened, every day for the past year. I could recite my story as easily as breathing. I allowed myself one more moment to breathe, to make sure I wouldn't open my eyes and completely unravel.

Slowly, I lifted my head and looked at them. These three strangers who came to my rescue and saved my life. These strangers who were so interested in me, who acted as if they knew me. I would tell them my story, then I would get theirs and hopefully things would start making more sense. My head turned slowly, finally making eye contact with the one they called Vander, reclined in a casual manner, his arm draped across the back of the couch. He was encased in shadows, as he had been practically every time I'd seen him since he saved me, but I easily found his eyes. I locked my gaze with his as I opened my mouth and began to tell my story.

CHAPTER 16
HAZEL

I explained everything to them. I explained how I was found out in the wilderness, traveling between towns, bleeding and helpless and completely out of my mind. I explained how I'd stayed with the healers as they tended to my wounds and tried to determine why I couldn't remember anything. I explained how Arlo had been the one to find me—how he had agreed to help me, take me home and nurse me back to health as we searched for my family. How he'd never left my side during any of it.

Then I explained, or rather tried to explain, my bright idea for the one-year anniversary of my accident and the pull I had to come back. Much of what had happened in the wilderness felt like a dream just right out of my mind's reach. It was a haze, a blur of moments of anxiety and excitement and longing. Any time I tried talking about Arlo much, it was like the words would slip away from me. The memories of his face—his touch—were fading. I stumbled over my words and struggled to hold my train of thought. By the end of my story, I started to wonder if Aermidh had truly healed all of me or if she should check me for a head injury.

When I was done, I looked around the room and waited. All three of them looked concerned and confused, like maybe they didn't believe a word of what I'd just said.

"That's it. That's the whole story." I wrung my hands as I waited for them to acknowledge me.

Bastian leaned forward, eyeing me like some bizarre creature he'd never seen before. "You said a year? You were there for a year?"

I leaned away, nodding cautiously as he shot a wary glance to the one cloaked in shadows across from us. I could have sworn those shadows grew as the creature within them watched me.

"But you've been missing from here for the past ten years..." muttered Bastian. His eyes never left his brother, almost as if he was saying it more to him than to me.

My heartbeat thrummed inside my ears, my mind working to process what he was saying.

"Wh—what did you say?"

Aermidh shoved an elbow into Bastian's side. "Now Hazel, this may come as a bit of a shock to you, and we don't want you to be blindsided." She threw a disapproving look at Bastian. "But ten years ago you were here, lived here. You grew up in a small cottage nearby and you've known Vander and Bastian since you were a child. That is, until ten years ago when you went missing." Her eyes danced warily between me and Vander. I couldn't tell if she was more concerned for me or him right now.

"You think... you think I'm from here?" I laughed at the realization. "I don't know who you think I am, but you have the wrong girl. I know nothing about this world, about magic. I think I'd know if I grew up in some fantasy land."

Aermidh eyed me, pausing before she spoke. "Would you though?"

Her words stung. Not because she'd said them to hurt me, but because she was right. I knew absolutely nothing about my past or where I'd come from. This *could* explain why it felt impossible to find answers back home, why no family ever showed up to inquire about me.

It couldn't be real, though. This was too much for even me to believe, too much for my mind to process. I wanted answers, but this couldn't be it. I'd expected to find some family, maybe estranged or far off and with no clue how to find me. I'd hoped for that reality, for somewhere out there where I belonged. But this? This was too impossible a reality to accept. Never in my wildest imagination had I questioned the possibility of something like this. I shook my head. "No, this is all too wild. I don't even know for sure that I believe in magic, in *you*. And you expect me to believe that I'm part of this, that I'm from here?"

"I don't expect you to believe anything, Hazel. I cannot imagine how hard this must all be for your mind to process. Especially when it's as damaged as it is already."

I began to argue back but came up short as I processed her words.

"What do you mean, *as damaged as it is already*?"

She leaned forward, tucking her legs beneath her as she slid to the floor beside me and took my hand. "When my magic checked your body for injuries, it checked your mind as well. There's a void there—a mark—something blocking your memories. It could explain why you don't remember anything about this land. About Tir Nadaar."

"Tir Nadaar?" My brows rose at the name.

"Yes, this land, our land, is called Tir Nadaar. The Land of Nature. Nature is the source from which all magic pours. And thus the namesake for our continent."

"Tir Nadaar." The word rolled off my lips like I'd said it a million times before. Yet it held no recognition for me. I stood up with a huff, walking toward the fire to warm my hands. *Tir Nadaar, faeries, shifters—such ridiculous-sounding things.* I felt like I'd fallen right into one of the books I'd borrowed from the library back home. I lingered, staring into the firelight dancing in front of me. Bits of embers popped and crackled around the flames.

The noise sounded so much like the fire Arlo had built us when we were camping in the wilderness. The fire's warmth reached out to me, brushed against me. I leaned into it just as I had leaned into Arlo's embrace as we'd lain beneath the open night sky. I'd promised him he wouldn't lose me. Yet here I was, a world away and desperately clinging to whatever shreds of memory I could conjure of him.

I just wanted to get back home, to find him and make sure he was okay.

"Let's just agree to disagree for now." I pushed off the warmed stone of the hearth and walked back where I'd been sitting on the couch. I couldn't help but notice the tense position the others were in, poised in careful observation of my movements. Aermidh's hand was placed firmly on Bastian's leg, as if holding him in place and signaling to give me time. I found myself drawn to the glowing eyes hidden in the darkness on the other side of the room, and it took all of my restraint to not meet them. He thought he knew me, but he didn't. I had to focus; I couldn't get distracted with their confused ideas of who they thought I was.

I needed to get back to Arlo. He would know what to do.

"My main concern right now is finding Arlo. He must be worried sick about me, and if those things are still out in the woods, then he's in danger if he shows up in the same spot I did. We need to find him and figure out how to get us back home."

"The Daeomi ran back home to its master. It shouldn't be a threat anymore." Vander's cold voice shocked me. This was practically the first thing he'd said all evening. "It should leave your male alone. It's your scent it wants."

My *scent*. He'd said it with such nonchalant ease, like he didn't understand or care how terrifying and cruel this world was to me. His casual demeanor infuriated me. I could barely contain my anger as I spat back, "Well, thank you for that comforting information."

Silence filled the room as the others went utterly still. Bastian moved ever so slightly, as if positioning himself to intervene. Fear crept over me as I remembered exactly who I was talking to. The shadows around him danced, as if sensing that fear—feeding off it. I could have sworn his lip curled up in the corner, a small wicked grin beginning to form, but it was gone before I could get a closer look.

We spent a little more time going over the attack in the woods. I learned that the oily black creature had been something called a Daeomi and his beast had been a depthhound—creatures from some other dark realm or underworld they called the Depths. It seemed as if they were some sort of package deal, separate entities but the same—like some sort of dark version of a familiar. And both, it would seem, belonged to a much larger and more powerful being that no one wanted to want to talk about.

I couldn't get a straight answer as to why they were after me. Bastian, this time, assured me they weren't a threat any longer and that I should just focus on healing up and getting acquainted—or *reacquainted,* in his words—to the house and the land.

"Why don't you want to let me leave?" My wariness of the three strangers around me was growing, their intent becoming more suspicious the more they argued to keep me here. "If I was healed by magic, then why do I need to rest? My leg is better, so let's just make a plan and start searching for Arlo."

"Are you going to run out there into the night, little spitfire? Are you going to brave through beast and banshee to find your male?"

Gooseflesh covered my arms as Vander's words washed over me. I tried hard to avoid meeting his gaze, but some unknown power compelled me to look at him. He still sat in his same place on the couch, watching, assessing.

"Not helping, brother," Bastian bit out through gritted teeth.

I gave myself one more moment to feel his icy stare cutting into my skin before I answered:

"If that's what it takes, then yes."

The intensity in his eyes lessened, something else flashing across them. Whatever spell forcing me to look at him finally broke and I searched desperately for something else to focus on.

"I'll send out some of my scouts tomorrow and have them begin searching," Bastian cut in. "Aermidh's magic can only heal so much, and your body still needs time to recover. Your injuries were not merely surface wounds. Your blood loss was great and as good as Aermidh is, that sort of recovery isn't going to be immediate. If you go back out there now, not only will you be hurting yourself further, but you'll be painting a large target on yourself and anyone who goes with you. Best to lay low for now, rest. We will search for your Arlo until you are able to go out yourself."

I sighed but eventually gave in, nodding in agreement. I was sure he was right on some level. My body didn't feel completely better yet and either my injuries, or the chaos that was this evening, was scrambling my mind and making it hard to decipher make-believe from reality. Silently, I decided I would stay and rest only long enough to gain my strength before going back out to those woods to find my way back to Arlo, with or without their help. I didn't care who they thought I was or what they believed to be true. I couldn't take their prying eyes or their nonsense talk any longer.

"I, uh—" I stuttered. "I think I'd just like to go to bed. If that's alright?"

I glanced nervously at Aermidh. It felt bold of me to assume they just had a room ready for me, but I was desperate to sleep and had nowhere else to go.

Aermidh stood, dusting off her skirts and shaking her head. "Of course! I'm so sorry we've kept you this long. I can't even imagine how you're managing to stay on two feet. Let's get you to your room. I made it up for you while you bathed earlier."

She rounded the couch and motioned for me to follow her down one of the hallways off to the left. Before I could go, I felt a sudden presence behind me.

Vander loomed over me, inches away and intently staring. The shadows somehow circled him—circled *us*—as he breathed in deeply and ran his eyes down the length of my body.

"I have a question for you, little spitfire, before you leave."

He paused, waiting for me to react, but I couldn't. I was frozen beneath the weight of his eyes on me, of his body so close to mine—shocked by the name he'd called me because it somehow felt oddly familiar.

"Did you see me before? In your dream the other night?"

A noise escaped my lips, something caught between a squeak and a gasp. I hadn't seen him up close yet, aside from the few moments before

I'd passed out in his arms when I'd thought he was Arlo. His slender form was much more intimidating up close. His dark hair piled in soft waves on top of his head, falling slightly in front of those glowing eyes. His jaw was firm, cheekbones high and defined. His arm flexed, showing off the bands of black ink embedded into it. One reminded me of what I'd noticed etched into his brother's forearm, but there were others that were entirely different, too. If I didn't know any better, it seemed like he was trying to contain some impulse to reach out and grab me.

I wanted to lie. I wanted to tell him that I had never seen him before, that nothing about him seemed or felt familiar, but that compulsion I'd felt under his stare earlier increased tenfold as the word floated out of my mouth and through the air.

"Yes." I held his gaze for a moment longer before I ripped my eyes away and forced my feet to carry me far, far away from him. I could feel his eyes lingering on me as I made my way down the hallway, feel him still watching as I followed Aermidh through the door to my room.

If Aermidh had magic capable of healing me, I wondered what kind of magic Vander possessed. I suppressed a shudder as my mind lingered on the question. A quiet, slow answer formed in the back of my mind, a warning that it may in fact be the kind capable of destroying me.

CHAPTER 17
VANDER

I watched as Hazlenn disappeared behind the door into her bedroom. I wondered if anything inside would trigger her memory. It wasn't like she'd lived here or anything, but my parents had taken her in as one of our own, kept a place for her whenever she'd needed it. I smiled briefly, remembering their kindness. Sometimes it was hard to believe they weren't still here.

The smile faded quickly as I realized Bastian was frowning at me. My face slipped back into a look of indifference as I met his gaze.

"What now?" I challenged.

"Don't you think she has enough going on without you giving off the sadistic evil bastard vibe?"

He moved to the small shelf at the edge of the room, pouring each of us a glass of sunbeam whiskey. The tonic was imported from Auris, the sun tribe. Their fermentation process with solar magic added just the right amount of bite to the alcohol. Bastian and I hadn't had a taste for anything else ever since our father had brought it back from one of his chieftain visits to their territory all those years ago.

I huffed out a laugh as I rolled my eyes. "Brother, I can assure you she's not paying attention to any vibes I'm giving off. She seems more mesmerized by Aerie right now than me—or you, for that matter. I don't think she's your biggest fan either right now."

"And what's that supposed to mean?" His voice raised slightly at the not-so-subtle accusation as he handed me a glass and took his place back on the sofa.

"It means she clearly has someone she cares about, who for all we know is out in those woods. And you won't let her go look for him."

"Three hours ago she was bleeding out in Aerie's greenhouse! Excuse me for not wanting to send her back into the Dark Woods. The Daeomi isn't the only thing she should be scared of out there, even if you supposedly took care of it."

My face hardened as I dipped my chin and leaned in closer to him. "I am the last person you need to remind about the nightmares of the Dark Woods, brother. It would do you well to remember that." I could sense my shadows growing, feel the room darkening at the tone in my voice. I willed my mind to calm as I sat back and took a deep breath.

"Besides, it should be Hazlenn's—" My voice faltered at the sound of her name—the name she no longer claimed, that no longer fit her. I cleared my throat, trying to work against the knot that was forming there. "*Hazel*'s decision. If she feels like she's up for a midnight trip to the Dark Woods, who are we to stop her?"

Bastian stared at me for several minutes, his face alternating between a look of shock and rage. He couldn't decide how to continue our conversation, that I had no doubt. The idea of the great big Chieftain of Talamh struggling for words had me trying to hide a grin.

"So you think she's telling the truth? That she's not Hazlenn?" Bastian said warily. "How could that be? She admitted to seeing you in the dream."

"I think she's exactly who we think she is." Before he could cut in, I added, "And a completely different female entirely."

Bastian scoffed, throwing back the amber liquid in his glass before putting his hands on his knees and pushing himself off the low sofa.

"Well, thank you for clearing that up, brother. Truly, that was some useful information right there. And what of her partner, the male? I suppose you're not even going to acknowledge that cruel twist from the Fates."

I didn't respond, taking a long, slow sip from my glass instead.

Bastian huffed out another laugh as he rounded the room. "I'm going to bed. I've already had enough to deal with today without trying to figure out just what it is you're thinking." He gave me one last concerned look, tapping his finger on the back of the leather upholstery. "Regardless of how you feel, regardless of how different things seem right now with her... Just remember what was."

He turned, trudging heavily toward his room as he called out over his shoulder, "And remember how much it was worth fighting for before you make the stupid decision to throw it all away in the name of self-loathing."

I shook my head as a sarcastic laugh slipped out. His words lingered in my mind far longer than I cared to admit. I sat there, staring at the dancing flames of the fire and mulling over Bastian's words—mulling over every moment of the day and every word, every look she had given me. She'd been right about one thing: none of this made sense. Anger rose abruptly and I threw my glass at the flames, watching it shatter against the stone, the shards falling into the glowing embers.

After a few minutes passed, I stood and rolled my shoulders. The time for self-loathing was over. The moon was high and the night was young.

It was time to hunt.

The sun had barely started peeking over the horizon as I made my way back to the house. I could feel thick, sticky blood coating my fur, drying in a matted mess as I prowled forward. I didn't mind it. It was a reminder of a night well spent, a few less nightmares circling our lands and preying on our people. Kahlis' creatures were getting brave—attacking more frequently—which only offered me more blood to take. If this was all I could do for our tribe, then I would gladly do it.

I planned to slip inside and head straight to the hot bath I knew would be awaiting me. Some time after Aermidh had moved in with us, Bastian had to tell her about my nightly hobbies. Back then it had mostly consisted of tearing apart the woods to find Hazlenn or any sign of what had happened to her. That lasted for a few years, until my hope began to dwindle and the markings on my skin started to demand more. The Mark had an insatiable thirst for bloodshed. To be honest, I wasn't sure if it was more so the Mark or me who craved it, but I gave in either way.

At some point in those years, Aermidh took notice of my... *condition* when I made my way back home come sunrise. She complained about the muck and blood I tracked in, inevitably making a mess in the house. I felt bad, or at least tried to, but there wasn't much I could do about it. It wasn't exactly like I could *kill cleaner* or anything. She would roll her eyes at me and storm off as if I was too much of a nuisance to deal with. Shortly after that, though, I started coming back from the hunt to find my bathtub full of hot steaming water, bits of petals and herbs floating along the surface.

I refused to acknowledge the gesture at first. I considered it Aerie's rude way of confronting me and demanding I clean up after myself. Eventually, though, I came to realize just how much those baths helped me after a night of hunting. It was like whatever concoction of magic and herbs she put into them wasn't only soothing to my body but soothing to my soul as well. It helped me recover in a way I'd never experienced before. It helped me feel a little more like myself and slightly less like the monster I had become.

I made my way through the house and toward my bedroom. I heard a soft click behind me and turned to see Hazel standing just outside her room, hand still frozen on the doorknob. Her mouth was gaping, eyes full of fear as she realized my presence in the hallway. I wasn't sure if it was my wolven form or the blood and gore smattered throughout my fur that she found so frightening. Both were probably a safe bet. My eyes lingered on her, watching how she stood out against this place, watching how she'd reacted to what I'd become. She no longer looked like she belonged here. Her skin was too pale, her body too weak to survive in a place like this. Her face looked sunken and I couldn't help but notice the dark shadows below her eyes, like she hadn't gotten a decent night's sleep in the ten long years she'd been gone.

She was nothing like the Hazlenn I'd known. She was too weak for this world, too weak for me. I stood there a moment longer, staring at her and letting her take me in, before a low growl escaped my throat.

I didn't necessarily want to scare her, but letting her see me like this felt wrong. It was like I was in a dream, or a nightmare, stripped bare with all of my deepest, darkest parts on display for her to see. She just stood there, unrecognizing and terrified. I needed her to get over that fear. If we were going to make any headway, she had to stop being so damned scared of me, of everything. I shook my head and turned back toward my room. I didn't know why I even cared, why I was thinking that we'd be anything more than what we were now: complete strangers.

She was different. I was different. There was no going back to what was.

I strode slowly through the doorway, making sure to shift just before letting the door swing shut behind me. Best to get it all out of the way now and not let her leave anything up to the imagination. Through the crack as the door closed, I caught a glimpse of her bright green eyes still watching me. This time, they weren't full of terror. They were round with amazement, her cheeks tinged red with what I assumed was embarrassment as she noticed my naked body. I let a small smile slip across my face as the door clicked shut. She'd always loved watching me shift before.

It appeared that she still did. My chest tightened, refusing to let the hope of what that meant creep in.

CHAPTER 18
HAZEL

I sat at a table in the kitchen, watching Aermidh and a couple other ladies as they prepped for the day's various needs and put myself to use by folding some of the linens one of them had brought in from outside. It seemed that Aermidh's staff was made up of various females, most of them appearing not entirely human. The one next to me was timid, almost dropping the basket when she realized I was standing in front of her and offering to help. Her nose was oddly shaped and the longer I let my gaze settle on her face, the more I realized her features reminded me of a doe. Not once did she speak to me, but she eventually let me take the basket and sat down beside me to start in on the folding.

I needed to do something. I'd spent most of the morning wandering around from room to room, trying to find anything that would distract me from my interaction with Vander or the reality of where I was. Before this morning, he'd made me feel uneasy. I couldn't tell what he thought of me, what his role in all of this was. If he an ally or something to be feared.

But after seeing him all blood-soaked and brooding this morning, I was downright terrified of him. I could only imagine what activities he'd been a part of to be covered in so much gore. The image of him attacking that creature in the woods—*the Daeomi*—flashed through my mind. I started to wonder if he'd actually attacked it for my benefit or because of some much darker desire. He'd been absolutely feral, as if he was wolf first and mortal second. It seemed safe to say that was a common state for him, especially after our interaction this morning. Yet I hadn't been able to tear my eyes away from him when he'd shifted—even when I noticed he was entirely naked, even when he held my gaze as he closed his door.

My hands stilled on the soft linen towel in my lap, remembering the look on his face.

"Morning, Hazlenn." Bastian's booming voice broke me from my thoughts with a little jump. Aermidh shot him a warning look as he realized his mistake.

"Shit, Hazel. Sorry, I forgot." He chuckled a little as he strode through the kitchen, shaking his head. "That's going to take some getting used to. Forgive me if I get it wrong once or twice?"

I forced a small smile, nodding in half-hearted agreement.

Bastian paused by the stove in the corner and poured something dark and steaming into a ceramic mug. *Good to know they still have coffee in the magical world.* Aermidh had already given me breakfast, but I was starting to smell the coffee even from the other side of the kitchen and it was making my mouth water all over again. Bastian saw me eyeing his cup and gestured to the kettle, offering me some. I nodded again, a little more eagerly this time.

I hadn't slept well last night. Surprisingly, no nightmares had come, but that was probably because I'd barely slept longer than a few minutes at a time. I'd tossed and turned until I was pouring sweat and sticking to the sheets. At that point, I gave up the idea of sleep altogether and paced my room, trying to make sense of everything that had happened in the last day or two. My restlessness was what drove me from my room as the sun was rising this morning, what caused me to bump into Vander in the hallway when I'd been convinced that no one would be awake yet.

I took the mug from Bastian and let the comforting aroma fill me as I brought it close to my face and took a deep breath. I was a tea lover at heart, but there was always a time and a place for coffee and today was one of them. I took a long sip before turning back to the towel still unfolded in my lap. I picked it up, carefully lining up the corners, and folded it over into a crisp, clean square. As I worked, I was aware of Bastian lingering just far enough away to not be considered overbearing or invading, and Aermidh's eyes darting between the two of us.

I set the towel on the stack of the others I'd already folded before making eye contact with him.

"What?" The word came out much harsher than I'd intended, but his lingering gaze was unnerving. Out of the corner of my eye, I saw the doe-faced girl flinch.

It took him a second to process I was talking to him, and his eyes went wide as he realized he'd been staring.

"Sorry," he said, shaking his head. "It's just been so damn long since I've seen you sitting in this kitchen. And you're just there, drinking coffee like it's any ordinary day. Like we haven't been hoping for this for the last ten years."

I didn't know what to say to that, so I gave a little shrug. I knew these people thought I belonged here, but I had no memory of any of them or this place. It was hard to be happy about something that didn't really feel like home, that didn't even feel real.

That wasn't true though, was it? If I was being honest, this world almost felt too real—the air too rich, the colors too vivid. It had been a large part of the reason I hadn't slept last night: I wanted to know more, needed to see more. I couldn't calm my mind or the desire in my bones to explore every inch of the house, to spend all day today learning as much as I could about this place. It might have been the realest thing I'd ever experienced.

I cleared my throat and took another sip of my coffee as an awkward silence settled in the air. "Have you found any signs of Arlo?" I asked, not really sure how to move on from his comment.

Something like grief passed through Bastian's eyes as he glanced at Aermidh then down at his coffee mug. "Um, no. Not yet. But I have some of my best sentries on it. If there's any sign of someone else out there, they will find him."

I nodded as we fell back into silence. I wanted to ask more questions. Who were these sentries and what were they looking for? How would they be able to tell if they found any signs of Arlo? Instead, I just sat and drank my coffee, letting Bastian continue to fill the space with awkward tension.

"Do you—" He started then stopped, trying to find the right combination of words. "Are you doing anything right now?"

I glanced at the half-folded basket of linens sitting next to me. I fought the urge to smile at the absurdity of his question. *I'm in a completely new magical world with no family or friends, no job or purpose. But yeah, I think I have time to pencil you in for this afternoon.*

As if sensing my thoughts, he let a small smile pull at his lips. "I mean, I know it's not exactly like you have a lot of plans at the moment. But I had something I wanted to show you, if you'd be okay with that."

That same familiar kindness seeped into his eyes and I was overwhelmed with the love I could sense he had for me, or at least for who he thought I was. That's why it was so unnerving to be around him, I realized. He was so passionate and happy and excited that I was here, like I was the key to some unseen puzzle he'd been working out.

What if I wasn't really that person, though? They all seemed to have such high expectations for who they thought I was, and I just wasn't convinced I was really who they were looking for. I didn't want to let them down. The way he looked at me now, with hope and love radiating from his eyes, it reminded me so much of how Arlo would look at me on one of my good days. It was like there was a crack in the clouds and he could see a light shining through, a glimpse of who I was, who I would be without all the darkness fighting to take over and snuff out what little good I had inside. It was hope in tomorrow and the next day and the days after that.

Who was I to take that hope away?

If they truly believed I was this Hazlenn person, then maybe I could give them the benefit of the doubt and play along, at least for a little while.

I glanced at Aermidh, still busily working across the kitchen.

"Go, have fun! We've got it covered in here," she said, waving a towel over the messy counters covered in flour and vegetable scraps.

I turned back to Bastian, forcing myself to take a deep breath before answering: "Alright, what do you want to show me?"

A massive grin split across his face as he stepped toward me and offered his hand. "Well, telling you would ruin the fun of the surprise, wouldn't it? I can't wait to see those eyes of yours light up when you see it."

With that, he grabbed my hand and led me through the house, turning and winding until I was utterly lost with where we were or where we'd end up.

Bastian didn't slow until we were so far within the house that I wondered if it was possible for us to be underground. A faint chill ran down my spine as I remembered this man, this male, was practically a stranger to me and perhaps running deep into his home with no one else and no idea how to get back wasn't exactly the best idea. Before I could question my decision-making process too long, Bastian came to an abrupt stop, turning to face towering double doors made of a dark, rich wood.

He was still wearing that ridiculous grin on his face, like a child given a giant piece of candy. He rested his hand on one of the copper doorknobs as he looked at me and paused.

"Are you ready?"

I huffed out a laugh, his excitement surprisingly contagious. "Ready for what? You to murder me?"

He scoffed, feigning insult as he put his hand to his heart. "I'll give you a pass on that one since you apparently have no memory of me. Although, now that I think about it, this probably wasn't the best way to go about this, given the circumstances."

His eyes shot nervously around the dark corridor we stood in, suddenly aware of the unease I felt. "No, I thought this would be a good room to show you since it was your favorite, you know... before." He hesitated on the last word and his voice sounded rough when it came out.

"Alright, well now I'm really curious. A mysterious room in the deep, dark depths of an ancient house isn't exactly what I would have pegged as being my favorite." I crossed my arms and threw a challenging look his way. "So let's see it then."

The concern melted away from his expression as he gripped the metal knob tighter and pushed against the heavy wood. The doors creaked as they opened, and I felt my stomach give a little flip in anticipation.

Bastian was careful to keep his eyes on me as he led me past the doors and into the room. No, *room* wasn't the right word. Atrium seemed much more fitting. At the far end was an expansive window that domed into part of the roof, allowing sunlight to pour in and fill every corner of the otherwise dark space. Beautiful stained glass hung in some of the panes, casting hues of light and silhouettes of various scenes across the rugged wooden floor. A canopy of deep green vines hung over the outside of the glass, making it feel like I'd walked into an enchanted forest.

It wasn't until we were several steps into the room that I noticed the books, shelf after shelf of books. Floor-to-ceiling bookshelves lined every wall around us. It seemed impossible for one room to contain so many books. I thought back to the little library that I'd spent most of my days in back home.

Okay, so maybe this would be my favorite room. I spun in a slow circle, taking in as much as I could.

Several intimate sitting areas were arranged throughout the space, made up of velvet sofas, elaborate chaises, and even some cozy-looking floor cushions. More formal study areas were located in the middle of the room, with sturdy-looking wood tables stocked with lamps for late-night reading and paper and ink for note-taking. I moved toward the middle of the space and ran my fingers over the rough wood of one of the tables. I felt something catch against my skin and I strained to see the corner of the table, where there was a small carving in the wood.

$H + V + B$

My stomach dropped at the sight. Could I have been the one who carved that H?

"I knew you'd still love it." Bastian stood by the door, smiling like a fool and watching my every move. Suddenly remembering his presence, I quickly took my hand off the table and turned back to him.

"It's... I feel like *amazing* isn't strong enough to describe this place." I looked around again, finding myself incapable of paying attention to anything but the beautiful room. "Thank you," I whispered. "Thank you for showing it to me." My voice was small; it was impossible to feel anything but, in a room like this.

"Yeah, well, I thought it would be a good place to start. Our entire history lives in this room. If there's any way to help jog your memory, this will probably be it. Not to mention it will help you get acclimated, you know, if your memory doesn't return."

I shot a tentative glance at him.

"Right away, I mean," he said, correcting himself. "I'm sure it will return eventually. I just thought maybe this would help."

He wasn't wrong. Seeing as how my biggest hobby back home was researching at the library, this probably *was* the best place to start. I had to admit, my heart was racing at the idea of learning more about this place. I didn't even want to consider the possibility of getting my memories back. I wouldn't let myself get my hopes up like that.

"So," I said, changing the topic as casually as I could manage, "how do you know where to start?"

Bastian's eyes shone as he raised a hand, and I watched in awe as a book floated off one of the higher shelves, hovering in the air. I stared far longer than what would be considered acceptable as he walked around the room and selected several more books, all of them floating off impossible-to-reach shelves, right into his hands. He explained how the library contained a kind of magic that helped its company find whatever they were searching for. Eventually, he had a sizable stack in his arms and he carried them back to the table I was standing by. I picked up a book off the top of the stack and was immediately impressed he'd been strong enough to carry them around the room. They weren't what I'd consider lightweight.

"These should be more than enough to get you started. I'll send Aerie up to check on you in a bit. She's, uh, better with this stuff than I am. You know, more… gentle and whatnot. She'll be able to answer any questions you may have." I could feel the shift in his demeanor. He was slipping back into that awkward space we'd been in before he'd brought up the library. Apparently he'd had one card to play and he'd played it well. Now he was out of things to talk about and was looking for a reason to excuse himself.

That was fine with me, though. I looked longingly at a cozy little alcove by a small window and headed toward it with a couple more books tucked under my arm. I preferred being alone anyway. I waved him off over my shoulder, thanking him again, and settled into the little reading nook. As he closed the doors, I let my gaze pour over the library, trying to take in every little magical detail.

This time, I didn't fight back the smile that spread across my lips.

CHAPTER 19
HAZEL

I spent most of the day lounging in the reading nook, poring over the books Bastian—or maybe it was the library?—had picked out for me. Aermidh appeared at one point with a tray full of delicious-looking sandwiches and drinks. We sat at one of the study tables and discussed some of the things I'd come across while reading. She looked over the books Bastian had given me and even added a few others to my pile.

"I had to give you a little more fae history. Remind me to give Bastian a hard time later for not being more thorough in his selection."

I grinned as she giggled and gave me a wink.

"Alright, tell me again what you've learned so far," Aermidh said, lounging back in her chair and tossing a grape in her mouth.

I took a deep breath as I gathered my thoughts, trying to decide where to begin. "So this land—this continent—is Tir Nadaar?"

She nodded, encouraging me to go on.

"And Bastian is the chieftain of one of the six tribes that make up the continent."

"We lead it together, but yes, he's the one with the fancy title." She rolled her eyes sarcastically as a small grin played at her lips. "Have you read about the other tribes yet?"

I nodded slightly and scrunched up my face, trying to remember the names. "Stratos, Auris, Scaldor, Vatr, and... Sgàil?"

"Very good." Aermidh let out a small laugh as she nodded in approval. "Air, light, fire, water, shadow. And of course, ours is Talamh, the earth tribe. The tribes are representative of the magic we pull from nature. You're picking up on things rather quickly!" She grabbed another grape and then pushed the plate of fruit toward me.

I took it, picking over what was left until I found a particularly ripe strawberry. I added it to my plate and looked back at Aermidh.

"How are you so calm about all of this?"

"All of what?" She shoved the last bite of her sandwich into her mouth.

"This," I said, gesturing to myself then to everything and nothing in particular. "Bastian has been teetering back and forth between what I'm assuming is excitement and nerves every time he talks to me, and Vander..." I let myself trail off, thinking about those glowing eyes that always seemed to be watching me, in either of his forms. "But you? You seem totally okay."

She eyed me as she finished chewing, then dusted the crumbs off her hands and sat up a little straighter.

"First off, Vander is Vander. He's a moody, brooding ass who's going to do whatever he wants no matter what's going on around him. His behavior hasn't actually changed all that much since they found you. And second, Bastian has the emotional maturity of a puppy dog, and probably the same attention span. He may play big, bad chieftain in front of everyone else, but here? Here, he's a softy and he's just excited to have you back home. Albeit a little too excited perhaps." Her eyes met mine, twinkling. "Puppy dog, remember? He just doesn't know the best way to show it."

I let my eyes fall to my lap, turning that information over in my mind. Aermidh reached out and placed her hand on top of mine.

"Give it time, it will get easier." She offered me a soft smile as she squeezed my hand. "And as for me, well, I wasn't around when the three of you were growing up, being thick as thieves and getting into all sorts of trouble."

My confusion must have been apparent, because she broke out into a laugh.

"Yup, you three were inseparable growing up, at least from what I hear. You know, Vander and Bastian are barely more than a year apart. They were so close as kids. Still are, I suppose. But it's different now."

She paused, letting her words hang in the air. "But then you came into the picture and instead of breaking up the duo, you just joined in. Became their shadow and followed them around everywhere, did everything with them. Bastian has told me some pretty crazy stories about what you all would get up to back in those days."

Her eyes sparkled as she spoke and I found myself smiling along with her.

"I would have given anything to see Bastian as a kid back then. Although I'm not sure it would be much different than how he is today. He's basically a massive child now. But no, I came into the picture shortly after you went missing."

The smile faded from my lips as her eyes darkened. It was easy to forget that these people had mourned the person they thought I was. I could see the pain, the worry laced through her features, for a past I couldn't remember. A past I wasn't even sure I believed in. Their emotions were so raw though, so present and obvious that it made it hard not to believe them.

"Bastian was a wreck back then. He'd lost you, who he'd looked to like a little sister. And in a way he'd lost Vander too. He was just gone. Here but not here. He'd leave for days at a time, months in the worst of it. Tearing apart every corner of the continent looking for you and doing Fates know what to get answers."

She shook her head a little, like she was trying to push away the pain of the memory. "Anyway, I met Bastian then and he desperately needed someone to help him find his way back. And I needed him just as much. I think it's probably easier for me to help you through all of this because I don't have a past with you. I didn't know you before. To them, you're Hazlenn, the girl they grew up with and loved and cared for and lost. To me, you're Hazel. A beautifully bright being who I cannot wait to get to know better."

My eyes widened in surprise as I looked at her. A ray of sunlight had broken through the large windows of the library and was casting her icy white hair in a hazy golden glow. I took in her presence, searching for any hint of dishonesty—and found none. Instead, genuine happiness shone from her. I couldn't help but smile back at her sitting there, offering me a hand. She was the image of divinity, my own personal answer to a year of questions and longing. All I had to do was accept it, accept them.

In some way, it made sense. If they really had known me before, if everything they were saying was true, I couldn't imagine how hard it had to be for them to look at me and know I wasn't that girl anymore. No wonder it was so much easier to be around Aermidh. All of those preconceived notions and expectations were nonexistent with her.

"Thank you, Aermidh, for being so kind to me. I can't wait to get to know you better too."

She waved her hand, getting up and gathering the dishes from our lunch. "Oh please, don't even mention it. It's been an absolute pleasure to do what I can to help. And call me Aerie, I mean it. We're friends, after all."

I smiled again at her words as I helped her clean up.

She shifted the empty plates and cups to a serving tray, casting me a sideways glance at the door. "Are you going to come back with me or do you want to hang out in here for the rest of the day?"

I glanced back at the little cubby I'd grown rather fond of and the stack of books I'd barely made a dent in. "I think I'll stay in here a little longer. I still have a lot of reading left to do."

"Alright well, I'm here if you need anything. And feel free to grab some books to take back to your room or anywhere else you might feel like reading."

"I couldn't imagine reading in a better place than this."

I glanced around the room again, still as utterly amazed by it now as I had been the first time I'd seen it this morning.

"Yeah, it has that effect on you." She stood with the tray balanced on her hip as she followed my gaze around the room. "Anyway, good luck. I'll come get you when dinner is ready. Happy reading!"

She waved at me as she made her way out of the room and I returned to my cozy little corner.

I was glad she'd come down here for lunch. It seemed like talking with her was going to prove the most useful of my options. I'd have to make a mental list of questions I wanted to ask her. Something she'd said prickled curiosity in my mind as I dug through the stack of books and found the one I'd been looking for. It was an ancient-looking book, the pages delicate and stained with age. It boasted a history of the Fates and seemed like a promising choice after the odd expression she'd used. I settled back into the cushions and let the book fall open in my lap.

Talking with her had felt so easy and I found my thoughts drifting back to our conversation as I tried to read. The warm sunlight poured through the window and pooled over my legs as last night's exhaustion pulled me under without a fight. I tried to focus my eyes as I read the same paragraph for the fifth time, but I was helpless to the lull of the quiet library. It didn't take long for me to drift off to sleep, my book still propped up against my thighs.

I woke with a start, the sound of someone clearing their throat echoing through the library. Vander stood a good distance away, stiff and indifferent as he watched me wake.

"Aerie sent me up to tell you dinner is ready."

I rubbed my eyes as I sat up, then ran my hands over my hair, suddenly aware of the mess of tangles gathering in the back. It took a second to remember where I was, what I had been doing. I glanced around the room, then back to the book in my lap. *Oh right, the Fates.* I hadn't gotten more than two pages into the book before passing out.

"That is, if you care to join us."

I realized at Vander's cold words that I hadn't given him a response.

"Oh." I paused, suddenly feeling self-conscious of his eyes on me. "Uh, yes, sorry. Dinner sounds wonderful."

"Fantastic," he deadpanned before turning on his heels and strutting out the door.

I sat, staring for a minute before I realized I should be following him. I had absolutely no idea how to get out of this part of the house on my own.

Vander's voice called from the hallway, "Better move your ass, Aerie doesn't like it when we keep dinner waiting."

His words spurred me into motion and I quickly tidied the area before grabbing a couple books to take with me and rushed to catch up with him.

We walked in uncomfortable silence for what felt like an eternity. His movements were smooth as silk as he strode confidently through the halls. I struggled to keep up. My head was turning in every direction as I took mental note of each twist and turn we made. I wanted to remember how to get back to the library without having to ask for someone to accompany me.

"So," I finally said, my voice sounding overly loud in the quiet of the hallways. "Are you um... okay? After this morning?"

A wicked grin played at the corner of his mouth. He didn't even glance my way as he coolly replied, "Quite. I apologize if I scared you. I didn't think you would be so... impressionable."

"I wasn't scared," I shot back, anger rising in my words.

Why did I care if he thought I was scared? I *should* be scared of him. I didn't really want to convince him otherwise. I wanted to keep him at a distance, not give him reason to interact with me more.

This time, his eyes flickered down at me as amusement spread over his face.

"Oh?" His eyebrows rose as he spoke. "Then maybe I'll have to try harder next time."

Silence fell back over us for the rest of our walk to the dining room. His words sparked something inside me, something icy and fear-ridden.

I slowed, allowing a bit of distance to form between us as we walked. He didn't seem to notice or care.

Good. I didn't want him to make good on that threat and I definitely hadn't liked the way his eyes had sized me up like his next meal to devour. I wanted to trust them—Aermidh and Bastian had been so kind to me—but Vander was, quite literally, another beast entirely. And a small part of me realized I'd never be as safe as I wanted to be around him. But there was nowhere left to run. As I watched him grin beside me, I realized: whether I wanted to or not, I'd have to trust Vander.

No matter how much the thought made my stomach churn.

CHAPTER 20
VANDER

I sat in front of the fire, swirling the glass of deep amber liquid in my hand. Bastian and Aerie argued behind me, but I had tuned them out several minutes ago. I couldn't take the bickering, the hushed voices as they discussed Hazel and the implications of the situation. It felt wrong, talking about her as if she wasn't just in the other room. She'd been quiet at dinner and excused herself for the night as soon as she'd finished eating.

I found my eyes lingering on her movements as she scurried off to her room. She was so scared all the time, so unsure of herself here. It bothered me in a way I didn't care to admit. So instead I took a long drink from my glass and turned back to Bastian.

"We shouldn't be discussing this without her," I said, my voice booming across the room, cutting Bastian off from whatever theory he was spouting off.

"I don't think we should fill her in until we are absolutely sure what's going on, Vander." Bastian's voice was rough, edged with the exhaustion

I knew we all felt. In between babysitting duties, the three of us had been running ragged all day, trying to reach contacts and get answers about Hazel's return. Bastian himself rode out to relay messages straight from The Dark Woods.

"The sentries have sworn there's no signs of anything out there. Not even from Hazel. We can't afford to divide their attention much longer. It's weakening our borders. There has already been an increase in Daeomi attacks amongst the outer villages. I think it's time to start considering the one real explanation for all of this, brother. We've thought this whole time that Kahlis had her. Why would that change now?"

I stared down at the rug, studying the intricate design of the woven fibers. I didn't have an answer for him, but I didn't want to consider the possibility that Kahlis had been holding her this entire time. Ten years at his hands was more than a lifetime of torment. Shadows danced around my shoulders as I let the anger rise.

"I want to believe her, Vander, I do. But you know our sentries are some of the best and if they say there's nothing out there, then there's nothing out there."

"It will break her," I said, unable to hide the pain in my voice. "To find out the very little bit she thought she knew wasn't even real. It would utterly ruin her. And she's already too fragile as it is."

Silence filled the room.

Finally, Aerie spoke: "Maybe it doesn't have to be one or the other."

Bastian contemplated in silence, trying to understand what she was suggesting. I could see the hopefulness stirring across his face at Aerie's words, wanting to believe she had the answers. She always had all the answers. Without her, who knows where we'd both be.

"We don't know any better than she does," Aerie continued. "This reality is what feels most plausible, most acceptable to us. That doesn't mean what she felt or what she experienced was any less real. Kahlis' magic is unique. It's not just implanting memories or dreams. It's reality-bending, mind-bending. He can create and take away at his will. It's what makes him so powerful, the closest thing to a god this realm has seen in centuries. I think the best thing to do would be to tell her the truth. The whole truth. She can decide for herself what's real."

"So you think it's possible?" asked Bastian incredulously. "This Arlo character actually exists and she actually traveled through some portal to the mortal realm? No one has ever traveled there before—"

"That we know of," Aerie cut in.

"All I'm saying," Bastian continued, lowering his voice. "Is that it seems much more likely that Kahlis forced these memories into her, embedded these experiences in her mind. Just for the sake of fucking with us."

Aerie worried her lip, glancing up to me for a brief moment. "I think both are equally possible and it's entirely *impossible* to know for sure at this point which is true. And I think lying to her further is only going to make it harder for her to trust us. She needs family. She needs us."

She turned to me, loose strands of her gold-flecked hair falling freely over her stern eyes. "Give her a chance to know the truth. She may just surprise you."

My eyes lingered on hers, that all-knowing gleam in them. I didn't know how Aerie was so wise, but she always played the voice of reason between me and Bastian.

"Aerie's right," I said resolutely. "You should tell her the truth."

Bastian scoffed at my words, shaking his head in disbelief. "Alright brother, it's your call. But I'll be damned if you're going to pass responsibility for this onto us. You want her to know the truth, you tell her."

Aermidh shot him a nervous glance but didn't chastise him. Which meant she knew he was right.

"Fuck," I huffed under my breath before finishing off the liquid in my glass, letting it sting the back of my throat as it went down. I stood, leaving my glass on the table by the sofa, and walked to my room.

I slammed the door behind me, shaking the frame with the force. I didn't care who heard, if *she* heard. I wanted her scared. Better to be scared and keep her distance than risk her trying to get close. Although I supposed now it wouldn't make a difference. I was going to have to confront her whether I liked it or not. I didn't want to be the one to tell her that there were no signs of her precious male out in The Dark Woods, that he might not even be real.

I threw myself down in a chair in the corner, dragging my hands over my face and then through my hair in frustration. I cursed loudly into the empty room, trying to satisfy the rage I felt building underneath my skin. It did little to quench the need and I quickly stood again and started pacing. At some point, I'd shifted into my wolven form. I hadn't even noticed until I went to curse again and was surprised by the deep growl that slipped out instead.

I was quickly reminded how my magic had a mind of its own, how it was not always easily controlled by my will. The Mark was calling for blood, whether I was listening or not. I shifted long enough to open my door before letting my primal form slip back into place as I prowled through the hallway. My body froze as my hackles rose. Awareness washed over me, a deep feeling of terror settling over my bones: not my terror, someone else's. Something wasn't right.

Moments later, a blood-curdling scream split into the air.

I didn't hesitate as I turned back toward Hazel's door and let my wolven form slam through the wood.

CHAPTER 21
HAZEL

Dinner had been fine, if not somewhat awkward. I'd excused myself as soon as I was finished eating, desperate to get away from all the eyes watching me. I slipped into my bedroom and closed the door. I let out a sigh as I closed my eyes and took a moment to calm my nerves. I hadn't been back in my room since this morning, and it was nice to have a space to disappear into. The bed sat to the right, covered in dangerously soft blankets and cushions. A fire crackled in the small fireplace, taking me by surprise. Its warm glow cast dancing shadows along the walls.

The room was donned in the colors of autumn, deep greens and coppery oranges complimented by touches of a rich black here and there. There was a bookshelf along the far wall, next to the fireplace. I hadn't noticed it before, but I strode across the room to get a better look. It was hard to read the titles in the night's dim light, but I ran my hand along the stacked spines anyway. I plopped down in the sitting area in front of the fire, placing the few books I'd taken from the library on the low table in front of me. I briefly wondered if it had been the deer girl I'd met earlier who'd made the fire for me. I'd have to remember to ask for her name. I imagined calling her *deer girl* would come across as a bit insulting. I leaned back, enjoying the warmth of the fire and taking a deep breath. However comforting my room was though, I found myself longing to go back to the library.

I sat there for a moment longer, letting my arms and legs get warm. Despite the nap I'd taken earlier, I found it hard to keep my eyes open. I debated trying to dive back into the book I'd started earlier but knew I'd just end up falling asleep before getting anywhere with it. Instead, I stifled a yawn as I made my way to the wardrobe by the bed and dug around for something to sleep in. Eventually, I came across a lilac-colored sleep set made out of a lightweight gauzy material. The fabric felt soft and featherlight in my hands and I eagerly peeled off the clothes Aerie had given me on my first day here and replaced them with the cozy outfit. The top had thin straps that were slightly too big and I found myself slipping them back into place as they took turns falling off my shoulders. The bottoms were breathable, flowy and stopping just above my ankles. They fit a little better than the top, but it all was a tad too big.

It didn't matter though, as I sunk into the bed and let the silky sheets envelop me. The pillow smelled like lavender and I took a deep breath in as I buried my head in the bed. I'd been too distracted yesterday to pay any attention to the extravagant bedding or the wardrobe full of clothes for me. I realized someone had made up the bed for me tonight; the sheets were fresh and clean rather than crumpled and heavy with the scent of sweat, as they had been this morning. It felt weird to have others in my room, tending to my needs without me knowing. It felt even weirder to see just how much these people cared about me... It made me want to believe, even for just a second, that I really was the girl they all wanted me to be.

I snuggled down in the bed, feeling my walls coming down with each deep breath I took. Despite everything that had happened today, I was actually starting to feel a little safe here.

That was my first mistake.

I stood, or rather hung, in a dark room. Chains cut into my wrists pinned above my head as I tried to find my footing on the slick, stone floor. The sweet, sickly smell of rot stung my nose, immediately causing my stomach to turn. I tried to calm the nausea, tried to will my body not to react, but it was no use. I turned my head to the side just in time as bile rose, burning my throat. I heaved again, my stomach trying hard to empty its contents. My body convulsed like that a few more times before I finally gained control.

A harsh laugh broke out from the darkest corner of the room. The light was too dim to make out who it belonged to. The air was damp with humidity and I looked around, desperate for a way to escape. The creature from the woods made his way forward, his body still in its mortal form rather than the oily black mutation he had turned into when he'd caught me.

"Hello again, little plaything."

His eyes danced wickedly over my body, still in the gauzy nightclothes. I cursed myself for putting on something so utterly scant. Not that I'd exactly planned on being kidnapped in the night, but I'd let my guard down. Come to think of it, I had absolutely no idea how I'd gotten here.

"How'd you find me?" My voice was raspy from the acid still burning my throat.

"We didn't find you. Well, not truly."

He stalked forward, letting his finger trace a line down my face and over my chest. I squirmed under his touch, incapable of getting away.

"You see, you're not here, not really. But boy, is it going to feel real to you."

His face beamed in cruel delight as his fingers dug into my waist.

"Enough."

A powerful voice sounded from all around us. The Daeomi went rigid at the word, immediately loosening his grip and backing away. His eyes didn't leave me, though. My relief was short-lived as another figure emerged from the darkness.

Everything about him was terrifying. A dark power radiated off of him, raising the hairs on the back of my neck as he made his way toward me. My eyes raced over every part of him, each one flooding me with more fear than the one before. His hair was a black pit, not in the silky smooth way I'd noticed Vander's had been, but ashen and lifeless. A singular streak of white cut across it, falling over his forehead. It wasn't the kind of white one associated with purity, but rather the kind of white that reminded one of lost souls, petrifying corpses, and the thick, sticky webs of a venomous spider. His eyes were black pools of pure evil, reminding me of the darkness I'd only ever experienced in my worst nightmares. I couldn't focus on them long without feeling a piercing ice creep down my spine.

My heart dropped as my gaze fell lower. His hands were stained a deep red, like some time long ago he had dipped his fingers, his palms, in a dark red ink and had let it sit there until it'd become a permanent mark on his skin. I noticed the way his arms faded from that rugged olive tone to the rust color around his wrists, down to that darker shade of too-deep red encircling the tips of his fingers. The color of nightmares. The color of blood, I realized.

I could almost see it dripping off each fingertip. I wondered how much killing one had to do for their hands to be permanently and visibly affected like so. Worse yet, I could see the even darker outline of his long, pointed nails, the almost black cracks and wrinkles of his knuckles, like whatever gore had caused the discoloration had dried there, unwilling or unable to be washed away.

He stepped forward, coming face to face with me.

"Hazlenn," he purred. The name sounded like a death knell on his lips.

A whimper slipped past my throat as I felt the first warm tear fall down my cheek.

He clicked his tongue in disapproval. "None of that now. I've been looking for you for quite some time. I won't have you waste our moments together on frivolous tears."

He leaned in close, picking up a lock of my hair and bringing it to his nose as he sniffed it deeply.

"You remind me so much of her, you know. You even smell like her." He let my hair fall back over my shoulder, pausing to fix the strap of my nightshirt that had slipped down. "I don't know what she saw in you though, why she worked so hard to hide you from me all these years. You really are a pathetic little creature, aren't you?"

His eyes slid over my body in a predatory way before landing back on my hair. Without warning, without any movement from him, an earth-shattering pain ripped through my head. I felt crushed beneath the weight of his invisible grasp.

"See how easily I could end you," he mused. The corner of his lip curled up as he watched me writhe in pain against the chains holding my wrists in place above my head. Images of every terrible thing I'd ever dreamt, ever felt, cycled endlessly in my mind. The sinister darkness felt like a tangible thing within me, snaking through me and creeping in for the kill, as I shut my eyes and tried desperately to fight through the pain. It was too much.

"Look at me, Hazlenn," he ordered.

The grasp on my mind grew stronger, becoming unbearable as a scream was ripped from my lungs.

He cocked his head to the side, as if he sensed something.

"Interesting."

I screamed again, on the edge of unconsciousness just as the creature before me, along with the room and everything in it, dissipated into thick, black smoke, leaving me alone in the darkness with only the sound of my screams piercing through the air.

I was screaming, trying to bring myself back into consciousness. I told myself to open my eyes, to wake from the nightmare, but it was like I was trapped. Somewhere in the recesses of my mind, I registered a crashing noise. Then, I felt something heavy settle along the length of my body. Fur brushed against my hands. The scent of cloves and smoke rippled around me and permeated my senses, guiding me back to reality.

Slowly, my vision came into focus. Vander lay on the bed in front of me. His wolven form was all but on top of me—his attempt to either help ground me or wake me. Deep, steady growls sounded from him as his nose nudged my head. The vibrations were oddly soothing and I realized my hands were grasped firmly in his silken midnight fur.

Breathe. Slow, deep breaths.

The words sounded through my mind and it sounded similar to something Arlo would say when he'd help me after a nightmare. That's what I'd experienced, just a bad nightmare.

Then why did my body still ache?

My breath slowed, eventually steadying as he pulled his head back and stared at me with those golden glowing eyes. The rings of black seemed somewhat less obvious than they had been before. I eased my hands out of his fur, not failing to notice the tufts that came with them from how hard I'd been grasping him.

He backed off as soon as I settled, staying at the foot of the bed. We stared at each other for several minutes, unable to move. I didn't know what to say, or if he'd even understand me while he was in this form. I opened my mouth to speak, but before I could say anything, Bastian and Aerie ran through the mess that used to be my door and into the room.

CHAPTER 22
VANDER

Kahlis. This had to be him. No one else was powerful enough to hold someone like that in a dream. Rage rippled through me as I felt the black ink pulsing on my arm. I couldn't take my eyes off her. I needed to be sure she was okay. Her screams had been dripping with fear. I had felt the pain in them.

Our eyes were locked, as if spellbound, when Bastian burst into the room, one of his axes in hand.

"What in the Depths is going on?" Bastian huffed out. Aerie was right behind him, eyes wide with worry. Breaking the spell between us, Hazel turned reluctantly to the doorway; I used the distraction as an opportunity to shift, wrapping a blanket around my waist. Nudity had never bothered me, but I figured Hazel could do without the shock of having a naked stranger in her bed right now. I had to suppress a shudder as the word *stranger* echoed through my mind. That's all we were now.

Bastian's eyes shot between me and Hazel before falling to the broken doorway and the shards of wood under his feet. Slowly, he raised his head to me.

"Brother, I'm going to need you to step away from her." His voice was calm and collected as he spoke, but I could sense the edge in his tone. I could see the gears in his head turning, calculating and assessing the threat. He thought I'd lost control, that my primal form—or the Mark—had taken over and was out for blood.

I scoffed as I rose from the bed, blanket firmly grasped in one hand. "Thanks for the vote of confidence, Bastian, but you'll be surprised to know this was not my doing." I paused, glancing down at the bits of wood. "Well, that was."

"He's telling the truth." Hazel's words were rushed and breathless. I bit back a smile at her urge to defend me. "It was a nightmare. Just a bad dream." Her head dropped as she spoke, embarrassment taking hold of her and whatever little strength she had left disappearing.

Bastian eyed us both again, verifying there was no immediate threat. "Sorry, brother." He offered me a small nod. "I heard her screams, saw the mess and you in your primal form... I just assumed the worst. I—"

I threw my hand up, cutting him off. "Save it, there's more important things to take care of right now."

I knew the conclusion he'd jumped to. I wasn't mad actually, I'd probably assume the same of me, given the scene he walked in on. Still, something inside me stirred at the reminder of the monster that lurked under my skin, of what even my own brother believed it was capable of.

I turned my attention back to Hazel.

"That," I said, gesturing to the rumpled bed she'd been thrashing around on not even five minutes ago, "was not a nightmare."

She tilted her head to one side, completely ignorant of the true danger she was just in.

"What do you mean?"

Instead of answering her, I turned to Aerie.

"We need to get her to the greenhouse. Now."

Hazel was too weak to walk, so Bastian draped her arm over his shoulder and half carried her through the house and out to the little greenhouse. If Kahlis had found her, then we needed to work fast to give her as much protection as we could.

Aerie guided her onto the bed in the corner. "Seems like this is becoming quite a favorite spot of yours," she offered with a little smile.

Once Aerie had her settled in, she moved around the room, grabbing various jars and a small stone mortar and pestle. She worked on a concoction before waving her hand over a nearby mug, filling it with warm water. Once her herbs had steeped, she carried the tea over to Hazel and made her drink.

"This should help restore your strength. Don't stop drinking until it's done. I'll make another one and you'll need to do the same again."

I watched as Hazel lifted the mug to her lips, her weary green eyes peeking out over the top. Her gaze shifted around the room in fear before finding mine and settling there. I wanted to reach out and comfort her, offer some sort of support. That wasn't my role, though—not anymore. I let the shadows grow around me as I slipped further back, letting Aerie take the lead.

When Hazel was well into her second cup of tea, Aerie turned to me and said, "I need you to start explaining and I need you to do it fast."

She could sense it too then, the impending threat. It felt like the air was crackling with dark energy.

"It was Kahlis."

Bastian's brows rose. "How? He doesn't know where she is. How could he dreamwalk to her without that information?"

"He doesn't need that information," I bit back. "He just needs something from her."

I watched as Bastian concentrated, trying to understand the situation. After a moment, his face fell in shock.

"The attack in the Dark Woods. They have her blood."

I nodded slowly, already having pieced that together myself.

"Fuck!" Bastian slammed his fist down on the table.

His curse was laced with the vibrations of a deep growl. I could sense his primal form threatening to come to the surface.

His panic echoed through me. If Kahlis had her blood, there were any number of things he'd be able to do to her, and no way to tell which he'd try. It was probably why the Daeomi had been so quick to scurry off. The rush of rage and regret flooded me once again, for not ending him when I had the chance.

"Ergo, why I said we needed the greenhouse. And Aerie."

I shifted my gaze to her. She was already grabbing new ingredients from her shelves for more herbal magic. I could tell by the way she moved that she was worried. It took a lot to unsettle Aerie, meaning I was right in believing this was a true threat.

"Can you do anything to help her?" I asked.

She was already at the shelves, searching for something with a swiftness that had the panic inside of me deepening. She pulled one of her books down and slammed it on the table, flipping hastily through the pages. I let my eyes fall to the various jars and bottles she'd laid out in front of us. Where her earlier ingredients had consisted of delicate looking petals and an array of green herbs, this collection looked like the stuff of nightmares, things found only in the darkest corners of our continent. Blood magic called for the strongest wards possible, meaning only the roughest and rarest ingredients could be used.

"Aermidh." Her name came out forcefully, betraying the panic I felt.

"Dammit, Vander, give me a minute."

Her cheeks were flushed as she continued to pull books off the shelf and compare pages. Finally, she slowed her work to give me an answer.

"I can try."

"*Try?*" I spat back at her. "There is no fucking *trying* with this, Aermidh. We either ward her or we don't."

"You need to step back, brother." Bastian's voice was a warning. He'd stepped closer to her, his hand itching to grab for the weapon at his side.

Aerie's tone was stern yet empathetic as she replied, "I know how serious this is, Vander. I'll do the best I can, but there's too many variables. It's impossible to protect her from everything Kahlis could do." Her eyes filled with remorse and worry as she waited for me to respond.

This time it was my curse that cut through the small greenhouse. I pushed off the table, running my hands through my hair in frustration. I had to think. There had to be something we could do to ensure the wards would work. My shadows grew around me as my rage built. I could feel the dark magic inside of me gnawing its way to the surface, demanding to be used. I stopped mid-turn as I remembered Hazel, perched on the bed and intently listening to every word we were saying. I lingered for a minute longer on her pure, ignorant face, before turning away. I cocked my head back toward Aerie as I paused in the doorway.

"Do what you can. Keep her safe."

With that, I pushed past the door and into the night. There was an itch I needed to scratch and I had a pretty good idea how I wanted to scratch it. Bastian's voice called out after me.

"What the fuck do you think you're going to do, Vander?"

I didn't wait to answer before shifting and taking off into the night. I could hear Bastian calling after me as I ran, even sensed him shift as he tried to catch up. But he wouldn't stop me. I could outrun him any day. That was one of the few benefits of the Mark: insurmountable strength. I was tired of sitting idly by and waiting for Aerie to find an answer. I'd given her time to figure out a solution, but we were out of time now. If Kahlis could get to her like this, then there was no telling what he'd do to her. What was the point of the Mark if I couldn't even keep my own family safe?

I might not be able to protect her here, but I'd be damned if I was going to sit by and do nothing to stop this. I wasn't afraid of what I'd have to fight—what I'd have to kill to get answers. While Aerie and Bastian waxed poetic about the natural balances of the lands, I knew in my gut one truth: there wasn't a single creature in the Dark Woods or Kahlis' lands I wouldn't enjoy ripping apart for her sake.

CHAPTER 23
HAZEL

I watched as Vander stormed out of the greenhouse. I didn't know what time it was, but the sun had long since set and I could only imagine what kind of things lurked out there in the cover of night. Bastian called to him without response before running after him. I could hear him yelling at Vander, could hear the desperation in his voice as he shouted. My eyes were peeled to the door, waiting for them to return. Somewhere inside of me, I felt a mixture of hope and dread rising as I waited to see if Bastian would return with him. I didn't know why I cared if Vander stormed off into the night in some fit of rage, but those emotions grew as I thought about the way he'd looked at me after I'd come out of the nightmare.

I could have sworn there'd been genuine concern laced in the depths of those golden shadows. He'd known how to pull me out, how to bring me back from the pit of whatever realm I'd disappeared into. The weight of his wolven form still lingered on my body. The vibration of his growls still rattled through my bones. Everything he did, I realized, was an effort to pull me back to reality.

Breathe. Slow, deep breaths.

The sound of those words echoed endlessly in my mind.

I didn't know if they had been my own thoughts or if his words had somehow penetrated the grip of the dream and slipped through my mind. I wasn't even sure that he'd said them out loud, if that was even possible. Although, I wasn't sure that anything seemed impossible anymore.

After what felt like an eternity, Bastian stormed back into the room. His lack of clothing was not lost on me, and I quickly averted my gaze as the memory of Vander's naked body slipping through his door lashed through my mind. Bastian had told me they were shifters, but this was the first time I'd actually seen him use that magic. I supposed I hadn't actually seen anything; however, his bare chest was a pretty good indication of what had just taken place. I was suddenly thankful for the worktable blocking my view of his lower half. This whole naked shifter thing would take some getting used to.

"That fool is going to get himself killed," Bastian growled as threw open the cabinet and pulled a pair of pants from the folded clothes and linens inside. He huffed as he walked, anger seeping out of every pore. I'd never seen him so upset. It felt completely contradictory to the loving, if not too eager, Bastian that I'd seen over the past couple days.

Aerie closed the space between them as Bastian finished fastening his new pants and leaned against the worktable, trying to gain some composure.

"What do you think he plans to do?" she asked.

"I don't know. That's the damned problem, he can never just stop and communicate a plan. He has to run off with some dimwitted idea of throwing himself at the problem, no matter the cost. One of these days his pigheadedness is going to catch up with him and he's going to wish he'd stopped long enough to at least tell me where he was going so I could save his ass."

Bastian spit the last words with a seething ferociousness. His chest rose in hot, heated breaths, unable or unwilling to slow. I could have sworn his body was shifting between mortal and wolven features the longer I watched him.

Aerie was insistent, pressing, "Do you think he could be going to Daravaana? To see Lennox?"

Bastian's body went rigid. His shoulders were stiff as his hands braced his weight against the wooden table. Tension hung around him like a dark cloud as his expression hardened.

"It's possible," he finally answered. "He's an absolute moron if he thinks he's going to get out of Kahlis' lands unscathed, though. Especially when Kahlis just tried to attack Hazel. He'll be expecting us to try something like this."

At the mention of my name, they both turned to me, as if they'd forgotten I was sitting here, listening.

We stared at each other for a moment, the air feeling too heavy to speak.

"Could someone maybe tell me what's going on?" I finally choked out.

Bastian huffed out a sarcastic laugh, shaking his head. "And after everything, the bastard left us here to deal with this mess. I swear, he only did this to avoid talking to you."

His eyes met mine as he talked. His face softened as he took me in, the lines of anger slowly melting away at the sight of me. I was sure I looked rather pathetic at the moment. I was completely lost in their conversation, like a naive child trying to comprehend adult things I had no business being a part of. My body still felt weak, although Aerie's tea had helped a lot. My head was throbbing after the nightmare, and my skin was sticky with sweat.

"I'm sorry, Hazel," said Bastian. "You deserve answers. This isn't how it was supposed to happen, but I suppose there's no more putting it off." He pinched the bridge of his nose as he concentrated on his words. "That wasn't a nightmare. Vander was right. What you just experienced is called dreamwalking, or at least some truly terrifying version of it. Vander said you've appeared to him in dreams before, yes?"

I nodded slowly, trying to understand what he was insinuating. My first night here, Vander had asked me if I'd seen him before, in a dream.

Had that been dreamwalking too?

"It's very similar to that," continued Bastian. "It's a rare piece of magic that takes years of practice and a lifetime to truly master. Which is probably why you were unaware you could do it, or at least control it."

I gaped at his words, confirmation of my own thoughts just moments ago. He must not have noticed my shock, because I barely had time to register what he'd said before he continued on.

"A creature named Kahlis dreamwalked in your mind and used blood magic to hold you captive. He's the same one who sent that Daeomi after you in the Dark Woods. That's how he got your blood."

Kahlis.

The name sounded familiar. I remembered the Daeomi using it when he'd spoken to me in the woods. I'd heard Bastian mention him before, and that must have been the name that Vander kept mumbling when they'd found me tonight. It was one of the things I'd been hoping to ask Aerie about, but I hadn't gotten the chance to yet.

"Why does he want me?"

Bastian shook his head as he shifted his weight. "We don't know, but he's had your scent for a long time and hasn't stopped trying. Won't stop until he wins."

My skin went cold as his confession sliced through me. Fear crept over me, tightening the grip on my chest. Kahlis' words came back to me from the nightmare.

"He mentioned in the dream—" I started, trying to remember what exactly he'd said. "He mentioned someone was trying to hide me from him. That I reminded him of her. Is she here? Can you take me to her? Maybe she knows what this is all about."

Bastian and Aerie exchanged nervous glances. Aerie moved around the table and sat down beside me, perched on the edge of my bed. Bastian scrubbed a hand down his face, letting out a sigh that expressed how tired he was, more than anything else.

"I would imagine," he said grimly, "that he was talking about your mother. Especially if he said you reminded him of her." His eyes lingered over my face, as if seeing someone else. "You are the spitting image of her."

My mother?

Hope welled inside me. A family. A mother. *My* mother.

I felt tears sting the back of my eyes as I tried to form a cohesive thought, but Aerie cut in before I could.

"Your mother passed away shortly before you went missing. I'm so sorry, Hazel."

Oh.

I swallowed, trying to let that news process in my mind. I hadn't known her, or at least couldn't remember her, so I supposed it wasn't hurtful news. Still, my heart had quickened at the idea that I might have an actual family somewhere. It was a short-lived hope that still stung despite being unable to remember her. Wave after wave of information was coming at me, knocking me down and threatening to pull me under in its tide. I had to concentrate; I had to push away that pain and focus on the real threat at hand. If I thought about it too long, it would paralyze me and I'd never find a way out of this mess. I could only handle one mess at a time.

I met their gazes, steeling my jaw. "In the dream, he hurt me. I don't know what he did, but it was like he'd crawled into my mind and was crushing me without even laying a hand on me."

Aerie's eyes widened. "We are very lucky that Vander was able to pull you from the dream, then. Kahlis comes from a line of very rare fae. His power does not conform to the laws of our land and exists outside of the tribal magic. He is one of the most powerful beings in our realm, which is what makes him such a threat. He can bend and break other's minds at his will. He can dreamwalk. He can fathom new realities and bend existing ones like a piece of clay in a potter's hands. It would probably just be easier to tell you what he can't do." Aerie's words slowed, as if recalling every terrible thing this Kahlis creature had ever done.

She attempted to suppress a shudder as she picked back up where she had trailed off. "And what he can't do, he finds ways to leech power from the earth or from others to do anyway. He was exiled from our lands centuries ago because of his direct disregard for the continent's laws, but that hasn't stopped him from trying to snake his way back in."

A dry laugh slipped through my lips. "You're really making me feel a lot better about the whole *this evil creature is after you* thing."

Aerie gave me a sheepish smile. She was trying to be honest and I appreciated that. It was hard, though, when everything she was saying terrified me to my core. The memory of Kahlis' hold on me in the dream was still painful and raw. I shuddered, pulling the blanket up to my chest.

"So you think Vander went after him?" I asked, my eyes bouncing between their worried faces. "If he's as bad as you're saying, how is Vander going to do anything to stop him?"

Bastian's deep voice grumbled in response. "We have a couple contacts inside Kahlis' lands, Daravaana. They are trusted members of our tribe who we sent to infiltrate his kingdom ever since Kahlis started attacking our borders. There's one, Lennox, who's especially close to Vander. It is possible he will try to make contact with him."

Bastian folded his arms over his chest, sighing. "Wouldn't be the first time he's acted on idiotic impulse without thinking it through first."

Aerie shot him a warning look. "It's impossible to say what Vander's plans are. Bastian's right, he doesn't often fill us in before taking off like this. But he always makes it home. I wouldn't worry too much about him."

She smiled, but it didn't reach her eyes. I could tell she didn't quite believe her own words. They both seemed more than rattled, which only made my stomach drop further. The silence in the greenhouse seemed to acknowledge the missing presence that had been there only moments ago. Vander was the most powerful creature I'd met since finding this world. If Bastian and Aerie were this worried about his safety, it made me wonder just how powerful Kahlis was—and if he'd actually be able to do anything to stop him.

I walked them through what happened in the dream, what kind of room I'd been held in and how just the scent of it had made me sick. I explained that the Daeomi from the woods had been there but the most terrifying of all had been Kahlis. They listened intently, their faces the picture of sympathy. At one point, Aerie started moving throughout the greenhouse, collecting tools as she gestured for me to continue.

"Keep going. Every detail is important and will help me strengthen the wards we will put around you." Her energy buzzed as she moved gracefully from shelf to shelf, then back to the work table. She sorted herbs and bottles as she dug through more books and eventually started mixing things together. I watched her as I spoke, finding the distraction calming.

Bastian was still leaning against the wall by my bed, patiently waiting for me to finish explaining the dream. His eyes never left me, like he didn't dare look away for fear that I'd fall back into Kahlis' hands.

I hesitated when I described the odd markings that had covered his hands.

"I've never seen anything like that," I said.

"Magic creates," said Bastian. He gestured to the onyx ink on his own skin. "All of us bear some mark of the magic we were given. It's how the tribes came to be."

Aerie stilled behind him, her hands falling idle as she listened to her husband speak. It almost seemed like there was apprehension in her gaze. Then she shook her head and returned to whatever she was measuring.

"It was meant as a gift," continued Bastian, "to be used to create and give life. But some in this world choose to use it for much darker purposes. And when those kinds of creatures abuse that power—abuse magic—it leaves a much darker mark. Stains like that, like his, come from bloodshed. And I don't mean the kind that happens in defense of yourself or those you love. I mean cold-hearted, brutal, bloodthirsty torment and killing." His eyes flashed with a distant memory, as if returning to a darker time. "And stains like his, well, I've never seen stains so dark. But

I can tell you it speaks volumes to the amount of evil he has done, the amount of innocent blood spilled."

Ice crept down my spine as I felt the color drain from my face. I could feel my body reflexively sink into the mattress, desperate for any kind of space to escape into.

"Okay, that's enough." Aerie's voice cut through the greenhouse. She was quiet but stern. "We don't need to terrify her even more than she already is. What she needs is rest. I think it's probably best for you to sleep in here tonight. I can keep an eye on you while I work."

She walked back over to the bed and stuck a bundle of herbs under my pillow, then handed me another cup of tea. "I'm making you a stronger tincture for future use, but it won't be ready for a couple weeks. The mixture needs to sit before it will be strong enough to help you. For now, we will just have to keep with the tea."

I took the cup, eyeing it carefully. It was much darker than the tea she'd given me before, and the scent was much more potent. Nausea still rolled over me and it took everything I had not to immediately gag at the idea of drinking the dark liquid.

"What's in it?" I asked tentatively.

Her face softened as her lips tipped up at the corner. "Some chamomile, valerian, skullcap, among other things. And reinforced with a little magic for good measure."

My eyebrows rose as she spoke. Aside from chamomile, I didn't know what any of the ingredients were. I looked back down at the drink, hesitant to take a sip.

Aerie offered a smile, sensing my apprehension. "It's to protect you while you sleep. It should keep you from dreaming, making it harder for Kahlis to dreamwalk to you."

I nodded, starting to understand what she was doing. "And the bundle you put under my pillow?"

"More of the same. It should hide you from him, cover your scent and mask your blood." Her gaze fell to the ground. "None of it is foolproof, I'm afraid. But I'm going to keep working, find everything I can to make sure you're safe here."

I nodded again as she reached out a hand and gave my arm a reassuring squeeze.

"It's okay to be scared, Hazel, but we are here for you and we won't stop fighting to protect you. This is your home too, if you want it. You deserve to feel safe here. You're not alone."

Tears pricked at my eyes. I glanced from Aerie to Bastian, who had come up behind her as a show of support. Together they stood before me, a united front, here to help protect me and give me answers I'd spent so long looking for. It was comforting in the most terrifying way. Despite that fear, I wanted to trust them, needed to trust them. No matter what I was leaving behind, I was here now. With a creature like Kahlis hunting me, I knew I couldn't go anywhere anytime soon.

And if what Vander had said was correct, it was my scent Kahlis was tracking, not Arlo's. Going back to him now would only put him in more danger. I had to trust that he'd be okay without me, for now. Leading that terrible creature to him was the last thing I wanted.

I'll find my way back to you, Arlo.

With that silent promise, I lifted the cup to my lips and drank deeply.

The tea wasn't nearly as bad as I thought it would be. It was delightfully warm and tasted like the lull of a summer afternoon spent dozing in the sun. My eyelids instantly felt heavy as I handed the cup back to Aerie. She helped me settle into the bed and then set the cup down on her worktable.

Aerie waved her hand to Bastian, who was sitting patiently beside me still. "I've got her, Bastian. There's no need for both of us to lose sleep tonight."

"I'm not leaving either of you. Not with Kahlis out there and Vander gone."

"We'll be fine," Aerie insisted.

Bastian ignored her as he made his way across the small room and planted himself firmly against the doorframe to the greenhouse. She gave him a frustrated look but leaned into his embrace as he planted a kiss on her forehead.

Watching them felt like an intrusion to some intimate moment I wasn't meant to see, but it comforted me. Seeing their love for each other, seeing their willingness to ensure my safety, it felt like home. I watched as Aerie returned to her books and Bastian settled into his position for the night. Their movements, mixed with the quiet buzz of the greenhouse, lulled me into a deep, dreamless sleep.

CHAPTER 24
VANDER

I stalked the edge of the Dark Woods, keeping an eye on the ever-moving hemlock trees. As much as these woods had become my home over the past ten years, I never felt at ease within them. There was always a threat, always something watching and waiting for its moment to strike. That was why I loved them so much, though: ample opportunity to fulfill that need for bloodshed.

The things that lurked here knew me by now, knew the shadow of the Grimm that clung to me like a parasite. Its mark was a death knell, a reminder to anyone who came too close that their end would be a messy and painful one. I could feel the magic pulsing beneath my skin, the black ink ebbing and flowing as I walked, whispering for me to use its power. My shadows reached out, searching my surroundings for the closest unfortunate soul to tear into.

I stilled my movements. Closing my eyes, I took a deep breath and willed the magic to calm. It was hard to control, especially when emotions were high. The curse of the Grimm was a separate entity at times, a mark with a mind of its own and a powerful magic to back it. I couldn't remember what it was like to not have that darkness within me. It had been so many years since I'd been able to think for myself, act on my own behalf. At first, the Mark had been its own thing entirely, something I had lived with and suppressed until it'd been safe to let it out. Now, it felt more like a piece of me than anything else. Its magic was still powerful and unruly, but I didn't know who I'd be without it. That scared me.

I watched the edge of the forest, where the trees thinned and stretched out to form the border to Daravaana, Kahlis' lands. The earth was cracked and gray with rot. What little vegetation was left had turned brittle and black long ago. Kahlis' magic had that effect on things. He leeched power from the earth greedily, not caring who or what he killed in the process. I could tell the Dark Woods were already starting to die off, the border between our two lands starting to diminish. We already knew that Kahlis was trying to weaken our borders, gearing up for something big—we just didn't know what. By the looks of it, he was starting to push out, take back the land little by little. I'd have to talk to Bastian about that. It had been quite some time since I'd come this far into the woods, and I cursed myself for not checking the border more regularly.

Finding a particularly large hemlock tree, I leaned into the shadows beneath it and waited for Lennox. I kept an eye on the branches above, stretching and bending to get closer as I let a shadow slip out to hold them at bay. I picked at the blood already drying beneath my nails as I waited. The journey here hadn't been without bloodshed, but the Mark wasn't complaining. I couldn't say I was either.

Lennox and I had a system for our little visits. I'd come to the border and let my shadows reach out until they found him. One benefit of the Grimm, I supposed. Its shadows had a way of calling to others, beckoning them to their death—or in this case, discreet meetings in the Dark Woods. It came in handy for sneaking around enemy lands and relaying messages from our spies.

Eventually, I could make out a form slipping between shadows and hiding in the darkness of night. Lucky for us, it was always night in Daravaana. Awareness washed over me and I prepared for the possibility of a threat, receding further into the shadows until I could be sure who it was making their way toward me. I eased my magic back as I caught a glimpse of that bright, shimmering eye, a telltale feature of Lennox's. Not a threat. Although one could never be too sure out here.

He hadn't seen me yet, and I hung in the darkness for a moment longer, letting a shadow reach out and ensnare him at the ankles. He fell to the ground in a loud thud, curses rippling through the air. I chuckled as I came forward and kneeled beside him.

"Letting your edge slip in your old age, Nox?"

"I just assumed you'd need some practice since you're sitting pretty back in Talamh while the big boys are out here risking our asses." A smile slipped over his face as he spoke.

It had been a long time since I'd seen him. His piercing silver eye was the same as ever, a stark contrast to the utterly black one opposite it. I'd only ever seen the phenomena on one other being in my lifetime, his twin brother Kirwan. The rest of his features were the same too. Although I could see how the years spent in this desolate place were starting to wear on him. He looked a little more ragged than before. His skin was starting to crease with either age or stress. His body looked tired, the darkness within him a little more present than it normally was.

I willed my shadow back as he brushed the dirt from his clothes.

"You look good, brother," he said as he gave me a once-over. "And... naked, as always."

I shrugged, giving him a hand and pulling him to his feet. "You know my primal form prefers the woods. It makes it easier to deal with the nuisances I come across on the way."

"And you couldn't think to pack an extra pair of pants for the journey?" He grabbed something out of the rucksack slung across his shoulder and tossed it to me. "Just because you're comfortable with nudity doesn't mean the rest of us want to be subjected to your naked body all day."

I chuckled again as I slipped on the pair of pants he'd brought.

"How sweet of you to pack for me," I chided.

"Trust me, it wasn't you I was thinking of, brother. Now what was so important you risked a visit to come talk to me?"

The reminder of the situation was sobering. My voice lost all edge of sarcasm as I spoke:

"Hazlenn's back."

His brows rose in surprise. That hadn't been what he'd been expecting.

"Well, sort of. It's her but it's not her. She says her name is Hazel. She claims she has this whole other life—a home, a male. She doesn't remember anything about Tir Nadaar, about us."

"Hmm," Nox hummed. He folded his arms across his chest, watching me carefully. "I'm sure you are loving the idea of her with some other male," he teased. "Please tell me you didn't bring me all the way out here to discuss your relationship issues."

I let a growl slip through my teeth. "This is serious, Lennox. She's only been back for a matter of days and Kahlis has already attacked her."

At that, he dropped the facade, his face slipping into an expression of solemn intensity. "You should have led with that."

"And you should have known what was going on. Isn't that your job as a spy? You're supposed to be relaying potential threats and sensitive information to us so we aren't blindsided like this." My voice shook with more anger than I'd realized I'd felt.

He gave me a warning look, closing the space between us. His face was inches from mine as he spoke. "It isn't my fault that I've been stuck here with little to no interaction from Talamh. How exactly do you propose I relay whatever information I collect without compromising my position when you're too busy stalking off into the night to feed your anger issues rather than doing your job and meeting with me?"

I stared at him, refusing to break eye contact. Rage boiled in my blood at his words, the Mark whispering to be unleashed. He was right, though: I'd been so busy sulking and hunting that I couldn't even remember the last time we'd had an actual meeting. Bastian hadn't questioned it because he didn't even like the fact that I'd signed up to relay messages from Nox in the first place. He'd thought it was too dangerous. Besides, Bastian's approach with me was always to allow me space to work things out on my own.

I sighed, pinching my brows as I tried to gather myself. "You're right, I'm sorry. Things are just... tense right now."

Nox backed off, letting the argument fall. "I'm fine here, really. There hasn't been much to report. It's been quiet for the most part. Well, quiet for Daravaana, which essentially means constant screams of anguish."

I eyed him as he shrugged and walked to the tree I'd chosen to hide beneath.

"You get used to it," was all he offered.

I was reminded once again of the evil to which Nox had willingly submitted himself. No one knew what went on inside Kahlis' borders. It was safe to assume the worst, though. I suppressed a shudder as I imagined Nox with his big heart in the midst of all that evil, trying to play *dark one* with Kahlis.

Nox filled the silence I left:

"Kirwan hasn't had much to report either, in case you were wondering." He threw me a pointed glance from beneath the branches of the hemlock.

Guilt started to spread within me as I felt color rising to my ears. I hadn't realized how far gone I'd been, how many others were suffering because I couldn't get my shit together. It wasn't just those in our tribe, the ones back home now safely cared for by Bastian. I had people out here too, people I'd given orders to back when I'd been acting chieftain, who were counting on me to still lead them, or at least check in every now and then.

"Shit, I—" Awareness washed over me once again, cutting me off midthought.

I turned, facing the direction Nox had come from. My body went rigid, listening and waiting for the smallest movement, the slightest disturbance amidst the decaying vegetation. My shadows reached out, searching as earnestly as my eyes.

Nox started to move forward, sensing my alarm, his hand reaching for what I assumed was his dagger concealed somewhere within the leather vest he wore.

I threw him back beneath the darkness of the hemlock tree and covered him in more shadow, trying not to compromise his position.

Before Nox could ask what I was doing, another figure stepped across the border and into the Dark Woods.

"And here I thought tonight's hunt would be a fruitless one. I was about to give up and find some entertainment back at the castle." The Daeomi chuckled. He slunk forward, slipping from one spot to the next. I prayed to whatever Fates might be that it hadn't seen Lennox. If his position was compromised, he'd be at the wrath of Kahlis. We already had enough to deal with, without him coming after more members of our tribe.

"Now, now, Vander, you should have known you wouldn't be able to sneak onto Kahlis' lands so easily. He's been expecting you, especially after he sensed you in Hazlenn's dream."

It took every ounce of restraint not to let a grimace slip across my face. I should have known he would have sensed me pull Hazel from the dream. I wouldn't give the Daeomi the satisfaction of the upper hand, though. I'd have to think about the ramifications of that later, of being foolish enough to let Kahlis see the connection we held.

"I couldn't let his royal darkness have all the fun," I said brashly. "Figured I'd show up and see what Daeomi trash strayed too far from the hive. Seems like you're the unlucky winner." I dipped my head as I let my lips curl back and reveal the row of teeth I could feel already shifting, eager to tear into the creature before me.

The Daeomi copied my movements, preparing for the attack, as he chuckled at my insult. He took several steps toward me as I tried to inconspicuously angle my body between him and the tree, where Nox was hidden. The Daeomi paused, cocking his head to the side and assessing my position.

Not inconspicuous enough, I suppose.

"Oh, come now, Vander. Don't tell me you brought the little play-thing along with you." He grinned as he peered into the darkness beneath the hemlock tree. "This is no place for a helpless little thing like her. Although..."

His words hung in the air as he took a tentative step toward the shadows of the tree. I crouched, waiting for my moment to strike.

"I'd love to finish what I started the other day. I haven't been able to get the image of her laying before me, all teary-eyed and bleeding, out of my mind."

Just as he landed another step, Nox lunged from the shadows, his dagger finding its target as they both fell to the forest floor. Nox found his footing easily and bounced back up. The Daeomi cried out in pain as the silver hilt of Nox's dagger shone in the moonlight, sticking out just below the creature's jaw.

"You stabbed him in the neck?" I deadpanned, looking blankly at the wild-eyed Nox now panting beside me.

"Sorry, brother, couldn't let you have all the fun. I've fantasized about stabbing that bastard more times than I can count. Feels so damn good to finally do it."

Between ragged breaths, a toothy grin broke across his face. I eyed him for a moment longer before shaking my head and turning my attention back to the Daeomi now writhing in pain amongst the muck of decaying leaves and dirt.

"That's all fine and well," I said, grimacing, "but what do you propose we do now? You can't exactly just walk back into Kahlis' kingdom after stabbing one of his most prized possessions from his inner circle."

"You'd be surprised what you can get away with in the name of anger and violence." Nox threw me a wink. "But I get your point."

As we contemplated the best course of action, the Daeomi threw a slew of curses and threats our way, letting us know just how dead we would be and how Kahlis was already aware of our presence within his borders. We watched a moment longer as the creature continued to cry out, no doubt in immeasurable pain from the enchanted blade of Nox's dagger—a little gift, courtesy of Aerie. I wasn't sure if we'd been paralyzed from indecisiveness or if we just enjoyed watching the filthy creature be tormented, but I started to worry his screams would draw unnecessary attention. I let a shadow slip around his neck and squeeze until the Daeomi's screams turned garbled and he slipped into unconsciousness.

We stood in the Dark Woods, on the border of Kahlis' lands, with the Daeomi completely at our mercy. The reality of it set in, shaking me into motion. I turned to Nox, equally as dumbfounded at the events that had transpired.

"What now?" I asked, waiting for him to make the decision.

He waited a moment longer, watching to ensure it was safe to take his eyes off the creature.

"I guess we need a plan," was all he offered before turning to face me and letting out a small chuckle. "I guess I'm coming home."

CHAPTER 25
HAZEL

The midmorning sun was warm on my skin. Aerie and I sat just outside the greenhouse on a patchwork quilt she had dragged out from inside. She'd invited me out with her to tend to the garden and bundle some herbs for drying. I knew it hadn't truly been a request; I hadn't been alone since after dinner last night. Still, I appreciated her effort to help me feel like I had some control over the situation.

After she'd collected the morning harvest, she settled in on the blanket beside me. Her basket was overflowing with various shades of leafy green plants. Yellow, purple, and white blooms stuck out from the bunch, creating little splashes of color amongst the earthy greens. As we worked, she explained the uses for some of the herbs and the process of hanging, drying, and shredding them before adding them to her shelves. It wasn't complicated work, but I was thankful for something to keep my hands busy, and it was interesting to learn what all the different plants could be used for.

"The land provides," she explained to me as we worked. "Food, resources, yes. But it's more than that. There is magic in the earth, power that courses through the dirt and the roots. Power that grows within the leaves of each plant, so long as we choose to listen to it. Let it tell us what power it holds and how we can utilize it."

Her voice was so eloquent, the words rolling off her tongue in a calming, natural way. It was a siren's song and I was hopelessly lost to it, leaning in for more as she continued on.

"The land provides our magic too. The fae often forget that; they are oftentimes too full of pride to admit their power isn't entirely their own. That's what I love about the tribes, though. They recognize the gift they were given, and honor the land with their actions."

She held up a skinny green branch with a burst of small white flowers at one end. They reminded me of the fluffy, white clouds hanging low in the pale, blue sky above us. Not at all unlike the flowers I found myself often stopping to admire on the path by the woods to Arlo's house—or the ones I found at the base of the archway I'd fallen through before winding up in this world.

"Yarrow," she informed me. "One of my favorites. It's an amazing little herb with so many different uses. It can relieve pain, heal wounds, help with blood circulation and even stop bleeding when needed. It's got quite the reputation on the battlefield; the healers always keep it on hand because of its versatility."

I took it from her, admiring its simplistic design. She watched me as I twirled it between my fingers.

"You want to know what I really love about it, though?"

I let the yarrow branch spin one last time before letting it fall to my other palm and then handed it back to her.

"It's something we call *cothrom*. It means the ability to balance, to work in ways that we may not understand or might seem contradictory to us. But it knows what it's doing and it holds the power to restore balance to the body, to help it normalize. Funnily enough, it can also mean to give something a chance or an opportunity. And that's what we do. We trust that it has the power to work, to fix what's broken. It's not that different from how we use magic. Sometimes we cannot understand everything. We get pieces and glimpses of the puzzle, but not the whole thing. And we have to rely on the power, the magic, to trust that it knows what it's doing and guides us as we use it."

My eyes lingered on the yarrow in her hands. It was so fragile, so breakable. It seemed like a plant that held so much power would grow thick and strong, making it impenetrable to the elements. It wasn't, though.

I wondered if a power like that could be hidden within me.

If I was in fact from here, it stood to reason that I should hold some sort of magic. Right? It had been a question I wasn't sure I wanted to ask. The dreamwalking was its own type of magic, I supposed, but it didn't feel like power. It felt like a curse that I would give anything to get rid of. I would be perfectly content if I lived my entire life without experiencing another dream ever again. That wasn't magic, it wasn't strength. Looking at the dainty stems in her hands, bending and breaking as she bundled them together, I didn't think I'd ever related to something more. It had me wondering if she'd chosen that plant specifically for me, made so weak and breakable to balance the power that lay within. *Cothrom.*

It had to be close to lunch by now. The sun was high and I found myself slowing down to close my eyes and breathe in the fresh spring air. It had been spring before I'd arrived here, hadn't it? That felt like a lifetime ago. I wondered if the seasons still applied to this magical world.

"Is it still considered spring here?" I asked Aerie, still seated beside me. "Or are there no seasons in Tir Nadaar?"

She giggled slightly at my question. "Doesn't it feel like spring to you?"

I turned back to the view of the rolling hills that stretched out past Aerie's greenhouse, the array of wildflowers and tall grass covering them. The sun felt warm, but not as hot as a blistering summer sun. The breeze was still slightly crisp with the chill of winter slipping away.

"Yeah, it does."

"So maybe you know more than you think you do." She gave me a small wink before returning to the bundle of comfrey in her hands.

I felt the corner of my lips turn up at her vote of confidence. We worked quietly for several minutes, the music of nature the only sound dancing through the air. After some time, I noticed Aerie's hands fidgeting, starting and stopping her work as if she were lost in thought.

One of the bundles slipped in her hands, cutting into her soft, delicate finger.

"*Aye, Cailleach.*" The words were a mumble under her breath. It sounded like a curse, but I hadn't heard the name before.

"What did you say?"

She squeezed the tip of her finger, sucking on it ever so slightly to stop the bleeding as she looked over to me.

"Oh, Cailleach? It's just an invocation of one of the old fae gods. They still pop into my head every now and then. Old habits die hard, I suppose."

"Who is he?"

"She, actually," Aerie answered as she went back to bundling the next bunch. "She was a guardian of sorts. She belonged to nature, the plants and the animals, the sky and the stars. And they belonged to her. We called to her when things happened in nature. A bad storm, an animal attack."

She raised her finger with a sly little grin. "A careless mistake with one of the more precarious herbs. I'm usually more careful, my mind has just been other places today."

I hummed in understanding.

"Is everything okay?" I offered as I finished tying the bundle I was working on.

"Yes, I just—" She paused, cutting herself off as she chewed at her lower lip.

"I wanted to talk to you about something. Something I think you deserve to know, but I realize it may be upsetting. Vander was supposed to talk to you about this, but with everything that has happened, well... No one's had time to really bring it up. But you deserve to know."

Her words worried me. What more could I possibly need to know?

There had been a constant stream of information since I'd gotten here. My brain was tired and aching from trying to understand it all already. It didn't feel like I could possibly retain any more information. I could see the worry etched on Aerie's face though, the way her brow creased as if it was important for me to hear what she had to say.

"Alright," I offered as I watched her mulling words over in her mind.

"Do you remember what I said about Kahlis' magic?" she asked, finally. "How he can create and bend reality?"

I did, although I hadn't really understood what that meant. I nodded as she continued.

"Well, the boys have a theory about that."

A small breeze danced around us, teasing at her hair and obscuring her face from my view. She worked the loose strands back in place, briefly swiping at her eyes as she did. Were there tears there? Something had changed in her tone, the melody of that singsong voice turning to something more somber.

"I know this is going to be hard to hear, so just bear with me, okay? Do you trust me?"

I nodded again because I did trust her. She'd been nothing but helpful since I'd arrived and I probably felt safest with her out of the three of them.

"Well, when you went missing all those years ago, Vander and Bastian immediately suspected Kahlis. He was already making moves to attack our tribe, all the tribes really. He wants to take over Tir Nadaar, return it to what it once was and sit as its ruler. It wouldn't be the first time they lost people to Kahlis."

I cocked my head to the side, curiosity rippling through me. "What do you mean by that?"

Aerie sighed, her voice falling softer than it had been a minute ago. "Vander and Bastian's parents were killed by Kahlis. They died protecting Talamh from an invasion ordered by him. Their sacrifice saved the tribe and strengthened our wards. It bought us a lot of time; the attacks haven't been as difficult to recover from, nor as frequent. But the boys were devastated by it—still are, truthfully."

It was starting to make sense now: why they were so set off by Kahlis' attack on me, why they felt the need to protect me from him—even why they thought he'd taken me in the first place. I could only imagine how awful it must have been to lose their parents like that.

"So you can understand why they'd suspect him," she went on. "They have a history there, yes, but it's more than that. Vander was with you when you were taken. He fought the Daeomi as best he could, but there were just too many of them. It wrecked him not being able to save you from them. Bastian has always said, he came back different that day, no longer totally himself."

I thought about what she was saying, remembering the dream Vander had referenced after my arrival, when I'd seen him in the clearing fighting those creatures, the ones I now knew as Daeomi. I remembered the explosion of power, the way it had sounded so much like my name when it broke through the forest as he watched something take off into the sky. As he watched me get taken. The realization of what I had witnessed in my dream so many days ago was jarring. I felt some pieces of the puzzle begin clicking into place.

I'd known that it was Vander, but I hadn't understood the gravity of the dream, what it was that I'd been a silent witness to. I hadn't spent much time thinking about it, what with everything else that had been going on. I thought about the look on his face when he'd finally turned to see me intruding on his dream. He had been so confused, so hopeful that I was really there. I wondered how many times he'd lived out that moment in his dreams, for me to be able to witness it in his mind all these years later.

Aerie watched patiently as the wheels in my mind turned, trying to understand the connections.

"Before I came here," I began timidly, "I had a dream. I didn't know what it meant then, but now I think I'm starting to."

I paused, trying to form words to describe what I was thinking. The sounds of far-off buzzing bees and the wind whistling through the tall grass were the only noise as Aerie waited for me to continue.

"I was at the edge of a forest, looking into a little clearing. Someone was there—well, lots of someones. There was a fight happening. I think it was Vander fighting the Daeomi. There were so many of them. He'd take down a few and ten more would rush him. It went on like that until this massive creature sprang into the air and just took off. It moved so fast and there was no way for him to go after it. I could feel his fear and his anger as he watched. Like, actually *feel* it. Then it was like his power exploded through the clearing, it flattened everything. The trees, the creatures he'd been fighting. I felt it rattle my bones. But I'd been fine, I was still standing there, watching. Eventually, he heard me and turned around. His grief was so heavy, I couldn't take it. I was pulled back, or maybe I chose to go back. I don't know. All I know is one minute I was there and the next I woke up in bed next to Arlo and knew I needed to follow that pull I felt."

Aerie waited to make sure I was done before speaking. "Vander told us you dreamwalked to him, but he didn't tell us what the dream had been about. It makes sense that you found him through that dream. It's a powerful memory. For both of you."

My head jerked up.

"Yes, for you too, even if you don't actually remember it."

I chewed nervously at my bottom lip, my mind working in overtime trying to connect all of the dots.

"Well—" I started. Aerie's reassuring eyes found mine as she locked in on what I was trying to say. "I may actually remember. To some extent."

I sighed, suddenly feeling tired. My head was full of wet sand. There was too much going on, too much to process. I was starting to wonder if I was forcing connections where none had been. Despite that fact, I continued.

"For the past year, I've had this recurring nightmare. Of being carried through the air by some massive creature with leathery wings. Of running through the forest being chased by it. It always ends the same: just when I feel like it's going to catch me, I'm ripped through the air and into nothingness... Then I wake up. What if..."

I trailed off, waiting for the courage to admit what I was feeling.

"What if it isn't just a dream?" I dared at last. "What if it's a memory? The same memory Vander dreams about. Of being taken by Kahlis?"

Aerie contemplated, her gaze drifting off to the grassy knolls laid out in front of us. She was silent for a long time. It took everything within me not to beg her to share what she was thinking.

Finally, she spoke. "I'd say, that is a highly probable theory."

The lack of commitment in her words irritated me. I needed validation, needed to feel like I wasn't losing my mind.

"Have you talked to Vander about this?" she asked.

I shook my head.

"No, I find it best to avoid conversation with him." My cheeks reddened at the thought of admitting something so intimate to the wolven beast.

Aerie let a smile slip across her face.

"Vander is all bark and no bite," she offered. Her brows furrowed as she thought about her choice of words. "Well, I suppose that's not entirely true. He's a lot of bite, as well. But not with you. You have nothing to worry about with him. You're probably safest with him, actually."

My head tilted, waiting for her to explain her meaning.

She winced as she realized what she'd said, before slipping a mask of indifference over her face and waving me off.

"We've gotten sidetracked. I wanted to talk to you about your time away from here."

I fought the desire to push her on what she'd admitted, but she clearly wasn't interested in continuing that point further. I let it fall away as I tried to focus on whatever it was that she wanted to talk to me about.

"Given what we know about Kahlis, his magic and his past attacks on our tribe. And given what we know about when you went missing, how Kahlis was no doubt involved." She eyed me cautiously before she continued. "It's not a far stretch to say that it's possible Kahlis has had you this whole time. It's only a theory, but it's one we wanted you to be aware of."

"But..." I shook my head, trying to understand what she was insinuating. "If Kahlis has had me this whole time, then where was he keeping me? Does he guard the door to the mortal realm?"

Aerie's expression was heavy with sympathy. I could tell I wasn't fully grasping what she was trying to tell me, which only irritated me more.

"Hazel, there *is* no door to the mortal realm. At least, not that we know of. There hasn't been a mortal realm for quite some time. We think, well..." She reached forward to take my hand in hers. "We think he created that reality to hold you captive, to make you incapable of making your way back to us."

My brows pinched in confusion. "But that would mean..."

I shook my head, unable to let myself understand what she was insinuating.

"No," I said, as the full realization of her words snaked through my mind.

No, no, no.

Aerie squeezed my hand slightly, drawing my attention back to her face.

"It's just a theory, Hazel. It doesn't mean that's for sure what happened. But it's a possibility and we thought you deserved to know. It would explain why you lost your memories, if Kahlis took them. So you couldn't find your way back to us, wouldn't question the reality you were experiencing. And it would explain why we've been unable to find anything out in the Dark Woods that signifies where you came from."

Why they hadn't found Arlo, she meant.

"What you're saying," I cut in, "is that none of it was real? But that's impossible. That would mean nothing I experienced in the past year actually exists, that Arlo—"

I couldn't say it. I wouldn't let myself admit that. He was real. No one would be able to change my mind. My thoughts drifted back to the pain I'd felt in the dream with Kahlis.

That had felt so real, too, though.

My head was spinning. I felt like I was going to pass out, or maybe puke.

"No," I repeated again. "I can't believe that."

"It's just one theory, and we could be entirely wrong. But knowing what Kahlis is capable of, we need to consider it. And even if it is true, it doesn't make anything you experienced any less real. It doesn't make *Arlo* any less real."

Tears pricked my eyes before falling in hot streaks down my face. Anger boiled within me. I wasn't mad at Aerie; she was just relaying a valid point about the situation. I was mad at once again feeling like I had zero control over myself, over my life. I didn't know what to believe, what to accept as truth anymore. I was so tired of feeling caught off guard, so tired of feeling like an outsider in my own mind.

Before I realized what I was doing, I stood and stormed off through the tall grass. Aerie called after me, but I ignored her.

I didn't have the courage to face her. Not now. Not while my entire reality was out of my hands. Not while the only person I'd ever loved, who'd ever protected me, could be a lie. How could I even trust that she was real? That any of this was? This is what my life had become, doubt and confusion racing through every fiber of my being, every aspect of my world. I was running from one nightmare to another—and I felt like I'd never be able to escape.

CHAPTER 26
HAZEL

I didn't know where I was going. I just needed to get away. Somewhere inside I felt that if I put distance between me and the news Aerie had just shared, maybe it would make it less true. Up ahead stood an old wooden stable. It looked like a good place to escape for a moment, so I altered my steps to disappear around the back of it. I was thankful that Aerie wasn't following but rather keeping watch from a distance and letting me have some time to process.

My head was spinning as I threw myself against one of the rough, wood-planked walls just inside the stable. I let the feeling of the splintering wood grain dig into my back, the feel of the sturdy structure somehow grounding me as I cried. I slid down, bringing my knees to my chest as I sat. Burying my face in my knees, I released the torrent I'd been holding back. Days worth of information and trauma finally came to the surface as I cried.

I cried for the knowledge I did not have, the feeling of not knowing who I truly was or where I truly belonged. I cried for the pain I'd felt over the last several days, the blood I'd lost and the torment I'd felt in the hands of Kahlis. I cried for the confusion that rippled through me every moment I'd spent here, never feeling like I could keep up. Mostly, though, I cried for Arlo.

I wanted him here. I didn't know how to handle this without him. Now, not only was he not here, but I'd found out he could actually not exist. I hated this world. I hated the magic and its ability to be so cruel and hurtful. No one should have that kind of power over others.

I cried for a long time, trying and failing repeatedly to gain my composure. Eventually, though, the tears stopped coming. The pain remained, but my body had given everything it had to grieve physically. I wiped my cheeks on my already damp dress. It was a gauzy light blue, one Aerie had let me borrow from the greenhouse, now streaked with snot, tears, and dirt from the stable floors. I'd have to apologize to Aerie later for ruining it so thoroughly.

A noise cut across the length of the stable, making me jump. I peered into the main room and found the little deer girl tending to horses in the various stalls.

Aerie had told me her name was Mirren. Her mother was from Talamh, the earth tribe, and her father had been from Sgàil, the moon tribe. Both had apparently passed away some time ago and Mirren lived here with them while her half-brothers were on assignment for the tribe. One of which, I remembered, Vander was supposedly meeting with right now.

I stepped out from the corner of the barn, catching the tail end of her flinch as her feed bucket clattered to the floor.

"My apologies, miss, I didn't mean to disturb you. I was just trying to finish the chores so I could give you a moment of privacy."

Her face was so innocent. It reminded me of a blooming rose, pink and fresh with the promise of years to come. She had to be younger than me, her body unmarred by the harsh realities of the world. I offered her a friendly smile as I walked across the stables.

"That's okay. I have to admit, you didn't catch me on my greatest day, but I won't let my misery keep you from feeding the horses. It's not their fault."

I stopped beside a particularly large and beautiful chestnut mare. Her temperament was calm and trusting as I laid a hand on her. I grabbed a handful of feed and let her eat it from my palm.

Mirren shifted nervously beside me. "You're good with her," she said, nodding to the horse eating happily from my hand. "She's not trusting, that one. Her name's Brigid. She's the chieftain's horse."

"*Brigid*," I repeated softly. Her name rolled off my tongue in a familiar way. It brought a smile to my lips as the horse leaned into my touch.

"You must be practiced with horses to keep her so calm with you."

"No." I laughed slightly. "I don't think I am."

Mirren gave me a bewildered look, but I didn't have the energy to explain my mysterious memory loss to her at the moment, even if it made me sound crazy.

I let the mare finish eating as I patted her side. The feel of her strong presence so at ease beside me was oddly calming. It reminded me of the effect Vander's wolven form had on me. The weight of the last hour, the last few days, suddenly felt less heavy as I stood here observing such a wondrous creature.

Finally, I turned back to Mirren. "Do you need help with the chores?"

She eyed me carefully, reluctant to accept my offer.

"Honestly," I pressed on, "you'd be doing me a favor. I have nothing else to do right now and I need something to keep my mind busy."

It was a half-truth. In reality, I had several things I should be doing: talking to Aerie, reading the endless pile of books sitting back in the library, searching the woods for Arlo. *Not that last one anymore, I suppose.* Grief gripped my chest as I remembered Aerie's words. I shook my head, refusing to let myself dwell on it any longer. As far as I was concerned, I had no more answers than when I woke up this morning. Until I had concrete proof that everything I'd experienced was courtesy of Kahlis, I wouldn't let myself go there.

After another moment, Mirren handed me a scoop full of feed and smiled. I let out a small sigh of relief, not realizing how desperate I'd become for the distraction. I wasn't sure if it was Mirren's innocent, kind presence or the warm comfort of the friendly beast in front of me, but I felt the smallest shift in my mind. I didn't know how to solve the problem I was facing, didn't have even a fraction of the answers I was looking for. But this, I could do. I could be here in the company of a new friend and take care of the powerful creature that seemed to lean into my touch. I could do my chores and distract my mind, even if it was the only thing I was capable of doing these days.

We worked in the stable for another hour, jumping between random bouts of conversation and comfortable silence. My initial impression of Mirren was altogether accurate. Just as her doe-like features indicated, she was timid and quiet. It took her several minutes of work to truly start conversing with me. I asked her simple questions like her age and what she liked to do, hoping to get her to warm up to me.

It surprised me when she shared that she was only sixteen. I'd known she'd been young, but it was shocking that she was truly still a child. My heart broke thinking about how hard it must have been to grow up without her parents by her side. I wondered at what age she'd lost them. She reminded me so much of myself, that same timid temperament familiar within me. She didn't talk at all about her parents but mentioned her brothers often.

I got the distinct impression that she looked up to them with adoration, twin flames shining bright for her in this otherwise dark world. When Bastian had spoken of Lennox, it'd felt as if there'd been an air of caution there, some sort of trepidation in correlation with the name. When Mirren spoke of him though, her face shone bright with pride and love. I felt myself smiling and laughing along with her as she told me stories of the twins.

I'd asked her about my room, wondering if she had been the one to tend to it the other night. She'd blushed at the question, the red in her cheeks answer enough. I thanked her for being so kind and told her it was not necessary if she did not wish to continue.

We finished tending to the horses, ensuring that each was thoroughly fed, watered, and groomed before we strode out into the afternoon sunlight. She led us back to the estate's side entrance that opened directly into the kitchen.

Aerie was at the far end of the kitchen, busily working to prepare what smelled like an amazing dinner. As soon as she heard us opening the door, she hustled through the room, closing the distance between us in no less than five quick strides, before enveloping me in a long, tight hug.

"I'm so sorry, Hazel," she whispered against my shoulder. "I didn't want to upset you, truly."

"I know," I choked back. Tears began to sting the back of my eyes once more as I let her warm embrace take over me.

She squeezed me a little harder before letting me go and gripping me by the shoulders.

"One day at a time, yeah? We will figure this out together."

I nodded, wiping away the single tear that had managed to escape with the back of my hand.

"The most important thing for you to remember right now is that you are not alone." She narrowed her gaze, making sure I understood the truth in her words.

I almost crumbled all over again. All I'd ever wanted was to find a home, family to call my own. Despite the grief I felt right now, somehow I felt like I'd found that here.

Aerie turned her attention to Mirren standing next to me, awkwardly shuffling to the side and trying to allow us space to talk.

"I'm glad to see you two connecting." Aerie nodded her chin back toward me. "Mirren is our beloved little fawn. She's something special to us."

She tenderly brushed the side of Mirren's face. Mirren's ears reddened, no doubt feeling embarrassed with so much attention being focused on her. I understood the feeling.

"Yeah, we bonded a bit while tending to the horses." I gave her a playful nudge, trying to make her feel more comfortable, as a small smile broke across her face.

"Well, while you're in the helpful mood, what would you say about helping with dinner?" Aerie broke away, heading back to the station she'd set up on the far end of the counter. It wasn't until she went back to work that I realized she was covered in flour.

"I know nothing about cooking," I admitted as I followed Aerie's movements across the kitchen. "But I'm all for chipping in. As long as you don't trust me with anything too important."

I grabbed a pastry from a plate of assorted breads, most likely left over from breakfast, as I leaned against the counter to watch Aerie. Crumbs covered my already-soiled dress as I bit into the delicious, buttery treat. My mouth watered instinctually, reminding me that I'd skipped lunch.

"Oh, don't tell me that. Stick with us long enough, Hazel, and we'll have you making a four-course meal on your own in no time."

Aerie's eyes twinkled as she made room for Mirren to join her and flicked a little flour at her face. Both of them giggled as they went to work kneading whatever dough Aerie had been working on.

They looked so content in their little corner of the kitchen. They laughed and joked with each other as I watched from the side, stepping in to offer help or move a tray when needed. Joy radiated off of them, a contagious feeling I was incapable of ignoring. Before I knew it, we all stood side by side by side, elbow-deep in various mixtures of dough and laughing so hard my sides hurt.

Without warning, the door to the kitchen blew open. Three dark forms stood on the other side, the setting sun behind them casting them in deep shadows. It took a moment for our eyes to adjust as they walked through the door, or rather stumbled.

"Nox!" Mirren gasped as she abandoned her spot in the bread line and ran to embrace her brother.

So that's Lennox.

I was instantly captivated by his distinct features, the sharp contrast of his different colored eyes.

She hadn't told me how long it had been since she'd seen him, but I could tell by the emotion on both of their faces that this reunion was a long time coming. My mouth split wide in an enthusiastic grin as tears threatened to spill from my eyes, mirroring the ones rolling happily down Mirren's cheeks.

It wasn't until I turned my attention to the other two forms that concern rolled through my body. Vander stood off to the side, bloody and covered in filth. I wasn't sure if the blood was his or not, but it surprised me to realize I was worried about him. Beside him was a dark form, rumpled and wounded and dripping blood on the kitchen floor. It took a moment to place him, for my eyes to adjust to the light and the look of him so distinctly opposite his prestigiously clean presence in the forest.

Held in the grasp of Vander's shadows, and entirely at his mercy, was the Daeomi from the Dark Woods.

CHAPTER 27
VANDER

I pushed into the kitchen, desperate for something to eat. I hadn't packed any food, nor had Lennox, since we'd had to leave Daravaana in such a hurry. The Dark Woods didn't offer much in the way of foraging opportunities, either. I forced the weakened Daeomi into the corner of the kitchen, ensuring that my shadows were still holding him captive. Daeomi were typically and unfortunately rather powerful parasites. Without Nox's enchanted blade to weaken him, I wasn't sure if my shadows would have enough power to truly hold him this long. They seemed to be holding strong, though.

Hazel stood on the opposite side of the kitchen, mouth gaping as she watched us. It wasn't an ideal entry, given what the creature had done to her not even a week ago, but there were more important things to worry about right now than tiptoeing around her.

"Hello again, little plaything."

The Daeomi's raspy words snaked through the room, rooting Hazel to the spot. I angled my head back toward him, allowing a shadow to grip the hilt of the enchanted blade still protruding from his neck, twisting it slowly.

"Quiet, filth," I growled.

I felt the corner of my lips tilt up, almost involuntarily, as I heard the creature's cry of pain in answer to my warning. *Utterly helpless.* That was exactly how I wanted him. We'd get more information out of him once we figured out what particular interrogation techniques made him squirm.

Aerie sprang to action, gathering some towels for us to use. It was not lost on me how she delicately slid herself between Hazel and the creature in the corner, as she handed me some cheese and a glass of water. I had positioned myself similarly, just in case he got any bright ideas while we stood here. I'd hoped the house would be empty upon our return, or at least the kitchen. I hadn't expected a welcoming party to greet us.

"Where's my brother?" I asked after draining the glass of water.

As if on cue, Bastian strode through the hallway and into the kitchen, whistling some irritatingly happy tune. His whistling dropped as he came to a halt in the entryway, taking in the scene.

"Vander," he said, his tone questioning. "Care to explain what you've done?"

He scanned the room, his eyes landing finally on the Daeomi in the corner offering him a sadistic grin.

"Now." No questioning tone lingered in the command.

I rubbed my jaw as I let out a sigh. "Well, once Nox stabbed him in the neck, it wasn't exactly like I could leave either of them in Daravaana, now could I?"

A short, breathy laugh squeaked from somewhere to my right and I forced my gaze to remain on Bastian despite how badly I felt drawn to look at Hazel. I couldn't stop the feeling of amusement that washed over my face at the way she'd reacted to me.

"And why exactly did Nox have to stab him in the neck?" Bastian plundered on. "Why did you even go there to begin with, Vander? Now you've not only compromised one of our spies, but you've brought an enemy into our territory! Not to mention, to Hazel!"

Lennox cleared his throat beside me, his arm still firmly wrapped around Mirren.

"Two spies," he said, his eyes darting between me and Bastian.

I shot him a cursory look.

Nox threw his hands up in self-defense. "I'm sorry, brother, but I had to let Kirwan know. If I'm compromised, then it's not safe for him to continue his mission."

"By the Fates, Vander, are you fucking kidding me?" Bastian's voice boomed through the kitchen, the room suddenly feeling overcrowded. "Do you think at all before you act? Or is this just your world and we're all living in it, subject to the consequences of whatever idiotic mess you get yourself into that day?"

Rage filled my bones. "Let me remind you that I am the older one here, brother. I will not stand idly by and be chastised like a child."

"And let me remind *you*, brother..." He filled the space between us as he brought his rage-tinged face nose to nose with mine. "That while you may be older, I am chieftain of this tribe. Protector of these lands. It is my job to ensure not only your safety but the safety of all who call Talamh their home. Or have you forgotten what position I hold?"

He spat his words with venom and anger, not realizing the insult he'd given until it was too late. Backing off, he flexed his hands and breathed deeply. I knew that look. His primal form was screaming to be released.

He was trying to gain control, force the beast back so he could finish this conversation like the civilized male he so desperately wanted to be.

Nox's words broke the silence, drawing everyone's attention to him:

"We, uh, have a plan. If anyone is curious."

No one spoke, so Nox took that as his sign to continue. "Vander's right. Neither of us could stay there after the Daeomi found us. Kahlis already knew of the deception before we were even out of the Dark Woods."

"Oh, he's well aware of your lies, traitor. The Dark One will peel your—" I willed my shadows to tighten around the Daeomi's throat, cutting off his empty threats and reminding him who held the power here.

"Right, uh, point proven." Nox cast a wary glance at the creature before continuing, "And the Daeomi would have just tracked us until we led him back here if we had let him go. Or worse, attacked us when we weren't expecting it."

I scoffed, disagreeing with the plausibility of the Daeomi filth getting the upper hand against either of us. Nox rolled his eyes and held his hand up, signaling me to shut it. Probably a wise decision.

"Vander and I figured why not take advantage of the situation? Bring him back here and tortu—I mean, uh..." His eyes swept across the room, taking into account the present company before he rephrased his words. "*Interrogate* him. See what information we can get and hopefully find a way to help Hazel."

His eyes found hers as he stepped forward.

"Hi again, Hazel. Lennox Raevynn, but I hear you won't remember me. I'll try not to take personal offense to that, although I've been told I'm kind of hard to forget." He gave her a little wink as he took her hand

and pressed his lips to it. My body tightened involuntarily as I watched their connection, rolling my eyes at Nox's ridiculous gesture.

Bastian stood in the middle of the room, still fuming. He was pouring every ounce of effort he had into keeping his primal form at bay. His power was palpable. Even the Daeomi had quieted down with his snickering and crude commentary.

Bastian looked between me and Nox, shaking his head in frustration. "Dammit, Vander. Fine. But if this plan backfires, it's your mess to clean up."

He pointed at me, his motions too rigid, too concentrated. I clasped him on the shoulder, making sure he looked me in the eye.

"I know the weight you carry, brother. It was once my job too," I reminded him, making my words as sympathetic as I could manage. "I'll make sure the Daeomi is cleaned up. Or"—I paused, an idea forming in my mind—"if you'd prefer to let off a little steam, you're more than welcome to help us... interrogate him."

My eyes flicked over to Lennox as he chuckled at my words.

Bastian didn't find it quite so humorous. "Just get it done and clean it up. I don't want him here any longer than he has to be, simply because you two are enjoying yourselves."

"Whatever you say, Your Majesty," I said, sarcasm dripping from my voice. My lips trembled with the effort it took to keep my grin concealed, as Nox made a dramatic bow next to me.

My control slipped as a small, familiar laugh that I hadn't heard in a decade sounded again from the other side of the kitchen. The pure sound of it brought a chuckle to the surface. Nox's laughter joined in as Bastian pushed past us and through the kitchen door, his face the picture of annoyance.

"Honestly," he said, exasperated, "you act like there's not a single century between the two of you. I'm the youngest of us and somehow I feel like the only responsible one."

Our laughter continued as he made his way into the dusky glow outside. I turned my attention from the doorway and through the kitchen as my eyes caught Hazel's across the room. I hadn't heard that laugh in over ten years. The commotion died down as I stared at her. The gleam in her eye was just the smallest bit brighter, a fraction more familiar than it had been when I'd left her a day ago. Despite the dire circumstances surrounding us, I was starting to wonder if she could in fact still be the girl I'd fallen in love with.

"You two are going to be the death of him," Aerie warned as she collected the soiled towels from me and Lennox.

"Ah, he'll be fine." Nox waved his hand toward the direction Bastian had stormed off. "He needs to let the beast out every now and then. It's not good for him to hold that in so much."

My eyes lingered on the door.

"Oh," said Aerie, her face wound tight with an exasperated look. "And I suppose it's your loyal duty to push him over that edge every once in a while?"

"Damn, right," I replied with a sarcastic smile. "What are big brothers for?"

Aerie scoffed, dusting her hands on her apron and mumbling under her breath in what I was almost sure was her ancient fae language.

Lennox and I dragged the Daeomi down into the root cellar, agreeing that was probably the best place to keep him. Aerie followed behind to start putting wards around the cellar as we secured him within. I stayed with the Daeomi while Nox grabbed some nullifying chains and a handful of other sinister tools from the estate's armory. Being the head family of a tribe came with some benefits, such as an armory full of magical weapons for situations such as these.

Aerie made quick work of warding the door before gesturing for me to step outside it with her.

"He shouldn't be able to hear anything outside the room now. Nor should anything be able to sense his presence here. But Nox needs to hurry with the chains before he figures out a way to contact Kahlis. If he hasn't already."

"Thank you, Aerie." I leaned down and planted a small kiss on her forehead. It did nothing to ease the worry etched along her face, though.

"There's something else, Vander."

I cocked my head, waiting for her to continue.

"I told Hazel today, about our theory. About Arlo."

I bit out a curse as I turned away, running a hand through my hair.

"I know, we said it should have been you to tell her, but I didn't know how long you'd be gone and I thought she deserved to know sooner rather than later."

I clenched my jaw, letting my teeth grind together in frustration.

"Yeah, you're right," I said at last, relenting "She does deserve to know."

I let out a breath that turned into a small laugh as I looked back to Aerie. "I'm sure that went well for you."

"As well as can be expected." Aerie mirrored my sigh. "I don't know that she believes it, but at least she knows now. Maybe it won't be as painful of a blow when we finally decide to stop searching the Dark Woods for Arlo."

My eyes narrowed at the mention of his name. I clenched my hands in fists, folding my arms over my chest to hide the reaction.

"You should talk to her."

Aerie didn't specify what I should talk to her about, but she didn't need to.

"She's got enough going on without having to worry about me and our *connection*."

"So it's still there then? The tether?"

I eyed her carefully, unwilling to say anything just yet.

Aerie continued: "Bastian told me you'd been worried it wasn't intact, wasn't as strong as it was before."

"I have to stop telling things to Bastian," I grumbled.

Aerie stepped forward, putting a reassuring hand on my shoulder. "If she deserves to know about Arlo, then she deserves to know about you too."

She had a point.

"I'll think about it. But my top priority right now is dealing with the piece of trash in there so we can make sure Kahlis can't touch her ever again."

"About that." Aerie let her hand fall to her side as she turned to face the dark doorway in front of us. The wards hung invisible between us as the Daeomi sat wounded and muttering just inside the room.

"I think I have an idea for where to start."

CHAPTER 28
HAZEL

The table was full at dinner that night, Lennox and Mirren rounding out the other half of the dining room. When I'd asked Aerie earlier why Mirren hadn't joined us for dinner that first night, she'd brushed it off, explaining how she didn't know if her presence would make me feel more comfortable or awkward. Looking at her now, though, I saw no traces of that timid, frightened girl I'd met my first day here. She was absolutely beaming, attached to Lennox's side every moment that she could be.

Lennox was not what I'd expected. His appearance was every bit the mysterious spy that Aerie and Bastian had discussed. His form was slim, but not in an awkward, lanky way. It was more similar to the fluidity of water, moving from here to there with a smooth motion of suave confidence, if not erring on the side of cunning elusiveness. His coppery hair was warm though, reminding me of the glow of a setting sun. My gaze lingered on it as he conversed with the others across the table, the glowing hues of orange shifting to show the occasional strand of yellow sunlight. The most striking of all, though, were his two-toned eyes: one as shiny and dark as obsidian, the other a bright icy silver, like that of a glowing full moon, hung low in the night sky.

The three males were busy catching each other up on various pieces of information from their time apart at the opposite end of the table. I picked at my food, trying to sort through the day's events. My fork scraped against the ceramic plate, the noise drawing more attention than I'd meant to. A self-conscious smile fell across my face as several pairs of eyes turned to me, the gesture feeling hollow. My appetite was long gone, my stomach heavy with apprehension. I watched the others around me, oblivious to the panic coursing through my veins. They were happy, despite the circumstances surrounding us. They joked and laughed amongst themselves, content to take joy in a good meal and re-united friends. It was so easy for them—to forget, to pretend. Although I supposed it wasn't their life that had been uprooted and used as a game piece amongst creatures of unfathomable power.

I distracted myself by mulling over snippets of conversation that had come up throughout the day, nothing too deep or serious. Despite my reluctance to accept the news that Aerie had shared with me, I found my mind struggling not to think on it. If I let my mind drift to those things, to Arlo, I could feel the icy grip tighten on my chest, stealing my breath and turning my hands to a stinging cold. I wouldn't let myself fall into that grasp, not here. I wouldn't let them see me come undone.

Instead, I focused on something else that had been creeping in the corner of my mind. In the kitchen earlier, Bastian had mentioned centuries between Vander and Lennox. *Centuries.* I didn't know how old I thought he was, but the idea of even one century seemed hard to grasp. It led me to wonder how old *I* was. Arlo and I had never discussed my birthday. I was sure I'd been asked at some point how old I was. Hadn't I? The more time I spent here, the harder it was to remember things about my life before, like it was some distant dream, just out of my memory's reach. I shook the thought from my head, hating to believe what that realization admitted.

Aerie leaned over, offering a gentle nudge. She lowered her voice to ask, "Everything alright over there?"

I offered her a soft smile. "Yeah, there's just something I'm trying to work out."

"Care to get a second opinion?" The twinkle of her eyes was endearing, making it impossible for me to not confide in her.

"Earlier, in the kitchen, Bastian made a comment about there being centuries between Lennox and Vander. It just made me realize, I have no idea how old I am. I don't even know when my birthday is."

Aerie patted my hand in a gesture of understanding and reassurance.

"That, I can help with." She eased herself closer, trying to give us a little more privacy as she answered, "Would you believe it if I said that *you* were a hundred years old?"

My eyes went wide. I stammered, trying to find my words as I looked down at my plate of uneaten food. "But Mirren told me that she was only sixteen. How could there be that many years between us?"

"Mirren is still just a child, however wise beyond her time she may seem. She's experienced many hardships in her sixteen short years, but she is still just that: a child."

Aerie's nurturing gaze fell to the other end of the table where Mirren was lost in admiration as her older brother recounted some tale of glory from long ago.

My gaze followed hers, struggling to make sense of it all. "I guess I just assumed that when she told me her age, I couldn't be more than a handful of years older than her."

"In many ways, you aren't."

When my brows knit together in confusion, Aerie let out a small laugh and continued, "Adolescence for your kind lasts about a hundred years. Despite there being more than fifty years between the two of you, you're not all that different from each other. Not to mention, you had just come into adulthood when you were taken. You've not had time to accept whatever power lies within, let alone begin to understand it. It could be why you were helpless against a magic like Kahlis'. I would imagine your powers were unpracticed back then, wild and uncontrolled because you'd only just begun to use them."

I didn't know what came as more of a shock to me: my age or the fact that Aerie'd just confirmed I had, at least at one point, had magic.

"What magic did I have, do you know?" I ventured, wondering if everything she was sharing could possibly be true.

She thought for a moment, her eyes tipping up as if to remember something from long ago. "I don't know that it's ever been mentioned to me. I know that you and your mother weren't born of the Talamh tribe, more like adopted into it. I'm sure Bastian or Vander would know if you—"

"No," I cut her off, grabbing her hand before she could signal their attention. "That's okay, I'm not sure I want to know. Besides, it's not like whatever magic was there still remains. It must have been taken along with my memories."

I'd meant it as a joke, but my words hung in the air with a heavy sense of hurt and anger.

Aerie stilled, staring at me for a long time. Her gaze was assessing, the warmth of her spirit spreading over her face and through the room to me. I got the distinct impression that it was her magic I was feeling, that primal urge to heal what was broken. I didn't know how to tell her that she couldn't fix me, that it was impossible to fix what was broken when the pieces were missing.

"Why is it so hard for you to believe you belong here, Hazel?"

Her words pierced me. I didn't have an answer, so I let my gaze fall to my lap, picking at the skin around my thumb.

"I know it's going to take time, but I promise this is where you belong. It may take a day or a year, but we will figure it out. We will be here for you, no matter what you need. We will fight to get your memories back if that's what you want. If you listen to anything we've told you, please just believe me when I say that we are here for you."

We sat there for a moment, her silence emphasizing the weight of her words. After she was sure her point had gotten across, she turned back to her plate.

"As for your magic..." She paused, taking a sip of the dark red wine in her glass. "That, my dear, has not gone anywhere."

My head jolted up, shock radiating through me. "What do you mean? How could you know?" I demanded.

"I can sense it," she said with an overwhelming amount of certainty. "It's still there, buried and forgotten after years without use. But it's still there, waiting for you to accept it."

My body buzzed, the sounds around me falling away as I turned within, searching for any sign of power. I was answered only with silence and self-doubt. Nothing there felt strong or powerful. All I sensed was a rather embarrassing amount of weakness.

She had to be wrong.

My thoughts and emotions circled like vultures, trying to convince me it wasn't true. I was so shut off from the room that I missed whatever Aerie had been saying.

"Hmm?" I asked as I willed my mind to settle. The bustling noise of the room came back into focus.

"Your birthday," she repeated. "It's been a while since we've celebrated Sol Litha properly. Perhaps it's time. The tribe would be beside themselves at the idea of a true solstice celebration again."

"Sol Litha?"

"The summer solstice festival," she said, smiling.

"How long since—" I started, but a gravelly voice cut me off from across the table.

"Ten years."

A chill crept down my spine as I realized Vander's shadowed eyes were distinctly tracking my every move.

Ten years.

They hadn't celebrated a summer solstice since I'd disappeared. Because it was my birthday. Because it was a reminder of my absence.

"Oh," I breathed out.

Something like guilt rippled through me. The understanding that an entire tribe had put a holiday on hold until my return was rattling. It was, yet again, a reminder of the expectations I felt I had to live up to, the existence of a past I couldn't remember.

Aerie chattered on about ideas for the festivities, excitement buzzing around her as she spoke. If she noticed the way I sunk into my chair, she did not show it. Apprehension clung to me. The idea of meeting others in the tribe, the attention that an event like that would bring on me was strong enough to have my hands trembling at the mere mention of it.

Vander's eyes didn't leave me as the conversation continued on, moving from one topic to another. I set down my fork and slipped my hands under the table to keep him from noticing how badly they were shaking. I tried to ignore the feel of his gaze burrowing into me, but the longer he looked the more I worried my thoughts were no longer my own. I wondered if he was somehow silently prying into my mind, eavesdropping on my most intimate secrets. I closed my eyes, pushing the thought away with all my might, and him along with it.

As if in answer to the question, he abruptly pushed his chair back, the legs scraping in a loud, intrusive sound across the dining room floor. He dropped his linen napkin on his plate and sauntered across the room.

"Come, Nox," he said, brushing past, "we've got a Daeomi to deal with."

Then he slipped into the darkness of the hallway, refusing to pay me any more mind.

I eased myself behind the heavy wooden door of my bedroom, alone for the first time since Vander had stormed into my room the night before. I was surprised to find my door back in one piece. It looked entirely the same and I couldn't help but wonder if it had been replaced or if someone had used magic to piece it back together.

The room was dark, the only light once again coming from the blazing hearth. A smile slipped across my lips at the site.

Mirren.

Her kindness was unmatched, the girl offering too much to someone who was no more than a stranger to her. The sound of her sweet laugh echoed through my mind as I remembered the three of us in the kitchen today. It felt like home, almost. The smile fell, though, as I recognized the quiet of my room. I had longed for this moment, expecting it to bring me peace. No prying eyes lingered on me here, no questioning faces or world-rattling information could find me here. Still, I could not find the joy within, could not find pleasure in finally having a moment alone.

I made quick work of changing into my nightclothes, another pair similar to the ones I'd found in my wardrobe the night before. This pair was a pale gray rather than the lilac purple I'd worn before. The room was warm with the heat of the fire as I sat in front of the small vanity mirror and worked on the tangled mess my hair had become. I was tempted to give up completely and retreat to a bath instead, but exhaustion gripped me as I worked, and the idea of doing anything other than falling into bed was repulsive.

As my fingers worked the comb through my hair, my mind finally released the floodgates of thoughts that had been only whispers throughout the day. Dark thought after dark thought pounded against my mind as I tried to steady the tide and keep from drowning in them. The room that had seemed so warm and inviting when I'd first opened the door, now felt dark and haunting. Panic and sadness threatened to pull me under as my breath quickened. The tightness in my chest felt unbearable as the first hot tear slipped down my cheek.

I knew this feeling, I knew the pain to come if I allowed it to take me over. What I didn't know was how to combat it without Arlo here. That thought only spurred on the attack as I became a heaving, sobbing mess. I sucked air into my lungs greedily, desperate for relief from the sting in my chest. It did nothing to tame the beast within though, each ragged breath being chased by another. The feeling of a million needles spread through my fingers and up my arms as I tried to stop their shaking, the comb falling from my hands and clattering on the vanity before me.

I stared at my reflection in the small dark mirror. My deep auburn hair hung in clumps around me, dull and matted from days of neglect. My face, streamed with tears, looked sunken and hollow. There was no stopping it, the feeling of free-falling into the darkness, the breath I desperately chased but could never find, the hateful thoughts crashing into me one after another.

Worthless. Lost. Nothing. Weak. Broken.

Despite the emotion so clearly taking me over, it felt as if there was a lack of something there, a missing depth of realness. As if, even now in my most raw moments, I was still only pretending. That made me hate the girl in the reflection even more. The numbness crept up my arms, washing over my chest, my face. It was not only skin deep, but rather sunk into my body until every inch of me was filled with it.

Numb.

It wasn't until my eyes fell to the small clipping of flowers sitting on the vanity that my breathing slowed, control taking over once more. In a small jar, tied together by the twine we'd used earlier that morning, were a few sprigs of yarrow sitting beside a steaming cup of tea. It took me a second to recognize it, its bright and happy presence a stark contrast to the depression hanging in the air. Aerie must have slipped into my room before dinner and left it for me.

Its presence brought a smile to my face, a whisper of happiness cracking through the darkness that had taken hold. I picked it up, turning the jar so I could view it from every angle. A small laugh escaped my lips, the ridiculousness of the situation hitting me. Tears still lingered on my skin, and yet here I was smiling at a silly little flower left in my room.

I set the jar back down, fluffing the blooms a little. I picked up the cup next, forcing down the somehow still-warm liquid in three deep gulps.

My smile fell. While the tea had made me feel warm and happy last night, it brought me nothing now. I couldn't feel the warmth it offered—or didn't want to. Something forced my vision to focus back on the mirror. My hateful gaze raked over the reflection, the girl I saw within. She was weak and scared—broken and powerless. I didn't want to be her, but I didn't know how to be anything else. My entire safety and survival had been reduced down to a nightly cup of tea and wishful thinking. The eyes in the mirror watched me tauntingly, almost as if to say it was all for nothing. How had I gotten here? How had I become so helpless? Slowly, I wiped my cheeks and finished combing my hair, refusing to look away from the reflection for even a second.

That was the girl Kahlis saw. That was the girl he wanted. He'd admitted as much when he dreamwalked to me.

See how easily I could end you. Those had been his words as he'd crushed me without lifting a finger. I stood no chance against him, against anyone. It wasn't some new revelation—I never had. Even in my life before this, I had lived every moment dependent on Arlo, and now, he wasn't even here. No, he wasn't even *real*. I had spent months in an imaginary library, living an imaginary life, and looking for a past that I wasn't sure I even wanted now that I'd found it. And the powers Aerie claimed I had, I couldn't even feel within me.

Despite how badly I wanted to be someone else, anyone else, I knew this was all I was. I had no power, no strength to fight. I was nothing like the little yarrow plant Aerie had left for me. I ripped my gaze away from the mirror as I headed for the bed and sunk into its soft linens, feeling the haunting hatred of the girl who had looked back at me.

I closed my eyes, willing sleep to pull my exhausted body under. It didn't, though. The only answer was a distant scraping and tapping, like that of a talon dragging across the door of my mind, searching for a way to slip in. The noise had been there all evening, whenever I let myself pause long enough to notice it. It set my teeth on edge, my body jerking with each tap of the dark appendage. I hadn't let myself consider it, didn't want to admit what it meant or how close he had to be for me to hear it. I reached under my pillow and clutched the bundle of herbs I knew Aerie had put there, along with the tea on the vanity.

I lay in the darkness, waiting for sleep to consume me.

Or Kahlis.

It was a dangerous game to play, waiting to see which would win, the herbs or the Dark One. But what was my life at this point but a pawn for others to play with? As the darkness of my room consumed me, I found it difficult to summon the energy to care. Eventually, my mind drifted, my body falling still as the tea took hold. I fell asleep to the distant rhythm of his tapping. Aerie's special tea blend may have offered me sleep, but it was a dark, restless one. Something full of fear and isolation, like slipping between this world and the next, like falling into a deep void of darkness with nothing and no one to save me.

CHAPTER 29
VANDER

Something resembling a gurgling cry escaped from the Daeomi's lips as Nox leaned over him, letting his knife slice into yet another part of the creature's skin. The root cellar was dimly lit. Aerie had created a few balls of fae light before she'd left us here to work, casting an eerie glow on the creature's body. The dirt floor had become muddied with the amount of bodily fluids he'd expelled. We'd been at this for a couple hours now, with nothing to show for it. It didn't bother me though, nor did it seem like Nox minded as he found another precarious spot to sink his blade into. To be honest, we were both focused more on causing pain than actually interrogating at the moment.

A smile pulled on my lips seeing the creature writhe beneath Nox's hand, but it was short-lived as Bastian's words echoed through my head. He was right, we didn't have time to waste. This was an unstable situation as it was. Not to mention attacks from Kahlis' creatures had increased against our tribe, claiming most of Bastian's time as chieftain recently. The longer this vile being was in our borders, in our home, the greater risk it put on Hazel, on all of us.

"That's enough."

I stepped forward, stretching my arm in front of Nox to keep him from slicing into the Daeomi again. I watched the heaving mess for a minute. The evil that shrouded me in shadows was nothing like the evil that lingered on him. The Grimm was dark, but it was fair. Death would come for everyone eventually. I offered balance to the world's chaos, restored wrongs and kept the scales.

That was the thing about my curse: there were always wrongs to be righted, never a short supply of lives that needed taking. So long as evil like this kept doing what it did, there would always be a rightful place for my rage to land. His disgrace of an existence had the Mark on my skin ebbing, the power crawling within me, desperate to be let out. Light could not exist without the dark to keep it balanced. No matter how dark my shadows were, I honored the land with my sacrifices. He destroyed it, leeching power and taking what he had no right to take.

He didn't look like much now, though. With each cry of pain, he'd lost control over his form, shifting sporadically into the oily black mutation and filling the cellar with his massive body and even larger wings. He was weak, pathetic—incapable of holding control over either of his forms. Blood pooled in shiny dark puddles on the dirt floor, mixed with a thick black substance that oozed from his wounds whenever he shifted.

None of us knew much about the Daeomi, aside from the fact that they'd originated from the Depths. They were Kahlis' creatures, the ones he used to do his bidding so that he never had to put himself in danger. It was rare to actually see Kahlis. Since he'd been exiled from the tribes, he'd made his home in Daravaana, building his kingdom off the backs of the most vile and detestable creatures in our land. Somewhere along the way, the Daeomi came to be.

Aerie had a theory, though, one that required some time for her to do some research. That was an area where we were happy to oblige. I stepped up to the pitiful, bleeding mess and knelt in front of him. His head hung low from the exhaustion the pain had caused. His face was swollen and discolored from the punches that had been landed during our session. Only one eye was visible still, the other swollen shut. He stared at me through that black pit, hatred seeping from him.

"Are you ready to play nice yet?" I asked.

A ragged, wet chuckle sounded from him as his head lobbed from side to side. "When Kahlis finds you, he will peel your skin off, limb by limb, for ever laying a hand on me. Then he will make you shift, just for good measure, so you can feel the agony of your changing form along the open wounds."

I laughed along with him. It wasn't a bad threat. I only gave him a moment to revel in it before lunging forward and grabbing him by the hair to lift his head toward the ceiling, so he could look at me as I towered over him.

I grabbed one of the herbal mixtures Aerie had supplied us with, something she'd said would cause terrifying hallucinations and debilitating pain.

I rolled it in my palm above him as he eyed the little burlap bag.

"I'm told your kind doesn't respond well to some of these things. A little belladonna, a sprinkling of hemlock, a healthy dose of black nightshade, all infused with salt and crushed selenite to purify. Let's see how well it works, shall we?"

The Daeomi's one good eye went wide with terror as I forced his mouth open and shoved the crushed herbs inside. I let a shadow slide through the air to force the herbs down his throat, causing him to choke and gag as they went down. My shadow lingered until I was sure he'd swallowed every last bit of the bag's contents. Maybe a little longer, just for good measure.

"That's a good boy," I said. "I like it when you swallow for me." I pulled back my shadow and landed a couple rough pats against his split and still-bleeding cheek.

Curses rippled from him as I walked back across the room to Nox and leaned against the cold cellar wall.

"What now?" asked Nox, one eye on the Daeomi still spitting hateful threats.

"Now, we wait. Make sure the herbs take effect. Then let him stew in his filth for a while. Maybe it will make him willing to talk. If not, we start over and do it all again."

"Damn, brother," Nox said, shaking his head. "I've seen some truly terrifying things in Daravaana—done some of them, too. But nothing can hold a candle to the look on your face right now."

"He hurt Hazel."

My body tensed at the memory of him standing over her bleeding body. As if I needed more of a reason to rip him apart. Nox hadn't been there, hadn't felt the pain burning through her limbs or the terror coursing through her veins when this evil bastard was looming over her, seconds away from tearing into her in more ways than one. My eyes remained fixed on the Daeomi. I knew exactly what he'd planned to do to her, and for that reason alone, I wanted to see the exact moment the herbs took hold—when his worst nightmares came alive. If I couldn't end Hazel's, at least I could make him pay for adding to them, and give him some of his own in the process.

CHAPTER 30
HAZEL

I spent the next several days wandering the estate and keeping to myself, or as much as they allowed me to. Vander was busy with the Daeomi, so I thankfully didn't see him very often. I was trying to avoid contact with both of them at all costs. Bastian had been called away to the border shortly after Vander's return, and I was trying not to think about what that meant for our safety. Kahlis already felt like an ever-present threat in my mind, but now, with the Daeomi Vander brought here and Bastian's constant battles at the border, it felt like he was *everywhere*.

Aerie was trying to give me space, but I knew she was keeping a watchful eye on me. I wasn't sure if it was because of the threat of Kahlis or because she sensed me pulling away. Either way, I found myself dodging into rooms and lingering in the shadows any time I heard voices coming toward me. I didn't want to talk, didn't want to face any of them—for fear of what terrible news I'd receive next. Instead, I poured all my focus on exploring the house and trying to distract myself with anything I could.

The estate was vast, its walls filled with ornate decorations and furnishings. Each room boasted a new array of emboldened colors and textures. Rugs woven with the finest thread covered the old wooden floors. Paintings, so beautiful they couldn't possibly be real, hung on the textured walls. With each new discovery, I felt like I'd happened upon some secret of old, like a book long forgotten on a library shelf, waiting to be picked up and dusted off. I wasn't even sure what half the rooms were used for or how long they'd gone untouched, but I kept exploring, kept sneaking through the twisted hallways in an effort to lose myself for a few hours.

It was magnificent, or it would have been if I could have brought myself to enjoy any of it. The distraction it offered was fleeting.

We think he created that reality to hold you captive.

Aerie's words echoed in my mind, like a constant weight, catching me and bringing me back down whenever I threatened to rise too high. The more they rang through my mind, the more I started to believe that she was right. I concentrated on the features of Arlo's face, the feel of his hand against my cheek, the way he looked at me just before he kissed me. It did nothing to abate my worry, and the longer I tried to remember, the more it faded away.

I'd retreated to the library for the afternoon, in hopes that its ambiance would comfort me and offer a moment of seclusion. Anger roiled through me as I failed for the fifth time to remember what shade Arlo's hair had been, and I threw the book that was perched in my lap across the room. It landed in a heap several feet from me before the magic of the library picked it up and set it ever so gently back on my lap.

"Thanks," I huffed out. It wasn't the first book I'd thrown today, but the library seemed to understand my pain, offering a gentle hand to help.

I chewed on the side of my thumb for another minute. I'd hoped to catch up on some of the reading that'd been set aside for me. The library seemed to be adding its own recommendations to my ever-growing stack. The sheer size of the collection was daunting, its presence lingering in the corner of my vision as a constant reminder of the amount of knowledge I still did not possess, things I still could not remember. Today was not the day, though. My mind was distracted with other things and being here, trying to understand this world that I supposedly belonged to—it was only frustrating me more.

I dragged myself off the velvet cushion I'd been propped up against and walked to the books spread out across the worktable. I found one or two smaller volumes that seemed easier to read before I stormed out of the library and back through the halls.

Aerie was working in the kitchen when I walked through. Her kind eyes found mine as I entered and she offered me a soft smile.

"Hi," I said awkwardly. "I was uh... hoping I could go for a walk?"

My eyes darted with unease around the kitchen before settling at my feet. Why was I asking her permission?

"Of course, Hazel. You don't need to ask." Her face was laced with concern, despite the gentle reassurance of her words. She wiped her hands on the towel draped over her shoulder as she stepped toward me. "Would you like some company?"

"That's okay," I said, the words coming out too fast. I took a step back, then paused, allowing myself a moment to settle my nerves. "I just wanted to get some fresh air, and maybe a little time to think."

A look of disappointment spread across her face, just for a moment, before she gave an understanding nod and went back to her work.

"Of course. I'll be here if you need me. The gardens are exceptionally peaceful at sunset."

"Thanks," I chirped as I rushed to the side door and slipped out.

I let it shut behind me as I leaned against it and closed my eyes. There weren't enough steadying breaths in the world to ease the vice grip on my chest. I hated pushing her away, hated making her upset after everything she'd done to make me feel welcome, accepted. Why was I doing this? I wanted so badly to be a part of the little family they'd built here. It's where I belonged, after all, wasn't it? If that was true, then why was it so hard for me to accept?

A clattering from Aerie's greenhouse pulled me from my thoughts. I snuck over to the door and peeked through its small windowpane, trying to get a glimpse of where the noise had come from. Just as I pressed my face to the glass, the door flew open, Lennox's mismatched eyes meeting me on the other side.

"Oh, fuck!" he exclaimed. "Sorry, Hazel, didn't see you there."

I looked past him into the greenhouse, trying to determine what he'd been doing inside.

"Does Aerie know you're in here?" I asked, not quite sure where my courage was coming from.

His hand pushed nervously through his coppery hair. He glanced over my shoulder, ensuring the kitchen door was closed before he answered, "Let's just say this is a little tradition of mine every time I come home. Aerie grows the best herbs I've ever had. Haven't found anything quite like it in all the lands I've traveled."

My eyes fell to his hands, a small burlap bundle in one and a small, wooden rectangular object in the other. I tilted my head to get a better look at it, trying to understand what it was.

"Well, second best. Nothing beats my mother's, of course." He flashed me a mischievous grin as he stepped through the doorway.

"Care to join me?" he asked, extending a hand. "From what I hear, you could use it after the week you've had."

I had no idea what he was talking about, but if he had something that could help me forget about the events of this past week, then I was all in.

"So," he said as we sat on a grassy hill a ways off from the house, watching the sun set before us. "How are you doing with all of this?"

He waved his hand around us, gesturing vaguely.

"Fine," I lied.

His fingers were delicately working at the rectangular object. It wasn't until I saw it up close that I noticed the intricate carvings along its sides. In the hollows of the wood shone stones of all different cuts and colors.

"Good." He nodded as he worked. "Now, let's try that again. How are you *really* doing?"

A small laugh escaped my lips as I pulled my knees into my chest.

"I don't even know where to begin to answer that."

"Noted. We can come back to it." He gave me a reassuring smile as he lit a match and held it up to one end of the wooden rectangle. An earthy aroma filled the air as he held the other end to his lips, letting smoke fill his lungs. "I swear, Aerie must infuse this stuff with her magic. There's nothing quite like it, at least not that I've found."

He handed me the contraption and I mimicked his movements. My lungs filled with the sweet, warming smoke. The heat of it stretched far beyond my lungs and I was suddenly hit with the sensation of love and light, like everything was just a little less heavy within me.

"I thought you said your mother grew the best?" I said, coughing a little as I exhaled.

"She did, yeah." A shadow of grief washed over his face as he turned his attention to the horizon, lost in some distant memory. "That stash is long gone now, though. She died a long time ago."

"Oh," I said, kicking myself internally for starting things off on such bad terms. "I'm so sorry, I didn't know."

"That's okay, it's been many, many years since then. Besides, I like talking about her." He held up the small wooden object between us, admiring the handiwork as much as I had.

"This belonged to her," he explained. "When we left our home to come here, I snuck it along with us. My father had been so heartbroken by her passing, he hadn't wanted to take any of her things with us. He wanted them to stay at home, with her." His lips twitched with emotion as he spoke of his home from so long ago. "She was an amazing healer and an even better mother."

"A healer? So you're from the Auris tribe?"

"Ah, and here I thought they said you didn't remember anything."

I blushed, his blunt demeanor catching me off guard. "I don't. Trying to keep up with everyone's conversations was proving to be too taxing, so I've been studying in my down time." I brushed my hair behind my ear, feeling slightly embarrassed at how easy it was for me to talk with him.

"Well, you were almost right," he said with a wink. "My mother was from Auris. My father, however, was a seer. He belonged to the tribe of Sgàil."

"So that explains the contrasting features." I gestured to his face and hair.

"I think you meant *devilishly handsome* features," he said, straightening up so he could puff his chest out a little.

"And your brother?" I asked, laughing a little.

"Well, I suppose he's devilishly handsome too, although I'd bet money on being the more striking of the pair."

"No," I said, full-out laughing now. "I meant, what about your brother? He's meant to be joining us soon?"

"Oh, well then—yes, he is. He should be here in a day or so."

I crooked my head to the side. "How do you know?"

He tapped the side of his glowing silver eye.

"It's a twin thing." He fixed me with a look of amusement as he spoke. "We were each born with a pair of contrasting eyes. His are the same as mine, only mirrored. They allow us to see what the other one wants us to see, allow us to communicate when we are not together. It's a piece of ourselves within the other. It's what makes us such an appealing option for tribe spy."

"Wow, that's... I've never heard of anything like that before. That's really interesting."

"You have, actually." He raised an eyebrow, waiting for me to catch his meaning.

"Yes, well. I don't *remember* hearing anything like that before."

He chuckled as he let the conversation die down. "Give it time, Hazel. You will."

I wanted to ask him how he could be so sure, but the silence that fell between us was too appealing. Within it, I could hear the whistling of the wind through the tall, silky grass. The scent of the rich soil beneath us filled my nose as I dug my fingers into it. In the distance, songbirds sang to each other as they settled into the towering trees for the night. I could feel the warmth of the setting sun along my exposed skin and I reveled in it. I wanted to stay in this moment forever, perfect and beautiful in every way.

I'd closed my eyes at some point and when I opened them, I found Lennox watching me. The faintest grin played at his lips.

"You know, you say you don't belong here, that you don't remember anything about us. Then you go and do shit like that and it's like looking right into the past. Like sitting beside the version of you from a decade ago."

Heat rose in my cheeks as I quickly looked away. I let the cool dirt slip through my fingers as I tucked my hands underneath me.

"I wasn't doing anything, just enjoying the sunset."

"That's exactly it. I don't think I've ever met someone who appreciates the beauty of our world as much as you do. How could you possibly belong anywhere else, Hazel?"

"That's easy to say when you're not experiencing the lows, too."

"So enlighten me. Tell me what your lows are."

I sighed, trying desperately to think of anything else to talk about. My mouth betrayed me, though, as it opened on its own accord to answer his question:

"I can't sleep. I ache. I'm caught between wanting to believe this is all real and wondering if it's somehow just a wild dream I'm trapped in. Every day new information hits me and I can no longer discern make-believe from reality. I've lost the only person who understands me, and now I'm realizing he may not even be real. I came here looking for answers, yet with each new answer I get, the more lost I feel."

I hadn't meant to share that much. I hadn't been so honest with anyone since I'd come to this world. Something about Lennox's spirit calmed me though. Much like Aerie, he had a way of making you feel safe, cared for, warm. He was quiet for a long time. Eventually, I forced myself to look up at him, wondering if he'd shut down altogether after my blunt confession.

His eyes were full of sympathy when I found them. Tears had formed along my lashes during my confession. I blinked to clear them away as one fell, betraying me, rolling down my cheek. He reached forward and wiped it away.

"What can I do to help?"

It was that simple—no long lecture about how I belonged here, no prying questions I didn't want to answer. He just offered himself, plain and simple.

I huffed out a laugh between my ragged breaths.

"I know everyone believes Arlo isn't real. Even I admit it makes sense. I just can't give up on him yet. I have to believe that the last year of my life, the only year I know, wasn't all a lie. That he wasn't a lie."

I paused, letting a few shaky breaths escape as I tried to gain my composure. "It doesn't matter though. I've overheard them talking. They haven't found any signs of him anywhere and I suspect they will stop looking soon, if they haven't already. Bastian's been mentioning an increase of attacks on the borders? They don't need to be distracted looking for Arlo when the tribe is being attacked. And besides, I think I'm starting to believe they're right."

The last words came out in a whisper, a confession I'd yet to make out loud.

Lennox was quiet for a moment, the lull in the conversation allowing me to get a hold of my emotions.

"Let me talk to Kirwan," he offered calmly. "He may be able to do some digging as he's traveling home. Take an extra circle around the Dark Woods just to see if there's anything Bastian's sentries might have missed or won't have time to find. It doesn't hurt to have a second pair of eyes there. The Dark Woods are tricky, always changing and shifting. It's easy to miss things."

The words lifted me, a gleam of hope growing within. It was a long shot: the woods had already been searched, and despite how badly I wanted Arlo found, I couldn't help but admit the reality of the situation. But I had to let him try.

"Thank you," I whispered, as more tears threatened to spill.

"Hey, what are friends for?" He put his arm around me and squeezed, the warmth of his embrace making that little spark of hope grow. "Can you do something for me, though?"

I leaned into his embrace, cherishing each ounce of sunlight glowing on the horizon. "Of course."

"Give Vander a chance. Let him in. Even if this Arlo exists, Vander once held an important role in your life. He deserves to at least have the chance to get to know this new version of you."

I scoffed, tucking my knees into my chest as I settled under his arm. "I get the distinct impression that he has absolutely no interest in getting to know me."

Lennox just hummed in amusement, the last rays of sunlight illuminating the small twinkle in his one silver eye as I stole a glance up at him. There was something there, something he wasn't saying. His fingers thrummed in consideration against my arm as the sun dipped below the horizon and cast a foreboding shadow over us.

"Impressions can be misleading."

CHAPTER 31
HAZEL

I stared at the ceiling above my bed, my eyes evaluating every detail of a particular notch in one of the wood planks. Whatever Lennox had given me earlier that evening was doing nothing to ease the frustration pulsing through my body as I tried to fall asleep, however it had made dinner much more bearable. I supposed its effects had long since worn off. That didn't explain why Aerie's tea wasn't working tonight, though. My skin was sticky with sweat from the countless hours I'd spent tossing and turning.

So many of the previous nights I'd spent just like this. Sleep had become a stranger, something I chased and chased until it turned on me abruptly and took me over like some blood-starved animal. To be honest, I wasn't sure if I was chasing sleep or avoiding it. The constant tapping of Kahlis' threatening hold on my mind was enough of a warning call to know what dangers were near, just within reach if he decided tonight was time.

The house had gone quiet several hours ago. I was positive everyone was asleep by now—except Vander. I rolled my eyes at the sound of his paws thudding against the hallway as he paced. He'd taken to the habit of lingering outside my bedroom door at night. I supposed he was checking on me, making sure I wasn't locked away in my mind, deep within Kahlis' grasp.

If only he knew how close Kahlis was. A rhythmic *tap tap tap* sounded, as if in answer to my thought. The sentiment of Vander's efforts would have been sweet if he'd bothered to say more than three words to me at any given moment. Why did he care so much about what would happen to me if he wasn't even going to take the time to acknowledge me?

That wasn't true, though. He acknowledged me just fine. That was part of the problem. I couldn't seem to get away from those guarded, glowing eyes and the set look of resentment on his face. He was constantly there, watching, judging my every move.

I shook out a shiver as his cold gaze lingered in my mind.

Unable to quell my discomfort, I lost patience with the bed and decided to try my luck at pacing. Perhaps a couple laps around the room would tire me enough that I could finally find sleep.

On my third lap past the window, I paused. Something in the depths of the night had caught my eye. I watched the almost-black trees in the distance, waiting for whatever it was to show itself. Everything was still, though. Not even the wind was moving. I lingered a moment longer, telling myself that I was officially losing my mind. I turned my head back to the path I'd begun wearing into the floorboards just as something moved beyond the trees. I spun, gripping the windowsill as I caught sight of it again.

It was just a small flash, a little bob of light amidst the dark forest beyond. It was gone as fast as it had come, but it had definitely been there. Curiosity spiked within me.

Forgetting about sleep altogether, I leaned against the window frame, eager to catch a glimpse of the strange sight. I moved further in; my face met the glass as my nose pressed in. It was no use; it was too far away, too elusive to see from the safety of my little window. I waited a few more moments, watching the small light come and go, dancing along the trees. It would slowly bob into the trees, then suddenly dart back within view, as if it was calling to me, asking me to follow it.

Then an idea settled within me. *Arlo.* Maybe he'd found a way to contact me. Maybe he'd found a way to summon me back through whatever doorway I'd entered this world. The idea seemed too ridiculous. Life wasn't that kind, couldn't be that perfect. Yet, as I watched the light dash back to the clearing just in front of the estate once again, I felt the same sensation that had carried me into this world in the first place, a pull from deep within. It wasn't quite the same, but similar enough. It didn't matter that I was in danger, that I had no knowledge of how to navigate the vast woods it was beckoning me toward. All I knew was that I had to follow it.

I grabbed a pair of boots I'd found in the old wardrobe and slipped them on. Making my way to the door, I stopped to listen for the sound of Vander's pacing on the other side. After a few moments of silence, I cracked the door open and peered into the hall. I let loose a sigh, realizing he wasn't there. He must have gone hunting. I slipped out from behind the door, closing it softly. Then, on tiptoe, I made my way through the house. I softened my movements as much as possible, worried that if anyone woke up, they'd stop me.

Guilt twinged in my heart as I made my last pass through the kitchen, knowing how worried Aerie would be if she knew what I was doing. My hand paused on the doorknob, the last remaining defense between me and the mysterious light waiting just beyond the estate. Bastian would truly mourn any harm that might come to pass from this risk I was taking. He'd worked so hard to get me back, and here I was running right back into the woods. And Vander... well, I had no way of knowing how Vander felt about anything.

But the last time I'd followed this call, it'd taken me from Arlo. I swallowed hard as my grip on the doorknob tightened and I pushed against the sturdy wood. Maybe this time, it would take me back.

The night was warmer than I'd expected it to be, a sign that summer was almost upon us. I walked toward the edge of the estate where the tree line began, the fae light in the house fading in the distance. I peered into the thick woods, as my eyes adjusted to the darkness. I looked frantically for the small ball of light dancing amongst the trees but saw nothing. Panic took over as I began to wonder if it had left, if it hadn't waited for me. I felt too exposed out in the night air, too vulnerable to whatever else might be lurking in the Dark Woods. Long, anxious moments passed with no sign of the little light and doubt took hold as I realized my stupidity in coming out here. I started to turn back to the estate, wondering what could have possibly come over me.

Just there, on the edge of the tree line, it slipped out into the open. Relief flooded me as I altered my path and made my way toward it. I was more convinced than ever that it was leading me to Arlo—leading me home. As I approached it, admiring its warm glow and playful manner, it vanished. A few paces away a new one popped up, bouncing around as if enticing me to follow it. I giggled, the sound not entirely my own, as I stepped past the tree line and into the woods.

We continued on like that for several minutes—me chasing each ball of dancing light, it disappearing just as I came upon it. It carried me deeper and deeper into the woods, the night growing ever darker. As I walked, I started to wonder if I had misunderstood the light's purpose for bringing me out here. My steps became less sure; my hands shook with nerves.

I looked around the Dark Woods, suddenly realizing I'd been a fool to believe Arlo was out here. Its towering trees shifted and creaked, the branches leaning in to grasp at my hair and arms, as I passed. The path had become overgrown, wild and unused. Cruel and violent noises sounded from every direction. Still, the lights remained constant in front of me. They grew dim, though, changing with each negative thought that began to echo through my mind.

I'm naive to believe Arlo's calling me.

I'm stupid to believe he'll be out here.

I've been a fool to believe he even existed at all.

A gray smoke snaked across the warm glow of the lights, taking them over and changing them to deep charcoal. Still, I didn't stop following them.

I don't belong out here.

I'm too fragile.

I deserve to be lost to the darkness of the woods.

The orbs dimmed ever further, a dark onyx shadow taking form. They no longer danced happily through the trees but rather pulled me greedily forward. Their presence was a demand, a need for me to follow them even deeper into the forest. I was helpless against them; my only purpose was to appease their call.

Their light brought me to the edge of a body of water. A dark lake was laid out before me. The water was as ominous and murky as the obscured balls of light and I instantly wondered what kind of creatures lurked below its surface. I stopped just behind the light, just at the edge of the water's reach. I waited for the light to show me what it wanted, tell me what to do. It vanished again, like it had every time, before reappearing a few paces away, hovering just above the water's surface.

I understood its meaning immediately. I took a step, the icy water seeping into my boot.

I'm not good enough.

I took another step, my second boot becoming immersed in the frigid water.

I don't belong here.

The water cut into my shins as I stepped forward again.

I don't belong anywhere.

I felt the water piercing my thighs as I made my way forward.

They don't want me; they want Hazlenn. They want someone I will never be.

The murky water reached my stomach, pulling me forward and willing me to go under.

They'll be better off without me.

It was up to my chest now, its pull nearly impossible to withstand. The ends of my hair dipped below the surface.

It would be so easy to slip under the surface and just disappear altogether. As easy as breathing—easier, even.

The water licked at my chin as I watched the onyx orb hang heavily above the water in front of me. Without warning, it plunged beneath the surface, bidding me to follow it.

I knew it was right. The lights had been a mercy, an offering to rid myself of the pain of this world, a path into the next life. They were helping me see clearly for the first time ever what I truly wanted. They offered an escape, the icy waters suddenly turning warm against my skin. Or perhaps it was just my skin turning numb against the cold. I was so tired of being numb.

Going under would break the numbness.

I took another step forward until I found my feet couldn't reach the ground.

I treaded water for a minute, letting the ice pierce into the rest of my body. My hair was heavy with the murky liquid behind me, my cheeks stung with the water's cold grasp.

Give up, Hazel.

Go under.

End the pain.

The dark liquid pulled on every part of me, my body too weak to fight back.

It's time.

We want you.

With that last thought, I slipped below the surface, welcoming the icy grasp of the watery grave below.

CHAPTER 32
VANDER

Awareness washed over me as my hackles raised, lifting my head to the wind and tracking her scent. I'd been trailing a particularly nasty breed of water sprite by the lake in the Dark Woods when I picked up her scent. Her unmistakable aroma of lavender and sage hung in the air. She couldn't be out here. I'd gone by her room before venturing out to the woods for the night. She hadn't been asleep, her body restless, tossing and turning in her sheets, but I'd been confident that she'd turn in soon. Aerie had left her the brew of tea again, as she did every night, and its effects would have soon taken hold, lulling her into a dreamless sleep. At least, it should have.

As my wolven form slipped easily through the trees, I reached out through the tether. It had been nothing but unreliable since she'd returned: there at times in full force, gone a moment later, or only offering a small window with which to sense her. Besides, I could tell it made her uncomfortable when I tried to use it. She might not remember that it was there, but I'd seen her eyes shift with unease the few times I'd watched her while reaching out through it. It was distant again, like she was only a whisper on the other end. It didn't stop fragments from slipping through, though.

Not good enough.

My blood chilled as I ran faster, my eyes piercing through the darkness searching for her amongst the blurred trees. The greens and blacks and browns of the Dark Woods merged together in a rush of ominous shadow as I picked up speed.

They want Hazlenn.

They want someone I will never be.

Terror overtook me as I heard her words ring out through my mind. I willed my body to move faster, power rippling into the ground with each stride I took. I tried to push back my own thoughts, begging her to snap out of whatever trance she was in. I screamed at her that she was enough, that I was sorry for ever making her feel otherwise. My words fell into the void, the tether not strong enough to carry them to her. I cursed at the frail connection as I pushed ahead.

Go under.

End the pain.

A howl tore out of me as I felt the torment weighing on her soul. It ripped through the trees, turning to a guttural growl and bringing a few to the ground around me as I ran—the power of the Mark surging through me, uncontrollable. My enraged form shook the ground with a strength I rarely used. I dodged out of their way, never slowing my pace. I would not lose her again.

I broke through the thick foliage of the forest to the water's edge as I shifted back to my mortal form. I didn't slow as the icy water splashed under my feet. The rocky bottom of the lake bit into my bare skin. It didn't matter. I pushed forward, desperately searching the water for her.

She was here. I could feel it—feel her—even if I couldn't tell exactly where she was.

I dove beneath the surface and swam further out, reaching through the tether for any sign. Off in the distance, deep within the water, I caught the faintest glimpse of light.

Fucking. Faeries.

The Wisps were dangerous enough for anyone to encounter, but Hazel probably didn't even remember what they were, let alone how to withstand their grasp. Even worse, the tether had gone utterly silent. I broke the surface, catching my breath and trying to get closer to where I'd seen the orb, before diving straight down with as much power as I could muster.

The water was even murkier this far down, the light of the moon unable to penetrate this depth. The only guide I had as I fought against the cumbrous waters was the distant glow of the Wisp, growing fainter by the second. I knew when it disappeared altogether that she'd be gone, lost to the Wisps and the depths of the lake forever.

My heart raced as I plunged deeper, arms stretched out and searching. She had to be here.

Dammit, Hazel, show me where you are!

My heart pounded in my ears, the ache in my chest telling me I was running out of time. If I had to break the surface for more air, it'd be too late; I'd never find her. My lungs burned as I scrambled to her through the tether one last time, demanding she answer. I was screaming into a void, nothing there but piercing, deafening black. I begged her with every fraction of power I had left in my body to come back to me, just as I had in those early days after Kahlis had taken her. As if the past ten years hadn't happened at all, I was right back in that clearing, watching her slip through my fingers.

I couldn't lose her again.

I felt the Mark coming to life against my skin, offering me the power I needed to keep going. I reached out a hand again, this time ordering the shadows of the dark waters to bend to me—tapping into a magic I wasn't entirely sure I owned. Suddenly, I felt something brush against my fingers.

Hazel.

The panic in my chest eased slightly as I followed the pull and wrapped her in my arms. I didn't wait to see if she was okay, didn't wait to see if she was even alive, before twisting my body back toward the surface.

She made no noise after we came up for air, no recognition that we'd escaped the grasp of the cold, murky lake. I swam for the shore, silently begging Hazel to hold on a little bit longer. My breath staggered as I laid her out before me on the moss covered rocks.

Her eyes were closed, the shade of her skin far too colorless to be okay.

I called to her, both out loud and through the tether, but she did not answer.

"Don't fucking die on me, Hazel." I lowered my mouth to hers, forcing life into her with every ragged breath. I let my shadows reach out and envelop her body, willing it to warm. I cursed at the Mark on my arm, bidding it to let her live. Its power growled within me, desperate to take the life it sensed slipping away. I would not allow death to take her, I would not make this sacrifice for the Mark. I laid a hand against her chest, checking for the steady rhythm of her heart, for the movement of her breathing, before allowing a shadow to push against her lungs, forcing out whatever contents lay within.

Her eyes fluttered open as she coughed up the black sludge of the lake. My breath loosed as I watched her fighting her way back to life. Slowly, color crept back into her cheeks. I sent up a silent prayer of thanks to the Fates for not cutting her thread just yet.

I pulled her into my arms, cradling her across my body as I trudged through the Dark Woods. My shadows wrapped tighter around her to trap in whatever warmth they could. Her lips were still too blue; her skin, too cold. The bite of it against my hands caused my steps to quicken. I let my eyes fall to her chest ever so often, making sure she was still breathing, making sure that beautiful heart was still beating its steady rhythm.

She didn't speak as we made our way home. Her body was in shock, slipping in and out of consciousness. When she was awake, the only sound between us was the clicking of her teeth against each other from the forceful shivers that overtook her body. She was soaked to the bone, and just as cold. I pulled her closer to my chest, trying to transfer my body heat to her. As I walked, I let the reality of the situation calm my racing heart.

She is safe.

She is here.

She is alive.

Still, it did nothing to relieve the pain that echoed through my mind. Her thoughts that had come through the tether earlier that night, the misery that I'd felt radiating from her, had rattled me. I knew she'd been struggling, but something deep inside burned with anger at the idea that those thoughts had belonged to her. She was hurting and a large part of it was my fault. Something within me shifted, like a fog lifting after a heavy rain. I would spend tonight and every night until the end of time making sure she never felt that way again.

CHAPTER 33
HAZEL

I nestled against the warmth of Vander's chest, lost to everything else around me. Walking through the woods, the thoughts in my mind, the feeling of sinking into the depths of the lake—they all felt like some far-off nightmare, one that I couldn't forget no matter how hard I tried. Even still, I felt myself fighting the urge to break away from his grip and run back to the lake, back to the all-consuming, endless cold I knew I deserved. I didn't know how Vander had found me, but I was so grateful he had. I wasn't strong enough to withstand this darkness. The reality of the situation was a chilling realization.

He saved me.

I avoided eye contact with him while he carried me back home. I knew I would have to talk to him eventually, but I didn't have the courage to admit what had happened. Shame rose within me as heat crept into my ears. How could I explain that I'd wanted to die? It seemed too terrible a truth to say out loud, and I hadn't really wanted that. No, death wasn't what drew me to those deep, troubled waters. The idea of disappearing, putting an end to the pain and suffering that had become every waking, and even unconscious, moment of my life? That had been the pull.

I'd drifted off again, my body exhausted from the incessant shivering. When I woke, we were back at the estate, walking through the kitchen and down the halls to my bedroom. Only, Vander passed my door and went several paces down the hallway. If exhaustion wasn't so heavily sweeping through me, I would have tried to argue. Instead, I let him carry me through his doorway and into his room.

He set me down in one of the chairs by his hearth. I was reluctant to leave his grasp but thought it indecent to ask him to continue holding me like a small child who'd had a bad dream. He walked to one end of the room, out of my vision. I didn't have the energy to turn and see what he was doing, but when he walked back over to me, he was fastening the buttons on a pair of pants. *Has he been naked this whole time?* I was going to have to get used to him constantly going without clothes. It seemed a common occurrence in a house full of shifters. He turned his attention to the fireplace. Within minutes he had a strong fire blazing, its warmth reaching out to lick at my frozen fingers wringing in my lap.

He leaned against the side of the hearth, shadows playing across his features. I couldn't tell what he was thinking. Tears threatened to betray my emotions as his gaze bore into me. I quickly averted my eyes, letting them fall to my lap. I was filthy, covered in mud and gunk from the lake. It served as an ominous mark of the night's horrendous events. I suddenly felt sick looking at the grime, like the depths of the lake were once again pulling me under. I began scrubbing at my hands, trying frantically to get rid of the dried mud. I needed it off; I needed any remnants of the lake's grasp far away from me, in case it somehow kept its hold on me. My breath quickened, my body impatiently amping up as I failed to get my hands clean.

"It's alright." Vander moved to me in two strides, stooping to force my eyes to meet his. He took my hands in his. "We'll get you cleaned up, just breathe. There's a hot bath right in there waiting for you when you're ready."

My eyebrows rose, surprise taking hold in me.

"Really?" I asked. I peered over my shoulder to get a better view of the bathroom.

"Yeah, Aerie has this thing about me coming home dirty from a hunt. She always has a bath waiting."

He brought me to my feet, refusing to let my hands go as he guided me to the bathing room. Just like he'd said, the bathtub was full and ready to be used. Steam rose in soft tendrils from the tub, the smell of peppermint filling the air. Several candles were spread around the bathtub, casting the room in a soft, warm glow. It was utterly different from the icy void that had consumed me in the lake, the one that still lingered in my mind. I didn't move—I couldn't. My feet were lead, rooted to the spot as I stared at the tub.

"Come now, Hazel. You don't have to be shy about nudity in the presence of a shifter." A smile played at his lips as he waited for me to undress and get in the bath.

"If it makes you feel better, I'll even turn around."

I thought he'd meant it as a joke, but his words proved to be sincere as he turned to face the opposite direction and leaned against the doorframe.

I looked down at the laces of my boots, then back to my still-shaking hands. My nightclothes would be easy enough to manage, the material loose and flowy, but my boots, I'd need assistance with.

"I can't," was all I managed to breathe out. He hesitated, almost unable to hear me with how quiet my voice had become. Slowly though, he turned and looked down at the shaking hands I held out in front of me. His expression softened as he made several measured steps toward me. He took my hands once again, turning them over in his and willing them to calm. Then he kneeled before me, unlacing my boots one aching foot at a time. I winced as he pulled them off, my feet still frozen from the cold of the lake.

When he stood, he tugged gently at the hem of my nightshirt, waiting for me to give permission before he continued. I nodded, avoiding his eyes as he slowly lifted the filthy fabric off my stomach and over my head. I folded my arms instinctually across my chest, shielding myself from the crisp air, and from his view. He moved to the waistband of my bottoms next, taking care to hook a finger along the side of my undergarment as he tugged. The gauzy material stuck to my legs as he pulled them down. He delicately peeled the waterlogged fabric off my calves before stepping back and allowing me space.

When he averted his eyes once more, I stepped into the tub, sending out silent thanks to Aerie and her magical, warm baths. The heat of the water sunk into my bones, instantly returning my body to its rightful temperature.

Vander moved to the side of the tub as I sat with my knees pulled tight to my chest. I said nothing as he grabbed the bar of soap and worked it over my skin. He started with my hands, working thoroughly to remove every speck of dirt. Then he moved to my shoulders and my back, both caked with mud and scraped and bloody due to the lack of coverage my nightclothes had offered while traipsing through the trees. I hadn't realized how the woods had torn me up, how distracted I'd been by whatever trance had taken hold of me. My arms ached as he scrubbed the wounds clean. Once he finished, he handed me the bar of soap as he picked up a comb and started working to untangle my hair.

I took the bar but couldn't bring myself to do anything with it. Instead, I sat there and let him take care of me. This was a side to Vander I hadn't seen before. It was one I had a hard time correlating with the beastly creature that haunted the halls at night and only offered me snarky comments and judgemental gazes. Lennox had asked me to give him a chance though, let him see the person I was now.

In this light, I could see why Lennox had asked that of me. It was becoming clear how much Vander cared for me, or at least had at one point. I just didn't think he would like who I'd become if I let him see her.

"Tell me what you're thinking, little spitfire."

The nickname that he'd used on me days ago had stirred so much anger within me. This time, it stirred something else entirely.

A smile played at the edge of my lips as I responded, "I'm thinking this isn't anything like what I thought you were."

His hand stilled against my hair. I turned to get a better look at him, instantly wishing I hadn't. Guilt and grief ravaged his features, making his shadows snake across the bathroom around us.

"I haven't been myself for a very long time," he admitted brusquely. "And I haven't been there for you like I should have."

His confession surprised me. I'd been waiting for him to ask me what had happened, to bring up the events of the night. Based on the way he was talking, I wondered if he somehow already knew. But if that was true, then why hadn't he cared before? He'd been keeping his distance since I arrived here, making sure to impress in me just how dangerous and indifferent he was toward me.

I turned back to the bathwater, resting my chin across my knees. He continued combing through the mess of tangles falling across my back. Silence fell around us. I didn't want to go there with him, couldn't imagine shifting the image he'd so thoroughly convinced me of who he was. I didn't have the energy to respond, to admit that maybe I was starting to see him differently tonight. Instead, I watched the flame of one of the candles dance in the darkness of the bathroom.

Its colors were beautiful, hues of burning orange and vibrant yellow shifting to let through the hottest shade of blue every now and then. The fire moved freely, ebbing and flowing to its own rhythm. It changed as it wanted to, growing smaller or larger at will. I hated it and loved it all at the same time. I wanted that freedom, that ability to change and shift around my environment without losing control or getting snuffed out completely. I wanted to let my emotions burn bright and be free without feeling like I was failing or falling apart. Instead, I felt like I was coming undone—like I would never be able to put myself back together. And if I couldn't, then who would? I couldn't put that burden on Vander, on any of them. As I watched it, I felt a tear slip from beneath my lashes, followed by another, and another.

If Vander noticed my crying, he did not mention it. Instead, he continued on, delicately combing out my hair until no trace of the lake was left in it. I was impressed with the gentleness of his touch, finding his busy fingers grounding as I felt him work. When he had finally finished, he set the comb down and let out a heavy sigh.

"Hazel, I never meant for this to happen. I can't begin to explain how badly I wanted you back home. By the Fates, you don't even understand the price I've paid—" He cut himself off, his breath heavy as he worked to find his words. "I've wanted nothing but this for the past ten years. But when you returned, you were entirely different. You had a life and a male and somewhere else you called home. I never imagined that's what you'd been doing this whole time. I got angry. I distanced myself because if I couldn't have all of you then I thought I wanted no part of you."

His breath shook as he paused. I was shocked by his words, but I didn't dare interrupt. I stared straight ahead at the small dancing flame as he continued, "But when I heard you tonight, when I felt your pain and I thought I'd lost you all over again, I realized something. I don't care what version of you I get. Hazlenn, Hazel, whatever else you may become. I want you. I want every version of you in whatever way I can. I cannot lose you again."

More tears fell down my cheeks, their salty warmth mirroring that of the water soaking into my skin. I didn't know what to do with his words, didn't know how to accept that kind of love. It was baffling, especially when an hour ago I'd been convinced that this world would be better off without me. Those emotions flooded my mind as I grimaced and turned away, tucking my face into the crook of my arm. I didn't want him to see my pain. I didn't want to admit how much darkness had consumed me tonight, how close he'd come to actually losing me forever. I didn't want him to see how much I hated myself for being drawn to him, when I still hoped Arlo was out there somewhere, waiting for me.

But he knows already, doesn't he?

"I'm not asking you to choose between me and Arlo," he went on, as if sensing where my thoughts had turned. "If we find him and you want to return to him, go back to whatever life you've built elsewhere, I'll live with that. But please, Hazel, don't stop fighting. Don't give up."

"What if he's not real?" The words escaped me before I could stop them. "I don't know what's real and what's not anymore. I don't know what to believe."

He quieted, seeming to debate what words to speak next.

"Then we will deal with that when the time comes."

He took my hand, gently relaxing my grip on the bar of soap so he could set it to the side. I'd forgotten I still held it and the bar's smooth surface was warped with grooves from how tightly I'd been gripping it.

He dipped his hands in the water before lifting my chin to his face and wiping the tears from my cheeks. The light of the candles cast shadows across his face as he looked in my eyes. Taking my hand and turning it over in his, he pressed his fingers into my palm slightly.

"No matter what else happens—what else you find out, Hazel. No matter what, please remember... This? This right here is real."

His words sucked the breath from my lungs, their cadence a familiar call in the depths of my mind. I couldn't place them, but I couldn't help but feel like I'd heard them before, like I'd clung to them in some distant memory.

I shook my head, letting the eerie chill run over my body, despite the warmth of the bathwater. The movement pulled me from his grasp and I took the opportunity to change the subject, not trusting myself to linger any longer on his words. His shadows rippled in response, as if they mourned the touch of my skin.

"You said you heard me before. In the woods? How?"

A look I couldn't quite place flashed across his face, like some unseen battle was happening within his mind.

"That's a conversation for another time," he said finally. "It's late and you're exhausted. You need rest." He stood and walked to the doorway, leaving a towel beside the bath for me. "I'll go get you a change of clothes while you finish up and dry off."

He lingered by the doorway, casting one last cautious glance my way before turning and disappearing into the darkness of the other room.

I quickly dried off and made my way back to the bedroom. The feeling of being in here alone was almost too much to bear. I wanted company.

I wanted warmth. I... I wanted *him*. The realization shocked me. He was a beast, a creature of violence and bloodlust. I shouldn't *want* him. I couldn't help but admit that something had shifted between us tonight, though. There was more to him than the monster he proudly played. There was something deeper—stronger—connecting us and pulling me in. And the more time we spent together, the more I noticed his absence and longed for him to be near.

But when I walked into the bedroom, he was nowhere to be seen. Instead, I found a stack of nightclothes folded neatly on a small table by the fire. Next to the clothes was another cup of Aerie's nightly tea. My face fell in disappointment as I turned to view the entirety of the room, just to be sure he wasn't there somewhere. What was happening to me? A day ago I was terrified of him, and now I was searching the shadows in hopes that he *would* be there? I squeezed my hands into fists as I took several calming breaths and turned back to the table. I pulled the clothes on quickly, comforted by the warmth they'd absorbed from the fire. Then I sat by the hearth and watched the flames crackle as I drank the tea.

I'd been expecting him to return—held out hope that he was perhaps just giving me a moment to collect myself—but when the cup had long since been emptied and the fire started to dim, there was still no sign of him. Exhaustion overtook me and I looked longingly at the simply dressed bed, made up with nothing but a singular pillow and a thread-bare blanket. The bed in my room had been made with much nicer linens, trimmed with soft, fluffy pillows and extra blankets. I couldn't find the strength to make it back to my room, though, not with the tea's effects taking hold. Nor did I necessarily want to sleep in there tonight, despite the comfort I knew it offered. If I stayed here, perhaps Vander would return eventually. Sluggishly, I pulled myself off the chair and trudged over to the bed. I sunk into it, barely staying awake long enough to pull the covers up.

Through heavy eyelids, I noticed the door creak open. Claws clicked against the floor as midnight fur slipped through the small opening. Vander, in his wolven form, stalked across the bedroom. He didn't seem surprised by my presence but rather settled onto the rug at the foot of the bed.

"Thank you," I whispered hesitantly as my eyes struggled to stay open.

I didn't know if he could even understand me when he was in *that* form, the form that took lives violently and stalked the halls covered in blood. I didn't know how I felt about sleeping with the wolf at my feet—if it was a safe or smart decision on my part. But I felt the need to thank him anyway, to stay despite every instinct telling me to put distance between me and the creature before me.

He'd let me in, shown me a small glimpse of what it looked like to be loved and to accept that kind of love. It did more to ease the ache in my soul than anything else had tonight. I let that thought consume me, the feeling of his gentle fingers still lingering on my skin as I drifted off to sleep.

When I awoke in the morning, Vander was gone. The events of last night hung in the recesses of my mind as I rubbed my eyes and rolled out of the bed. It had taken me a moment to realize I was still in his room, wrapped in the comfort of his sheets. His familiar scent clung to the fabric, or maybe me. Either way, I inhaled deeply, longing to breathe more of it in.

The bright morning sunlight streamed in through the window. I hadn't been able to see much of the room in the darkness of the night.

Today I looked around, taking in the rich, earthy tones of the bedsheets and drapes. Where my room was soft and vibrant, his was stark and empty. There was little more than the bed, a couple chairs by the fire, and a few books strewn around the room. No decor, no sentimentality.

On the small table by the now cold hearth was another neatly folded set of clothes waiting for me. I yawned as I made my way across the room and grabbed the light material, letting it unfold in a cascade of fabric as I held it up. He'd left me a dress—a white cotton dress. It was simple and beautiful and unlike anything I would have picked out for myself. It was too pure, too pretty for someone like me to wear, especially after the darkness I felt last night.

Before I lost the courage to try it on, I slipped out of my nightclothes and pulled the flowy fabric over my head. I was surprised by how well it fit, and I gave a little spin to admire the way it draped down my body. I smoothed my hands nervously over the tight-fitting bodice, wishing momentarily that the scoop of the neckline wasn't so revealing, and tried to get used to the feel of the long flowy sleeves that hung off my shoulders. Giving up on the frilly material, I tiptoed over to the door and peered out into the hall. There were no signs of him anywhere—no sign of anyone, actually.

I slipped out into the hallway and padded along the woven rug lining the floor, making my movements quiet as I went. Luckily, the dress hung just above my ankles, or I would have been tripping over the excess material. I could hear some distant commotion, something like arguing coming from the dining room. I headed that way, slowing my steps at the entryway. I paused, making sure I remained in the shadows as I heard Bastian's voice rumbling with anger.

"I don't know what you were thinking, Nox. It's one thing to raid Aerie's cabinets, but to include Hazel? You had no business offering her anything, especially with the risks going on right now. We're already dealing with increased Daeomi activity along our borders, not to mention the very real attacks that Hazel has experienced!"

"You need to relax, Bastian. Let the girl cut loose a little. She's not going to get any better with your overbearing tight ass constantly looking over her shoulder, telling her what she can and can't do. That much is clear after last night."

I could see the ends of Lennox's copper hair just past the edge of the entryway. His tone was casual, unbothered, but I couldn't help but feel bad that he was getting chastised for something we'd done together.

"If you had respected my overbearing tight ass, she wouldn't be in this mess in the first place!" Bastian's words echoed through the halls.

"Oh, please. Don't act like she succumbed to the Wisps because of me. If anything, smoking helped her withstand them for as long as she did last night."

Bastian huffed through what I imagined was gritted teeth. I couldn't see him or anyone else in the room, but his anger was palpable.

"Be that as it may." Aerie's voice lifted the tension in her typical singsong way. "Hazel's mental state is delicate at the moment. Not only is she struggling within herself, she also has Kahlis watching, waiting for the tiniest opportunity to snake his way back into her mind. Which means we need to be careful about what we subject her to. We're lucky the incident with the Wisps didn't render her helpless to another attack from Kahlis."

A scoff sounded at Aerie's words. I couldn't see who'd made the noise, but I'd bet good money on it being Vander.

"It didn't feel quite so lucky when I was pulling her from the depths of the lake."

Yeah, that was definitely Vander.

I chewed on my bottom lip, debating if I should make my presence known. It felt wrong to eavesdrop, but they were talking about me, my life. It wasn't wrong if it was about me, was it? I debated with myself a little longer before finally deciding to step forward. As I made my way to move, Lennox's words stopped me in my tracks.

"So I suppose telling her Arlo wasn't real was you being careful about what we subject her to?"

I quickly retraced my steps and pressed my back firmly against the wall. I gathered the skirt of my dress in my hands, pressing the flowy material to my body. I squeezed my eyes shut, silently praying no one had caught sight of me.

As I slowed my breathing, I heard Aerie release a long sigh. "I didn't want to tell her. None of us did. But she deserves to know what she's up against. What the reality, or possible reality, of the situation is."

"All I'm saying," urged Nox, "is maybe you didn't have to try so hard to convince her he wasn't real. If you're that worried she's so fragile, if you're that concerned about her mental state, maybe don't convince her that the entire last year, or ten years or whatever, was completely fake."

"She deserves to know," Bastian bit back. "And she deserves to hear realistic expectations, unlike the empty promise you made to send Kirwan on a wild goose chase."

Nox shifted, his tone turning frigid. "She deserves to feel supported and accepted as she is, not like some outsider whose opinion is irrelevant to you. She's not the same girl we lost ten years ago, and you need to be okay with that."

Lennox's words hung in the air, the room going eerily quiet.

"I agree," Aerie finally said. "She's not the same girl. And it's time we stop treating her as such."

"Thanks for the support, Aerie," said Nox, his eyes flickering to Bastian, "but it wasn't exactly you I was referring to."

This time, Bastian scoffed, banging his fist against something hard. "Oh, that's great, Nox, blame it all on me. Fates forbid you ever do anything wrong. For fuck's sake. Vander, you've been awfully quiet over there. Care to join in? Tell me how much I'm blowing it?"

"I think," Vander said with a slow, precise drawl, "that we should let her speak for herself."

As he spoke, a shadow snaked across the dining room floor, and reached into the darkness of the hallway around my feet, drawing me forward into the room.

Three sets of eyes looked up at me, each loving and pitying in their own ways. The fourth, Vander's, was not visible. His back was to me, his attention aimed away from the group and toward a small window off to the side. There was no possible way he could have seen me listening in the hallway. He'd told me after the incident in the woods that he'd heard me, *felt me* in the forest. I didn't understand how that was possible, but I was starting to believe that there was more to his magic than what I grasped.

I shook my head, realizing my gaze was drilling into his rigid, muscular back. I forced myself to meet the other eyes watching me carefully.

"Uh, hi," I said awkwardly.

Aerie offered me an amused smile. "Let's get you some breakfast. You must be famished after everything that happened last night. Eat first, then we can talk."

She hustled out of the room and into the kitchen to prepare me a plate. I lingered by the hallway a moment longer before taking a seat at the table, suddenly feeling self-conscious. When I finally seated myself, I let my eyes drift around the room. Bastian was still seething, his arms tense and awkward as he simmered in the corner, but he was trying to keep his cool now that I was here. Lennox leaned against the opposite wall of Bastian, picking at his nails with a look of indifference across his face. My eyes finally landed on Vander, the one whose gaze I'd been avoiding, the one whose gaze I wanted to see most of all.

He'd turned away from his perch at the window, leaning against the wall and watching me closely. Even as he stood there, his body swayed toward me as if he was drawn to me, couldn't help but be near me. His eyes were two obsidian stones, though, firm and unyielding as he took me in. The gold in them was barely visible this morning. His arms were folded across his chest, the same chest I'd nuzzled against last night after he'd saved me, only this time he was clothed. Heat rose into my cheeks, giving away my embarrassment at the memory. His face betrayed no emotion, his features just as stone-cold as his eyes. I could have sworn, though, that as my gaze met his—as I remembered the feel of his warm skin against mine when he'd carried me back to the estate—the corner of his lip twitched, tipping up ever so slightly into something like a smirk.

It was gone a heartbeat later.

"Hazel," he greeted me with the smallest of nods. "Glad to see you're feeling better this morning."

CHAPTER 34
HAZEL

All eyes were on me as I carefully picked at my breakfast. Usually, I'd be devouring the bacon in two bites and grabbing for seconds, but I felt more than awkward trying to eat while everyone else sat and waited. I was torn between just pushing the food away and demanding they talk or continuing with my breakfast in a painstakingly slow manner, weary of whatever it was we were about to discuss.

After another painful minute of silence, I laid my fork down.

"Can we just get on with it? I can't eat with all of you ogling me like this."

I could sense the amusement creeping across Vander's face from his seat next to me and it took everything in me not to snap a snide comment at him. I could feel the heat rising in my cheeks just at the thought of his gaze burrowing into me, and I sent out a silent prayer that he didn't notice.

Thankfully, Aerie leaned in. "How are you feeling after last night?"

Embarrassment stirred within me as I looked down at my lap. I knew this was what we'd be talking about. I'd just hoped I wouldn't have such a large audience as we discussed the nightmare that was last night.

"Okay, I guess. It almost doesn't feel real, like some sort of fever dream."

Memories pulled on my mind like the icy water of the lake. I tried my best to repress a shudder, the weight on my body feeling eerily similar to what I'd felt going under the surface last night, thick and heavy and impossible to hold up.

"Do you remember anything about a creature called the Wisps?"

Bastian spoke this time. His question almost made me laugh. He was still so confident that I'd remember something, anything from here. His hopefulness was almost an encouragement, if I hadn't found it so annoying. I didn't know how many more ways I could explain that I had absolutely no memory of anything from this place.

I simply shook my head and waited for him to continue. He folded his bare arms across the leather vest that hung from his chest. The tunic underneath was rolled at the sleeves to allow those dark inky marks a chance to peek out.

I could have sworn the smallest bit of disappointment played at his features, but he didn't let it linger as he continued, "That's what you encountered last night. They are a type of old magic, a breed of faerie that roams the Dark Woods and preys on troubled souls. Calling them out to the Depths until they consume them completely."

His words wrapped around me, sending a chill up my spine as the thoughts from last night still rippled through my mind, haunting me. A lump formed in the back of my throat.

"So it was them that I heard? Not my own thoughts, but theirs that drew me to the lake?"

My voice was quiet. I would never admit what I'd heard, what I'd thought and said to myself, about myself. I had to know though, if it had been my own dark desires that pulled me out to the water last night, or the magic of the Wisps.

"Right," Bastian said with a sort of finality.

Aerie threw him a disapproving glance from where she sat before turning back to me and reaching across the table to hold my hand. "The magic is what called you out there last night. But the Wisps cannot conjure something that is not already there. Whatever you heard, whatever you experienced—it had to already exist within you in order for the Wisps to manipulate it. They look for the fractured and hurting and prey on those pieces we bury deep down, hoping that nobody will ever see them. They take that darkness and echo it tenfold in our minds in an effort to bring their victims out and convince them to journey to the Depths. So to answer your question, yes and no. Their magic called to you, but it was your own struggles you wrestled with in the Dark Woods last night."

Somehow that was even less comforting than believing it had been entirely them or entirely me. It felt like dark magic, like something that no one should be able to do. It felt like Kahlis. Refusing to linger on the truth it revealed about me, I veered the conversation in a different direction.

"You said they were a type of faerie? I thought you said the fae were rare."

"They are," Aerie agreed. "Back when our world was created, the fae ruled abundantly. They were the most powerful creatures and most were not kind with that power. Mortals were taken from their realm and enslaved here, held in brutal captivity. Creatures with lesser power were looked down on and lived a life of poverty and torment. It was a cruel world. A harsh one, even for the fae, because violence and chaos ran rampant. We were at war constantly. Despite being immortal creatures, death was everywhere."

She paused, her hand falling slack in mine as her mind lingered somewhere distant. She gave her head a quick shake before she continued, "The Fates weren't the only gods of that time—I've mentioned one of them to you before. But when the old gods and goddesses started to die off... when the land itself started to die off, the Fates stepped in. They offered the gift of magic to those who did not have it and forced those who did to abide by the laws of nature in order to use it. It was the first and only time they have intervened in our world. They tore down the border between realms and brought the most powerful kingdoms to ashes. It leveled the playing field, allowed order and peace an opportunity to flourish. Mortals began mating with fae and other magical creatures until the fae as a whole were practically extinct and the mortals died out completely.

"In their place rose a new breed entirely: something no longer mortal but also not quite fae. I think that was the Fates' intention all along, to make a world where not one kind of magic held rule and rank, but one where many lineages and types of magic were respected and treated like a gift. Despite their efforts, some of the old magic still lingers, mostly hiding in the Dark Woods."

Bastian stepped forward, leaning against the table next to Aerie as he took over the conversation: "That's how the tribes came to be. They ensure that order and balance remain. That's why each tribe has a purpose, and together we govern to enforce the laws that have been put in place to protect the land and its inhabitants, to ensure the old magic does not grow too powerful. Because, while magic is a gift, it also leaves a mark, and it is our duty to care for and protect it and its source."

I couldn't help but notice how Vander shifted in his seat beside me, crossing his arms so that the marks on his skin were no longer visible. Bastian's own marks flexed against his skin as his arm stayed firmly planted against the table, holding his weight. I let my eyes trail the pathways of ink, the intricate pattern of something resembling roots and vines.

"And that's why you have the marks on you?" I said, utterly in awe. "The imprint of whatever magic you've been gifted?"

I let my gaze fall from Bastian's markings before subconsciously drawing my eyes to my bare skin.

Lennox sat on my other side, watching my movements and no doubt taking note of the inference I'd made while looking at my pale, unmarked arms. He'd been uncharacteristically quiet this morning. One of his legs was draped casually across the other, his face the picture of indifference—until now. He suddenly sat up straighter, uncrossing his legs.

"The marks appear once we come into our powers, as we leave adolescence and enter adulthood," he explained. "You're still young. Your lack of markings is not a sign of your abilities."

"Or lack thereof," I muttered under my breath.

A small, knowing smile played at Aerie's lips from across the table, but she didn't press me further. I supposed everything they were telling me was stuff I would have learned if I had actually invested time into the endless pile of reading waiting for me back in the library, instead of sulking around the estate as I had done for the past week. Silently, I chastised myself for not prioritizing the reading. In a land where all sorts of dark power lurked, it seemed like learning and understanding the threats that existed should have been high on my to-do list.

Aerie's soft voice broke me from my silent criticism. "You've been through so much in such a short amount of time. It's natural for you to feel confused and hurt and even be struggling with it all. We had thought maybe giving you space was best, but now I'm wondering if a different approach would be better."

I eyed her cautiously, waiting for her to continue.

"I think..." she started. "I think working on your mental blocks would be best. I can help break them down and dig for whatever is left of your memories. That is, if you'll allow me. It would be the best defense against Kahlis, teaching you how to keep him out. And it would help with the other things you're struggling with as well."

I hadn't the slightest idea what working on my *mental blocks* entailed, but the subtle *tap tap tap* in my mind was answer enough that she was probably right. His presence was growing stronger, especially after last night. Suddenly, I realized how much of a fool I'd been for not telling them sooner. Unease settled in my chest as I tried to find the courage to admit the presence I'd felt lingering in my mind ever since Kahlis' first attack.

"Actually," I ventured, "there's something you should know."

I pulled my hand back from Aerie, dropping my head toward my lap again for fear of seeing their reactions when I told them.

"I can feel him. In here." I tapped at my temple as I spoke; my words were heavy and quiet. "Ever since he dreamwalked to me, I've been able to feel him trying to pry his way back in."

Silence hung around us. I wrung my hands nervously, waiting for them to respond, but no words ever came. I slowly forced my head up as I swallowed around the lump in my throat, ready to take in the frustration and anger I was sure would be waiting for me. Instead, I was met with pale faces, leached of color. They were shocked—if not terrified—but not angry.

"I'm sorry I didn't say anything," I added before anyone could speak. "I was just so scared to admit he was really there. The wards are working, I think. He hasn't been able to get through."

"Not well enough," Aerie admitted. "If you can still feel him, then he still holds power over you. For all we know, he could have sent the Wisps to you last night. It's just a matter of time before he finds a way to slip through. That's probably why the tea hasn't been helping you sleep as much at night."

I wondered what else she'd silently observed over the past few days. My eyes darted nervously to Vander, praying he wouldn't betray the more intimate details of our night together. As if in response, I felt a sudden rush of heat as Vander fixed me with an intense stare.

Out of the corner of my eye, I noticed Bastian's features give way from shock to anger as he cocked his head toward Vander.

"Have you felt him?"

Why would he be asking Vander that?

Vander leveled his gaze to Bastian, gritting his teeth. I could feel the reluctance in his answer, like he was admitting to something he didn't want voiced.

"No." The single word slipped through his clenched jaw, irritation radiating from him.

"Okay, let me rephrase. Have you *tried?*"

The brothers sat in a sudden and visceral silence. Vander folded his arms over his chest, the air charging with an inexplicable energy. His boot drummed against the floor of the dining room in a rhythmic *tap tap tap* of annoyance at Bastian's question.

I was caught in the middle of some silent argument that I did not understand. Aerie rolled her eyes as she sat back, waiting for them to finish whatever battle was taking place.

Finally, Vander's incessant tapping came to a stop as he leaned his elbows against the edge of the table. "I'm not having this conversation right now, brother."

"Why not?" Bastian's voice rose. "Are the stakes not high enough for you? Are the risks not worth it? You could help with this!"

"It's not your decision to make." Vander pushed his chair back and stood.

"It's not yours either," Bastian bit back.

Lennox was smirking next to me. He leaned over, his voice low enough that only I could hear. "I love it when mommy and daddy fight."

He gave me a little wink as he plucked a piece of bacon from my abandoned plate and leaned back in his chair, tearing into the strip of meat as he casually crossed his legs again.

"Bastian, I'm warning you," Vander growled. Shadows snaked out around his tense body, as if to deepen the threat. "Leave it alone."

"She deserves to know!" Bastian threw his hands up in an exasperated manner, his eyes turning wide and wild in the height of his frustration.

My back stiffened. Gooseflesh covered my arms and I slowly turned my head toward Vander.

A muscle in Vander's jaw ticked as he stared down Bastian. Bastian recoiled slightly, as he realized what he'd done, but he stood his ground, refusing to let it go.

A low whistle sounded from the seat beside me.

"You still haven't told her, brother? That's messed up."

Lennox's sarcastic tone rang through the air, but I couldn't take my eyes off Vander. He'd told me last night that he'd heard me, *felt* me in the Dark Woods. I hadn't understood it then; I'd been too exhausted to truly question him about it. My mind raced, thinking of all the times in the last week I'd wondered if my thoughts weren't entirely my own. I thought of the night I dreamwalked inside the mind of the terrifying, if not slightly gorgeous, creature in front of me. I thought of the echo of my name on the wind, calling me into the wilderness, away from Arlo. The final piece of the puzzle settled into place in my mind.

My voice was quiet but firm when I finally spoke.

"Tell me what they're talking about."

Then, as if to test the theory brewing somewhere within me, I let a single word radiate through my mind.

Now.

Vander's face recoiled at my thought, his composure slipping for a fraction of a second as shock etched into the deep lines on his face. He stumbled back, so slightly I wasn't sure I hadn't just imagined it entirely, before pushing the chair out of his way and turning his back to Bastian.

Vander's face had gone utterly pale, but he refused to let his composure slip. "This conversation is over."

The only sound echoing through the dining room was the fall of his footsteps as he made his way down the hall and out the door.

"Well." Lennox's cheery voice broke the silence as he clapped his hands together and stood. "That was painfully awkward to watch. Might I suggest we table this discussion for a later date? I have a filthy Deaomi calling my name and I've decided on some explicitly cruel ways I'd like to torment him, so if we're done here." He patted me on the shoulder as he made his way out.

I looked at the plate of food sitting in front of me, no doubt cold by now. It didn't matter: my stomach had turned and I couldn't bring myself to take another bite.

"As if I don't already have enough on my plate," Bastian murmured under his breath, storming out.

I had heard from Aerie about Bastian being held up at the border, but I didn't notice until he made his way around the table the blood that covered his clothing or the exhaustion under his eyes. He must have come straight here this morning from his position at the the borders. I suddenly realized I was staring, and forced my gaze to stay trained on the table instead. I was sure I didn't want to know the extent of what he'd been through the last several days, but nausea sunk low in my gut as I realized that there was likely a sinister reason for his absence around the estate when I'd left to follow the Wisps last night.

Only Aerie lingered, watching and waiting for me to make a move. I couldn't though: I was paralyzed, my mind running in endless circles trying to make sense of what I'd just realized.

"When you're ready to talk, I'll be here." She patted my hand as she stood and grabbed the plate of food. "And if you want to take me up on my offer to work on your mental blocks, you know where to find me."

She turned to make her way back to the kitchen but lingered for a moment by the doorway.

"If I could suggest something." Her voice was soft, reassuring and full of love. "Go talk to him. Neither of you will get anywhere if you both keep avoiding each other. Bastian may have spoken out of turn, but his advice was not off base. And I don't think Vander is capable of making the first move. Not right now."

She tapped her fingers idly on the frame of the door, watching for a moment longer to be sure I'd heard her, before disappearing into the kitchen.

He had been the one to make the first move though, hadn't he?

I thought about what he'd admitted to me last night, how he'd so tenderly cared for me, revealing a different side of himself in the process.

I stood from the table, my hands trailing along the polished wood as I made my way toward the direction Vander had stormed off.

Aerie was right. I needed to talk to him. I didn't care who was making the first move anymore. I was done playing games. I just needed answers, and he would give them to me, one way or the other.

CHAPTER 35
HAZEL

I stormed out of the house and into the bright morning sunlight. The heat was already growing to an uncomfortable level and I was suddenly thankful for the lightweight dress he'd left out for me, even if it was blowing hard in the wind and making it difficult for me to run after him. I shaded my eyes with my hand as I looked out across the open fields, searching for Vander. Off in the distance, I could make out his tall form stalking toward the Dark Woods. Shadows were snaking around him as he walked, indicating just how upset he was.

It didn't matter. He wasn't going to get away from me that easily.

I took off toward him, hoping to reach him before he dipped beyond the tree line. No matter how badly I wanted answers, I wasn't sure I was ready to step foot back into those woods quite yet. I shouted after him, despite knowing he had already sensed my presence. He didn't slow though, his stubbornness winning the battle within him.

I shouted at him again and again as I closed the distance between us.

"Hey, asshole," I spat.

He paused at my crude language, the words apparently shocking him enough to finally wait for me.

I grabbed his arm, forcing him to turn to me. "Tell me what that was."

He began walking again, easily slipping out of my grasp as a smirk slid over his face. "It's nothing, little spitfire, go back to the house. I'm sure Aerie has use for you somewhere."

It was an effort to keep up with him, my short legs not offering nearly as much strength as he had. It didn't stop me from trying.

"I have no interest in what Aerie has use of," I threw back. "I have interest in you."

He raised an eyebrow at me without slowing his pace. "Is that so?"

I rolled my eyes as I stomped through the foliage, trying to keep up with his wide strides. "That's not what I meant. You owe me some answers. You don't get to just storm off like that."

"Oh, but see, that's exactly what I'm doing, little spitfire."

"Stop calling me that!"

He slowed his steps, letting me catch my breath. "Then stop being so emotional. Though, I do find it rather adorable."

Rage fumed as I huffed, breathless from trying to catch up to him. He put up a good facade; it would be easy to say that he was completely unbothered by the morning's events. I knew the truth though; I'd seen the shock and anger on his face when he'd walked out of the dining room.

"You aren't going to get out of this, Vander. No amount of pighead-edness or insufferable sarcasm is going to distract me. I'm not going to let it go."

He stood in front of me, arms crossed and eyes cold. He glowered, his mouth setting into a hard line and betraying his true emotions. After a minute of silent evaluation, he turned and began walking again.

I stared after him, shock and irritation rooting my feet to the ground.

He is impossible.

"If it's answers you want," he called out over his shoulder, "then I suggest you try and keep up." He stopped short for just a moment as he looked back at me. "Little spitfire."

I clenched my jaw in irritation as I forced my feet forward. I didn't even try to be graceful about it as I stomped after him through the trees. I didn't know where he was taking me, and he was annoyingly skilled at staying just out of reach. I cursed my short, weak legs as I pushed them to catch up, but it was no use. No matter how badly I wanted to be, I wasn't in control anymore. We were on his territory now and there was no keeping up with the shifter as he made his way through the trees he called home. I could walk away now and avoid this whole conversation, avoid running the risk of him losing his temper and turning that rage on me out here in the seclusion of the Dark Woods. But I still wanted the truth—*needed* the truth. More than I needed to keep my distance or ensure my safety. Ignoring the burning in my legs, I pushed on after him. It was time to get answers.

I stumbled in his wake as we made our way down the tree line. I let loose a sigh of relief when I realized we weren't going further into the Dark Woods; but after several minutes of trailing along the border, I started to wonder if he'd chosen this path simply so he could laugh at me trying to navigate the overgrown roots and tricky foliage. Several times I broke from the tree line and back into the warm morning sunlight in an effort to catch my breath and give my exhausted legs a break, but the hemlock trees were too thick and heavy to see Vander when I did. Eventually, I gave up trying to find an easier way around the woods and just conceded to the path Vander was weaving, huffing and puffing along the way. His movements were smooth like silk, his body simply flowing from one stride to the next as he navigated the woods. He made no noise as he climbed over the enormous roots and slipped in between trees. Not even the snap of a twig or the rustle of leaves sounded beneath his feet. I, on the other hand, was a noisy, breathless mess.

I could hear him chuckling up ahead, but he never once turned to watch me or make sure I was keeping up.

Arrogant ass.

By the time he slowed his steps and stopped at the edge of a clearing, I'd already come up with a whole slew of insults to throw at him.

Glowering at his back, I mumbled, "If this is your idea of a practical joke, I'm going to hit you so hard."

He smirked as he leaned against one of the gigantic hemlocks, taking in my exhausted form. My breath was ragged as I leaned over, my hands falling to my knees as I greedily sucked down the warm, damp air of the woods.

"You need to start training. You never know when you're going to have to rely on your body's strength to protect yourself. And looking at you right now, I'd say you'd be dead in two minutes if you ever had to."

I peered up at him from where I leaned over, still unable to fully catch my breath. I didn't even have the energy to strike back, so I just threw him an obscene gesture as I panted.

"Make that one minute," he corrected as his eyes trailed down my pathetic body, before shaking his head at me and pushing off the tree, closing the space between us. My eyes widened as I overcorrected myself and stumbled back, nearly tripping. He caught me by the arm and pulled me forward.

"Hands up," he said as he gently lifted my wrists above my head. "Stand up straight, keep your arms up like this. There you go. That will allow your lungs to fully open as you breathe. You'll recover faster that way."

I wanted to rip my arms out of his grasp and tell him I didn't need his help, but after just a few breaths in the new position, I could already feel a difference. That made me hate him even more. Who was he to drag me out here, to infiltrate my thoughts and mind, and then have the audacity to try and help me? I didn't need his help. I didn't need anything from him other than the answers he still hadn't given me. I glared at him openly as my breathing slowly regulated, thinking of all the ways I wanted to hurt him.

He tried and failed to hide the smile tugging at the edge of his lips as he watched me. "Arrogant ass, am I?"

My face went from rage to shock as he repeated my own thoughts back to me.

"Are you ever going to explain how you can do that or are you just going to keep freaking me out?"

He thought for a moment, the mask of stone he typically wore slipping away to reveal a cool amusement beneath, before he turned on his heels in that annoyingly smooth way he always did.

"I'll think about it," he answered with a shrug. "First I want to show you something."

I stomped after him, fully intending to rip him a new one for still avoiding my questions. But as we slipped past the tree line and into the little clearing, my mouth gaped open, the words on the tip of my tongue forgotten as I realized where we were. In front of us, all around the small clearing, were uprooted and decaying trees. It looked like the heart of some dark explosion of power. It looked like Vander's dream.

"Is this…" I started, my body turning slowly as I took in the extent of the damage to the woods around us. "Is this where it happened?"

I tried to find words to specify what I was referring to, but as my head turned to find him once again, I knew I didn't need to.

The emotions were covering every inch of his face, the agony and grief and rage all fighting for dominance as he looked back at me. In an instant, it was like I was back in that dream, watching him fall to his knees on the forest floor. The pain I felt as I looked at him was a dagger in my chest.

He didn't answer my question. He didn't have to.

I forced my eyes away from the devastated landscape, desperate to understand what kind of power could leave such a mark. Instead, I made my way to where he stood in the middle of the clearing. He didn't look to the flattened trees, or to the disrupted earth around us.

He was focused solely on me.

"I haven't been back here since it happened." His voice was quiet, so much like it had been the night before when he helped wash away the haunting remnants of the lake from my cold, shaking hands. "It was too hard to come back here. To remember how you were torn from my arms and there was nothing I could do to stop it. Reliving it in my dreams every night was enough of a reminder, enough of a torment."

A cloud of darkness ebbed around him. I didn't know what to say, how to help him. I couldn't remember the night I was taken, but I could feel his pain. I'd felt it in the dream and I could feel it now. I reached out a tentative hand, letting it fall softly against his forearm in an attempt to comfort him.

His arm tensed at my touch, the muscles in his body going rigid.

"That was the day I earned that," he said softly.

His words confused me, until I noticed my hand had somehow landed on one of the strange markings on his skin. I'd meant my gesture to be comforting, but I realized I'd somehow been tracing it subconsciously, as if it called to me. He had several marks similar to that of his brother's, inky black roots winding up his arm to signify his place in the Tribe of Talamh, but this one had always perplexed me. It was so different from any I'd seen on Bastian.

My forehead creased as I concentrated on the jagged markings my fingers were tracing over. It was a brand of sorts, his skin feeling rough and raised beneath the markings. A bold circle with hard lines jutting out in all directions was surrounded by a crescent moon, and in the middle sat a sunken skull, tying it all together in one dark mark. Not just a sun or a moon or a skull, not three separate things, but one solid creation to signify whatever it was that he had gone through, whatever magic now coursed through his veins because of it.

"What does it mean?" I cocked my head, examining it more thoroughly.

Vander abruptly pulled his arm away, tucking it slightly behind his back to obscure my view.

"The Mark of the Grimm. Shadow is born in the presence of both light and dark. It's a curse and a promise to make me repay for the lengths I went to try and save you."

I stared at him blankly, not fully understanding. I could feel the power radiating behind it, though—could sense the darkness lingering in his words. It was nothing good. Something Bastian had said earlier that day snaked its way through my memory.

"Magic may be a gift, but it always leaves a mark." The words slipped through my lips, almost absent-mindedly. His shadows danced around him as if in answer to my statement.

Vander nodded slightly as I let my eyes linger on his now half-hidden arm.

"What did you do, for the magic to leave that kind of a mark?" My curiosity was getting the best of me.

He let his eyes fall from me before he answered, "It doesn't matter. It didn't work."

What kind of magic could be that dark and still not work to save me?

Before I could say anything else, he started walking to the far end of the clearing.

He moved quickly, as if unable to linger on the topic any longer. "This isn't why I brought you out here, though."

Without any more explanation, I followed as he strolled to the other side of the woods and back into the thick canopy of branches.

Off in the distance, I noticed a cozy stone cottage tucked between the trees. It was overgrown by the foliage of the forest and long abandoned, but it was warm and inviting nonetheless. The roof was covered in a thick, dark moss and a beautiful green ivy weaved its way up one of the sidewalls. The door had a crescent moon window set within it, and though the paint was old and peeling, it still radiated a deep slate blue hue. It felt somehow familiar, though I couldn't remember why.

He turned back to me, walking backward toward the house with frustrating ease. He didn't even so much as stumble over the tricky terrain.

"I thought you should see your home, the home you grew up in."

For the hundredth time today, I felt the air escape my lungs, leaving my chest empty and burning. My eyes went wide as I looked to him, then to the house behind him. My feet carried me to the door, the small porch full of overgrowth, before I'd even realized I was moving. I placed a hand on the wall of the cottage, the rough-cut stone cool to touch.

Home.

The word felt foreign to me. I couldn't imagine growing up here, sitting on the porch or playing in the woods surrounding it. I'd just assumed I had lived at the estate, with how Aerie talked about Vander and I growing up together. I would have never imagined I had an actual house here. I let my fingers run over the little moon window, wiping the thick grime from it so I could peer inside. I couldn't make out much, the window far too dirty from years of neglect. I turned back to Vander to ask if we could go inside but stopped short as I noticed the wildflowers growing along the sides of the house.

Yarrow. So much yarrow.

Tears stung my eyes as my throat tightened around the lump forming there.

Of course there would be yarrow growing here.

Vander stepped forward, close enough to reach out and touch me, comfort me, if he'd wanted to—but he didn't. He stood and watched, letting me process the emotions crashing through my mind in wave after endless wave, as I took in the beautiful scene.

My voice was rough when I finally spoke, hoarse and ragged with the tears I was trying to hold back. "I don't think I remember it."

"That's okay," Vander answered, but I could tell the hint of disappointment in his tone, threatening to betray him. "Even if you couldn't remember it, I thought you should see it."

He gently took my hand, his touch feeling electric as the roughness of his fingers rubbed against mine. He shoved against the door a couple times before it finally gave way, no doubt stuck with years of neglect.

I took a deep breath, then we stepped into the darkness.

CHAPTER 36
HAZEL

I couldn't hold back the torrent of tears as I looked around the house, my house. It was like stepping back in time, to weeks or even months ago—before any of the chaos that was this magical world had come into my life. I might not remember my childhood here, but I knew the house well. I knew the faded armchair in the living room that I'd spent countless days splayed across, buried within a book. I knew the kitchen where I'd eaten countless meals and enjoyed endless cups of tea.

This was our home—Arlo's and mine. The image of him standing there not even two weeks ago flashed across my mind, his head bent and hair falling in his face as he made me a cup after a particularly rough night. I pushed forward into the cottage, longing to be back in a familiar place.

A chill settled over my skin, despite the musty feel of the air. It was eerie being here, returning to the only home I knew, but not really returning. The house was so similar, so much like the one Arlo and I had occupied together, but the longer I took it in, the more evidence I saw of a different life lived within these walls. There was an emptiness here, a void, and it forced a shiver down my spine as I pressed my palm to my cheek, catching a single tear as it made its way down the side of my face.

I dragged my eyes across the living room, making note of the things that stood out from my memories. I moved to a nearby bookshelf full of familiar stories I'd spent my days reading in Arlo's home—no, *my* home. I realized as I ran my fingers over the spines that every book I had ever borrowed from the library back with Arlo was sitting here on these shelves. I picked up a particularly well-used children's book about an elf named Willow. Willow Meyers. The illustration of the mousey creature on the front cover sent a chill creeping over my skin as I recalled the kind, shy lady at the Guard's office who had snuck my record to me. Her bravery and kindhearted help had been the reason I'd found my way back here, having handed me the map that would eventually take me to this world. Yet, she hadn't even been real. Just a distant memory of some book I must have loved as a child. I couldn't remember it, but the sentimentality was a strong presence in my mind and I tucked the book back gingerly on the shelf, careful not to damage the already fragile binding.

If she had been nothing more than a storybook character, then what did that say about Arlo? Another bolt of pain pierced my heart, turning away from the books and searching desperately for something else to focus on. The scene as a whole tugged at something distant in my mind, something outside of my life here with him. I tried to place it, but it was too far off, too buried in the recesses of my mind to be able to unearth it. All I could remember was an overwhelming sadness as I examined the room and looked to the empty couch, to the table beside it littered with little amber bottles, overturned, dried out, and long-abandoned from their intended purpose.

Something caught my attention amongst the bottles on the table, a small leatherbound book. The leather was faded and cracking with age. The binding was coming undone; it looked almost too fragile to handle. I moved to pick it up but caught sight of the bedroom first. I shoved my way out of the sitting area, closing the distance toward the singular bedroom and away from the coffee table in three desperate strides, knowing already what I'd find in there. It didn't stop me from searching, eyes wide with panic as I let them take in every inch of the room once. Then again for good measure. I'd almost expected to find him sitting there, waiting for me and smiling at some secret joke I hadn't been let in on, but there was no sign of him here. No proof that he'd ever existed outside of whatever imaginary world I'd been trapped in. The bathing room was tucked into the far corner, its presence a dark reminder of my ever-constant struggles, the sleepless nights I'd spent within its four walls as I tried to push out the nightmares taking over my mind. It was our home, Arlo's and mine, despite not seeing a single trace of him here. I couldn't think of it any other way.

I backed out of the room and stopped just within the doorframe, unable to stand another moment in the dark, empty space. Within seconds I was transported back to that bedroom Arlo and I had left behind as we ventured into the woods, on a journey to find answers about who I was. I supposed I had found them now, but it didn't help to numb the pain of losing Arlo in the process. I couldn't be in the room, *our* room. I couldn't bring myself to sit upon the bed against the opposite wall, to run my hands over the soft linens now dirtied with age—not when that space was ours, and he wasn't here to experience it with me.

Vander's presence hovered behind me. He didn't speak, didn't ask any questions, no doubt assuming the tears I shed were for some distant childhood, lost along with the rest of my memories. He'd be wrong, though. I had long since begun to realize that the world I'd just come from, the world I'd left Arlo in, had been compiled of indistinct, gray monotony—and the very few pieces of it that I'd loved had truly just been small beacons of lights from my past, a way to guide me back to reality and call me home.

The realization was oddly comforting while simultaneously gut-wrenching. This whole time, even on my darkest days, my subconscious had been trying to tell me where I truly belonged.

How was I so easily deceived?

I became suddenly aware of Vander's presence, that I was not alone.

"Are you listening to my thoughts right now?" I accused, tilting my head toward him. I couldn't bring myself to look at him, though—not until I found out what he could hear.

"No." The answer was more like a growl of frustration. "It's not a constant connection, at least not anymore."

My only reply was a firm, singular nod. *Good.* He didn't need to hear this confession, didn't need to know how thoroughly I'd been deceived even after days of acknowledging the trick that had been played against me. It was humiliating to understand the depths of the lies I'd believed, to still feel like, despite everything I knew now, that maybe it had somehow been real.

"But I can feel you," Vander amended softly. "I can feel the pain you're feeling. And it's tearing me apart that I can't do anything about it."

His words chilled me to the core. Within an instant his body was behind mine, his chest close enough to brush against my back with each breath he took. With painstaking precision, he moved his arms around me and unfolded my hands from where they clasped at my chest. He slowly nudged my body to move, to turn to face him. Even as I did, I couldn't bring my eyes to his.

"Do you want to know why I call you *little spitfire?*" He guided my back against the doorframe as he leaned over me. He lifted his hand to my face, wiping away the stream of tears now sliding down my cheek. His face was so close to mine, I could feel his warm breath dancing over my skin. "Because your emotions are so raw, so strong. They're a tangible entity and when I feel them, it's all I can do to keep from falling to my knees as they wash over me. Do you know how hard it is, to sense everything you do? To feel the cascade of endless emotion that's not even my own? To not be able to do anything about it?"

I didn't dare look at his face, to see the way he was no doubt looking at me. I kept my eyes trained solely on his chest as it rose and fell in a steady, hypnotic rhythm.

"I could feel your pain when you walked in here, could feel you shut down and push me away. Just as I can feel you now, your heartbeat racing and your curiosity growing. Tell me, little spitfire, what is it that you're so curious about?"

"How?" The word was rough against my throat, my voice unrecognizable. "How are you able to sense my emotions, hear my thoughts?"

His breathing slowed, tension rippling through his body with my question. It was only after a long moment of silence that I forced myself to look up at him, forced myself to demand answers.

With his body so close to mine, it was a struggle to see him. I'd known he'd been tall, but so few times had he been this close for me to truly acknowledge his size. It made me swallow hard as I arched my back to get a better look at his face. I expected the usual mask of stone, features void of all emotion, but what I found was so different. He looked at me with a tenderness that I'd never imagined him capable of, but it was more than that, too; there was real pain there, pain like what I was feeling in this house—pain from having lost the one you love.

Maybe we were more alike than I realized.

"You told me you'd give me answers if I came with you today."

My words were a challenge, a reminder of what he'd promised.

He pushed off the door frame from where he'd been leaning over me and scrubbed a hand down his face. Apprehension wrestled across his features as he put space between us. The silence in the house was deafening as I waited for him to answer, but no answer came.

I let out a frustrated breath, turning my head back to the dark bedroom.

"I don't get it," I said, relinquishing hope. "I don't get any of it. The way you can read me. The way Aerie can heal and you and Bastian can shift. The way I'm completely helpless to Kahlis invading my mind... I don't understand the magic. I don't understand how it works and I hate it with every fiber of my being."

I tried to stop talking, to hold back the dam that had seemingly broken—but the words just kept coming:

"I'm tired of feeling powerless, like the helpless victim at the whim of whatever magical being I stumble upon. I miss my home. I miss Arlo. I miss the safety I had there. Maybe I didn't know who I was, but at least I felt *safe*." I choked on a sob as the words rushed out of me.

A muscle in his jaw ticked. "I suppose if it was up to you, you'd just scurry back to your male in that little make-believe prison. Hide there in ignorance and deny all of the answers you've so desperately been trying to find. It may have been safer, but it wasn't real. And it robbed you of that power within you, crippled you in the process of keeping you hidden. If you truly believe you are powerless, then you are believing a lie."

My body went rigid at his accusation.

"And *I* suppose that would make you mad. After all, you worked so hard to get your precious Hazlenn back," I argued, letting pure venom run through my words. I wanted him to see my pain, to see how deep those roots of disappointment went.

I stifled a squeal as he moved, quick as lightning, back over me.

"It would be quite... grating... to lose you again, Hazel. But make no mistake, I did what I did to save *you*. No matter what version of you that may be." Vander's eyes slid over my body in a primal way.

"You. Are. Enough." Each word was punctuated with force as they slipped through his gritted teeth, almost like it pained him to admit. "Not who you were before, not who you'll be in the future. You. Always and forever, you."

Something about his gaze sent my heart racing again, but for entirely different reasons. His shadows reached out around us, cloaking us in an even deeper darkness as if in response to the heat pooling in my core.

"It doesn't matter if you don't like what you found. It doesn't change the truth— doesn't change who you are." He lifted his head, something rolling through his body before he let a smirk settle across his lips. "Nor does it change the desire I feel growing within you right now."

I scoffed, trying to argue back. It wasn't fair that he could hide everything from me and I was as transparent as glass.

He cut me off, pressing in ever so slightly to bring my attention back to his eyes. "If it's safety you want, then it's safety you'll get. I promise I will do everything in my power to keep you safe, for however long you choose to stay here. Because it is *your* choice. I will be anything you need me to be, little spitfire, but you have to promise to keep fighting. You have to keep talking to me and not shut me out."

I tried to look at the house around us, but my eyes only met the darkness now ebbing from Vander. I needed to gather my thoughts, needed space to think about what all of this meant without the distracting scent of him permeating my senses. But he just smelled so damn good. I could get lost forever in that clove and citrus musk if I didn't force myself to concentrate. He was so close, so honed in on me and my emotions. And he was watching every inch of me in this secluded space he'd made for us. There was no point in trying to hide anything from him.

I'd been feeling a pull, a piece of the tether tying me to this world since before I got here. It had been with me all along, constantly nudging me back toward this place. It made sense, but more than that, it felt *right.* For once in my life, I just wanted to feel right. I wanted things to be easy and simple and I wanted to let my mind choose what it wanted. I was so tired of people telling me what was real and what wasn't. I was tired of feeling like an outsider, misunderstood and treated like a fragile piece of glass. Even Arlo, on his best days, had walked on eggshells around me.

Vander was different, though. He didn't do that. He didn't play it safe or act like I was powerless. If anything, he pushed me to be stronger, to fight harder. Even if said fighting was with him. No one had ever done that for me before. He pushed me to my limits but never past them. I'd felt terrified around him before, but now? I was starting to realize Aerie was right when she said that I was safe with him. He was here and real and felt like everything I'd ever wanted and more, even if that scared me.

I let out a shaky breath as I looked back up to Vander. His deep black eyes glowed with swirls of golden shadow.

"The past week has been one of the most confusing weeks of my life," I confessed, my voice shaking. "I have no idea anymore what is real and what's not. My memories are gone and the few I have, I'm starting to accept may in fact not be real. This...." I gestured around me, even though our bodies were still heavily cloaked in shadow. "This was the house I lived in, back in the other world. It's the same, down to the frayed tear in the armchair back in the living room."

A small laugh escaped my lips, the confession feeling strangely ridiculous as I said it out loud.

"I don't understand how. I can't make sense of it. It shouldn't be
possible and yet here it is." I shook my head in frustration, failing to find
the right words to explain everything racing through my mind. "I know
it sounds absurd, but some small part of me was holding out hope that
it had all been real. That I'd have something to return to, if I decided to
try and go back. Being here now, seeing it like this... it's a blunt, painful
knife piercing through that hope. It's a cruel example of how wrong I've
been."

I took a deep breath, trying to muster the courage to finish my
thought. "The fact is, I don't think there's anything for me to return
to, *anyone* out there waiting for me. How could I stand here and deny
it when the very house I thought I lived in for the past year was actually
from some fragment of a memory I don't even remember having, pulled
from the depths of my subconscious? How could I have been so naive?"

My body shuddered as I tried to suck down the musty air of the
cottage. I felt myself rambling, but I didn't know how to stop. Words
just kept coming; admitting to him the battle that had been raging in my
mind turned out to be as simple as breathing. I'd thought it would be
impossible to share, but it was the most freeing thing I'd done in a long
time.

"All I know," I continued, avoiding his gaze, "is that somehow, despite
being a world away and having no memories of my own, I was still being
called back to here."

My eyes finally rose to his as I leaned in slightly, even now feeling the
pull between us. "Maybe even back to you."

Hope sparked in his eyes as he searched my face for any hint of hesitation. When he found none, he slid his hand into my hair. Gripping

the nape of my neck, he tilted my face up toward his and moved in even closer. I could feel the movement of his lips, so close to my own.

"You have no idea how fucking long I've wanted to hear you say that."

His breath brushed ever so slightly across my lips as I leaned into him in response. Without another moment of hesitation, his lips crashed against mine. Every piece of doubt and worry fell away, replaced only by the feeling of him on me. I wanted him. I wanted this. I wasn't sure that anything had ever felt more right.

His mouth was warm with desire, the taste of him just as rich as his spicy scent that overpowered my senses as I breathed him in. His hand lingered in my hair for a moment, tugging slightly to keep my head tilted up and my mouth on his, before trailing down my side and grabbing at my hip, his other hand planted firmly against my lower back, refusing to allow even the slightest bit of room between us. My fingers bunched in his tunic as I grasped desperately for more. A small noise escaped me as I parted my lips, allowing his tongue to slip between them. It danced greedily over mine, as if he was claiming me as his own. As if in answer to my own noise, a deep, guttural growl vibrated against my body, the power behind it causing lightning to skip over my skin.

I could feel every ounce of longing in his movements. Every kiss, bite, lick showing me just how badly he needed me. We were lost to each other, the world around us completely gone as we became more entangled in one another. My knees gave way, lost to the desire pooling at my core. He didn't relinquish control, though. Instead, he grabbed my hips, lifting me slightly as he pushed his thigh between my legs to hold me up. The sensation only deepened the need within me.

His fingers slid up my thigh, bunching the cotton material of the dress he'd picked out for me and trailing across the skin on my hip, my stomach, pushing the fabric up. He ran a calloused thumb over the peak of my breast as I arched my back into him, a silent plea for more. I felt the smile spread across his lips as he kissed me.

"Do you like that, little spitfire?"

Words escaped me, my breath ragged and my mind incapable of forming an answer. When I tried and failed again to reply, I simply nodded against his cheek as he nipped and licked at my neck.

A barreling thunderclap shook the house around us, making me jump and pulling me out of the trance I'd been lost to. It was only then that Vander backed away, allowing my legs to find the ground once more. Our breathing was ragged, the noise filling the otherwise silent cottage.

"Shit," Vander bit out as he leaned to glance out the window. "Looks like a bad storm."

He turned back to me, desire radiating from his gaze. "As much as I'd love to keep you here and ride out the storm doing—well, a lot more of whatever that was"—his hand gestured to the doorframe I was still leaning against, trying to catch my breath—"we better get back. You shouldn't be outside the wards for too long. It's not safe."

The reminder of the constant threat against me was sobering, the need within me slipping away the more distance Vander put between us. I took several deep breaths as I turned my back against the haunting feel of the bedroom and made my way back into the main part of the house, following Vander's gaze out the window.

I gave the house one last, long look. He was right. It was time to go back to the estate. I grabbed his hand, lacing my fingers through his as he turned his attention away from the window and back to me.

I offered his hand a little squeeze, hoping he could feel every wild emotion coursing through my veins as I said, "Then let's go home."

CHAPTER 37
HAZEL

The rain poured down as we made our way through the woods and back to the estate. Luckily, the thick canopy of trees kept most of the rain at bay. It was easy enough to sidestep the steady streams of water as they found ways to break through the small gaps of the leaves and branches. The rich scent of petrichor filled the air and I took my time moving through the trees, closing my eyes and letting my head lob back to bask in the almost perfect ambiance around us. Vander's pace was slower this time, more patient as he waited for me to catch up. I knew by the way he grimaced at our steady steps that this speed was killing him. He didn't fight it though, didn't sneer or laugh as he helped me over the more difficult spots, now muddied by the rainwater breaking through.

Before I knew it we were back to the tree line, staring out at the estate beyond. It was barely visible through the torrential downpour.

"Ready?"

His question referred to more than just the trek through the rain to get back inside the house. Things had shifted between us, changed in a way I couldn't quite explain. It exhilarated me as much as it terrified me. I stayed for a moment longer, admiring the strong cut of his jaw as he surveyed the land before us, no doubt planning his exact movements to get back to the house as smoothly as possible.

When he noticed me staring, the corner of his lips turned up and heat rose to my cheeks. It wasn't embarrassment I felt, though. No, with him, I didn't have to be embarrassed or ashamed. I felt safe. I felt seen.

"Stop looking at me like that."

"Like what?" I asked, feigning innocence.

"You're going to have to keep a much tighter rein on your emotions if you want to try and hide them from me."

He spared me one last glance as his smirk tilted up into a full-blown smile, like he could tell exactly what kind of intimate thoughts were circling my mind right now.

Okay, now I'm embarrassed.

I shook my head slightly, trying to pull myself back to reality.

He took off into the rain, pulling at my hand as he went. I lunged into the storm, my feet slipping in the muddy grass as he half dragged me along. He let out a deep chuckle, a pure, raw noise that brought warmth to my cheeks as he quickly worked to help steady my feet before continuing the short run up to the side door of the house. Beneath the walkway between the kitchen and Aerie's greenhouse, we stopped to catch our breath. Despite the short distance between the woods and the estate, we were both soaked to the bone. I was no longer grateful for the white dress that clung to me in a wet, heavy mess. Its fabric had gone practically translucent from the rain. Droplets ran down my cheeks and through my hair as I tried to stop the laughter from stealing the air my lungs were trying to suck down.

Vander was laughing too, trying to wipe his face clean of the rainwater dripping off of him. He shook his head as he closed the distance between us. Grabbing at my waist, he pulled me close to him and swept the dripping clumps of hair away from my face.

"Your laugh may in fact be one of the most intoxicating sounds I've ever heard."

I blushed again, seemingly unable to keep the color out of my cheeks when I was around him. I tried to avert my gaze, find something else to focus on, but he didn't let me. He hooked a finger under my chin and brought my eyes back to his, lingering for a moment to study me. I knew there'd be questions and watching eyes as we made our way back inside. I didn't want to deal with that yet, so I let him pull me even closer as he made his way to kiss me one more time.

Suddenly, the door behind us burst open as Bastian stormed out, stopping short once he realized what he'd just interrupted.

"I—sorry, I didn't mean to intrude."

"Then why are you doing so?" Vander's words were laced with irritation as he turned his head to look at Bastian, not relinquishing even a whisper of space between us as he did.

Bastian's eyes darkened.

"Where the fuck have you been?" The tone in his words stunned me, concern and anger radiating through him.

"What's it matter to you? What has you in such a mood?" Vander's face remained casual, but he let go of me and turned his full attention to Bastian as he assessed his brother's worried movements.

"You're going to have to put whatever this is on hold." Bastian's body quaked with anger, or maybe it was fear? "We have a problem, brother. A big one."

Bastian's words spurred Vander into motion, pushing past him and gliding through the kitchen. Bastian followed in a powerful wake of frustration. I trailed behind them, utterly confused. Up ahead, I could hear Mirren and Lennox talking, their words eager and excited as they bustled around the living room. A third voice I didn't know sounded through the hall, one that seemed faintly similar to Lennox.

As we walked, I realized Kirwan must have finally returned. The thought brought a smile to my face, knowing how overjoyed Mirren had to be to have both of her brothers home at last. Her giddy laughs were an answer to my musings, causing my smile to grow as I made my way into the living room behind Bastian.

Both Bastian and Vander stopped short in front of me, their frames far too large for me to see beyond them. Vander's shadows grew around him as I felt his anger intensify.

Why would he be so angry about Kirwan's return?

I knew Bastian had been angry upon Lennox's return. Perhaps the reality of losing two spies had finally dawned on Vander, causing a similar reaction. Still, it didn't seem necessary. Mirren was so happy; how could he not find joy in her small giggles and excited movements? She was a little ray of sunshine dancing around the living room. Vander didn't need to bring her down by starting another argument about the twins' return.

I moved around him to say as much, opening my mouth to speak as the full length of the room came into view. The words fell away from me as I took in the other form standing across the way, the one Vander had been blocking with his shadows. My mind took several moments to catch up to what my eyes were seeing, treading through the heavy confusion that now swirled around me. He stood in front of me, no more than a few paces away and every bit as chivalrous as I remembered him being, broad-shouldered and firm in the middle of the room with that gentle gaze that had brought me back from the brink of hysteria time and time again. His honey eyes assessed me carefully, that golden hair falling slightly over his brow, just like it always did. My throat was raw, unable to voice what I was seeing.

"Arlo."

I staggered backward, Vander's rigid body the only thing keeping me from falling over.

"How—I..."

There was no way to form a cohesive thought as I took in the image of him standing before me.

Real. He is real.

Shock and joy poured from every part of me. All of those sleepless nights, all of those struggling moments, wondering if any of it had been real—it was all gone in the blink of an eye. He was here, no one could deny that now. A blinding rage took hold inside of me, overpowering me and making my knees buckle once again. It wasn't my own emotion I was feeling. I didn't understand how, but I could feel it building behind me, Vander's shadows growing along with it.

I glanced back at Vander, as stone-faced and rigid as ever. The joy I'd felt mere seconds ago was replaced with fear—fear that Vander wouldn't be able to contain that rage, fear that Arlo wouldn't want me anymore after everything that had happened to me here, fear that I no longer knew where I belonged or what I was supposed to do. My worlds were colliding and I didn't know how to even begin to process it.

He wasn't supposed to be real. They'd all convinced me he hadn't been.

I looked back to Arlo as I backed away from Vander and into the middle of the living room, into the middle of their standoff. It was only then that I noticed the similarities between them. A small gasp escaped my lips. I didn't know how I hadn't connected it sooner. Their features were so similar, their build mirror images of each other. The only difference between them was the shade of their hair, the glow of their eyes. Arlo was pure light to Vander's dark shadows. I covered my mouth with one of my trembling hands, as I gawked at them standing there, staring each other down.

"Seems like someone's got some explaining to do."

I vaguely registered Nox's words from somewhere behind me, his usual tone of sarcasm sounding just slightly off—slightly worried. The others must have noticed the same because an eerie type of stillness crept across the room.

Aerie stepped forward. I hadn't even noticed her presence in the room when I'd come in. I was thankful for her here now, her arms wrapping around me to help keep me from collapsing altogether.

"Vander, what did you do?" Her words were heavy, as if she already knew exactly what it was he had done.

Vander made no movement to answer her; he just continued to stand there like a statue. His hands balled into fists at his sides, the only hint at the rage still building within him. It was overwhelming, feeling him so fully. It threatened to pull me under, turning my vision red and demanding I put action to the emotions simmering beneath both of our skin, reaching a boiling point. I couldn't contain it. I needed an outlet for it before it crushed me completely.

"She asked you a question, brother."

Bastian made his way toward where Aerie and I stood. His hand rested against the battle ax strapped to his side, like he was preparing for the worst. I wasn't sure if he was more concerned about Arlo, the stranger in his home, or his own brother, whose darkness now consumed the entire half of the living room in which he stood. Some part of me noticed Kirwan and Nox shifting in the corner, backing away from the growing shadows and tucking Mirren behind them in a protective maneuver. They were all on edge—all sensing the threat in our midst—but I didn't understand what, or who, it was.

Slowly, Vander's gaze dragged across the room to where Aerie stood next to me.

"You already know what I did, Aermidh. Why bother asking?"

"I've had my suspicions." Her voice shook slightly, not with fear but raw emotion. "But I'd hoped you hadn't been stupid enough to actually do it."

Frustration spurred me into motion, the rage within me spilling out as I finally stepped forward, finding my voice.

"Can someone tell me what the fuck is going on?"

Silence fell over the room at the anger in my words. I was so tired of feeling like I was one step behind, never fully understanding the conversations going on around me. I'd felt darkness before, but this was different. This was hot, violent bloodlust and it would take and take if I let it out. I *wanted* to let it out, to feed it and watch it grow as it sought revenge for every pain I'd ever felt. I'd give it anything it wanted in order to feel like I had some sort of control over the current situation.

"He split his soul." Aerie's words were quiet in my ear as she pulled me back from the brink of that rage, wrapping me even further into her embrace. "In a desperate attempt to protect you when you were taken. He made a deal with Death itself and split his soul so it would attach to you."

Vander's gaze didn't leave me as he waited for my response, watching my every movement to gauge my reaction.

My eyes swept across the room to where Arlo stood. I expected his face to look as shocked as I felt. Instead, I found his gaze still fixed on Vander, silently assessing the creature before him.

Bastian's voice cut through the air, harsh and bitter. "*That's* how you got the Mark? Fuck, Vander, I knew it was bad, but I didn't know it was *this* bad. How could you do this? How could you not tell us?"

Bastian's nagging continued on, but the words blurred together in an endless string of curse words and insults. My vision darted between the two of them, my brain incapable of accepting or understanding how they were both standing here in front of me, seemingly two sides of the same coin. Even if I'd wanted to comprehend what was happening, the hatred and anger still building inside of me was blinding, casting too thick a fog to concentrate on any one detail for long. My stomach turned as I tried to get the emotions to settle. I felt like I was going to be sick.

"Did you know?" The one question that kept coming to me, finally slipping out into the tension-filled air of the living room and cutting Bastian off. I didn't know who I'd meant it for. Arlo? Vander? Perhaps both of them?

Arlo was the first to answer.

"Yes." His affirmation cut into my skin, slicing at the last remaining fragments of the sanity I was clinging to. "At least, partly."

Arlo's composure slipped slightly as I watched him, the lines in his face going slack as he shook his head and softened his features before turning to me. "I was created to protect you, at all costs. So I did. And I tried my best to keep you from this place until you were ready to return. It wasn't always clear what our past had been, what was reality or not. Traveling back through the Rift has cleared my mind some, made it easy to see through the haze and remember."

I forced myself to look at him, to really look at him. He was Arlo, but not quite the same Arlo from before. He was calmer, more sure of himself, and his eyes lacked that common edge of worry they usually held. In fact, they seemed oddly empty now that I was taking time to really look at them—so unlike the depth I'd come to recognize in Vander's eyes.

"I didn't know everything," he continued, "but I knew enough to come looking for you after you disappeared. I knew that you'd come home and that meant you were in danger here."

Arlo tensed, seemingly fighting a compulsion to reach out for me, just as he'd done so many times before. He'd grown to recognize the signs of my hysteria, the little tells I had when I felt like I was beginning to freefall into that deep, black abyss—the tells I'm sure were plaguing me now as I felt more and more control slip from my grasp.

"I'm sorry I misled you, Hazel. I was just trying to keep you safe."

He took a step toward me, causing me to recoil slightly. Aerie steadied me as she put a hand up, signaling him to not come closer. I closed my eyes, steadying myself in Aerie's grasp as I tried to fight through the nausea. There was so much to unpack there, so many questions I needed him to answer, but I couldn't form them here, not with everyone watching me. Not with so many conflicting emotions fighting to break through the surface.

"And you?" I turned my head to Vander, moving on before I let myself linger too long on what Arlo had admitted. "You told me you'd done something to save me, that it cost you the Mark of the Grimm." Aerie's muscles tensed, clearly uneasy about the invocation of the Mark. "But you said it hadn't worked."

His face was still cold as stone, but he was refusing to give way to the shadows now ebbing around him, threatening to cast the whole room in darkness. I was suddenly aware that his mask might not be a mask of indifference, but rather a way to clamp down on that darkness building to an unfathomable level. Perhaps that was the darkness I felt—not my own emotions, but rather his own struggle to control his. He'd told me before that he could sense my emotions—*feel* them as if they were his own. Maybe it worked both ways and he'd finally let his control slip enough that I was feeling him now.

The idea didn't seem to bring me any comfort. The extent of his anger burned so fiercely that he terrified me all over again. Gone was any trace of that vulnerable, tender male. In his place was something dark and hauntingly similar to how Kahlis' magic felt. I hated knowing how deeply his violent need ran, hated even more that I was now feeling it as my own without any way to control it.

"It worked," he finally answered. "Just not in the way I'd hoped. Instead of protecting you from Kahlis, I lost you. To every good part of myself." His eyes slid over to Arlo's body, hatred seeping from his gaze. "To someone I can never become again."

I shuddered at the tendrils of obsidian that slithered down the tether with his words. Darker than anything I'd ever felt from him, something so cold and black that it caused my skin to prickle—strangled my own emotions and snuffed them out altogether at its mere presence until I felt nothing but bitter, endless black. It was impossible to comprehend that this was the same creature who'd teased me mere hours ago, who'd helped me face the depths of my own feelings and had finally let his guard down enough to be vulnerable with me. How was this the same creature who'd pulled me from the lake when my own darkness had consumed me? Had that all been a mask, and this was who he truly was? Or was this darkness, this depth of cold rage the mask? A show he was putting on to distance us—distance me—from getting too close?

For the first time I felt like I was seeing the true depths of his darkness, the true hold of the mark on his soul, or what was left of it. I wasn't seeing Vander, I realized.

I was seeing the Grimm.

CHAPTER 38
VANDER

I wanted to rip the head off the male standing in front of me and watch until every drop of blood sputtered from his limp body. It didn't matter if he was somehow a piece of me. I tamped down on the power burning within me, willing it to calm. It did nothing to settle it, my body barely able to keep it at bay. I knew Hazel had felt it too—the confusion at her own anger so evident as she spoke, the horror she now felt at the true darkness of the Mark coiling through the tether. She wasn't used to feeling me, still learning to discern my presence in her mind from her own. Still learning how to control it, too. And I could see now how it terrified her to feel me so... fully.

I would not lose control—for her. If I let go, even a fraction, she'd snap. I needed to reign in the Mark for both our sakes. She would never forgive herself if the Mark unleashed itself through her. There was no coming back from that kind of torment. The only thing holding me back from making good on my desires was the small spark of joy I'd felt from her when she'd realized he was here.

Arlo.

I'd known he'd existed. I didn't want to admit it; I'd let Bastian and Aerie run down their theory about Kahlis and his magic being responsible for whoever Hazel had thought existed. It was wishful thinking, though—a fool's game. I'd known deep down that he'd been real. I'd known from the moment my power exploded in that clearing; I'd known as I watched her get carried away; and I'd turned deep within myself, telling my power, the Fates, the earth—whoever would hear—that I would pay whatever price necessary to keep her safe. It was a bargain with Death itself that split my soul. There'd be no forgetting the depths of that darkness. Just in case I hadn't known, there was the Mark that was seared into my arm, the shadows that overtook me and the power that called me to do its bidding. They served as a crude reminder of just how steep a price I'd paid.

I watched her wine-red hair, still damp from the rain, falling over her shoulder as she chewed at her bottom lip, remembering the feel of my fingers in its silken strands not even an hour ago. She was still soaked to the bone. Her white dress, the dress that had always been a favorite of mine from her time here before, was still plastered to her body, hugging every curve and dip. I'd been a hopeless fool for leaving it for her this morning, no matter how much desire it had stirred within me to see her in it. I cursed myself for bringing her back here. I would have rather taken my chances with Kahlis than return her to the arms of the abomination standing across from me. I didn't regret what I'd done, if it indeed had protected her all these years; but I didn't want to let her go now that I'd finally gotten her back.

Arlo stirred across the living room, moving toward Hazel again.

"What do you think you're doing?" My head cocked to the side as the words slid out of my mouth, hate dripping from them.

"Comforting her, she's clearly shaken by all of this."

"You will not touch her." The shadows around me grew, emphasizing the threat in my words.

"You don't get to decide that," Arlo said with determination, his steps solid as he strode toward her. "She's with me now."

"Like fuck she is." I stepped forward in warning.

"I think we should all just let her have a minute." Aerie's soft voice felt unnatural compared to the instability of the room. Despite the way she was looking at me, I was grateful as ever for her voice of reason. Even if it meant I couldn't touch Hazel, at least Aerie was keeping that *thing* from her.

Bastian stepped forward. "Our problems lie well beyond your complete lapse in judgment, and whatever the fuck we are going to have to do about this." He waved his hand toward Arlo. "Though, don't mistake the change in topic as my acceptance of this. We *will* talk about this later and you best be prepared to have some fucking answers."

I bit back my retort, all too aware that letting even the slightest amount of control slip could have a deadly reaction for those around me. The Mark writhed against my skin, a dark force fighting against my restraint.

Aerie led Hazel to one of the sofas next to us, a silent invitation for everyone to calm down and take a seat. Thankfully, she draped a wool blanket over Hazel's shoulders. Her body had started shaking. Whether from cold or shock or trying to fight through my emotions raging through her, I wasn't sure, but it was making my blood boil to watch her suffer and not be able to do anything about it. As her body calmed, so did a fraction of the shadows growing around me.

The tension was settling somewhat, or perhaps just pivoting its attention in a different direction. Kirwan, flanked by Nox and Mirren, took a sofa for themselves. In the midst of all the chaos, Mirren had lost her giddiness about Kirwan's return. Instead, she clung to Kirwan and shied away from my shadows edging across the room. Bastian moved to sit next to Aerie as Arlo walked forward and leaned against the back of the sofa where Kirwan sat.

I didn't move. I wouldn't act casual, like a threat wasn't lurking within our very walls. He might have been a part of me, but that was ten years ago. I didn't know what he was now, what he'd become. I didn't trust him, and I wouldn't play nice.

"Care to explain how he got here?" I tilted my head toward the male looking so comfortable next to Kirwan, refusing to take my eyes off him.

Kirwan leaned forward, shifting nervously. "I got Nox's message about looking around the Dark Woods before coming home. I was already deep within it, so I didn't think it would be too much grief. That's when I stumbled upon him—and the Rift."

My gaze faltered at his words, finally turning my attention to Kirwan. My brows furrowed in confusion. "The what?"

Kirwan cleared his throat, adjusting in his seat as he began to explain what he was talking about. "In the Dark Woods, there's this thing I found. A rift, a crack. Some sort of dark power splitting the air apart. That's where I found him, disoriented and frantically searching for Hazel." He turned toward the other couch, where Bastian and Aerie loomed protectively over Hazel. "Honestly, Bastian, I don't know how your sentries missed it. I could sense it from miles away. The smell alone was potent enough to guide me to it before I even saw it."

Bastian winced where he sat across from Kirwan.

"Well, they, uh—they haven't been out there in a few days. It's been hard to find able bodies after the last few rounds of Daeomi attacks. We needed to concentrate what was left of our sentries on the weakened border." He glanced awkwardly around the room before letting his gaze fall to the ground, too ashamed to look at Hazel.

"You said it smelled?"

Hazel's quiet voice surprised me as I looked back at her. I hadn't expected her to be so eager to talk, not after the shock she'd just experienced.

"Yeah," Kirwan answered. "Like death itself. Why do you ask?"

"When I awoke in the Dark Woods, when I first got here, there was this *thing,* like a crack in the air itself. It reeked of decay. I'd barely remembered it until you said something."

I hated the doubt I felt coming from her. I couldn't imagine how hard this all had to be on her. To constantly doubt what your mind was telling you, to not be able to discern the memories in your brain from reality—it must all be so confusing and frustrating to live with. Still, she was here, she was trying. That alone had me wanting to fall to my knees and worship her. She was so much stronger than she gave herself credit for. Even in the midst of my anger, of the Mark somehow influencing her through me, she still had the ability to fight through it and cope. I would push her every day to find that strength, if I had to. It was the kind of strength she'd need to fight against a creature as strong as Kahlis.

I reached out through the tether, testing to see if it was currently intact.

Are you okay?

Her head jerked toward me, rage shooting at me like daggers as she pushed back a thousand curses my way.

Good. I could deal with her anger. It was better than her giving up, shutting me out. It was better than nothing at all. It was a sign that she was still here, still willing to fight.

"So what does that mean?" I shifted my weight, letting my body relax a little as I leaned against the hearth and waited for someone to answer.

Aerie sighed. "I can't say for sure, especially without seeing it, but I would assume it's a rift in our world, a Rift leading to wherever Hazel was. And power like that is a parasite. It cannot be left unchecked."

Of course Aerie knew what this was. She had the most experience with weird and dark magic out of all of us combined. I really hated the fae, but sometimes it was a fucking Fates-send having her here.

"You're right," Kirwan said, "it's killing the Dark Woods. Leeching power and life from everything around it. It's one ugly motherfucker, too. My guess is that it's going to keep growing the longer it's left untouched."

"So what do we do? How do we close it?" Bastian, finally regaining his composure, had turned to Aerie, waiting expectantly for her to answer. In fact, all of us had turned to face her, the faerie clearly being our only source for understanding this mess.

"Well," she started, taking a deep breath in as she pushed to her feet. She moved across the living room, joining me by the hearth. There was no need for a fire, not with the humidity of the summer storm still pelting the windows of the room. Still, she leaned over it, waving her hand across the logs, leaving a warm fire crackling in its place. "It's tricky, I'll have to dig through my books to see what kind of spells would be required to shut down such a dark magic. It will be more difficult without the presence of the one who created it."

She lingered by the fire, kneeling and watching the flames dance. Their orange glow reflected in her light blue eyes. I could tell she was worried, the weight of the situation falling solely on her and her abilities.

She looked up at me, grief and frustration radiating through her face. I could tell she was hurt by the confessions of the day, by what she and

Bastian had realized I'd done. The look on her face right now was a large reason I'd never told either of them. I knew they'd be disappointed, and I couldn't explain to them why I'd done it. There weren't enough words to describe the pain I'd felt losing Hazel, the desperation that swarmed within me as I offered up a piece of my soul in exchange for her protection, in exchange for the Mark.

She stood again, turning back to the room. "But I'll start digging... along with the work I'm doing to find a way to keep Kahlis out of Hazel's mind in a more permanent way. It seems we have two impending threats now."

"Oh, good." Nox's sarcastic tone slipped through the room. "Because I was getting so bored with just the one."

Aerie let out a small laugh as she leaned into the warmth of the fire.

"And what do we do about that one?" Bastian asked warily, tilting his head back toward where the abomination stood. Aerie pressed her lips together in a firm line, but Hazel was the one to answer.

"He stays here, for now. He may have insight about the Rift that we need."

She wouldn't look up as she spoke, wouldn't dare a glance at either of us. An involuntary growl vibrated in my chest, though. I didn't like the sound of that, but I wasn't sure I had much say in the current state of events. Aerie's narrowed eyes confirmed that theory, and I clamped down once again on the anger building within me.

Arlo cleared his throat, moving around the low sofa. "I'm sorry, but why would closing the Rift be more difficult? We have the source of the magic."

His voice caused my jaw to clench. Slowly, I turned my attention back to him, the eerie presence of his too-familiar features causing my skin to crawl.

"I was unaware you had the Dark One in your back pocket." My words were laced with promised violence. Every moment I lingered in his presence was a moment closer to me letting the Mark have its way with him.

He sneered at me, obviously unaware of the real danger he was currently facing, how he was one wrong move away from a grisly death. "Kahlis isn't the one who made the Rift, smart ass."

The room deadened at his words. All attention was on him now, waiting for him to continue.

"You don't know?" His gaze darted around the room before landing on Hazel, his vexed features softening some as he looked to her.

She looked back. The longing in her eyes had my shadows growing all over again.

"If it wasn't Kahlis, then who?" Her voice was rough with emotion, the events of the day no doubt weighing on her mind even now.

Arlo moved closer to her, causing my own feet to take several steps forward. Aerie put her hand up, signaling me to give them a minute. I gritted my teeth as I watched him close the distance between them, his eyes looking to hers in a tender way that had me wanting to vomit.

He took her hand and brushed a stray strand of her hair out of her face.

"You did, Hazel."

CHAPTER 39
HAZEL

*N*o.

It couldn't be true. I had no power, no magical ability.

"You must be mistaken." I shook my head in utter disbelief. "Kahlis did this, you all said so. I couldn't have possibly made something like that."

My eyes darted around the room, looking for confirmation. I found none on their faces, wary and watching as I wrestled with the news Arlo had shared.

How could I have made the Rift? The other world?

Even if some power was hiding deep within me, Kirwan said the Rift was a dark, powerful magic. It would have taken something equally dark and powerful to create it. It had to have been Kahlis.

Yet, no one denied what Arlo claimed. I'd already begun to accept this world as my home, but in this new light it was impossible to deny I was the girl they all missed so desperately. It had always been me. And I couldn't remember a single thing about her. My eyes found Vander across the sitting room, searching for answers I was sure he still held. His face was hard, a wall of control and isolation refusing to respond. He didn't meet my gaze but rather focused on where Arlo kneeled in front of me, still on guard.

Vander had lied to me. I couldn't comprehend the lengths he went to in order to save me, the piece of himself that he sacrificed in my name. Yet here he stood, cloaked in darkness and marred from the Mark. He was dark and dangerous and deadly, and I'd let him in. I'd believed him when he told me everything had not been real, that Kahlis had caused all of this.

Had he known about this too? Had he known that it was my own power that created the Rift, the other world? Had he known and tried to hide it like he tried to hide the truth about Arlo and the evil that resided within him?

My hands began to shake. I tucked them under my legs to try and hide the involuntary reaction.

Arlo spoke, his voice a soothing lull against the storm raging in my mind. "I know you don't remember, I can only imagine how hard this is for you to understand. That's why I tried to keep you away, Hazel. You didn't want to be here, to be a part of this. When I came to you, Kahlis' creature had you in its grasp. You were desperate and hurting and so scared. When we finally got away, you let that pain and fear push through until you found your power. You wanted to escape."

No, no, no.

I wanted him to stop talking, stop admitting the depth of the darkness inside me. They would all be so disappointed, so hurt that I *chose* to leave. I didn't want Aerie to look at me the way she'd looked at Vander tonight. I shook my head fervently, as if the motion would turn back time and keep any of this from happening. Arlo reached under my legs and took my still-shaking hands in his. His touch was warm, familiar. Yet it did nothing to subdue the uncontrollable reactions raging through my body.

"So much had happened," Arlo continued on, pleading. "I didn't know all of it, didn't know what was causing that pain, but I could tell you wanted nothing more than to disappear. You carved out a little piece of safety and we retreated into it, Kahlis and his creatures nipping at our heels as we went. You breathed life into the Rift, breathed life into me. My darling divine."

His eyes shone with pride. I could hear the emotion in his voice, the desperate need for me to understand what had happened and why he'd kept this from me. This was his way of begging me to forgive him, of hoping I'd grasp the reality of the danger we'd been in, and why he'd done what he'd done.

"We barely made it," he said, voice wavering. "Another moment in this world and you would have been torn apart. I didn't understand it all at the time, but I knew I needed to protect you, knew my one purpose was to keep you safe, keep you from the pain and fear of this world."

His voice echoed through my mind, barely registering the words. Single details slipped through as I tried to keep focus. The world around me was blurring, my eyes burning from the tunnel vision that had begun. A steady, high-pitched ringing had settled within my ears and it was all I could do to stay upright. Arlo's hand brushed my arm in soft, simple strokes, trying desperately to calm me, to ground me.

"No, no." I shook my head in disbelief as my stomach turned.

Had I wanted that badly to be rid of this world?

The hatred I'd felt so often for magic burned in my mind. In the short week that I'd been back, how many times had I found myself turning bitter toward that power, wishing it didn't exist?

As if a far-off memory was begging to be unearthed, a mantra of sorts circled within me:

A world without magic. Safe. Calm. Hidden.

Perhaps that had been the mantra I'd repeated to myself when I was escaping Kahlis. Perhaps I had heard it in my dreams every night for the past year and just refused to acknowledge it, for fear of remembering... or perhaps I was grasping for straws in a world that kept making me doubt my sanity.

"So if Hazel made the Rift, then why are her memories gone?" asked Nox. "And why does it reek of Kahlis' magic?"

Aerie answered, "It may not be Kahlis' magic that it reeks of, just dark magic in general. The amount of power it would take to make an alternate reality, a new world... It goes against our laws. That kind of magic would leave a deep mark."

Aerie had once again joined me on the sofa, trying to let her warmth and calm stretch out over me. It was no use, just as Arlo's touch had been. I let my gaze fall to the ground, my eyes focusing on the intricate grooves of the woven rug beneath our feet.

Aerie added, "You may have created a new world, a safe haven to escape Kahlis, but this world wouldn't let you go unscathed. And just as there's a Void in your mind, the Rift is a curse on our land. I'm afraid—" Her words cut short, her voice hesitant as she stopped them.

"Say it." Vander's cruel tone dripped with malice. I wasn't sure who he was angrier with in this exact moment, Arlo or Kahlis—perhaps even me for causing all of this in the first place, for leaving him after he gave every piece of himself to save me.

"I'm afraid," continued Aerie carefully, "that just as the Rift threatens to take over the land and leech the life out of it, so will the Void in your mind keep taking from you. Neither will stop and your power—your stability—will not be restored until the Rift is mended."

Silence fell over the room, the air heavy with the weight of her words. The crackle of Aerie's magical fire was the only sound for a while. I felt the color drain from my face, the nausea reaching a tipping point in my stomach. Still, I kept my eyes trained on that spot on the rug.

Bastian's voice finally broke the silence. "So we close the Rift. That should solve everything, right?"

"Perhaps," Aerie offered, though her tone wasn't convincing. I noticed from the corner of my vision the way her head inclined slightly toward Arlo. "But I can't say anything for certain without doing more research on the subject. Hazel, I know the timing of this is just awful, but we need to start working on your mental blocks as soon as possible. It could hold a lot of the answers we need."

I nodded absent-mindedly, trying and failing to ground myself. I couldn't hold it in anymore, the shock taking over my body in a trembling wave of nausea. I stood abruptly, carefully avoiding eye contact with any of the others sitting around me.

"I— I need a minute."

I took off toward the closest bathing room, incapable of holding back the reaction. I burst through the door, barely making it to the toilet in time before heaving up every ounce of substance I had in my stomach. I wanted it out, wanted it all out. I wanted the betrayal and lies and loneliness gone—felt them churning my stomach with each convulsion. With each thought racing through my mind, each pitiful, aching realization at the truths that had been revealed tonight, I felt myself retreating into that all-too-familiar darkness.

It felt like it would never end—the secrets and scheming and magic forever morphing to keep me in the dark, to keep me questioning my reality. The pain was too much to bear, the sense of being utterly and completely lost and alone. I would have given anything to not feel it all. I longed for numbness to wash over me, willed the disconnect to find me as I escaped to the darkest recesses of my mind. Even as the mess turned to bile and dry heaves, my body did not slow its purge. It went on, violently roiling and trembling as I cried into the cold porcelain bowl and prayed no one followed me in here to witness the wreckage I had become.

CHAPTER 40
VANDER

I leaned against the cool stone wall of the cellar, watching the Daeomi. He was a bleeding, drooling mess, slumped over in his own filth after losing consciousness during our most recent interrogation. I was grateful for the dim lighting of the room. This evening's events had spurred on a pounding headache, mostly from the effort it took to keep my power at bay—to keep the Mark at bay. I was even more grateful for the reprieve the root cellar offered from prying eyes and invading questions. I wasn't in a talking mood—that is, unless the Daeomi felt like chatting.

Aerie had pulled me aside after our little family heart-to-heart in the living room and told me of a particular spell she'd come across. She thought it was a possible way to strengthen the wards against Hazel and explained what she'd need. Funnily enough, we didn't even need any information from the Daeomi, just his blood taken specifically while he was shifted into his primal form. She urged me to end things with the Daeomi too, the events of the evening apparently rousing some sort of worry within her.

As she spoke to me in hushed, urgent words, I realized Arlo had disappeared, most likely trailing the path Hazel had made toward the bathing room. I gritted my teeth as I turned my back to the direction they'd gone and came straight here, to the root cellar. I needed a release, something to soothe the Mark still straining and fighting within me. I forced the Daeomi to shift, pinning his skeletal wings to the back wall with more of Aerie's enchanted blades to make sure he stayed put in the right form while I made him bleed.

Aerie had hurriedly explained she'd learned that Kahlis must have used blood magic to summon them from the Depths. I didn't care about the details; all I needed to know was that Kahlis had used his own blood. It had been a risky move on his part. Doing so made them more powerful, strengthening them with magic similar to his own and deepening their connection to him. However, he had to realize how dangerous it would be if anyone ever captured one. I supposed he was cocky enough to think they'd never get caught. Still, it didn't sit well with me that we'd been able to capture one so easily.

I grimaced as the door to the root cellar creaked open, keeping my eyes peeled to the Daeomi filth sitting in front of me. *Sitting* was being generous, actually; the daggers pinning him to the wall were forcing his body to hang in a seated position. A smirk settled over my face as I eyed the daggers sunk securely in his wings, the steady stream of blood still pouring from them into the collection bowls I'd placed on the ground.

"I thought I'd find you here." Nox's easygoing tone sounded from behind me as he reached forward and handed me a glass of dark amber liquid. Fates bless him. I took a greedy swig from the glass as he settled into the room and closed the door behind him. "So Aerie had a bit of a breakthrough then? As much as I've enjoyed tearing into this one, I'd be lying if I said I wasn't ready for a break."

I grunted, unable to return his sentiment. If anything, I was a little disappointed that our fun with the Daeomi would be coming to an end, especially now when I had so much anger to satisfy. At least the Dark Woods would always be there to quench that bloodlust.

"I came in here to see how you were doing with everything, but that look on your face, and the shape he's in... I'm going to go ahead and assume you don't want to talk about it."

"Do I ever?"

"I suppose not." He leaned against the wall beside me, crossing one ankle over the other as he drank from his glass. "But you're going to have to start talking to someone, brother. That shit will eat you alive if you just keep bottling it up."

"It hasn't yet," I deadpanned, turning to meet his gaze.

He blinked at me—unconvinced—taking in the sight of my blood-splattered clothes.

"All I'm saying," he said slowly, diplomatically, "is that I'm here if you decide you ever want to talk about it. Any of it."

I huffed out a laugh, rolling my eyes. "Please spare me the late-night, bleeding-heart confessions. We've had enough of those today."

"Normally I'd agree with you, but today was some heavy shit. And I know you better than any of them. I just don't want to see you shutting us all out again. Now that Hazel's back, you've actually started to come out of that brooding, asshole shell you'd turned into."

"I doubt that," I mocked. "If you'd like me to stab you just so you have a little reminder of how much of an asshole I am, I'd be more than happy to oblige."

I pulled a small dagger from one of the sheaths along my chest and flipped it in my hand, making sure to let the silver blade gleam in the dim fae light. It wouldn't hurt Nox, not really. The fast healing that we'd inherited from our fae ancestors, combined with our immortal life span, would make sure that he'd survive much worse than that.

"Okay, fine, you're still a brooding asshole. I'd hate to ruin your carefully curated reputation." He let silence fall between us for a moment as we watched the unconscious Daeomi. "I just think that given everything that's come to light, you should talk to me. Or better yet, go talk to her."

I stiffened involuntarily. Her scent still lingered on my clothes, the unmistakable aroma of sage and lavender. I could still taste her mouth on mine, feel her fingers bunching against the fabric on my chest. I *had* talked to her. I'd tried, at least. I'd come so close to admitting everything. Thank the Fates I hadn't. Now with Arlo here, with the things that had come to light—that would have only complicated matters further. My lips pressed together in a firm line, remembering the look she'd given Arlo, the way he'd touched her, and she'd let him.

"She has her male back. I'm not needed anymore."

The Daeomi began to groan in front of us. I stepped forward, preparing the methods I'd planned to slice and pierce him. Maybe I only needed his blood, but that didn't mean I couldn't enjoy the collection process.

"Aren't you, though? Didn't you tell her? That you're—"

"Like I said, it doesn't matter anymore."

It didn't matter what Nox was saying, didn't matter how badly I wanted to tell her. I could live with the pain of not being with her, the feeling like the very breath had been stolen from my lungs. I was suffocating and I would never find air without her by my side, but it was a sacrifice I was willing to make if it meant she was safe and happy with the male that was worthy of someone like her.

I debated where to land my first blow, eyeing the Daeomi's wing: just to the side of where it was pinned to the wall, and close enough to the joint where it jutted out of his back—to know I'd be hitting some of the larger nerves. I had half a mind to rip them out entirely. If they were anything like the wings of some of the shifters that I'd encountered, it would be an unimaginable pain.

I turned my back on the vile creature and looked to where Nox stood, shaking his head.

"You can try to bury it all you want, Vander, but I know you. Just like I know this won't end well if you keep lying to yourself. And to her."

He slipped out the door without waiting for my reply. I palmed the jagged knife I'd picked up from the table, his words echoing like a spirit through the room. The Daeomi had fully regained consciousness and was now groaning at an irritating volume. The noise set my teeth on edge as I clamped down my jaw and let the Mark take over my body. Without another thought, I lunged at the Daeomi, slamming the jagged knife into his wing and ripping it down the length of the joint in the leathery appendage, shredding it in the process. The creature's screams radiated throughout the room, fueling the Mark as its power crawled under my skin.

It was no use trying to keep it at bay any longer.

CHAPTER 41
HAZEL

Arlo had found me a sweating, sobbing mess, curled up on the bathing room tiles. He came in and wrapped his arms around me, rocking me ever so slightly and stroking my matted hair as I cried and cried. I fell asleep like that. I supposed he carried me back to my bedroom because when I awoke in the morning, we were in my bed. He was passed out beside me, his arm draped over me as if he had tried to protect and comfort me, even in his sleep.

Seeing him here, in my bed after I'd all but convinced myself that he hadn't been real, after I'd allowed myself to move on, allowed Vander to—

No. I couldn't worry about that now.

Besides, he'd lied to me. About everything. They both had.

I forced myself to sneak out of the bed before I could let the thought linger too long, tiptoeing past Arlo's sleeping form to grab a pair of dark leggings and a gauzy mauve tunic out of the wardrobe. Then I slipped out the door, not wanting to risk getting ready in there—in case Arlo woke up. I made my way through the quiet hallways, stealing a moment in the hall bathing room to change and clean myself up as best I could. Thankfully most of the house was not awake yet, so I didn't have to worry about bumping into anyone.

I looked in the mirror, finding myself still in my dress from the previous night, the one that had been rain-soaked and splattered with mud and muck from our trek through the woods. I couldn't help but notice the scent of clove and citrus that still lingered on it. I blocked it out, refusing to let my mind think about *him*.

I peeled off the soiled, once-white fabric, attempting to put as much distance between myself and that day as I could. Instead, I pictured Vander standing in the living room, rippling shadow and rage—forcing my mind to replace the more intimate idea I'd started to have of him with that terrifying image from yesterday. He didn't just have the Mark of the Grimm. He *was* the Grimm. I'd come to realize that as I felt his very own brand of darkness overtake me. He and the Mark were one, and no matter what he'd convinced me of, I needed to remember that simple, terrifying fact.

The clothes I'd pulled from the wardrobe were soft and smelled of lavender. Their feel against my skin helped calm the nerves now racing through me. I tried my best to smooth down my hair as I looked in the mirror, before balling up the soiled dress and emerging from the bathing room. As I opened the door into the hallway, I ran right into a bright and cheery Aerie.

"Oh," she said in an annoyingly chipper voice. "Just who I was looking for! I wanted us to get started on the mental work right away today." She eyed me curiously, noticing the bundle of dirty fabric tucked up under my arm. "That is, if you're feeling up to it."

I nodded slightly, easing the bathing room door shut behind me so I had some room to back up.

Before I could object, she grabbed the dress from me.

"Here let me take that, I'll drop it with the washing I have to do today."

With one swift movement, she turned on her heels and started off toward her greenhouse. I let out a heavy sigh as I allowed several paces to separate us then started after her. I knew she'd said this would be important, but I didn't have the energy to try with it today. I just wanted to bury myself in the library and spend the day napping in solitude.

As we passed through the kitchen, she tossed the dress in a nearby basket, then grabbed an already prepared plate of food and a mug of what smelled like coffee, gesturing to me to follow her to the greenhouse. Once inside, she sat me down at her worktable, clearing away some of the ancient-looking books so there was room for the food. She took a seat across from me and then pushed the plate my way.

"Eat," she said. It wasn't a question. "You're going to need your energy for what we're doing today."

I eyed her cautiously as I picked up a piece of toast.

"And what exactly is it that we are doing today?" I asked before biting into the warm, buttery bread. Food here was so much better than whatever world I'd come from.

"Today," she said matter-of-factly, "we are going to learn what the inside of your mind feels like."

Dread pooled in my stomach. That didn't sound like anything I wanted her to know.

She must have noticed the fear in my eyes because she quickly added, "It's just for you, so you can understand how it will feel to put up mental blocks. It's hard to build a wall when you can't even see the land you're building on."

I nodded like I understood what she was saying as I took a bite of the eggs on my plate, but I honestly had no idea what she was talking about.

"Think of it like this," she added. "When you walk into a house, you must first find the door, correct? In order to learn how to protect your mind, we must first find the door." I nodded more confidently this time, finishing off the last bite of toast and taking a sip of the gloriously rich coffee. She tidied up the table as I ate, giving us more room for whatever work we were about to do.

"There are some things we will have to do once inside that door, seeing as how *your* house comes with some missing pieces and dark scars, but the idea is still the same."

At that, I pushed the plate away. My appetite had disappeared, being replaced by a sickening sense of foreboding.

Setting aside my dishes, she dusted her hands on her apron and gave a lighthearted laugh. "Now don't go getting all shy on me. I promise it will be okay, and I'll be right beside you the whole time."

I tried to summon even a modicum of courage, pushing my fear into the recesses of my mind. I had to do this. If it meant protection from Kahlis, I *would* do this. I would do anything to not feel that weak and helpless again.

"Now," she said, clapping her hands together, "let's begin."

My elbows pressed against the rough wood of the worktable, my head heavy in my hands. My vision blurred as I tried to find something to focus on around the room. I hadn't realized just how much Aerie had been working to find something to help me. Ancient looking tomes and spell books were scattered on every available surface of the small greenhouse. Handwritten notes and objects grabbed at random sat as placeholders amongst the open books, marking the more important things she'd come across. Now with the Rift growing unstable, she'd be twice as busy. I grimaced as I let my head sink further into my palms. We'd spent the morning working on the void in my mind, and the steady throbbing that had settled directly behind my eyes was reaching frightening levels.

"Are you up for trying one more time?"

Aerie's soft voice pulled me from my thoughts as I lifted my head, the movement intensifying the ache. We'd been at this for hours and the only thing she'd managed to help me find was the headache pounding in my skull. I had half a mind to just give up, tell her it was useless. I looked around the cluttered room, though, and reminded myself just how hard she was working to help me.

I nodded slowly as I stretched my hands out for her to take again.

"Okay, let's try a different approach this time."

She took my hands and guided me over to the small bed in the corner, gesturing for me to lay down. She slid a soft cloth over my eyes as she bustled around me. I heard the crackle of something being lit as she set it on a small table beside us. A familiar smoky aroma twined around my head, filling my nostrils.

Incense, the same she'd burned the day they found me and brought me here.

She knelt beside the bed, pulling something from a box in her lap.

"This time, we're going to flood your senses, as a way to drown out this world and allow you to turn fully within your mind."

She placed a cold, smooth stone in each of my hands, closing my fingers around them. A weight settled in a single line down my chest as she placed more stones upon me. Somewhere close by, a steady ticking started up. I remembered seeing a pendulum on one of her shelves when I'd been in here before. I wondered if that was what I was hearing now.

I let the fragrant smoke and the rhythmic ticking carry me as I gave way to the darkness behind my eyes. It was oddly comforting, feeling lost to this world, floating within myself. It was like a thousand weights had been lifted from my chest. The pounding in my head was starting to ease the further I retreated into this space.

Aerie's voice floated to me, found me in the black escape of my mind. "Focus on your senses, letting this world slip away as you think only on what your body is experiencing." She waited a minute, letting me drift further within myself. "Good, now I want you to focus, look for that spot in your mind. It should feel dark and confusing, maybe even a warning to stay out. Push through it. Go to it."

I let her words guide me through the recesses of my mind. It was calm here, peaceful, and I found myself getting easily distracted in the comfort.

"Keep going." Her words were an encouragement, snapping me back into focus as I drifted even further.

A cold shiver snaked its way down my spine, shifting the stones Aerie had laid across my chest and stomach. I'd found something, a spot buried deep down that boasted nothing but pain and ice. Despite every instinct screaming at me to turn around and run, I pushed through, toward the chill of the darkness just before me.

"That's it." Aerie's words echoed in my mind as I forced myself to keep going. I could almost picture her hands hanging in the air just above me, her senses stretched out to follow the path I was forging.

Tendrils of dread and agony wrapped around my legs, gliding over my skin as they settled upon my shoulders and tried to drag me down. I could feel the tears pooling in my eyes, but I wouldn't let them stop me. I kept pushing, kept digging deeper into that dark place inside my mind.

The Void.

I was there. The air felt different, nothing like the warmth and comfort I'd felt when Aerie began the ritual. This was something else entirely. It was cold and empty, hateful and bitter. The emotions raged through me as I felt them all individually before they came together in a chorus of despair and hopelessness.

The tendrils that had wrapped around my body and tugged at my shoulders tightened, threatening to pull me under fully—to where, I didn't know. I wondered if it was possible to get lost in here, to never return to the world beyond my mind. A small voice whispered to me, telling me how much I wanted that.

"Focus, Hazel. Don't let it distract you."

Aerie was my anchor, my beacon of light in this dark, dark place. I let her words radiate through me, let her magic stretch out around me and ease the tendrils of self-loathing and doubt back as I made my way forward. Something else echoed in the darkness.

Hazlenn, my Hazlenn.

I felt the brush of a hand against my cheek, despite the darkness that consumed me. My breath quickened, looking around for wherever the motion had come from.

"Keep going, Hazel, you're doing great."

I swallowed around the lump forming in my throat, nodding as I tried to focus on what I'd heard. The darkness lifted around me, shapes and colors coming together to take form. It wasn't like real life. It was fluid and blurred, like a dream, but I could still make it out. I was back in that cottage in the woods, kneeling beside the couch in the living room.

Someone lay across it in front of me, but it wasn't Arlo. I tilted my head to the side, leaning in to understand who I was seeing.

Her hand took form as it brushed my cheek again, brushed away the tears now freely flowing down it. I didn't remember when I'd started crying. I took her hand in mine as a pain settled in my chest. I realized as I took note of her labored breathing that I was watching her slip away, into the next life. More tears flowed as I looked around desperately for anything to save her.

"It's okay, Hazlenn. It's time." Her words drew my attention back to her as I clasped her hand firmly, holding it against my face and cherishing the warmth it offered. Too warm, I realized. I'd always thought at the end of one's life there would be nothing but bitter cold. There wasn't now, not from her. Her hand blazed with a fevered fire, something more terrifying than the cold I would have expected, like at any moment she'd burn up and be reduced to nothing but smoldering ash.

"I'm so sorry, baby." Every word was like sandpaper as it came out of her mouth, the pain it caused her written all over her graying face. "I'm so sorry that we didn't have more time. There's so much you don't know yet, so much you still need to understand. I should have told you sooner. I thought—" Her words were cut off as she succumbed to a ragged fit of coughing.

I grabbed a cloth off the nearby table and dabbed at the spittle now sliding down her chin, noting the red stain it left on the white linen as I pulled it away.

"I thought we'd have more time." Her eyes were full of sorrow and love as she looked at me. Given their milky appearance, I couldn't tell if she could actually see me, or if she just somehow knew where I was.

"I'm sorry, I don't know what you're talking about." My voice was shaky, admitting how lost I was.

"You will," was all she answered.

"What should you have told me? What don't I know?" My voice rose in desperation as I pleaded with her to keep talking. She only patted my cheek as she began to fade away, the memory slipping from my grasp as I began yelling for her to tell me what she knew. I grasped at her, my hands finding nothing but smoke as she disappeared into darkness. I rattled out a line of curses, pushing my mind to not let her go. I screamed—at her, at myself, at the world within me and the one outside of me. It was no use. The vision was gone and I was left to the dark and bitter cold of the Void, the tendrils snaking around me and tightening their grip.

I gasped for air as Aerie lifted me off the bed to a sitting position and pressed a hand to the pendulum to stop the rhythmic ticking. My skin was ice-cold as her hands pressed into my forearms, the warmth of her touch felt like fire against me. My breath was ragged as I tried to let the world around us come back into my view.

"Slow, deep breaths," she told me. "Note the things around the room, the smell of the air, the feel of the bed, things like that."

I nodded, unable to speak, as my eyes darted around us. The incense was still thick in my nostrils, so I focused on the feel of the sheets as they slipped through my fingers, the rough wood floors as the grooves dug into my bare feet.

She watched me for a moment longer, panic laced in her pale blue eyes, before moving through the greenhouse and grabbing a small dish.

"Here," she said. rushing to my side and pushing something between my lips. A tangy, sweet flavor filled my mouth as I sucked on the hard treat she'd forced on me. "That should help."

I didn't understand how sweets could help with whatever was happening to me, but before I could argue, I felt my breathing regulate a little and the warmth return to my arms. I flexed my hands, urging the blood to flow through them as the tingling sensation spread down my arm and into my fingers.

"What just happened?" I asked, stunned.

"I think you found the Void."

CHAPTER 42
VANDER

I stormed into the greenhouse, footsteps heavy with the exhaustion of the night before. I'd stayed up through the night, letting the Mark have its way with the Daeomi. I hadn't wanted to venture back to my room, past Hazel's door. I didn't want to know if Arlo was with her.

I let the pail I was holding land with a thud on Aerie's worktable. It wasn't until I raised my head that I realized either of them were here. They both stared up at me, gaping as they no doubt took in the blood and black bile splattered across my clothing and coating my boots. I looked down at my feet, only now noticing the mess I'd left in my wake.

"I uh—sorry, I didn't think anyone would be in here." My eyes narrowed as I looked back to them, realizing the state Hazel was in and how Aerie was kneeling beside her in a concerned manner. Hazel's face was leached of all color, her lips a shade too blue for comfort. "What in the Depths happened?"

I fought the urge to go to them, to let my more primal impulses take over to ensure her safety. I took a single step forward, my feet clearly not on the same page as my brain, then planted them firmly against the wooden floor at the sight of her recoiling away from my movement. My eyes pored over her body, scanning for whatever threatened her.

"I could ask you the same question." Aerie's tone was short, irritated by my presence interrupting whatever was happening between them.

"You said you needed blood." I gestured toward the pail sitting on the table, a single obsidian bead of the thick, sticky liquid now creeping down the side from when it had no doubt sloshed at my careless movement. "So, I brought you blood."

Aerie's face twisted in horror. "I said I needed some of his blood, not a whole Fates-damned torrent. What did you do, bleed him dry?"

I choked back a chuckle at her outcry, realizing far too late how stunned Hazel looked, her gaze lingering on the bucket like it was a fucking severed head.

The smirk that had begun to form on my lips settled into a firm line as I turned back to Aerie, irritation growing within me. "Look, do you want it or not? I'm just trying to be helpful here."

She shook her head, letting out a long sigh as she turned her attention back to the bed where Hazel sat, pale as a spirit. "Leave it there, I'll deal with it in a minute. Grab a towel and wipe your mess up as you go, though. I don't want bloody boot prints all over my floors."

I muttered under my breath, but I did as she said, moving to a stack of nearby linens and finding a towel amongst them. I moved the towel over the dirtied floor with the tip of my boot, so I didn't have to get on my damn hands and knees as they watched me.

I worked my way back to the door, throwing the soiled towel toward a basket for dirty linens once I finished. I paused before I left, looking back at the bed.

"Is she okay?" My voice was low, concern coming through stronger than I'd wanted.

Her eyes shot to me then. Anger and pain coated the daggers she was throwing at me.

"*She's* fine," Hazel bit out.

My jaw clenched at the tone of her voice, the molten rage spilling from her words. I gave a curt nod before turning on the balls of my feet and striding back out into the mid-morning sunlight.

"Wait." Aerie let out a frustrated sigh. I could hear her lean to Hazel and exchange words in a hushed tone, as if they didn't want me to hear. Aerie knew better though. If my shifter blood wasn't enough to pick up their whispered conversation, my shadows no doubt would.

"He'll be able to tell you more about the vision than I can."

"I don't care, I don't want to hear what he has to say."

I kept my back to them, pretending to be oblivious to their words, but the muscles in my back went rigid as Hazel spat her disapproval my way. Her words were an icy contradiction to the way she'd melted for me just yesterday. Funny how quickly things could change. I supposed with Arlo here now, she had no more use for me.

She's better off without me, anyway.

I clamped down on that thought, letting the pure self-hatred distract me from the pain of not having her, and dissolve the lingering memory of her lips on mine.

After a few more moments of hushed arguments, Aerie called me back into the room. I turned slowly, carefully trying to avoid Hazel's gaze. When I finally lifted my head, I found her eyes steadily trained on the rough wood floor in front of her, fully ignoring my presence.

Fine, two can play that game.

I said nothing as I crossed my arms and leaned against the doorframe. Aerie looked cautiously between the two of us, clearly waiting for Hazel to say something.

When several moments of silence had passed, Aerie let out a small sigh. "Hazel and I have been working on her mental blocks today, trying to find the Void in her mind that's causing... problems."

I scoffed, earning a narrowed gaze from Aerie. *Problems* was a rather nice way of describing the absolute mindfuck that had become our lives.

"We've made some progress. There was a vision, a possible memory, of what I suspect was Hazel's mother. I don't know anything about her though, and I thought we could use some insight." Her eyes lingered on me, sharpening as if in warning to behave, before she added, "From you."

"I'm at your disposal," I deadpanned.

Aerie, again, waited for Hazel to speak, but quickly realized it was a lost cause and took over. As she filled me in on the vision, I steadily watched Hazel, her eyes so dutifully trained on anything that wasn't my face. It took real commitment to avoid someone that blatantly. It almost made me smile, the muscles twitching at my lips.

Little spitfire, indeed.

Her eyes shot to me as the nickname I'd given her radiated through my mind, as if she could hear it clear as day. It was the first time she'd truly acknowledged me since last night, since she found out everything.

Well, not everything.

Thank the Fates for that. Still, my chest tightened as if I had been stabbed by a poison dagger, the venom slowly creeping through my body and tearing me apart. Killing me slowly.

Aerie's questioning tone broke me from my thoughts. "Do you re-member anything that Hazel's mother may have been trying to tell her? Any idea what she would have been referring to in the vision?"

I held Hazel's spite-filled stare as I thought, recalling the horrible day that was seared into my brain. I let the silence hang there for a moment longer, reveling in the unspoken challenge that now grew between our unfaltering eye contact.

"The day you were taken, the day you disappeared," I finally answered, "your mother was on her deathbed. You asked me to come, to help you as you said goodbye. Because you didn't want to be alone when it happened."

My words faltered, my voice going quiet and my gaze softening as I took her in. Her face looked stunned by the heavy pivot our conversation had taken.

I dared on. "I waited outside during her last moments, close enough to be there if you needed me, but far enough that you had some privacy. I don't know what she said to you, what happened then—but when you came out, you were shaken. More so than just from her passing. You'd learned something and you were spiraling out of your mind with shock and fear."

Her face turned from stunned confusion to sorrow and horror. A tear slipped past her lashes, followed by another, and another. My chest twinged with pain. I didn't want to be the reason she was crying, but Aerie gestured for me to keep going.

Dammit if her eyes weren't the most vibrant shade of green, the tears pooling there working to bring out the emerald hues swirling in them. They did something to me, the pain in my chest dipping lower, turning to something more primal.

I cleared my throat as I shifted uncomfortably against the doorframe. "I, uh—I never got to find out what had you so spooked. Kahlis and his men showed up right after that. And well, you know the rest."

I waved off the memory with a motion of my hand, but the shadows around me darkened as the scene of carnage and destruction flashed in my mind.

Aerie let out a breath, clearly hoping I would have been more helpful. Hazel let her gaze fall back to the floor, wiping away the tears that now trailed down her cheeks. Aerie thanked me as she turned her attention back to Hazel, ushering her to drink some brew of tea that was still steaming in the cup beside them.

"Right well," I began awkwardly, feeling suddenly useless, "I—have things to do, so... let me know if you need anything else, I guess."

Aerie waved me off as she rose from her spot and dove into one of the million books that lined every surface of the greenhouse. I turned to walk back to the house but stole one last glance at Hazel before I left. Her lips were still tinged with blue, the only color on her ashen face. Her hair was a knotted mess above her sunken, hollow eyes. She looked rough; more than that, she looked like she was on death's doorstep.

It was a look I was quite familiar with, being death's personal omen and weapon. Ice filled my veins as I stared a moment longer. The shadows behind me deepened as the Mark on my arm cried out, begging to claim its victim. Far too often had the Mark cried for me to claim her lately. It made my stomach turn, anger flaring at the power scratching at my skin. I needed Hazel to find her strength. Fates knew I was using all of mine to hold back now. She could barely keep herself together, let alone handle the power of the Mark.

If death didn't claim her first, I was terrified the monster within me would.

CHAPTER 43
HAZEL

Days passed after that first session in Aerie's greenhouse. Everything lost its meaning, its purpose. I didn't eat, I barely slept. It was like finding the Void had stripped me of any substance. Arlo's return was supposed to bring me peace, but I'd never felt so lost. I was a hollowed-out shell, an empty tomb on legs as I drifted through the days—or maybe it was weeks? I'd lost all sense of time. I avoided Vander at all costs. Even the thought of him sparked pure, agonizing rage within me.

At least it was something, though, something besides the unrelenting numbness.

I'd known from the moment I'd come here that I should have kept my distance from him, had known he was dark and deceitful, his shadows hiding more than just the blood on his hands. It hadn't stopped me from letting my guard down, letting him edge his way in before sticking a knife in my back. I was hurt by his lies, even if what he did was to save me. It didn't justify what he'd done, didn't change who—what—he was now.

He was a beast, a creature capable of doing dark and violent things. And no matter how much distance I put between us, I could still feel his anger simmering just below the surface. He kept his distance as fiercely as I kept mine, as if he was disgusted by this weakened version of the female he used to know.

Arlo tried to talk to me, tried to pull me out of the cave that I had withdrawn to, but even that effort was short-lived. Within a day of his return, we'd fallen back into our old patterns. I lost the motivation to find answers, lost the will to learn of whatever power lay within me. I'd lost interest in much else besides accepting that this was just my life now. The hurt and confusion of Arlo's return combined with the fruitless efforts of Aerie's sessions with me were too much. I didn't discuss things further with Arlo, didn't press him for an explanation like I'd originally planned to—or blame him for the lies he'd told me. If anything, he was just as much of a victim as I was. He fell in stride with my behavior, not knowing a different version of me existed, had been coming alive over our time apart. That fire had gone out, though, and I sunk into the familiar comfort that he offered.

I was grateful that Bastian was too preoccupied with chieftain duties to continue playing the overbearing big brother. It had allowed me the ability to slink through the estate without worry of running into him or being interrogated about Aerie's progress, or lack thereof, with the mental work. Although his absence served as a bleak reminder of Kahlis' ever-growing presence within the tribe's borders. The few times I'd seen Bastian as of late, his body sagged in exhaustion and more often than not he was covered in the thick black muck of Daeomi blood.

Aerie was determined, the sessions in her greenhouse filling most of my time. We hadn't had much of a breakthrough, though, after that first day. No matter how deep I searched, how hard I pushed, it was always the same thing: the vision of the woman we believed to be my mother, dying in front of me and telling me how much she wished she had more time to explain things to me. I was always inches from death as I emerged from the session, my bones rattling with the cold as my head pounded incessantly. Aerie speculated that it was the effects of the Void, a sign of how deep I had to go in my mind in order to reach it, how dark the magic had been to leave something equally dreadful behind. No matter how determined she was, she never let me push too far, never let me grow too close to death's doorstep and always had some sort of remedy waiting to help revive me as I emerged from the trance.

Despite the pain that those sessions brought me, I looked forward to them. Aerie's presence was as warm as the tea she made me each day, the small glimpse of peace that I desperately clung to in the otherwise all-consuming darkness that had become my life. I found myself often counting down the hours until our next session, lingering outside the greenhouse, longing for another dose of her calming company.

I awoke in bed, the bright summer sun already streaming in through the window across from me. My back was to Arlo, his large form curled around me. He'd practically been my shadow over the past week, the only time apart being my time in Aerie's greenhouse. I sent up a prayer of thanks to the Fates or whatever powers above for that little reprieve. We hadn't slept together since his return, barely even kissed. I tried, but no matter how similar things seemed now, something had changed between us. It was always him leaning in, his lips brushing across my cheek or pressed against my forehead. The gestures should have been sweet, loving. Instead, they set my teeth on edge and pushed me further into the emptiness that had begun to consume me.

I slipped out from under his hold, careful to soften my movements so that I didn't wake him. I dressed in near silence as I kept a watchful eye on his steady breathing. Sometimes I wondered if he knew I was trying so hard to avoid him, if he ever woke up while I tiptoed my way through my measly morning routine and just pretended to be sleeping because it was easier than addressing the shift in our relationship.

I tied my hair back with a black ribbon, taking in the mere echo of the girl who stood opposite me in the mirror. I barely recognized myself anymore. I no longer felt hatred for the reflection, no longer felt anger or pain. I just... was. The strands of wine-red hair were pulled messily back, the length of my ponytail falling across my back. Even tied back, I couldn't hide the knots that gathered in it, the oil and dirt from lack of washing. I hadn't had the energy to care lately. I took a deep breath, prying my eyes away from the haunting reflection before I crossed the room, my bare feet padding softly along the smooth wood planks of the floor.

"Trying to sneak out?" Arlo's voice was heavy with exhaustion as he pushed to sit up in the bed.

My hand hovered above the doorknob, my teeth grinding together.

"I just didn't want to wake you." I hated the way my voice sounded, full of shame and fear. I hated that it reflected who I was becoming with each passing day.

"You don't have to avoid me, Hazel. I'm here *for* you. Let me help you, please."

I nodded, refusing to meet his gaze.

"I'm fine, promise. Just late to meet with Aerie. Go back to sleep."

I didn't wait for his response as I eased the door open, slipping through as quietly as I could before closing it behind me with a soft click. I turned to the hallway ahead, my eyes set on the familiar path to Aerie's greenhouse, when a small squeal escaped my lips. Vander stood just in front of me in his wolven form, his midnight black fur close enough to reach out and touch. I could have sworn a smirk stretched across his muzzle, those wolf lips curling back to reveal his dangerously large canines. In an instant, his movements flashed and he shifted to his mortal form. His shadowed golden eyes never once left mine.

"Were you out here spying on me?" The words felt thick on my tongue. We hadn't spoken to each other in weeks.

"Don't flatter yourself, little spitfire. I was just returning to my room after a night of hunting." He strode past me, too close for comfort as I suddenly remembered just how naked he was. The shadows in the hallway darkened, as if in answer to his statement.

Hunting.

What he meant was killing. I suppressed a shudder as my mind turned to the Mark on his arm, the brutality I'd learned it signified. However, I'd seen him return from hunts before, covered in gore and filth and reeking something awful. That wasn't the case now. I backed away as I turned to watch him stroll casually back to his room. My bare feet landed on the spot in the rug he'd been occupying moments ago, finding the ground warm, too warm for him to have only been here mere moments. Shock rolled through me as it occurred to me: he'd slept outside my door last night. My eyes shot back to him, the rigid muscles of his back so much more noticeable without the cover of a tunic.

"Enjoying the view?" His words dripped with wicked sarcasm. His mouth curled into a smile as he looked back over his shoulder, reaching for the door and disappearing into his room, leaving me gaping and confused in the hallway.

What just happened?

The question radiated through my mind as I made my way through the estate to Aerie's greenhouse. I'd barely spoken to Vander in the past couple weeks. He'd made even more of an effort to avoid me completely. As much as I hated him, even feared him after the things he'd revealed about our past, about himself, I'd gotten the impression that he was even less thrilled with me right now.

Had he truly slept there all night? Had he done it before, without me even realizing?

The questions distracted me as I opened the door to the little greenhouse. Aerie greeted me from within. I nodded to her, still evaluating his words, the looks he'd given me in the hallway.

Aerie watched as I took a seat on the bed, noting the distraction but not pushing me to share anything with her. She was standing at the worktable, leaning over a particularly ancient-looking tome.

"What would you say about taking a break from the memory work for today?" She eyed me carefully, noticing the surprise, and bit of disappointment, that was no doubt washing over my face. "I've got a better idea, and I think you could use a little rest from all this."

She waved her hand over the room, the bed where I was sitting.

As much as I cherished our time together, the pounding in my head was already growing and we hadn't even begun yet. A break could be good. I nodded again, slightly hesitant to discover what other plans she had for the day. Before I could question her, Mirren appeared in the doorway with an oversized basket that looked almost impossible for her to carry.

"Ready?" she chirped, shifting the weight of the basket between her arms, which were hooked through its handles.

I cocked my head. She'd been practically nonexistent since Kirwan and Lennox had returned, not that I could blame her. I was happy to see her, though a little confused.

Aerie didn't answer my questioning stare, just simply smiled a wide, graceful smile as she grabbed her own bundle and turned to Mirren.

"You bet," she answered as she strolled through the room and motioned for me to follow.

CHAPTER 44
HAZEL

Aerie led the way past the estate and down a path I hadn't traveled before. I'd noticed Bastian and Aerie using it often, sometimes Mirren or another one of the estate workers accompanying them. I didn't know why I hadn't explored it before, why it hadn't seemed to matter. As we walked, Aerie explained it was the path to the main village for Talamh. I realized how shockingly little I'd seen of this place. I'd barely been outside the walls of the estate, only really leaving for the occasional stroll in Aerie's garden or a walk through some of the grassy knolls to clear my head.

Or to visit my home with Vander.

I shook my head, clearing it of the painful memory. I didn't want to think of that right now.

It was only a five-minute walk to the village, the short distance surprising me with how quiet and secluded the estate felt. The village was bustling, full of life and laughter. Creatures of all sorts were strolling the busy streets. I noticed several shifters, similar to Vander and Bastian, roaming in their primal forms; sprites and dryads flitted through the crowds, along with several types of magical beings I couldn't even identify. Vendors lined the walk-ways of the busiest part of town, selling everything from assorted foods and magical items, to handcrafted jewelry and some of the most breathtaking artwork I'd ever laid my eyes on. I was mesmerized by it all, the energy buzzing through the crowd seemingly contagious as it pulled me from my cave ever so slightly.

There appeared to be some sort of market day going on, so the towns-people were out in full force. The sheer size of the crowds would have usually made me stop in my tracks and run back home, but for the first time in my life, I didn't feel the need to isolate myself. Aerie stopped several times to check on various members of the tribe who were affected by Kahlis' latest attack, so Mirren and I browsed the nearby stalls to give them some privacy. Quarreling voices caught my attention at a jeweler's stall, and I lingered close by to eavesdrop on the heated discussion.

"What need have I for jewelry at a time like this?" the louder voice shouted. She was a rough looking-female, clearly irritated with the vendor trying to lure her over to the stall. At her words, I looked around the booth. It was surprisingly empty for how packed the streets had been—especially given how beautiful the pieces were. I ran my fingers over a necklace that had caught my eye: a crescent moon set with an obsidian stone.

"Ah, such a great selection." The vendor's sultry voice caught me off guard, having turned their attention back to me so quickly.

"Oh, sorry—I'm just looking. It is beautiful, though."

"And such a fitting piece for a creature as strong as you."

I laughed, impressed and taken aback slightly by the vendor's efforts to make a sale. The creature was cloaked in cloth and shadows, to the point that I could barely make out their face. I leaned in, examining both the necklace and the creature who was now holding it up for me. Aerie's soft voice pulled my attention away as I realized Mirren was no longer beside me.

"Thank you for your time, but really, I'm just sightseeing today." I turned away before they could respond, but even as we made our way through the busy street, I could have sworn I felt the merchant's eyes following me. I shook the feeling from my shoulders, refusing to let the paranoia ruin one of the first lovely days I'd had in weeks.

Everyone we passed greeted Aerie like an old friend, oozing with their love and admiration for her. I supposed I wasn't the only one who couldn't resist that warm magic of hers. She was an idol to them, but she was also a friend, a sister. I didn't think anyone else could possibly hold such a deeply respected role amongst these people, being both revered and beloved.

She stopped at a small shop—a bakery, I realized, by the intricate sign hanging above the door. It was just one shop in a long line of them, occupying a larger building made of limestone. The inside was packed with patrons waiting for their orders to be filled. Aerie opened the door for us to shuffle our way inside, the smell of fresh-baked bread and sugary pastries wafting around me. I inhaled deeply, closing my eyes and reveling in the delicious scent.

When I opened my eyes again, I found Aerie watching me. She couldn't contain her smile, looking to Mirren before they both lost themselves in a fit of giggles. I joined in, the sound of my own laughter surprising me. I couldn't remember the last time I'd truly laughed, let alone giggled. I was about to say as much when a loud voice broke out over the crowd, pulling everyone's attention.

"Well, my, my, my, if it isn't our Lady, Aermidh Darroch."

A tall, slender female emerged from behind the counter, the crowd parting to give her room. She was beautiful, her skin a shade of green that reminded me of dewy moss creeping across the forest floor. I wondered what manner of magical creature she was. Something like a forest dryad seemed like a safe bet. Her inky black hair was long, trailing down her back in a sheet of pure onyx as it swayed to match her steps. Flour and batter covered the linen apron she was wiping her hands against as she stopped in front of us.

"I'm surprised you could pull yourself away from that fancy house long enough to grace us with your presence."

Her words shocked me, but there was a twinkle in her eye. Aerie giggled again, pulling the flour-covered dryad in for a hug.

"It's good to see you too, Rosalind."

Rosalind laughed, pulling back and clutching Aerie by the shoulders to give her a look-over. "You need to come down more often, we miss seeing you! And it's not fair for you to keep little Mirren here from us. It's the highlight of my week when you bring her in with you."

She nudged Mirren playfully, and I was surprised to see that Mirren, for once, didn't look uncomfortable at being noticed.

"I know, I know. We've been a little preoccupied lately, though." Aerie's eyes slid over to me, finally drawing Rosalind's attention to where I stood. She took a step back, sucking a breath through her teeth.

"Hazlenn, is that you? By the Fates, girl. I thought I'd seen a spirit." She pressed her hand to her chest, as if trying to steady a racing heart, as she closed the space between us. "It's so good to see you again. I've missed having you in my shop."

Aerie cut back in, offering me some relief from Rosalind's questioning gaze.

"She actually goes by Hazel now. It's been quite an adjustment since her return, so we've been keeping a low profile back at the estate. Lots of ordered rest and calm environments for this one." She hooked her arm around mine, bringing a small smile to my lips as I still carefully avoided Rosalind's eyes.

She nodded in understanding at Aerie's words, an unspoken warning not to pry or draw too much attention to me.

"Well." Rosalind turned, clapping her hands together. "I've got just the thing for you today, had I known you were coming in, I would have had it already boxed up and waiting for you." She threw a wicked grin back at Aerie, to which Aerie just rolled her eyes and followed in Rosalind's wake.

Rosalind slipped back behind the counter and bustled around the stacks of pastries. There were so many delicious-looking treats lining the shelves and counters between the waiting patrons and the busy staff: breads twisted in intricate designs, handheld pies filled with jams and creamy custards, and small cakes decorated with the most decadent-looking icing. Within minutes Rosalind was making her way back to our side of the counter and handing Aerie a large box of assorted pastries tied up with twine.

"Only the best for you, Lady Darroch," she said with a wink.

Aerie returned her wink, thanking her for the treats and slipping some coins onto the counter.

"You know I won't be accepting that," Rosalind said, refusing to touch the silver coins.

"And you know I'll be leaving them anyway," Aerie answered in her singsong voice. She turned to make her way back through the crowd. As I moved to follow, Rosalind laid a hand gently against my shoulder.

"For you," she said, handing me a small box, big enough for a single pastry.

I blinked back, surprised. "Oh, thank you, but I don't have any money."

"Consider it on the house, in memory of your mama. And as a welcome home gift."

Her words were warm despite the grief I noted behind her smile.

"You knew my mother?"

Words caught in my throat as I thought of a hundred questions to ask her. She must not have heard my question, seen the longing in my eyes, because she didn't respond. Instead, she pushed the box into my hands, refusing to take no for an answer. She ran her eyes over me once more, settling back at the box I now held.

"It was her favorite. You both would come in at least once a week to buy some." Her gaze flitted back up to my face, the glint of tears beginning to shine in them. "You look so much like her, Hazel."

Something like pride beamed from her as she took me in one more time before waving a hand to dismiss me.

"Alright now, go before Aerie loses you in the crowd."

I shook my head, her dismissal pulling me from whatever trance I'd been in. I turned on my heels, throwing her another quick thank-you as I rushed through the crowd to find Aerie and Mirren waiting for me at the door. I hesitated a moment, the desire to run back to Rosalind and ask for every detail she could remember about my mother burning inside of me. Before I could, Aerie ushered me out to the busy street as she made eye contact with Rosalind across the shop, giving her a small nod of appreciation before she let the door close behind us.

Apparently, a visit to the village wasn't the only plan Aerie had for the day as she led us out of the town and down a path through the woods.

"Where are we going?" I asked breathlessly after another half hour of walking through the trees. Sweat had long since broken out across my forehead and was now dripping down my spine. The heat of summer was upon us, spring slipping away like an old memory. I wondered how many more days there were until Sol Litha, the summer solstice celebration... until my birthday, as Aerie had so kindly informed me. I grimaced, remembering what she'd said about restarting festivities for the holiday, and sent up a silent prayer to the Fates that she didn't intend to go through with it.

It had been spring when I'd first returned to Tir Nadaar, the warmth of the days only lasting a short while, as the mornings and nights encased them in a brisk air. There was no telling, though, just how far into spring it had been, or if the seasons passed on the same timeline as the world I'd come from. The thought had me on guard, worried and wondering if my birthday was closer than I'd realized. Perhaps with everything else going on, it would be forgotten altogether. The idea of any of them trying to celebrate me right now, with all of the conflict and danger encircling us, seemed absolutely absurd.

"You'll see when we get there. It's not much further," Aerie said.

I grunted in frustration as I wiped the sweat from my brow. I paused, panting for a few moments before realizing how far ahead they were getting. I quickly scrambled to catch up.

Just as I reached them, Aerie slowed.

"Here at last," she said, swiveling her head to look at me.

As I came up beside her, out of breath and trying to wipe the sweat out of my eyes, I stood up straight to see where exactly she'd insisted on taking us that required such an exhausting trek through the woods. Out ahead the trees opened up to reveal a small meadow, the grass rolling in velvet waves on the summer breeze. Wildflowers popped up amongst the grass, like a patchwork quilt. I could have sworn the air was sweeter here, and I took a deep inhale to confirm my theory. It was breathtaking.

Aerie smiled freely as she watched me take in the beautiful landscape.

"Come on," she said with a slight laugh, urging me forward into the tall grass. "This isn't even the best part."

She trudged through the grass, somehow making it look as graceful as gliding across water. Mirren ran up ahead, not waiting for either of us to take off into the meadow. I was careful with my steps, worried about damaging the undisturbed beauty as we made our way through. On the other side of a grassy knoll was a spring, as clear as glass and surrounded by the most unique-looking rocks. Crystals, I realized as I got closer to the water. Boulders of the purest amethyst and smoky quartz shined in the afternoon sun, a gleaming beacon to anyone near. We walked up to the water's edge, the grass giving way to the rocky sand that surrounded the spring. No, not sand... I knelt, letting the roughness of the rocks dig into my knee as I plunged my hand into the grains, letting them slip through my fingers and back to the ground. They were more crystals, the finest grain of crystal I'd ever seen. Hues of purple and white and smoky gray mixed together to create a texture so similar to sand, the naked eye almost couldn't detect it. I would have missed it entirely if it hadn't been for the varying sizes of stone surrounding the waterline.

I dropped the remainder of the crystalline sand as Aerie came up beside me.

"I used to bring Mirren out here when she was just a little fawn, letting her play in the grass and swim in the waters of the spring until she was exhausted. She used to have so much energy, I couldn't find anything to channel it through. Until we found this spot." The warmth of fond memories radiated from her eyes as she looked back to where Mirren was, now setting out a blanket for us.

I couldn't think of what to say, didn't know how to explain the gratitude I had for her showing me such an intimate, sacred place.

"It's beautiful," was all I could muster, refusing to pull my eyes away from the beauty that lay before me. Aerie hummed in agreement, enjoying the ambiance just as much as I was despite seeing it countless times before. It seemed like the kind of place one would never grow tired of, never stop appreciating.

"Come," she said finally. "Let's eat."

CHAPTER 45
HAZEL

Aerie had prepared quite the spread for us: finger sandwiches with the most delicious fillings, exotic fruits, more cheeses than I even knew existed, and of course, a large pot of tea brewed by her and kept warm with some piece of her own magic or enchantments. By the time we'd finished eating, I was thoroughly stuffed. I couldn't remember the last time I'd eaten so much.

I lay back on the blanket Mirren had set out for us, propped up on my elbows behind me. The sky was a deep blue, full of cotton clouds that seemed too white to be true. I closed my eyes and listened to the meadow, the birds dancing through the air and the insects singing as they moved through the soft grass. It was peace, utter bliss. I let my thoughts drift to what Rosalind had said about my mother, imagining days spent just like this with her when I was a child.

Mirren and Aerie chatted beside me, something about her training and magic. I peeked an eye open, intrigue pulling me back to their conversation. Aerie had leaned over a small patch of grass just beside our blanket, waving her hand over it with a calculated twirl of her fingers. Beneath her hand a new patch of wildflowers formed, small buds at first, but grew and grew until they were beautiful full-sized blossoms.

"Remember," Aerie said as Mirren leaned in close to admire the flowers. "Look within. Feel that hum of power inside as you envision what you're wanting to do. Your power only flows if you accept its presence. Welcome it and will it to do what you want."

Mirren nodded knowingly, as if that was an instruction Aerie had given her a million times before. Mirren closed her eyes, her chest heaving with the deep breath she took as she focused. I watched her carefully, analyzing every move she made as she concentrated on another patch of grass close by and waved her hand just as Aerie had done. She moved it once, twice, and a third time before finally coaxing a single bud to grow from the earth. It wasn't quite as impressive as the bundle of flowers Aerie had summoned, but it was beautiful and strong. Pure joy rippled across Mirren's face as she squealed in delight.

Aerie laughed, clapping her hands. "Very nice, Mirren. That's quite an improvement from our last lesson!"

I watched them in awe, realizing just how much of a motherly role Aerie filled for Mirren. Something inside me ached as I watched them—Aerie's praise pouring over Mirren, Mirren looking back to Aerie with love and pride and admiration. I was happy for them—for her, remembering the horrific past Mirren had come out of—but something like jealousy twinged inside me too. Their unfiltered love for each other was a stark reminder of just how much I lacked something like that. Maybe I'd once had it, but I couldn't remember it and that hurt all the more thoroughly. Rosalind's words echoed through my mind. The grief of my mother's memory shining in her eyes had made me feel utterly shameful for not being able to feel it too.

Aerie nudged me, drawing me out of the vicious cycle of thoughts in my mind.

"Do you want to try?"

"Me?" I balked. "No, no—I have no idea how to do something like that."

Aerie pulled me over, rolling her eyes.

"And you won't know how until you start trying," she urged.

"It feels weird at first, but I promise it gets easier," Mirren offered, her amber doe eyes twinkling with encouragement.

I took a steadying breath, keeping my eyes on Mirren as I said, "Okay, what do I need to do?"

If Mirren could find the power within her after everything she'd been through, then I could at least try, for her. I already knew nothing would happen; I hadn't been able to sense any magic within me since Aerie first mentioned it to me weeks ago. But it felt wrong to deny them when they both sat there, watching me with hopeful encouragement.

Aerie was practically giddy. "Alright, I want you to close your eyes. Remember how we begin our sessions for the memory work. Clear everything else away, focus only on what you feel inside."

I did as she said, pushing out everything around me, acknowledging the sounds one at a time before letting them fall away. I slowed my breathing, letting only Aerie's voice distract my focus.

"Good, now just as we've searched for the Void before, I want you to search for your power. It's hard to explain, but you'll know it when you feel it. It feels different for everyone, but mine feels like warm sunlight on my bare skin, the feeling of steaming tea sliding down my throat."

"And mine feels like plunging my hands into rich soil, the smell of the trees after it rains," Mirren chirped in excitedly.

I nodded, taking in their words before letting them fall away, too, and searching within for anything that felt familiar to what they'd explained. Within my mind, I could feel the Void, cold and dark and haunting. I made sure to stay far, far away from it as I kept searching. I tried to think of warm memories—the feeling of Arlo holding me, a lazy afternoon spent reading together in our living room. It felt warm, felt like love. Maybe that's what they had wanted me to find, so when Aerie asked if I was ready, I nodded.

"Good, now reach your hand out over the grass and picture whatever you want, will it to grow beneath your hands."

I held out my hands above the grass, opening my eyes only enough to see where they extended in front of me, shaking as they hovered in the air. I moved as she had moved, but nothing happened. I remembered how Mirren had moved several times in order to get her magic to flow, so I copied the movements, going again and again. Still, nothing happened and I dropped my hands to my lap in a frustrated huff.

Silence hung between us for a moment before Mirren reached out and grabbed one of my hands.

"It's okay, Hazel," she insisted. "It took me a while to get it too, and that was a *really* good job for your first attempt." The smile she offered me was kind; I smiled back at her before I could stop myself.

"It will take time," Aerie agreed. "It takes a lot of work to find that power, to learn to master it. Don't get discouraged. You did great for your first lesson."

I started to reply, to argue that Mirren was only sixteen and could muster more magic than I could with a century under my belt. I wanted to tell her how I didn't think there was any powerful magic in me anymore, that she had been mistaken about still sensing its strength within me because there was no possible way I could feel this weak if anything powerful enough to create the Rift still lingered inside of me.

Instead, I let my gaze fall to my hands in my lap, letting out another sigh.

"Yeah, okay," I said, without truly letting her words reach me.

By the time we returned to the estate, it was late. The sun was starting to set and Aerie jumped into the kitchen to help the estate staff finish up preparations for dinner. I didn't have much of an appetite. The picnic lunch Aerie'd made for us had thoroughly filled me, and the pastries from Rosalind's bakery had left me feeling sleepy, each motion feeling like trudging through wet sand.

As I slipped out of the kitchen, I told Aerie I was going to skip dinner and just head to bed. She watched me with a careful precision as I walked out the doorway, but simply said, "Okay, let me know if you need anything."

I waved my hand in acknowledgment as I moved quietly through the house and hoped I didn't run into anyone else before I made it to the peaceful escape of my bedroom.

As I closed the door behind me, I breathed a sigh of relief to find the room empty. I was half worried Arlo would be in here, waiting for me to return. As I let my eyes scan the room, though, I relished the quiet that greeted me. I walked over to the stack of books collecting dust on the small table by the fireplace, untouched since my last visit to the library. I picked up a couple from the stack, wondering if I had enough energy to read before falling asleep tonight.

I settled on one about the Fates, realizing how little about them I actually knew, before tossing it on the bed and quickly changing into nightclothes. I slid into the sweet comfort of the fresh sheets as I settled back against a mound of pillows and let the book fall open across my raised knees. My eyes adjusted to the fluid script on the paper as I dove into the world it described.

The Fates, also known as the three sisters, are the deities of our world—gods, in their own rights. They record our life threads, weaving the story of our world into an endless tapestry across the cosmos.

Despite their ever-growing power and wealth of knowledge about the inner workings of our universe, they do not intervene in our world. We pray to them, ask that they bless us with an easier life journey or protect us in more dangerous prospects, but ultimately, they only use their power to document the timeline and ensure balance remains.

They protect the gift we've been given, the power our magic draws from, ensuring that the earth is cared for and our laws are followed.

Legend has it that before them existed other gods and goddesses, during the time of Fae rule and the carnage that it became. Many died off, due to the fae's abuse of magic and the land, their reverence and respect long-forgotten. The one whose passing left the Fates to rule and marked the beginning of their watchful reign over our lands was Cailleach, the Divine.

Upon her ascent into the cosmos and the utter destruction of the Old World, the Fates stepped forward as our guards, to balance the scales and record our stories. No one knows their purpose for recordkeeping or just how deep their power runs, but it is blasphemous to question the entities that rule over us.

Lesser supportive names for the

> *Fates include things like the Fu-*
> *ries, the namesake insinuating*
> *that rather than ensuring order*
> *they often are the cause of the death*
> *and destruction that plagues our*
> *world. Some theories actually sug-*
> *gest they caused the downfall of the*
> *Old World, killing innocents and*
> *bringing carnage to anyone who*
> *questioned them. It is a crime to*
> *insinuate such things, as they are a*
> *holy entity that ensures the safety*
> *of our world and it is law to revere*
> *them as such.*

My eyes grew heavy as I tried to keep reading. As much as I wanted to learn about this stuff, as much as I wanted to try and bring old memories to the surface, it felt impossible to get through the sheer depth of information. The words blurred on the page in front of me as I let out one last deep yawn, stretching my hands above my head and sinking into the soft bed just a little more. I fell asleep dreaming of a vast war in the sky, the Fates blurring between the orderly picture of grace and safety and the more grotesque, horrible creatures some called the Furies bringing carnage to those on the earth below.

When I awoke, I rubbed my eyes, trying to clear away the sleep so they would focus. I was aware within moments of the darkness of the world around me and the lack of Arlo's presence beside me. It seemed odd that he wouldn't be here with me, given how dark it was, how late into the night it had to be.

"Arlo?" I called out to him softly, thinking perhaps he was in the bathing room. I sat up, pushing against the soft material of the bed. No, that wasn't the feel of my bed. Cold, damp stone bit into my hands as I propped myself up. The chill in the air finally registered as I wrapped my hands around my bare arms.

My eyes slowly adjusted to the lack of light, the stone cell slipping into view and radiating through my memory as my entire body shuddered in realization of where I was.

"No," I gasped, my breath a foggy tendril on the icy air.

A deep chuckle vibrated from the corner of the cell, the towering form emerging from the shadows. "Yes, little one. I'm afraid so."

He knelt before me, those bloodstained hands reaching out to grab my chin.

Kahlis.

My whole body started to shake, the movement involuntary and apparently unstoppable as I tried and failed to will myself to still, begged my body to not show fear.

He only laughed harder, deeper, as he watched me squirm and shake beneath his grasp.

"You've been hiding from me, little one. I don't appreciate it when the things I want try to run from me." He paused, cocking his head to the side

as he took in the terror on my face. His nostrils flared as he inhaled deeply, smelling the fear coursing through my body.

"Although," he drawled, "it does make for such satisfactory moments as this one."

I opened my mouth, unsure how I found the courage to speak. "You don't have me, not really. This is a dream. You can only find me by dreamwalking, which means you're still limited."

"For now." A cruel smile curled across his lips. "Tell me, did you enjoy my little gift, the Wisps? They are a nasty little creature, aren't they?"

His lips pressed together in a hum of approval as my body shuddered at the memory of the fae lights calling me out into the lake and urging me to succumb to its frozen grasp.

"Ah, you weren't aware that they had been a gift from me? How unfortunate. I thought my intentions were quite clear." He stood, circling my weakened body and eyeing me from all angles as if to assess just how pathetic I was.

"What do you even want from me? Why not just come find me? End all of this?" I didn't care if it was foolish to challenge him. I was so tired of his games, I just wanted answers.

"All in due time," he mused. "Your protectors have made it difficult to step foot on their lands. Not impossible... but difficult. And when my powers reign strong on so many different planes, why limit myself to only the physical?"

I forced a smile up at him. "My protectors are ten times the male you will ever be. And they won't stop until I'm safe from you, fully and eternally."

It was a bold statement, but it was one I found myself clinging to in the midst of the musty, freezing cell.

"*No matter, I'll find another way to reach you. I will always find another way.*" *He stooped to me, his breath hot against my ear.* "*I'm getting closer each day, can you feel it? Can you feel my presence tapping against your mind and whispering all sorts of nasty things to you?*"

As if in show of just how true that statement was, I felt him slip through my mind, making my whole body writhe as he preyed on that darkness inside me, amplifying it and pushing it through every inch of my body. I screamed in agony, the thoughts raging in my mind too much to bear: promises of things he would do to me, things he'd make me do to myself. A creature made from my worst nightmares took form and slithered through my vision as it clawed at me, piercing me with fire from the inside out. I could feel his hand on my mind, those sharp nails scraping against it and peeling it back, layer by layer.

My eyes caught sight of that cruel, hateful smile as I continued to writhe on the frigid stone floor. The pain was excruciating, unlike anything I'd ever fathomed possible. I was lost to Kahlis, at his mercy and trapped in this never-ending torment. I didn't want to die. I didn't want it to end like this. I fought through the darkness and the pain, clearing the thick, smothering fog just long enough to generate one original thought, a silent cry for help down the tether.

Vander, please.

CHAPTER 46
VANDER

I lay across the rug in the hallway, the solid wood floor beneath it offering no comfort as I tried to sleep. It didn't matter if it did, it wasn't what kept me up. I'd slept in far less comfortable places than this, the cold stone of the caves and rock formations buried within the Dark Woods often supplying me with rest when I'd needed it. No, my inability to sleep now was due to something else entirely.

Hazel hadn't been at dinner. Aerie gave some half-assed excuse about them having a long day, but I didn't miss the concern in her eyes. Just as I hadn't missed the countless meals Hazel had been skipping lately, the lack of effort she'd put into anything these past couple weeks. I thought backing off would help, taking myself out of the equation and letting Arlo fill whatever role he'd offered her in their previous time together. I wasn't used to her being like this, but it appeared this was normal for Arlo. Despite his efforts to help, there'd been no difference in her mood and I had half a mind to rip his head off just for failing her so miserably, for being okay with this version of Hazel.

I hadn't helped her either, though, and I was just as angry at myself for not being able to take away that pain that laced through her mind every second of every day. The tether was working, better now than ever, but I found myself having to shut it down to silence the pain I felt pouring through her.

I'd taken to sleeping outside her door—outside *their* door—because I didn't entirely trust Arlo yet and wanted to keep a close eye on him. Nox had laughed at me when he found out, claiming I was only doing it to creep on them. I punched him in the stomach for suggesting such an invasion of privacy, then smirked a little as I told him it was an idiotic suggestion, since they weren't doing anything worth creeping on. At least that was some small victory.

I shook my head, my fur swaying as I readjusted my paws against the cool floor and leaned back into the wall behind me. I'd just closed my eyes, sleep finally welcoming me, when a scream broke out through the hallway. I was on my feet within moments, assessing the hallway, despite knowing exactly where that scream had come from. Another one pierced the air, followed by more. It was a cascade of terror, each scream overtaking the next one as they crashed against me.

A moment later, another voice joined them.

"Hazel—Hazel, wake up. Please! Come on, wake up!"

Arlo's cries were muffled in the wake of Hazel's screams. I imagined him on the other side of the door, shaking her in their bed as he loomed over her writhing form, just as she had been the night I pulled her from the nightmare Kahlis had trapped her in. I froze for a moment, waiting to hear her wake at his command. When the screams continued—grew even more pained, more desperate—I barreled through the door.

My breath was ragged as I paused just on the other side. The splintered wood fell like rain around me. I stared at the bed, assessing the extent of the danger waiting there. Any desperate brute would have run in, leapt on the bed without another thought. I was a honed hunter. Years of training lingered in my mind, rousing to life at the first hint of a threat, but it was more than that: the Mark calmed things in me, stilled my movements even in the most dire circumstances, allowed me the time to think before acting, and had saved my life countless times because of it.

Arlo was indeed leaning over Hazel, shaking her violently in an attempt to pull her from the dream, and to no avail. She lay there stiff and unhearing. Her lips were twinged that shade of blue that provoked ire deep inside me. Her screams echoed through the room even as they continued to build, one on top of another. Arlo's eyes shot to the door, several seconds too late if I had actually meant him harm. I tucked that information away for later, in case I ever needed it.

His eyes were laced with terror as he took me in, my wolven form. I wondered if he was familiar with it, knew or remembered the feeling of shifting, the freedom it offered. Slipping into my wolven form was like slipping into a warm bed after a long day. It was as simple as breathing and I often hated the feel of forcing myself back into the mortal form that I spent most of my time in. Arlo hadn't shown any signs of magic since he'd been here, and I was starting to wonder if he was without any altogether, seeing as how my power hadn't suffered at all since the split.

The terror in his eyes turned to pleading as he backed off the bed.

"Help her," he begged me.

I would have reveled in the look he gave me, the desperation and powerlessness in his eyes, if it hadn't been for the cause of those feelings. I turned my attention back to Hazel, her back arching so hard off the bed I was worried it would snap in two if I didn't act quickly.

I moved across the room swiftly, putting a paw on the bed, hesitating only for a moment before another scream ripped from her throat and through the room. In one smooth motion, I lay my wolven body across hers, holding her down as I brought my muzzle close to her face and let my warm breath heat her cheeks. I closed my eyes, blowing out a deep breath as I concentrated.

I pushed through the tether, breaking down the walls I had slipped up earlier that day, calling out to her.

It took me a minute to find her, her essence buried so far within herself, her mind another world away and trapped by Kahlis. I pushed harder, calling her. I willed her to answer me, to follow me back to the real world. I almost vomited when I finally found the withering, flayed remnants of her mind that were screaming and trembling in agony from what Kahlis had done to her. Her physical body would show no wounds, but the way she looked here was enough to suggest that she'd never be the same again. What Kahlis had done was solely to her mind, to her soul. He'd known where to strike, known her struggles and how he could hurt her most. And he'd shown no mercy when he ripped her apart.

Her emerald eyes shone up at me, tears streaming down her face as she recognized the safety that I offered. She let me approach, and I latched onto her—guiding her back to reality, and far, far away from the grip of the monster that had done this to her.

When I opened my eyes, her hands were clutched in my fur, her head buried in my scruff. Sobs vibrated from her as she refused to let go, refused to open her eyes and admit she was home at last, safe and sound.

"I'll uh, go get Aermidh." Arlo's voice was rough with emotion. He disappeared from the room a moment later, head hung low.

He'd realized the same thing I had just now: the tether, the connection between us, was only present between me and her, despite Arlo being born from my own soul. I would be the only one who could save her from these nightmares with Kahlis, the only one who could pull her back to reality when she was trapped within his grasp.

She continued to cry into my fur, not loosening her grip for even a second. I nuzzled against her body, a silent promise to always be here to lead her back from the depths of darkness, no matter what complications lingered between us. I let that singular statement ripple down the tether, hoping that she could hear it, would accept it. Her tightening grip around my neck and the slowing of her sobs were the only reply I needed.

CHAPTER 47
VANDER

Aerie was in the room within moments. I'd already shifted back to my mortal form and cradled Hazel in my arms as I pushed past Aerie into the hallway. The look on her face mirrored the terror pulsing through my blood. She gave me a stern nod, understanding passing between us. It was bad. We made our way to the greenhouse without ever speaking a word, Arlo trailing behind.

I set Hazel down on the bed in the corner, careful to not rouse her too much in my movements. She whimpered against my chest as I moved, my face falling into a grimace at the pain laced in the noises she was making. I backed away, letting Aerie take over. She was already busily preparing an herbal mixture, but she moved to Hazel's side as soon as I set her down. A warm glow emerged from her hands as she stretched them over Hazel's shaking body.

I turned back to the door, realizing Arlo was still behind us. His face was ashen as he watched Hazel grimace in pain and fear while Aerie worked to help her. I knew that look, knew what it felt like to be so helpless in the wake of her pain. Despite my hatred for the male in front of me, I found my gaze softening. I strode through the door, closing it behind me and pushing him back into the heat of the summer night.

"Come on," I said, gesturing for him to follow me back into the house. "It's best if we give her time to work."

Incapable of breaking free of the daze he was in, Arlo followed me absent-mindedly into the house. His hands ran through his hair and over his face, as if he could scrub hard enough to erase the horror he'd witnessed tonight. I moved toward the bar just outside the kitchen and poured us each a deep glass of sunbeam whiskey. I grabbed the bottle in one hand and the two glasses pinched between my fingers in the other, handing Arlo one.

We made our way back to the kitchen, opening the side door so that we could still have eyes on the greenhouse, now glowing with Aerie's power. I wanted to know the moment we could go back in there, check on her, and know the truth of the situation. I took a long sip from my glass, leaning against the kitchen counter as I watched the glow from the windows ebb and flow.

"How are you holding up over there?" My eyes didn't leave the greenhouse as I spoke.

"Oh, uh—" Arlo stuttered, trying to piece together some form of a reply. I knew he wouldn't find one, knew my question was pointless. I knew what seeing her like that did to him, did to me.

"Drink," I told him. "It will help."

His eyes drifted down to the glass in his hand, apparently unaware that I'd even handed it to him. When he realized what he was holding, he brought the glass to his lips and didn't stop until he'd drained every last drop of the burning liquid. When he set the glass down on the counter, I grabbed the bottle I'd brought from the bar and refilled his glass, topping mine off too, before setting the bottle down between us.

Bastian made his way into the kitchen, eyeing the bottle of spiced amber liquid before grabbing a glass of his own and pouring himself a drink.

"I fixed the door," he said tightly. "Again."

I nodded to him in acknowledgment.

"You do realize you could just use the handle, right? There's only so many times I can stitch the wood back together before we'll just have to make a new one."

I rolled my eyes, both of us knowing that wasn't true. Bastian's powers were strong, despite the fact that he barely ever used them.

"And for fuck's sake, could you please put on some pants? Other people live here too." He threw a bundle of clothing at me, something he must have grabbed from my room while he was fixing the door.

"I thought marrying a fae would make you less of a tight-ass, not more," I hissed through my teeth as I pulled the pants on and fastened them in place. "I'm sorry if my mind is concerned with other matters besides modesty right now."

Bastian threw me a narrowed gaze but knew better than to argue further. Silence fell as we waited for Aerie to finish her work. Arlo refused to look to the greenhouse, couldn't do anything other than pace annoyingly through the kitchen.

"How—what—"

He couldn't find the words, so I just sighed and shifted my weight as I took the liberty to answer the questions I knew he was trying to ask.

"Kahlis. He's been trying to get to her since she returned. We had her warded, but he's using blood magic against her. It's... complicated to ward against. Aerie just started on a new approach, but it isn't ready yet."

Arlo cursed, his pacing quickening with rage. "This is why she should have just stayed in the Rift. It was safe. *She* was safe. Dammit, why didn't she listen to me?"

His question was to no one in particular, but I inclined my head toward him.

"You would have preferred she stayed there and slowly withered away? You heard Aerie, the Rift is draining her power. The Void it caused in her mind won't stop growing until she has nothing left."

My words stopped him in his tracks, his stare fighting between shock and more anger.

"Of course not, I just— it's my job to protect her." He let his gaze fall as he went back to pacing. "I just don't know how to do that anymore."

My wolven form bristled beneath my skin, ire coursing through me as I stepped in front of him in one swift motion.

"Protect her?" I scoffed. "You coddle her. You turned her into the disempowered, frightened mess that she is! Maybe you protected her for a time, but you cannot cage her in the name of protection. She outgrew that world, outgrew the Rift. And now she needs to learn how to overcome it before it steals everything from her."

Arlo flinched at my words, running a shaking hand through his hair as he stared at the ground.

"Perhaps this isn't the time or the place, brother." Bastian's words were a quiet presence as he set his hand on my shoulder.

I clamped my jaw down, gritting my teeth to keep from chewing the male out further. Instead, I turned my attention back to the greenhouse just as Aerie opened the door and motioned for us to join her.

I was first through the door, Arlo close behind as we trailed into the greenhouse. Hazel still lay on the bed, her eyes closed and the color in her face at last returning.

"I had to put her under, the pain was too much for her to bear," said Aerie. "My magic is still working, so don't touch her."

"What happened?" Arlo's plea was desperate.

"Kahlis got to her again. This time was much worse than the first."

"The first?" Arlo's shocked gaze darted between me and Aerie. "This happened before?"

I refrained from answering, disgust rising in me at how little he knew about Hazel, how little he'd even asked about her time here since they'd been reunited.

"Yes, but it wasn't nearly as bad. Thank the Fates Vander got to her in time. I don't understand why it was worse this time, though. What changed?"

Aerie's body shifted toward me as she waited for my reply.

I eyed Arlo cautiously, debating how to answer.

"It's my fault," Arlo cut in. "I was trying to wake her; I knew something was wrong. She's always had these nightmares. I thought it was just another one of those until she started screaming bloody murder and her fucking body felt like it would break in half if she didn't stop thrashing."

Aerie's brows knit together in confusion as she looked at Arlo, then back to me. "Oh," she said as her jaw fell open in realization, finally understanding what both Arlo and I had in that moment.

"That's when Vander came in," Arlo finished, refusing to elaborate further.

He didn't need to. A silence fell over the room as one thought rang true in all of our minds.

Despite Arlo being a piece of my soul, the tether existed between me and Hazel alone.

We watched her in silence as Aerie continued working her magic to repair whatever Kahlis had done. As she worked, she explained what her magic was sensing. The only way she knew to describe it was that Kahlis had flayed her mind, skinned her alive. Despite the fact that her physical body remained unmarred, the pain she felt was very real. It was just another annoying factor of the mindbender's endless power.

Hazel woke soon after that, bringing everyone in the room to attention as she cried out, either in fear or in pain.

"It's okay, Hazel, you're safe. We've got you." Aerie knelt beside her, gripping her hand tightly as she spoke and no doubt sending more of that warm light through Hazel with her touch. It made no difference to Hazel's trembling, the pure look of terror in her eyes growing as she shrunk away. Aerie looked to me, urging me to test the tether to help calm her.

I hated how many people were watching us right now. Bastian had woken Kirwan and Lennox as well, requesting their presence in case things went downhill—well, more downhill than they already were. I sighed, making my way across the room as I rubbed my jaw. A pain had begun to bloom there, the stress of the night's events apparently manifesting within me. Aerie moved to make room for me but remained close by in case her help was needed.

I reached for Hazel's hand, but she jerked away, terrified of me, of everyone. I met her stare, those wide eyes radiating fear. They looked at me with no recognition, just as they had the day I found her in the Dark Woods. I sucked in a sharp breath, disturbed to see the true extent of

Kahlis' hold on her. I tried to reach out to her again, relying only on the tether this time, rather than physical touch.

I'm here, little spitfire. You're gonna be okay.

I repeated the words, pushing them down the tether over and over in a gentle promise of safety. Slowly, the light returned to her eyes. The trembling slowed, then stopped altogether. The room breathed a collective sigh of relief as her terror fell away and settled into recognition of where she was, who we were.

"Vander," she whispered, her eyes locking on mine as she reached out, at last letting me take her hand.

I brushed my thumb in reassuring strokes across her hands as she let go of the last grips of pain still holding onto her.

"I'm here, Hazel. I always will be."

CHAPTER 48
HAZEL

I sat in Aerie's greenhouse, knees pulled tight to my chest as I drank deeply from whatever kind of tea Aerie had brewed for me. Pain still riddled through me, fear threatening to pull me back under, but I let Vander's words repeat on an endless loop in my mind.

You're gonna be okay.

His words anchored me to reality, helped me keep a grasp on the here and now rather than slipping back into that dark place where Kahlis had kept me.

It was still shocking, the pain he could inflict without even touching me, the fear he managed to push through me without even being in the same territory. His power was truly horrific, something dark and vile that had my skin crawling all over again as glimpses of what he'd done to me flashed through my mind. I forced myself to look at my arms, my legs, noting how they bore no marks from him. It hadn't been real, but the pain still haunted me, the feeling of absolute isolation as he willed the very skin on my bones to peel away in an angry inferno of red. I winced at the memory, trying my best to focus back on what the others were discussing.

"We're out of time," said Bastian, impatiently. "If the Rift affecting the land wasn't reason enough, Hazel's own safety is now in danger. That was too close a call. We leave for the Rift as soon as possible."

He had shifted into full chieftain mode. His words were commanding and final, fuming at no one in particular. He wasn't mad at any of them, I realized. He was just furious at the helplessness he felt in the wake of all this. As I looked around the room I noticed they all seemed to share that sentiment. My eyes caught on Arlo, his usually large frame hunched and sullen in the corner. He didn't argue with anyone, didn't attempt to contribute to the discussion.

"She's in no condition to travel," Lennox argued back from where he leaned against the doorway, pointing toward my pitiful form still fighting to stop the shakes reverberating through my body. It was like attempting to stop shivering in the bitter cold of winter; the more I fought it, the stronger it grew. "Aerie, talk some sense into him. Tell him she can't travel like this."

Kirwan and Vander stood beside Lennox, the three of them barely fitting in the entrance for the greenhouse. The latter had been eerily quiet during this discussion and I found myself lingering on his dark form, the shadows deep around him.

Aerie inclined her head toward me, mulling over Lennox's words. She sat perched on the edge of my bed, offering a constant supply of warm energy and fresh tea.

"Normally I'd agree with you Nox," she admitted, "but there are extenuating circumstances here. Kahlis' attacks have grown more frequent, both on the tribe and on Hazel. He's getting too close, too bold. There seems to be a connection between her and the Rift and Kahlis' attacks.

The longer we go without closing the Rift, the more at risk she is for this happening again."

She eyed Vander carefully, glancing for a moment at Arlo, before continuing.

"Next time she might not make it back to us."

I shuddered involuntarily, a tendril of ice snaking its way down my spine. She squeezed my knee, sending another wave of warmth through my body in an attempt to suppress the chill.

"So it's settled," said Bastian firmly "I'm done playing the waiting game with this. We go fix that damned Rift and we get things set right again. Then we find a way to stop Kahlis once and for all." When no one argued, Bastian pushed off the worktable and came around to where Aerie sat and took her hand. "Aerie, my love, can you show us what you've found? Do we have a way to close the Rift?"

Aerie sighed, but I didn't miss the hint of color that rose in her cheeks as she let him pull her to her feet and planted a soft kiss on her cheek. She walked toward one of the books on the worktable.

She opened it but paused, leveling an assessing gaze at Bastian. "We won't know anything for sure until we actually can try it. This isn't exactly a scenario we can find in a history or spell book. But I've found a spell or two that should help us close it."

Her fingers flew over the pages of the old book as she tried to find what she was looking for. Bastian joined her at the table, his large form leaning over her as she read, almost swallowing her in sheer size.

"I think I have everything I need here," Aerie said at last. "It will take about a day to collect it all and prepare the spellwork."

"Great," Bastian boomed as he clapped his hands together. "Then we leave at the next sunrise."

I peered out one of the windows from where I sat, noticing the periwinkle hue growing on the horizon.

By the Fates, it was already morning?

"Bastian, I—" Aerie chewed on the edge of her lip as she debated what she was going to say. "Even with the spells—even if we tried every one of them—I'm not entirely sure it would work."

"Why?"

Vander's voice finally rang out through the greenhouse, forcing my gaze back to him. He kept his eyes trained on Aerie as he stepped forward, his shadows falling across the room, dimming the already low fae light that hung here.

Aerie took a deep breath before answering, "Because I'd be the one performing them. And it wasn't my magic that opened the Rift. In order for it to work, Hazel may have to be the one to perform them."

What?

My eyes widened, the color once again draining from my face.

"Me? But I thought I just had to be there." Another surge of shivers rattled through my body, bone-deep as they shook me.

"You may. Your very presence there may be enough to help close it. But we need to be realistic about the possibility that it won't work. Not unless you close it yourself."

"But I—" I stuttered, my words falling out in jagged, sharp breaths as I tried to speak. "I can't do that—can't *close* the Rift. I don't know how. I don't even have magic anymore."

"I mean..." Lennox started to argue, drawing out the words in a long singsong way.

"Not the time, Nox," Bastian cut in, shutting him down before he had another moment to finish his line of thought.

"I'm not expecting you to close the Rift, Hazel," said Aerie, "especially not after all you've been through tonight. I just need all of us to be aware that it might not work with my magic."

Aerie's eyes scanned the room, as if to make sure each and every one of us understood her meaning. When they landed on me at last, her gaze softened.

"But we will try." She offered me an encouraging smile.

I tried to return it, but the mutation that slipped across my lips probably resembled more of a grimace than an actual smile. I quickly buried my face back into the warm mug in my hands, inhaling the scent of herbs rather than look to any of the eyes that now bore into me.

"Everyone pack your shit," Bastian abruptly announced. "We leave in the morning. Try to get some sleep before then."

The shuffle of feet sounded through the greenhouse at the finality of the chieftain's orders, pulling a sigh of relief from my chest as I chanced a glance toward the door. Lennox and Kirwan were already gone; Arlo lingered in the door, seemingly unable to decide if he should stay or go.

"You," Bastian ordered, pointing at Vander. "Do not leave her side."

My skin went cold at his words. The idea of having to be so close to Vander after... well, after everything that had happened between us, was nerve-racking, to say the least. I'd tried so hard these past couple weeks to avoid him altogether. There was still so much left unsaid.

I felt like he was hiding from me, like I'd be a fool to trust him. Despite that fact, I couldn't help but notice the way his shadows shifted, lessened at Bastian's command.

Bastian planted another kiss, this time against Aerie's forehead, before stalking across the room and to the door. He threw one last look toward Arlo before leaving.

"You, too. Two sets of eyes are better than one. So are two armed bodies." He pulled a sheathed dagger from his side and tossed it to Arlo. "Vander can show you how to use it if you don't know already. And take you to our armory, should you feel like you need more."

A muscle in Vander's jaw ticked as he gave a curt nod at the firm order of his chieftain. Bastian was truly done playing around. I settled back into the bed, feeling the effect of Aerie's herbs starting to take hold. I didn't even know what she had given me tonight, but it felt much stronger than anything she'd used before. I found myself relaxing as I watched the periwinkle sunrise just outside the greenhouse windows. The remaining males moved around the small space, trying to put as much distance between them as possible. I suppressed the urge to smile at how rigid both Vander and Arlo looked, realizing this meant I was now required to be under the watchful eye of not one, but two males with whom I had a very complicated relationship.

Well, this should be fun.

I hadn't meant for Vander to hear my thoughts—hadn't even meant to think them. Aerie's herbs must have been *much* stronger than what I was used to. But despite my loopy state, Vander's eyes darkened as they locked on mine—an unspoken challenge hanging there.

Yes, it should be.

CHAPTER 49
HAZEL

Vander gave Arlo permission to leave just long enough to pack his things for our journey, stressing with both his words and his shadows the need to hurry back and not linger about the house. I tried to stay awake and discuss the various aspects of our tasks over the next several days, but Aerie insisted on letting me get some sleep before we left.

She gave me a dose of the potion she'd made with the Daeomi's blood, my first round of it since the potion had needed time to brew. I sent up a silent prayer to the Fates that this would work better than the teas had over the past few weeks, and took every burning drop of the liquid fire with gratefulness, refusing to let the pain it seared into my throat register.

When I awoke again, the greenhouse was empty, save for Aerie who was bent over the worktable and mixing a slew of ingredients in one of her copper bowls with fierce concentration and precision. She didn't let her eyes wander from what she was doing, even when I forced my aching body out of bed and pulled up a stool beside her. I watched her in silence for several minutes, finding her actions hypnotic as she measured and mixed things of all nature into the bowl. The only sound was her occasional muttered words as she poured a new ingredient into the mix or the flare of her magic as she reinforced the spellwork with her own power.

Eventually, I pulled my eyes away from her steady movements and looked around the room.

"Where's Vander?" I asked.

I hadn't expected him to disregard his brother's orders so quickly, despite his inclination to walk to the beat of his own drum—or rather, prowl.

Without taking her eyes off the jar she held, of what I could only hope wasn't accurately labeled *Dessicated Bone Powder,* she answered:

"He's just outside, claimed he needed to stretch his legs."

"Oh," was all I managed to respond. I don't know why I had hoped to see him, why it annoyed me now that he was making up reasons to not be in the same room as me.

"Arlo's helping the rest of the group prepare some things before we leave, but he should be back soon too. I told Bastian it was unnecessary to have them both here with us, what with me tending to you and the wards on the greenhouse being the strongest in the territory."

A shameful heat reached my ears as I averted my gaze, Aerie's eyes finally leaving her work to throw a sideways glance at me.

What did it say about me that I didn't even think to ask where Arlo was?

I tried to brush it off, tried to lie to myself and fabricate a whole list of excuses for why my mind didn't immediately recognize his absence.

Before I could voice any of them, Aerie had already returned to her work and I fell back into the hypnotic silence of watching her skilled hands.

"So where did you learn all this stuff?" I asked, impressed by the precision and wisdom that something like this line of work required. I'd seen her mix a mean cup of tea, seen her use herbs in ways I didn't even know could be used, but what she was doing now was even more meticulous than anything I'd watched her do before. Her face indicated as such, the lines burrowing across her brow only coming from a place of deep concentration.

"I mean," I continued, pressing closer, "I know your magic can heal, but this is different, right? This is more than just whatever power you possess."

She nodded absent-mindedly as she continued to work.

"I was raised in a fae household, one of the last remaining pure-blood families. When the First War broke out, our bloodline went into hiding to ensure they could carry on their fae heritage or some nonsense like that."

She sighed slightly as she flipped through a nearby spell book, then grabbed another tome and cross-referenced something before adding another ingredient to her bowl.

"I never bought into any of it," she admitted. "I sympathized with what the Fates had done, wanted desperately to escape into the world of New Magic and be freed of the oppressing hand of my father, my family. I was my father's only heir, though, his only chance to continue the bloodline, and he had big plans for what that meant. So, before he could marry me off and trap me in their corrupt world forever, I found a chance to run away, a way to escape his cruelty once and for all."

A wave of her hand had the bowl glowing with threads of her warm golden light. It snaked its way through the contents within, appearing to bind them together and bring them to life.

"Once free of them, I found the New World to be rather cruel in its own right, the creatures of New Magic not being particularly fond of my kind. That's when I found the coven, a sisterhood of witches buried within the woods. They took pity on me and brought me into their fold, taught me everything I know. I looked to them like family, and they raised me as their own." A glowing sense of pride radiated from her as she dusted her hands in front of her before settling them on her hips and turning to me.

"Where are they now?" I asked, a smile growing on my lips to reflect the one already spread wide on her face at the mention of their memory. It fell quickly, being replaced by something like grief and guilt.

"They've been dead for quite some time now. My father eventually found where I'd escaped to. Instead of stealing me away and forcing me to return home, he—"

Her words were cut off by the slightest crack in her voice, a sob forming somewhere in her throat. "He thought it would be a better lesson to tear them apart, uproot and demolish the coven that I called my family, and leave me behind to burn in the embers of what remained. He assumed that the weight of guilt would be its own death sentence, that he hadn't needed to deliver the final blow with his hands when he'd done so with his actions against my sisters. The fae consider witchcraft an abomination; he wouldn't touch me once he'd realized what I'd turned to, what I'd become."

Something inside my chest cracked, realizing the level of pain and anguish she had experienced all those years ago. It made me suddenly appreciate her so much more, her efforts and her craft. I couldn't imagine how hard it had to be for her to use the skills that her sisters had once taught her, the skills in and of themselves being a constant reminder of their absence in her life. My heart broke for her, but my respect grew tenfold, too.

"I'm so sorry," was all I could think to say, as the fae female with silvery white hair and piercing blue eyes stood before me, her very essence dripping warmth and love and kindness. I couldn't imagine how anyone could hurt her like that, how anyone so capable of evil had had a hand in bringing her into this world.

She brushed away a single tear that had slipped past her lashes as she waved a hand in the air and grabbed an empty jar from the shelves behind us.

"It's alright, it was a long time ago. I carry them with me, bringing their light to life every time I use what they taught me. Besides, I have a new family now, one that I'm so thankful for."

I thought of Bastian—the way that he doted on her, the way that he looked at her every moment she was in the room with him, the way he handled her with gentleness, not because she was delicate but because she was a deity deserving of that level of graceful care. Their love was unlike any I'd ever seen and I hoped one day I'd be lucky enough to have someone who loved me with that kind of ferocity.

When I looked up, though, I realized she was looking at me, talking about *me.* It was yet another attempt of hers to try and get me to understand how much I belonged here, how much this hodgepodge group of misfits loved me and accepted me as one of their own. I stifled a smile as I thought of the Chieftain of the Tribe of Talamh and his family: a young shifter still trying to understand how to rule, his brother with anger issues and a fractured soul tying Death itself to his being, a runaway fae with more wisdom than probably the rest of Tir Nadaar combined, the twin flames with the Fates know what powers, and their half-sister who was innocence embodied—and whatever I was.

It definitely was an eclectic mix.

"Does it ever feel like you don't belong?" I winced, embarrassed by my blunt question. "I mean—you're fae and... the Talamh tribe seems to have a grudge against the fae. And yet you lead them with grace and kindness and understanding anyway. I just wonder... if it ever feels like you don't belong."

She continued packing the contents of the bowl into a more portable container, mulling over my question. She let out a small sigh as she secured the lid on the container and wiped her hands on her apron, turning that understanding gaze toward me.

"Sometimes I do feel like a bit of an outsider here. I think that's why it's so easy for me to keep busy around the estate." She gestured to the greenhouse and the gardens beyond. "Sometimes it feels easier than trying to go into the village and relate to everyone. But these people are worth trying for."

I let my head dip low. That was a sentiment I could relate to. Aerie had been my closest friend since coming back here, the one person I'd been able to lean on. With what she'd just confessed to me, though, I realized how similar we were, how our struggles had been the same in some ways. I knew all too well the crushing weight of expectations and the fear of letting those around me down.

Perhaps she realized that too, because she reached out and gave my hand a reassuring squeeze, the motion pulling my attention back to her.

"Enough talk of this for now," she said gently. "We have a long journey ahead of us and I need a few moments with you to go over the spell work."

I nodded my head, the movement shaking off any lingering thoughts.

"Alright," Aerie said, turning back to the jar now sitting full of whatever herbs and obscure ingredients she'd mixed together. "Now this is a little tricky. I couldn't find much to help our exact situation, so I had to piece some things together until we had spellwork that would actually accomplish what we need."

I gaped at her, my jaw falling slack at her nonchalant tone.

"What?" she asked.

"You didn't just find a spell. You *made* a spell?"

"Well, I took parts and pieces that we needed from a variety of—"

"You. Made. A. Spell." My words cut her off, each one punctuated for emphasis.

Color rose in her alabaster cheeks, whether from embarrassment or pride, it was hard to tell.

"Yes," she said, her words light and amused as they rolled off her tongue, "I suppose I did."

I scoffed as a wide smile grew across her lips, the pride breaking through in thorough display now.

"You never cease to amaze me, Aerie. You are such a badass."

"Right, well," she said, the pride fading against her worry, "let's just hope it actually works."

She let out a shallow breath as she turned to the spell books laid out across the table and walked me through the more minute details of what she'd done and how it was supposed to work. Most of it went over my head, but what I gathered as she walked me through everything for the thirld time was that she had found a way to channel my energy through her power, in order to close the Rift. The spellwork would act as a catalyst, strengthening our efforts to close it and essentially mend the tear in time and space, and whatever else that the Rift had caused.

"Now, when the Rift is closed, it should mend the Void it caused in your mind. It should help with the things you've been struggling with and it will make you less of a target for Kahlis."

I winced at the statement, unable to feel anything but helpless against him after our last encounter. Acid tore through my arms and legs, as if the sheer memory of his time with me provoked those wounds to reopen within my mind. I found myself yet again hating how powerful he was, thinking how no one should be able to hold such titles as mindbender.

"Sorry." Aerie's eyes laced with sympathy as she noticed my reaction. "How are you doing, after last night?"

I could sense her trying to reach out, trying to use her magic to check on my wounds that she no doubt had healed several times over.

"I'm fine," I lied, trying to brush off the fire pouring through me as the blows Kahlis had delivered still echoed in my mind. I turned back to the books in front of us, desperate for anything to distract myself with. Something in one of the smaller books buried beneath the open pages caught my eyes. I pulled it to the surface, flipping through the pages as I skimmed the words.

"Have you—" I let the question fall away as I read deeper within the text.

Aerie nodded as she leaned over me, eyeing the book I'd picked up.

"Yes, in the very little free time I've had, I've been researching the Mark of the Grimm, trying to figure out if there's a way to remove it from Vander. I knew it was a long shot, but he doesn't deserve the evil that the Mark proclaims. I've been researching here and there for years, but now that I know *how* he got it, I figured I may be able to uncover something new."

I nodded absent-mindedly, feeling a cold chill snuff out the fire that had been burning through me only moments ago.

"And—" I stuttered, fumbling over the words. It had been a question on my mind every day, every moment since we'd understood what exactly it was Vander had done—if for no other reason than my own personal guilt regarding the situation. The question had been on the forefront of my mind during every single one of our memory work sessions together, if only I'd found the courage to ask it.

"Have you found a way? To remove the Mark, to mend his soul?"

I knew what I was asking, knew that mending his soul would ultimately mean losing Arlo in the process. It was why I hadn't asked her sooner. I couldn't choose between them, couldn't even fathom condemning one so that the other could live. I had to know, though. I had to know if there was even the slightest chance to fix all of the turmoil I had caused.

Aerie looked at me a long moment before answering, her head cocked to the side and her eyes watching in an unbiased, understanding way.

"No, Hazel, I haven't," she said, finally.

The answer should have brought me relief, should have filled me with joy to know that was a decision I'd never have to make: which life was worth saving. Instead, something tightened in my chest as I felt the pricking of tears behind my eyes. I swallowed hard, trying to tamp down on the emotion threatening to well up.

Aerie opened her mouth to say something just as the door opened and Vander prowled in, putting an end to the conversation entirely. I slipped the book discreetly back under Aerie's things as they spoke, careful to make sure Vander wouldn't see its contents.

CHAPTER 50
HAZEL

The day went by quickly, in a blur of preparations and packing. Vander was my silent shadow, his only absence being the short reprieve he took outside the greenhouse while Aerie and I talked. Despite his constant presence, we barely spoke. I didn't know what to say to him, how to acknowledge the things that had passed between us during the chaos of the previous night. Instead, I focused on the small list of preparations I'd been put in charge of until night fell.

I slept in the greenhouse, truly only getting a couple hours of rest. Vander stalked the small room in his wolven form, his perked ears signifying that he was on alert. Every few minutes he'd pause, his ears twitching and his head tilting to the side, as if he was listening, assessing the territory for any threats. I could tell he was restless, on edge, and his movements made it impossible for me to get any sleep.

Arlo joined us in the greenhouse once he finished whatever preparations he'd been given and helped Aerie finish packing up the last of her things, sliding into the small bed beside me when they were done.

Dawn came with a vengeance, the twilight glow illuminating the shadowed faces of our little group. Our movements were slow and ragged as we met at the stables to depart. Mirren was there, arguing with Kirwan and Lennox, as Vander, Arlo and I made our way from the greenhouse.

As we drew closer, I overheard their argument about Mirren staying at the estate. Kirwan insisted that she was too young, and any trip into the Dark Woods was a dangerous one. I understood why they didn't want her to join us, why they insisted she stay inside the wards and safety of the estate. Still, something in my chest cracked a little at her frustration. I knew what it felt like to be treated like a child, to feel powerless and useless and not in control.

"I can handle myself out there," she spat at Kirwan before swinging her head back to Lennox. "Tell him, tell him how you've been training me. Tell him that I can go!"

"Mir, I—" Lennox's sullen voice was cut off by an aggravated huff from Mirren.

"I. Am. Not. A. Child. I've been making decisions for myself in your absence for years. I can take care of myself."

"I don't doubt that." Kirwan looked at her with sympathy in his eyes.

Lennox hung his head low, as if ashamed. "But we are here now, Mirren. We have to look out for you. We need to have all of our efforts focused on the task at hand and not making sure that you're okay. You're safer here, within the wards. Please, just listen to us."

Mirren didn't answer; she only rolled her eyes as she grunted her frustration and stormed off back to the estate, mumbling a string of curses that would have put Vander to shame. I couldn't help but smile, her fiery spirit so opposite of the sweet, innocent girl everyone claimed her to be. I gave her a reassuring look as she passed me, mouthing the words *I'm sorry* as she slowed her movements just in front of me.

Despite the anger coursing through her, her features softened as she took me in.

"You've got this, Hazel. I can't wait for your return."

"I'm not sure I have any bearing on the situation," I replied honestly. "Aerie's the one doing all of the work. But thank you for your encouragement. Stay safe, Mirren. If you get bored waiting for our return, there's always the library. It's helped me lose track of time on some of the longest days I've spent here."

I gave her a small wink, hoping the words would do something to ease her boiling rage. She shot another hateful look toward her brothers, but simply nodded as she leaned in and gave me a firm hug.

"Be careful out there," she whispered into my shoulder as she squeezed me tighter. "And come back to me in one piece. I'd hate to lose a sister so soon after finding her."

Her eyes twinkled as she pulled away and a lump formed in my throat at her kind words. *Sisters.* That's what she considered us to be now, just as Aerie had told me I was family.

I nodded in agreement, unable to find anything to say as she let her hands slip through mine and turned to make her way back to the estate.

We closed the distance to the stables, joining Lennox and Kirwan.

"I still think she should come with us," Lennox grumbled. His head was still hung low, more so in irritation now as he argued with his brother in hushed tones.

"I'm not having this argument again, Nox. It's safer for her here."

Lennox looked like he might push further, but instead, he let Kirwan make his way into the stable as he slowed his strides and joined us while we walked in silence.

Inside the dimly lit stable, Bastian and Aerie waited for us. Aerie held the reins for a silvery white horse, strapping down the last of her things to the saddle. The animal looked just as graceful and powerful as Aerie. Bastian held the reins for a massive chestnut mare, the same one I had bonded with all those weeks ago. She whinnied at me as I made my way toward her and I gave her a couple reassuring pats.

"Hi again," I whispered.

Bastian watched me, surprised at the horse's easy temperament toward me. "You know, it would be a lot easier for me to walk. I have more power when I shift and I'd feel more comfortable being on the ground and on guard, in case anything should happen."

He handed me the reins, refusing to drop his hand until I took them. I was stunned: the Chieftain of the Tribe of Talamh was handing over his warhorse to me, choosing to stalk through the woods as some sort of lowly guard rather than ride like the leader he was.

"I couldn't possibly—" I shook my head, trying to hand the reins back.

"Sure you can, you'd be doing me a favor. I need to stretch my wolven legs anyway. Besides, Brigid clearly prefers you."

He chuckled as the strong mare tousled my hair with her muzzle. I gave her several pets to appease the beast, leaning into the familiar warmth she provided.

Without much more discussion, our group made our way out of the stable and toward the Dark Woods.

Kirwan joined me and Aerie on horseback. Arlo, apparently deciding to ride with me, had settled against my back atop Brigid. Lennox, Bastian, and Vander circled us on foot, the latter two having shifted into their wolven forms. Despite the rising sun, the world grew dark around us as we slipped behind the tree line of the woods. It was as if the trees knew exactly what we had come here to do, and shadowed us in darkness as a warning to turn back, a mark of what was to come.

Our first day through the Dark Woods was rather uneventful. Most of the creatures that lurked there left us alone. I wondered if it was the presence of a chieftain that kept them at bay or if they could sense the Mark of the Grimm as Vander weaved through the trees and shadows in his wolven form. His head was low, his movements precise as he watched the thick foliage for any sign of a threat. I noticed that he kept a wider berth than the rest of the group, pulling away often to dip deeper into the trees for a while, and circling back around or emerging up ahead several minutes later. Watching the way he moved like silk stirred something within me and I found myself shifting in the saddle trying to force my mind to other things.

In addition to Vander's distracting presence, Arlo's movements were setting my teeth on edge. He kept readjusting his hold on me, his grasp too gentle, too delicate. It was like he was worried he'd hurt me if his fingers lingered too long in one spot. My back went rigid against him as he moved his hand for what felt like the thousandth time, debating the best way to hold onto my waist.

"I'm not made of glass, you know," I barked at him, my voice laced with more poison than I'd intended. I couldn't stand how he was treating me. It had always felt like he was walking on eggshells around me, but ever since last night, he'd been acting like an utter ass.

"I'm sorry, I'm just trying to be mindful not to hurt you after..." His voice trailed off, but I knew where his mind was: after last night, after everything Kahlis did to me. He didn't even know the extent of what had happened to me, and still he acted like I was too fragile to touch. If only he could have seen just how bad it had been. He probably wouldn't even be riding on the horse with me now. Probably would have insisted I stay back at the estate with Mirren altogether.

I rolled my eyes, reaching back and grabbing his hand to plant it firmly around my hips.

"See? Doesn't hurt. Aerie healed me so you don't need to treat me differently, just act like normal," I lied as I turned back, my face wincing slightly at the pain that tore through me after the rough movements. I could handle it, though. I reveled in it, letting the flames spur me forward.

"I am acting normal, Hazel. I'm just trying to take care of you." Silence fell between us as I realized how right he was. This was how he always treated me, only I was just now realizing how little I wanted it.

"I don't need to be *taken care of*." My words shot like arrows toward him. I was trying to calm my anger, confused at where the deep well of it had come from.

"I'm not weak," I added, almost as an afterthought. Almost as if I didn't quite believe it.

If Arlo had heard my words, he didn't reveal it. We rode in silence for a long time after that, his hands staying firmly planted where I had put them. I could tell my comments had wounded him though, could feel the way he gave my body as much space as allotted with us both restrained to the leather saddle.

When we stopped to make camp for the night, the wolves prowled the immediate area as Aerie set up wards to guard us from whatever creatures a night in the Dark Woods might summon. Once the wards were up and a border established, we made quick work of setting up camp and starting a small fire to heat the stew that Aerie had packed for us. It would last us a meal, maybe two if we ate it sparingly. We would most likely resort to hunting for our food at some point in this journey if we had to linger out here for any length of time. I cherished every bite of the succulent meat and creamy sauce, not wanting to think about what kinds of animals one would hunt for food in the Dark Woods.

As soon as I finished eating, I retired to our tent, claiming exhaustion from the events of the last several days. It wasn't a lie—I *was* exhausted—but I was more concerned about getting a moment to myself, away from the watchful eyes of Arlo. He hadn't spoken to me since our heated discussion earlier, but I couldn't seem to shake his gaze. A smattering of canvas tents lay spread out around the fire. I made my way for the one Bastian had pointed me toward and ducked behind the canvas flap. It was the first time all day I didn't feel like I was being evaluated and assessed.

I didn't bother with changing; a night in the woods didn't exactly call for comfortable nightclothes. Instead, I pulled off my boots and slipped into the covers of the small pallet Arlo had set up for us. I lay in the quiet darkness of the tent, mulling over what the next day held. With any luck, we'd find the Rift and begin working on it. I let my mind wander to the Rift itself, what little I remembered about it and how Arlo had claimed it was my magic that had created it. I held my hands above me, their silhouettes almost indistinguishable in the darkness of the tent.

I let Aerie's lesson with Mirren play over in my mind, remembering her words as I turned my hands through the air so I could examine them. *Your power only flows if you accept its presence, welcome it and will it to do what you want.* Those had been her words to Mirren, but I wondered if she'd meant for me to hear them. I'd been so adamantly against the idea of any power lying within me, so sure it couldn't possibly have been my own hands that made the Rift.

But what if I was wrong?

I closed my eyes, letting myself wander within my own mind, searching for that power that Aerie insisted she'd sensed in me. She was so adamant, her belief moving to something even stronger, even deeper within me. The memory of her constant comfort and warmth wrapped around me, her magic spurring me on to push further and find my own. Something deep within sparked, a beacon begging me to keep pushing. I followed it, letting the spark grow as it spread through my veins and down my arms into my fingers. I could have sworn a soft glow radiated through the tent from behind my closed eyelids, but before I could find the courage to open them and confirm my theory, I heard shuffling outside.

I dropped my hands to my chest, sinking them deep within the blankets now tucked up around my chin as I pinched my eyes closed even tighter.

Arlo swooped into the tent. I breathed a slight sigh of relief and pretended to be asleep. He settled in next to me, his movements seemingly as stiff as my body felt. He said nothing as we lay in the darkness, most likely assuming I was actually asleep. I made no motions, no indications to let him know he was wrong.

My eyes grew heavy with exhaustion the longer we lay there in silence. I found myself drifting in and out of consciousness as I listened to Arlo's breathing grow steadier. Just as I let my body slip back under the cloud of exhaustion, I heard Arlo whisper into the darkness.

"I know you're not weak, Hazel. I just don't know how to be the kind of strength you need anymore."

CHAPTER 51
HAZEL

Arlo's words washed through my dreams in confusing waves as they split apart and converged into new nightmares. Visions of me curled at the feet of Kahlis, bleeding and sobbing, played over and over again. When he spoke, it was Arlo's voice, telling me I was weak and no one would be there to save me. The vision imploded on itself, crashing together in a swirl of black smoke before becoming something new. Then I was sitting in front of my mother back at our cottage, her voice once again Arlo's as the words repeated over and over: *You are weak. You are weak. You are weak.*

When I awoke, I was covered in a cold sweat and my breath was ragged. I felt like I had just run for hours, the hot shallow breaths doing nothing to abate the sting growing in my chest. I looked around the tent for the midnight fur that was supposed to be my guard during our time in the Dark Woods but found nothing aside from darkness and the quiet sounds of Arlo's snores. I rolled my shoulders and shook my hands, trying to get my body to ease. It was no use and within another moment, I was crawling out of the tent with my boots in one hand to try and get my mind to settle. Kahlis might not be able to find me in my dreams anymore, thanks to the potion Aerie had made for me, but that apparently didn't stop the nightmares from still finding me.

Just outside my tent, a dark form perched on a fallen log. The fire had died down to mere embers, casting him in deep shadows where he sat. He moved, bringing something up to his face as an orange hue glowed in the moonlight, the contents of the pipe burning in a subtle crackle as I closed the distance between us. Not Vander.

"I didn't expect you to be up, Lennox."

I dropped onto the log beside him, my movements still shaky from the nightmares, as I bent to pull on my boots.

He nodded to me, not taking his eyes off the tree line beyond my tent.

"You're not the only one with nightmares that haunt them, Hazel." His voice was distant, his tone stunning me as it lacked its usual sarcastic edge. I was suddenly aware that I had walked into a moment I was most likely not intended to see.

After several minutes and another pull from his pipe, he finally dragged his eyes over to where I sat.

"You can call me Nox, you know. You did before."

"Oh," was all I offered, thrown off by his blunt words.

"Alright," I said.

"Alright," he replied.

He took another drag off the pipe before half-heartedly offering it to me. I shook my head, declining due to the backlash it had caused last time. I wasn't here to smoke; I just wasn't ready to be alone quite yet. Going back to the tent felt like an impossible task right now. He didn't push me, but the longer we sat in silence, the more the visions I'd dreamt of haunted my mind. Tremors shot through my hands as I searched the campsite for that familiar glow of golden eyes.

He offered the pipe again, looking at me with intent this time.

"Trust me, it will help."

I hesitated, but took the pipe from him and let the earthy wisps of smoke fill my lungs.

"I was right about where you are, half an hour ago. Now look at me." He waved a hand over his sullen form. "The picture of mental stability."

I smiled at him. He returned the sentiment, but I didn't miss the way it didn't reach his eyes. I could only imagine what kind of nightmares must have plagued him. I was captured by Kahlis in my dreams, experienced his explicit form of torture more than once, but Lennox had *lived* there. He'd been in that world and dealt with him firsthand.

"Thanks." I held the pipe back out to him, but he shook his head, not even bothering to take it.

"Nah, I've had enough. Best if I stop now. We have work to do tomorrow. Besides, if I smoke anymore while I'm on guard duty for you, then Vander will have my balls."

"For me?" I tilted my head toward him, trying to understand his meaning.

His lips pressed together in a firm line, as if he'd accidentally let something slip. "Yeah, Vander had... an itch to scratch. I told him I'd keep an eye on you while he ventured out."

My irritation spiked. I knew he hunted these woods often, but was it really so hard to take one night off? We had more important things to focus on than his violent impulses. Bastian had given him an order to stay with me and this was the second time in less than a day where he'd wandered off.

"Which way did he go?"

Lennox didn't answer, just nodded in the direction of the tree line behind my tent, the same spot he'd been focusing on since I sat down beside him.

I gritted my teeth, reaching down to ensure that the dagger Arlo had purchased for me all those weeks ago was once again strapped to my side. I'd made sure to pack it when we were preparing for our journey, back at the estate. Given how many trained and armed members were in our little caravan, I didn't think I'd actually need it. Still, I figured it was better safe than sorry.

I stood in one swift motion, the herb from Lennox's pipe acting fast to steady my nerves. If Vander could disobey Bastian's orders and stalk off into the woods, then so could I. What if I'd needed him tonight? What if my nightmares had been sent from Kahlis rather than the ones that typically plagued me? He would have been out in the woods doing unspeakable things while I was here, lost to Kahlis and stuck in a nightmare being tortured. Or worse, killed. I took several steps toward the woods, fueled by the anger of the *what-ifs* that could have happened tonight. I half expected Lennox to grab me or at the very least, object. When he did neither, I turned back to him.

"Aren't you going to try and stop me?"

He put his hands up. "Hey, I'm not your keeper. If you want to trample about in the Dark Woods after midnight, far be it from me to stop you. Besides, with Vander out there, you aren't in danger. He'll sense you a mile away. He'd know if you started bleeding and needed help."

I smirked at him. "Real comforting, thank you. Don't you think Vander would have your balls for this just as much as for the smoking?"

"I'll handle it if he does." He gave me a wink, motioning for me to go after him.

"Thanks... Nox," I said, before pivoting toward the tree line and disappearing beneath the canopy. His deep chuckle faded behind me as I edged my way deeper into the woods and away from the safety of our campsite.

The Dark Woods were quiet. They had been quiet for much of our journey, but now as I slipped through the black cover of night, I felt as if the quiet was growing. It was otherworldly; even the trees had gone still in my presence. I had become accustomed to their swaying, sentient movement. Despite the way it had made my skin crawl when I'd first noticed their mannerisms, it quickly became normal in my mind. This, however—utter stillness, as if time itself had stopped—was not normal.

The subtle glow of the campfire was swallowed by the deep black of the woods. I clung to what little bit I could see, what small sounds stayed with me from the campsite, for as long as I could. They had quickly fallen away though, leaving me to fend for myself as I assumed a path through the foliage to find Vander. I was going to chew his ass out for leaving. The deeper I retreated into the woods, the more my anger grew. How could he be so selfish? How did he not understand that he was basically the only thing I had to rely on for protection at this point—my last line of defense? Only he could pull me back from Kahlis' dreamwalking. Only he could lull me out of that terrorizing state. Now, because of him, I was out in the Dark Woods in the middle of the night with no clue as to what I was doing and probably putting myself in even more danger, just to prove a point. If he wasn't going to take this job seriously, then I would find him and force him to.

I stopped trudging through the overgrowth, my head swiveling around to determine which direction I should go—or which I'd come from. I had all but decided to give up, worried I was drifting too far from the camp, when I realized I couldn't make my way back, even if I wanted to. Fear gripped my chest as I let out a frustrated huff.

Maybe coming out here was a mistake.

I wouldn't even be out here if Vander could go five seconds without killing something.

I pushed the fear down, letting my irritation and anger smother it as I took a few deep breaths and finally settled on which direction to go. I took a single step forward, my foot not even finding time to sink into the soft, mossy ground of the woods before a hand clamped down around my mouth, stifling a scream as it tightened around my lips.

CHAPTER 52
VANDER

"You shouldn't be out here, little spitfire. All kinds of things slither through the night in the Dark Woods. It's no place for an unobservant pain in the ass."

I felt her terror give way to rage as she realized whose hand was clamped around her mouth. I leaned into her scent, lingering for a moment longer against her back before dropping my hand and letting her scurry away from me.

She spun fast, landing a punch to my gut. I would have been irritated at the action, her arm packing a surprising amount of strength, if seeing her like this didn't stir something deeper within me.

"You gave me a heart attack, Vander." Her breath was ragged, head shaking—as if she was trying to brush off the feeling of my phantom touch still lingering on her.

"Serves you right for coming out here," I said, trying to recover from the loss of breath her punch had caused. "What were you thinking?"

"I could ask *you* the same question," she bit back, eyes flaring with emotion.

She stomped over to where I stood. It was so hard not to laugh when she was angry like this. It was like watching a rabbit try to take on, well, a wolf. I had to give her credit though; she had guts coming out here like this. Most of Tir Nadaar avoided the Dark Woods like a plague.

"Relax, I was keeping an eye on you. I knew the moment you slipped away from the campsite and I've been tracking you ever since. I just wanted to see how far you'd go before you admitted you were lost."

The glare she threw me dissolved the smirk that had settled on my face.

"This isn't the time for games, Vander." Her voice shook, trembled, and I immediately scolded myself for not realizing how scared she'd be if she woke to find I was gone. It wasn't anger I was seeing in those round, green eyes—it was fear. "Bastian gave you an order to watch over me and you're out here playing villain of the night instead of making sure that Kahlis doesn't find a way to get to me again."

A low growl rumbled through my chest in warning as I stepped closer to her. She might be scared, but it was unfounded, irrational. If she thought I'd really leave her unguarded, after everything that she'd been through... Her chastising was like a flood of ice water, dousing whatever heat had begun to stir within me.

Insufferable female.

A tremor of pure rage rippled through her body as she heard the words I'd sent down the tether. Before she had time to throw back a retort, I blazed on:

"Do you really think I'm not taking this seriously, Hazel? Trust that I know what I'm doing. I know how to protect you, even if it may not look like the overbearing, disempowering methods you're used to."

She picked up my meaning without missing a beat, throwing the insult right back at me:

"At least Arlo is doing *something*. At least he cares!" Her words boomed through the trees, so loud and full of accusation, but I couldn't help but notice the questioning tone in her voice or the doubt in her eyes, as if she was trying to convince herself as much as me. "You walk around here like it wouldn't bother you one bit if something happened to me."

My movement slowed, my voice dropping low as I circled her and whispered, "You and I both know that isn't true. Don't confuse my ability to ensure your well-being from afar with indifference for your safety. Just because I don't have to be breathing down your neck to ensure you're safe, doesn't mean I don't care about it."

I stepped in close behind her, letting my shadows wrap around her as I bent my head toward the exposed skin of her neck.

"Or perhaps you'd prefer I did," I breathed out, letting the weight of my words settle against her ivory skin. It was impossible to miss the gooseflesh that rose from her smooth, silky skin.

She lingered a moment, rooted to the spot by either fear or something more wicked. It took all of my restraint to not reach out and kiss her, taste her. Despite the dark coverage of the canopy, her skin shone in the moonlight that leaked through from above. Seeing her out here, in my environment—it did something to me. It fed the primal urge that I'd been fighting every day since her return.

Before I could do something stupid, like act on it, she mercifully broke the silence and pushed away from me again.

"Or perhaps *you're* making up excuses so you can slink off to the Dark Woods and sink your teeth into something."

My smirk returned. She was completely unaware of how much truth her words held in this moment, just in an entirely different way than she was thinking.

She huffed, clearly irked by my lack of concern. "Need I remind you what happened last time I had to wait for you to show up and pull me out of the nightmare Kahlis had me trapped in?"

I inclined my head toward her, assessing her meaning as she pelted daggers at me with her eyes. Her fear was heavy, despite the front she was putting up. She didn't need to remind me. Nothing would ever burn the memory of her, hollowed and flayed after Kahlis' torture, from my mind. It didn't matter that none of it had been real, that her body hadn't physically been hurt. She'd felt every last drop of pain from what he'd done to her in that nightmare and it was a wonder that she was here at all, and not lost to insanity within herself.

"Do you think I was out hunting last night? When Kahlis found you?"

Her demeanor shifted, her body recoiling slightly as she realized that she'd assumed incorrectly.

"I know how to control myself, Hazel. I know how to control my urges. Despite what you might think, I am not a wild animal. I was at the estate when it happened. Right outside your damn door, as I have been every damn night since your encounter with the Wisps."

"Every night?" Her echo of my words was breathy, stunned. Her jaw fell slack as her eyes went wide. I let the confession wash over her, assessing if the knowledge would comfort her or scare her more. When she refused to speak, I went on:

"The reason it took me so long to find you last night is because Arlo tried first. I broke into your room when I heard your screams, his frantic desperation to save you. I thought..." I broke off, dropping my eyes to the forest floor, anger and shame rolling through me at the weight of my mistake. "I shouldn't have waited, shouldn't have hesitated to save you. I just had to know if he could do it."

I sighed as the truth came out. "I had to know you needed me. Not anyone else. Just me."

Hazel battled for a moment, the callousness she'd stormed out here with slipping ever so slightly to give way to something softer, something more tender and vulnerable beneath. I took it as my cue and stepped toward her, hoping she wouldn't retreat again. My movement must have shaken something back into place because in an instant that cool anger snapped back over her features.

"And instead of understanding the importance of that, you take off on the first night to go hunt?!" Her voice rose as she closed the distance she'd put between us. "It's that hard to put up with me? That hard to just suck it up and make sure I'm okay?"

"You're so self-centered, you realize that?" I scoffed, shaking my head.

I let a beat of silence pass between us. She crossed her arms over her chest and tapped a foot, waiting for me to explain myself.

I rolled my eyes, huffing out a frustrated breath as I finally let go of the last bit of dignity I had left. "Fine. Yes. It is *that* hard for me to be around you, Hazel. I can't stand it and Fates spare me if that requires the occasional break from your never-ending presence in my life."

She gasped, clearly offended. She opened her mouth to argue, but I held up a hand to cut her off.

"I can't stand being in your life as just another person, to sit back and watch as someone else touches you, holds you. I can't stand the pain and anger I see within you whenever I let my own emotions, the feelings of the Mark, seep into the tether. I can't stand causing that pain in you when you already have so much pain to manage. I'm just trying to figure out how to cope with the roles we play for each other now, trying to navigate how exactly to be what you *need* me to be when it isn't even close to what I want us to be."

She took a step back, eyes darting to the Mark on my arm. "You know? That I've been feeling you through the tether? Feeling the Mark?"

I nodded, but her gaze was trained on the crude marking on my skin, writhing and crying out at the attention it was receiving. She shuddered in response, no doubt feeling it flare. I pinched the bridge of my nose, trying and failing to gather control of the dark magic making its presence known. This was the exact problem with *us.* I was too strong, too violent. I loved seeing her emotions untamed, hoped that perhaps that fiery spirit could help her handle my power. But so far she couldn't manage feeling the tether, let alone the Mark—and I couldn't tamp down on its power hard enough to make it nonexistent to her.

"I don't know how to be what you need either," she said through a whimper. *I don't know who I am on my own... without Arlo.* Her thoughts radiated down the tether, barreling into me with the surprised suddenness of an unexpected, thick fog. I suppressed the urge to scoff, forcing myself to take in the full extent of the darkness she was trying to let me see. Her head was hung low, shoulders slumped, like she'd been carrying the weight of this confession for far too long.

She must have noticed some reaction in me, though, because she felt the need to defend her thought. "You don't understand. You weren't there during the worst of it. You talk this big talk about feeling my pain and it hurting you to know I feel it. But you weren't there when it was at its worst, when I didn't know up from down, life from death, nightmares from reality."

Tears were now welling behind her lashes, her voice rough as she whispered through the night air, "Arlo *was,* though; he held me countless nights as he patiently tried to piece me back together. He was the thread that single-handedly held my sanity in place." She shook her head, burying her face in her hands to try and hide her sobs. "How do I walk away from that? Who am I *without* that?"

Perhaps I'd read her wrong. Perhaps it wasn't her fear of the Mark keeping us apart. Perhaps it was her fear of letting me see the true extent of *her* darkness that was keeping her at arm's length—of letting somebody in after already sharing that with someone else. There was so much more here to unpack than I'd realized; I didn't even know where to begin. But if anyone knew that struggle, it was me. My heart ached for her, ached for the wonderful creature she couldn't see in herself. I wanted to hold her, to show her all the ways that I knew she had strength—and all the ways I understood her darkness. She just had to believe it—and accept it.

"Maybe it would just be best to keep our distance," she said, swiping at the tears running down her cheeks and clearing her throat. She took a step back, collecting herself as she forced more distance between us—in every way. "I don't know how to do this, how to make this work. With Arlo, with the Mark. Maybe we should just go our separate ways and be done with all of this, Vander. "

"I can't!" The words were out of my mouth before I could register what I was about to admit. This wasn't the right time, nor the right place. But I couldn't take another second without her knowing. She wanted to show me her darkness? Fine. I'd show her just how aware I was of every aspect of it. And how it changed *nothing*. "I can't because we're fucking *Fated*, Hazel. I can't just *choose* not to be around you. Our life threads are woven together. For all of eternity. And there's nothing I can do to change that, no matter if I wanted to or not. No matter how many times you reject me, no matter whoever else you decide to be with instead of me: we are in each other's lives forever, regardless of what we want."

Her eyes widened, taking in each word like a slap to the face—cold, bitter pain.

"Fated?" She echoed my words, her voice shaking. "I don't—I don't understand. How could we? How are we supposed to...?" Her voice trailed off but I could tell by the way she was once again sizing up the Mark on my arm what she was thinking. There was a reason the Fates had woven our lives together. A reason we felt so drawn to each other. And I thought, just maybe, she was starting to understand that too.

Her voice had gone utterly quiet, barely a whisper in the night:

"Fates be damned."

If only it were that simple. There were still so many things about this world that she didn't remember, didn't understand in her current state. So I supposed it was my place to enlighten her. I leveled my gaze at her, closing the distance she kept putting between us. My steps were slow, calculated; each one reverberated through the ground with my power as I let my shadows reach out and wrap around her, forcing her closer to me.

"No, I don't think you do understand, little spitfire."

Two more steps and we were face to face, chest to chest. I greedily breathed in her scent again, letting the familiar aroma ground me and give me strength to continue.

"Your entire being echoes through my soul, Hazel. I *want* nothing more than to have you wholly and eternally. Darkness and all. It's not a simple matter of what the Fates decided for us. It is in my very essence to be near you, to sit at your feet and worship the ground you walk on. When you were gone, I was so lost. I was out of control and out of my mind without you. I became whatever the fuck I am now: a dark, purposeless shadow who only lives to inflict pain and death as a way to feel something. *That's* who I am without you, *that's* how badly I need you. Make no mistake though, that darkness would never, *could* never be turned toward you. You feel it so strongly because you recognize it, just as it recognizes the darkness in you. You are my life's breath, the fire in my veins, and I would tear this world apart if it meant giving you peace of mind."

She shuddered but didn't pull back, didn't move a singular muscle.

"But then you had to go and fall in love with that other part of me. You depend on him. And I don't know what to do about that. I don't know how to act around you *because* of that. He's not me. A piece of me, yes, but not the whole thing. He's a piece that I can never get back. And he offers you a form of protection that I never will. You say you don't know who you are without him? How am I supposed to demand you be with me instead of him? When he keeps you safe and he's all the best parts of me. I'm not worthy of you. No matter how much I burn for you, I could never deserve you. Not before, when I was whole, and certainly not now. When all that was good and lovely and wholesome was stripped of me, and walks and talks separate from my body. Not with this damned mark on my skin and the darkness that slithers beneath its surface. Not when even being near you causes you to recognize that same darkness within yourself."

I let my eyes pore over her form, taking in every beautiful piece of her, every piece that I would devour if given the chance. We were so alike in so many ways, but she wouldn't accept that, wouldn't accept me, until she'd realized it for herself.

"No, Hazel, I don't deserve you. And as much as it kills me to live this half-life now, I'd do it all again if I knew it meant saving you. Because even still, I feel your anguish, your darkness threatening to consume you. And somehow he seems to keep that at bay. Probably better than I ever could. And I won't take that away from you. I could never."

CHAPTER 53
HAZEL

I wanted to tell him how wrong he was, how it might have been like that at one point between me and Arlo, but that had ended the moment he'd shown up at the estate. I wanted to tell him how tired I was of everyone making decisions for me about what I could handle, what I needed. I wanted to tell him how much he helped that darkness inside of me in a way that Arlo never could. I didn't say any of that though, as my brain was still reeling from what he'd admitted.

Fated.

I had known there was a connection between us—the tether, or whatever he called it. I knew there was something there, but I thought it was just more magic that I couldn't comprehend. I hadn't realized we were Fated, hadn't even realized what that meant or just how deeply our connection stemmed. No wonder I couldn't get him off my mind, couldn't avoid him or deny the way he made me feel. I'd thought he hated me, was pining for some far-off version of the female I used to be.

He'd told me, though, that night after the Wisps: he told me then that he wouldn't lose me again, that he'd take any version of me he could have.

"How long have you known?" I couldn't bring my eyes to his.

He'd kept this from me, even after the Wisps, even after our moment in the old cottage; and that stung worse than the icy tendrils of the Void in my mind.

He let out a long sigh. I could tell by the way his hand twitched at his side that he was restraining himself, trying to resist the urge to touch me.

"I didn't know for sure until I lost you, until I felt like my very soul had been ripped out of my body. I didn't know if things would be different after you returned. If Arlo might..." he trailed off, but I caught his meaning. He wasn't sure if Arlo being here, being real, may have shifted whatever it was that tethered us together. "Fated mates have a bond unlike anything else in this world," he explained in a hushed tone. "They aren't meant to survive without each other."

I couldn't move, couldn't breathe.

"That's why you split your soul, so you could protect me even after we'd been separated?"

I felt the motion of his head moving in agreement, incapable of admitting it out loud.

Finally, I let my eyes meet his, let them acknowledge the battle raging there—a battle between fear and hope after all he'd admitted before me tonight.

"But"—I shook my head, still not quite understanding—"*you* survived."

"Can't you see, Hazel?" A muscle in his jaw twitched as he looked down at me, letting me see every part of him: every flaw, every scar, every dark shadow, dripping with self-loathing and rage. "I didn't."

I swallowed hard, looking into the glowing golden eyes of the male I'd seen so many sides of before tonight. It was as if they all were coming together, converging to click into place something that I'd long ago forgotten. Tears welled in my eyes as I tried to understand what exactly it was I was feeling, what my heart was telling me it wanted.

"It doesn't matter if you don't want it, don't want me," he said, sounding defeated. "I've just waited so Fates-damned long to tell you. It doesn't matter if you've chosen another. I needed you to hear it, needed to say it at least once."

Vander took a step back, finally releasing the tension that had built between us. He'd taken my silence as rejection, a sign that I didn't return his sentiment. I wanted to tell him how wrong he was; I wanted to scream at him that I felt it too. I couldn't, though, my body paralyzed with shock.

He turned, making his way back toward camp. "Come on, we'd better get you back before Arlo wakes to find you missing. Wouldn't want him to think you got taken by the shadows of the Dark Woods."

Arlo. Every time I started to let my mind drift to the possibility of me and Vander, there Arlo was to make things more complicated. I didn't know what to do. How was I supposed to walk away from everything Arlo was to me? How was I supposed to survive without him by my side—the very thing that had been holding me together this past year? My mind hurt from trying to understand it all, trying to figure out what I was supposed to do—and I felt that familiar darkness threatening to pull me under.

I forced my feet to move, to follow the path Vander was making for us as we walked in silence back to the campsite. Hot, frustrated tears fell in silent streams down my face. I made sure to stay in Vander's shadows as we walked. I didn't want him to see me cry. Within minutes, the glowing embers of the campfire broke through the trees. Lennox was still sitting on the log by the diminishing fire when we broke through the tree line. I beelined for my tent, refusing to say anything else to Vander. I needed time to think. Nothing about this was fair, and I couldn't manage discussing it any further tonight. I sent up a silent prayer of thanks that Arlo was still fast asleep as I sunk into my blankets and brought my knees to my chest. I wrapped my arms around them as I lay on my side and watched the warm glow of the dying fire through the canvas of the tent.

Lennox and Vander's voices drifted through the summer night's wind, hushed.

"So I take it that didn't go well."

A growl vibrated through the air.

"Maybe she just needs time." Nox's voice turned softer, a thread of sympathy weaving through it.

"I'm not holding out hope. I wasn't trying to get her back, I just needed her to know." His voice dripped with anger and disappointment. "Now she does."

My eyes shifted from the glow of the fire to Arlo's serene face across the tent. He was such a great male. There had been so many times in the past year when I'd wondered how I ever deserved him. Now, I didn't know what I deserved. I'd been so cruel to him lately, so off-put by everything he'd done for me in the past weeks. I thought he'd changed, become more overbearing and intolerable, but maybe it was me that had changed.

I squeezed my eyes shut as another wave of grief tightened around my chest, pulling a new torrent of tears from behind my lashes. My breath quickened, my lungs incapable of pulling enough air to satisfy the piercing pain radiating through them. I gripped my legs tighter as the tremors started to roll through me and my body gave way to the hysteria.

I knew what I felt for Vander, Fates or no Fates, but that didn't mean I wasn't still afraid of him—or rather, still afraid of being with him. It didn't mean I was ready to let Arlo down and walk away from all the safety and care he offered. He'd done so much for me over the past year, how could I just walk away from that? It would break me to hurt him so thoroughly. I didn't even know if I could survive without him, or if I'd simply crumble without his steady hand to hold me. But even as I lay next to him, peacefully asleep beside me, all I could think of was the male just outside the tent and everything he'd admitted to me tonight.

CHAPTER 54
HAZEL

The tremors and tears must have subsided at some point, lulling me into a deep, dreamless sleep, because when I awoke, daylight streamed into the crack of the tent opening. Arlo must have already woken up because I was alone amongst the blankets. I dug my palms into my face, trying to rub away the pain that I felt building behind my eyes. As I let the counterpressure push away the oncoming headache, I noticed the commotion of the others outside the tent.

Arlo ducked around the canvas flap just as I sat up to find out what everyone was doing. "I brought you some breakfast, but you'll have to eat quickly. They're already packing up."

He handed me the bowl before turning to his blankets and rolling them up into a neat bundle. The bowl was full of steaming, thick porridge. It didn't look the best, but the smell wafting from the bowl had my mouth watering as I dug in. Arlo paused what he was doing, baffled by my apparent appetite. He didn't say anything, most likely scared if he took note of it that I'd throw the whole bowl away out of sheer embarrassment. His gaze just darted from me to the bowl I held close against my chest as I shoveled the remaining bites into my mouth.

He shook his head, as if to clear the confusion from his mind, before turning back to his packing. He'd finished with his bedroll and moved to work on mine as I scooted off the blankets.

"You let me sleep in?" I asked, wondering how long the rest of them had been up.

His hands hesitated, his body stilling and muscles going rigid.

"Seemed like you had a rough night. I thought you could use the extra sleep."

My skin went cold, my spoon hovering in the air, midbite.

Did he know about last night? How *much* did he know?

"I—" I stuttered, trying to decide exactly how much I wanted to reveal.

"I know, I know, you don't need me taking care of you. Although, I don't think letting you sleep in after a particularly restless night necessarily counts as taking care of you. It's just common sense."

I shook my head slowly, remembering the way I had jumped down his throat yesterday for being too scared to hold onto me as we rode through the woods. Guilt curled in my stomach. I needed to make amends for how badly I'd been treating him lately. I set the spoon back down in the bowl, pushing the dish aside as Arlo finished packing up the last few things in our small tent.

"Arlo, I'm sorry. For yesterday."

"Hazel, don't." He sighed, shaking his head in frustration. "You were right. You are far more capable than I give you credit for and it's time I realize it. I just... I got so damn used to you needing me. And I'm scared of what we will look like when you don't anymore."

His head hung low, his fingers fidgeting with the clasps of the bag in his hands.

"I'll always need you, Arlo." Even as the words left my lips, it felt wrong to say. There was no point denying the shift that had happened between us. He gave me a half smile, the gesture seeming inauthentic.

"No, you won't. But that's okay. You are destined for so much more than what we had, our little life together."

I cocked my head to the side, confused."Why do you say that?"

"Because I know you, I know you are destined for great things, Hazel. I just wish I could help you achieve them."

"Arlo, you're scaring me. What are you talking about?"

I grabbed his hand, not wanting to let go until he explained the nonsense that was coming out of his mouth. He laughed dryly, shaking his head as he pulled his hand back.

"Nothing, just getting sentimental about how far you've grown in the short time since you've been back. That's all."

I wrapped my arms around my chest, not knowing what to do with my hand now that he'd pulled his away.

"I haven't changed that much." I could feel myself shrinking, hating how his attention had shifted solely to me.

His eyes pored over me, starting at the very top of my head and working their way slowly all the way down to my bare toes before coming back up to my eyes and landing there.

"Okay, Hazel." There was a gleam in his eye, something that made me think he had so much more to say but had decided against it. I was going to push him on it, demand he explain what he meant, but Bastian's voice boomed from outside the tent for us to get a move on.

"Come on," Arlo said. "I'll get everything else packed up if you want to go give Aerie a hand."

He held the tent canvas open for me as I collected my bowl and made my way into the morning sunlight. I stood with one hand against the material, holding the tent open so I could watch him for a moment longer.

This was the male who had taken care of me, who held me on my worst nights and laughed alongside me during my best ones. He'd spent the last year keeping me safe, watching me cry, piecing me back together after each and every one of my episodes. I still didn't understand how he was here, how his being actually came into existence, but I was so glad it did. Against all odds, he'd found me and protected me. He'd done his job well and I didn't know how I would ever show him how thankful I was for him.

"Hey, Arlo?"

"Hmm?"

"I love you."

His hands stilled over one of the burlap rucksacks he'd been stuffing with our few remaining things.

"I know." A small breathy laugh slipped through the tent as he nodded slightly. "I love you too, my darling divine."

It didn't take us long to find the Rift. Kirwan had been right; the smell of decay was strong throughout the Dark Woods, and once we were in the general area, it was easy enough to use the scent to lead us right to it.

It had grown since I'd last seen it. It had been alarming the first time around, but now it was downright terrifying.

It took us several tries to get close enough to inspect it, the smell being almost too potent to approach. Everything within a mile was either dead or dying. Crude, black veins reached out of the grotesque crack in the air, penetrating the ground and literally sucking the life from the earth. The disruption in reality crackled and sparked as we neared it, as if it knew exactly what we were here to do.

I swallowed hard, my throat working against the knot that was forming there.

I created this?

It was dark and ugly and felt as though it wouldn't stop stealing from this world until there was absolutely nothing left. It was some of the darkest magic I had encountered over the past few weeks, and my stomach turned at what that insinuated about myself.

Lennox came up beside me, letting a long, low whistle slip between his lips as we looked up at the ebbing magic together.

"You weren't kidding, Kirwan. That is one ugly motherfucker."

"Yeah, and it's only gotten uglier since I last saw it." Kirwan pulled up on my other side and the three of us stood there staring at the dark hole in the very fabric of reality before us.

"Alright, enough chitchat. The longer we're out here, the more at risk we are," Bastian called from behind us as he helped Aerie unpack the jars of herbs and pages of notes she'd need for the spell.

"Right. Plus I don't like the way it's looking at me," Lennox called over his shoulder, without taking his eyes off the Rift.

"It's not looking at you, jackass." Kirwan rolled his eyes. "It's not a sentient being."

"You sure about that, brother?"

The twins' bickering words flowed around me and I couldn't help but smile at the stride we fell into so naturally as a group. Even here, even in front of this hideous thing, it was comforting for things to feel so normal.

I couldn't help but wonder if they were doing it intentionally to ease my spirit.

The twins fell back, stalking into the trees with Vander as Bastian ordered them to set up a perimeter. Aerie joined me in front of the Rift. I hadn't been able to take my eyes off it, hadn't been able to move from my spot as I drank in every detail about it. It terrified me, but the longer I watched it, the more it intrigued me, too.

"You ready?" Aerie laid a soft hand on my shoulder, pulling my attention away from the *thing* in front of me.

I nodded my head. "Are you? You're the one who has to do the work."

Aerie laughed in a way that conveyed nerves more than anything else. "Yeah, well, here's hoping that will be enough."

She handed me a bowl of salt and herbs and told me to make a circle just in front of the Rift, big enough for both of us to stand in. I did as she directed while she took another bowl with similar-looking contents and formed a line directly to the Rift, connecting my circle with the magic sparking just up ahead. It was the closest any of us had gotten to the Rift so far and I found myself holding my breath as she worked, nervous for what getting that close might do to her. When she walked back to me, unharmed, I let the breath go.

"All clear on my end," Lennox called as he strode out of the tree line.

"Likewise." Vander's even voice was much closer than I'd realized, causing me to jump slightly as he took his place beside me and Aerie. Bastian took the empty bowls from Aerie, packing them away before readying his weapons and standing to the other side of Aerie, opposite Vander. Arlo stayed quiet, directly behind us.

"Where's Kirwan?" Bastian asked brusquely, turning to watch the trees for the last member of our group. As if the question had summoned him, Kirwan slunk out of the woods.

"Everything alright, brother?" Bastian's tone was curt, assessing, as his gaze lingered on the tree line behind Kirwan.

"Yeah, yeah. I just thought I heard something." Kirwan turned his gaze back to the woods as he walked, watching the same spot as Bastian. "Wanted to be thorough. Must have been one of the Dark Wood's creatures, because it scurried off."

Bastian waited a moment longer, ensuring there wasn't anything following Kirwan's movements, before nodding slowly and turning back to the Rift.

Kirwan and Lennox served as a sort of lookout just beyond the circle we'd formed, taking up their spots and pulling their weapons. Something warm grew in my chest to see them all here, fighting for me, on guard for me. I didn't even have to ask them to show up; it was just understood that this is what we would do, to save me. I inhaled deeply as I turned back to Aerie.

"Okay, what do we do now?"

She took my hand, then turned so both of us faced the Rift.

"Don't let go, okay? I'm going to use you as an anchor and a catalyst. I'll need your touch to help close the Rift, but I'll also need you here to help ground my power should it become too unstable."

I nodded again, chewing nervously at my lip as she raised her free hand to begin.

"Mending a rift... shouldn't be that different than mending wounds, right?" She let out a small sigh that conveyed just how little she believed her own words as she evaluated the sheer size of the Rift one more time. Finally, she closed her eyes, her brows pinched in concentration as she began her work.

A minute passed, then several. I didn't dare interrupt, didn't want to break her concentration, but the only thing she appeared to be doing was making the Rift angrier. I didn't know that I agreed with Kirwan's assessment. The rip in reality in front of us seemed pretty sentient to me.

After another minute, I leaned over and whispered, "Aerie?"

She dropped her hand, shaking it as she rolled her shoulders, as if she had to let her magic stretch and flex.

"Let me try again," was all she offered.

She closed her eyes once more and threw her hand up, the muscles in her arm flexing as if straining at the weight of this task. I knew then, I knew as I watched her pouring every ounce of effort into her magic, that she wouldn't be able to do this. No matter how hard she tried, how powerful she was or how many spells she used, it wouldn't close for her.

"Aerie..."

My voice became less questioning, as she tried for a third time to will her magic into the Rift. It didn't budge, didn't even so much as spark with her efforts now. It was as if it was mocking us, laughing at the trivial attempt we'd managed. It was an impenetrable force in front of us, an unmoving wall of magic that Aerie could do nothing about. She dropped her arms in defeat, letting my hand slip through her fingers.

"Hazel, I'm sorry, but I think—"

Her words were cut off by Vander, a deep guttural growl that was definitely more wolven than mortal sounding from somewhere inside him.

"We've got company."

Those were the only words of warning before several dark forms slipped out of the woods to the right of us, the last of which appeared like black smoke on the wind before coming together in a cascade of swirls to form the living, breathing version of my worst nightmare.

Kahlis.

CHAPTER 55
HAZEL

Kahlis stepped forward. His features were even more terrifying in person. Before, he was just a vision in a nightmare a world away. Now, he was flesh and blood before me, a very real and tangible threat that was all too eager to inflict more pain upon me. He walked as if the very ground rose to meet each step... or was forced to. He dripped with power and it was impossible not to tremble beneath his gaze.

No less than seven Daeomi slithered through the trees and around us as we watched in stunned horror. My eyes shot to Vander, his body sliding instinctually between me and where Kahlis stood. Kahlis took another step forward and in a heartbeat, Aerie's hands shot out and threw a barrier between us and him. A dome of golden light arched above us, encircling the rest of our group and separating us from the snaking dark forms quickly working their way around the wards.

Bastian was beside Aerie without a moment of hesitation.

"How long will your wards last?" His voice was clipped, hushed.

"Not long," she said, her usual calm tinged with panic. "They are strong, but he *will* break through them if he tries long enough."

Bastian cursed, turning to Vander in an effort to form a plan. We knew there'd be risks coming out here, but we'd hoped the Daeomi blood would be enough to mask our time beyond the tribe's borders. Regardless, the males had been sure to bring their weapons and prepare for a fight.

"Don't stop on my account."

My blood went cold at that voice, the same one that was a constant in my mind, reaching me in my nightmares more times than I cared to admit.

"You know, a little birdie told me something about this." He strolled casually over to the Rift, raising an eyebrow as he reached out an assessing hand. "Imagine my surprise when I found out it was created by none other than our very own Hazlenn. I have to say, I'm impressed. It was a truly *fantastic* hiding place, dear girl."

He clapped his hands together as a dark chuckle permeated the air. "It is a bit ironic, though... isn't it? After everything you lot have done to exile me, claiming my power is too damaging, too harmful? Then one of your own goes and creates this."

He threw his hands up on the last word, admiring the grotesque magic flowing from the Rift. He chuckled again, rubbing his hands together in delighted amusement.

"Why are you here, Kahlis?" Bastian asked, his voice low.

Kahlis smirked, pausing for a moment to look at the chieftain in a patronizing way, before clicking his tongue. "That information is a bit above your rank, Bastian Darroch. All in due time, though," he said, throwing a wink my way.

Bastian moved even closer to Aerie. He was shifting into full primal mode, protecting what he cared most about. I knew Kahlis knew it too, judging by the way he eyed Aerie.

"Ok," Bastian's words were slow, calculated. "Let's try this instead. How did you find us?"

"Oh, that's the best part!" Kahlis mused. "Forgive me for not starting with that. You see, your efforts were most valiant. It was cute to see you try so hard to deter me—and I will admit, you found a way to do it. We had just started tracking that Daeomi you stole from me—well, rather the one I let you have so it could lead us through your wards—when you fell off my radar completely, Hazlenn. Tell me, how did you do it?"

"Daeomi blood," Vander answered. "I have to admit, I did quite enjoy cutting into one of your most prized vermin to get it, too."

Kahlis fixed him with a look that could have melted me on the spot, pure evil incarnate. "Yes, well, I suspected as much when I arrived at your estate to find the dried-out husk that used to be one of my beloved creatures."

The color drained from my face as I turned to look for Kirwan and Lennox.

"Mirren," they said simultaneously. They both raised their weapons as they stepped to the edge of the barrier Aerie was still holding in place.

The wicked smile slipped back over Kahlis' face. "I will admit, the warding you did on the estate made it rather difficult for us to find our way in, even with my connection to the Daeomi. But we got there eventually. And don't worry, the little fawn wasn't there. She was, however, trailing you, and was most helpful in leading us here—unwittingly, of course. See, you may have hidden yourself from me, but her? Her we found with delicious ease."

He snapped his fingers as another two Daeomi slinked out of the cover of the Dark Woods, a crumpled, bleeding body in their hands.

"We followed her. From the shadows, of course," Kahlis drawled. "We didn't want our little fawn getting scared and throwing us off your tracks. That is, until we got close enough and I decided to let my Daeomi have some fun with her. They were most thorough in showing their... appreciation for her help."

My heart plummeted as I took in the sight of Mirren's battered body. She could barely stand as the Daeomi pushed her forward. The typical cotton dress she usually wore was shredded, the remnants barely hanging on her body. She stood, painfully slow as tears streamed down her face.

"I'm so sorry, Hazel. I didn't mean to lead them to you. I just wanted to be here to help."

I shook my head, my mind not wanting to make sense of what I was seeing. Bruises peppered her face and arms; her lip was split and one eye was so swollen I wasn't even sure if it was still there. I let my eyes drift over the rest of her body just as I heard Lennox and Kirwan scream in rage at Kahlis and the Daeomi that held her. She was covered in blood and dirt, every available surface of skin painted with the story of their violence against her.

No, no, no.

I was going to be sick. This couldn't be happening. Sweet little Mirren—innocence incarnate—at the mercy of Kahlis and his monsters, was far worse than anything I had expected when the vile creature had strolled out of those woods. Everything happened so fast, the world was spinning, my stomach was roiling, I couldn't hold back the ringing that had begun in my ears. Mirren was sobbing her apologies, gasping and bloody and utterly helpless. Kirwan and Lennox were yelling in the background, either at Kahlis to let her go or at Aerie to let them through the wards.

Time was moving too fast; there wasn't enough of it to get to her, to stop Kahlis. They were trying, but it was like running through wet sand while watching the world speed around us. Just as it reached a climax, just as the pressure reached unfathomable heights, it stopped. With the simple snap of his fingers, time itself froze. A blood-curdling scream pierced the air from where Mirren stood, just as that sadistic smile grew to new depths on Kahlis' face. I watched in horror—we all did—as the world stood still and we were forced to witness the torment he was putting Mirren through. Her screams reached cataclysmic levels as pressure built in my chest, knowing what would happen if he didn't stop, if we didn't stop him. There was nothing to be done. He'd stopped time itself, just so we could see the exact moment he crushed her mind, releasing it in a mist of gore that showered Aerie's wards in ruby-red droplets.

The moment her body fell to the ground, time returned to normal. Kirwan screamed in agony, as Lennox fell to his knees beside the wards that Aerie hadn't even had time to bring down. He placed a hand to the golden glow now splattered with Mirren's blood. Her body was only inches away, the wards being the only thing that stood between them.

"Drop them now, Aermidh. Drop the fucking wards *now.*" Kirwan's voice was a guttural, brutal command. Aerie faltered, just enough to pull them back into a tighter formation as Lennox, Kirwan, and Vander slipped beyond their borders and into the carnage on the other side.

Aerie whimpered as her eyes fell to Mirren's body but pulled herself together long enough to call over her shoulder to me. I was by her side within seconds, my entire body shaking with terror.

"You have to close the Rift, Hazel. It will only close for you."

"For me? But I can't—"

She cut me off, not interested in whatever excuse I was trying to come up with. "Kahlis wants *you*, Hazel. We cannot let him get to you. And we cannot leave until the Rift is closed. We won't last long against them. We're outnumbered and overpowered."

"I don't know how," I whispered. It wasn't an excuse, but a plea for help. I would try—for them, for Mirren, I would try. They were out here because of me. She was dead because of me. A sob escaped my throat as the thought radiated through me. Dead. Mirren was dead, for no other reason than to show he could do it. She was too innocent, too sweet. She didn't deserve this, none of them did. So, for them, I would try.

I turned back to the Rift, swallowing the nausea that was building in my gut.

"Yes, you do, Hazel. Remember, it was your power that made it in the first place. That power is still inside you. You just have to try. But I can't let the wards down. I can't anchor you."

"I'll do it." Arlo's voice vibrated around me as his warmth encircled me. He was at my back within a heartbeat, and I breathed a sigh of relief at the strength his body brought me. I found myself leaning into him as I raised my shaking hands in front of me and looked to Aerie for directions. She eyed Arlo for a second too long, something unspoken passing between them, before nodding at him.

Bastian had shifted to his wolven form, a wall of russet and amber fur in front of Aerie, his broad shoulders still prominent even in this form. He stood before her, her own personal pillar of protection as he watched his brothers fight the Daeomi just outside the wards. His eyes were locked with Kahlis, who stood opposite us and watched with that same wicked gleam in his eye. Kahlis didn't move a muscle, did nothing to fight the males raging war upon his Daeomi. He only waited with a twisted sort of bemusement, like a god watching his pawns play out a game of his design. That grin deepened as he challenged Bastian with his stare.

Ice snaked its way down my spine as I heard that voice from somewhere inside whispering to me, doubting my capabilities for the task at hand. I shook free from the thought, turning my attention back to the Rift and letting Arlo ground me as I closed my eyes and waited for Aerie's instructions.

"Concentrate, Hazel." Her soft voice filtered in, just like it had in our sessions "You're going to have to go into the Void. Deeper than you've ever gone before."

I nodded behind closed eyes, letting my consciousness sink back into that place that had become all too familiar as of late. I didn't slow as the tendrils of ice and agony snaked around me; I didn't slow as familiar visions danced around me and tried to distract me as they attempted to pull me in.

"Arlo, keep your hands on her, don't break the connection." Aerie's voice was the only one I would allow to penetrate my mind; hers and Arlo's.

He leaned into me and whispered into my ear, "You're doing great, Hazel. Keep going."

I moved deeper and deeper into the Void, the cold here making my bones brittle. It was a cold that only came from complete and utter darkness. I didn't let it stop me as I pushed further. I thought of Arlo and his dedication and warmth. I thought of Vander and how he never stopped pushing me to dig deeper, become more. I thought of Bastian and Aerie, who showed me what it looked like to have a family.

Mostly though, I thought of Mirren. She had shown me what true unconditional love looked like. She'd called me her sister and believed in me, even though she knew barely anything about me. And now she was gone and Kahlis was here and nothing felt right or whole. I wouldn't let her die for nothing, I wouldn't let Kahlis kill any more of the ones I loved, the ones I'd begun to call my family.

I could feel the warmth building somewhere inside, flowing through my veins as it snaked down my arms and out beyond me. Arlo's stifled gasp was the only confirmation I needed that it was working. A smile pulled on the edge of my lips as I let it grow, let it unfold in front of me and concentrated it solely on the Rift just ahead.

I could hear the crackle of energy, feel the Rift respond as my magic flowed around it, into it, and slowly began to repair it.

The tug at my lips split into a full-fledged grin as I willed it to keep going, completely astonished that it was actually working. That joy flooded out of me a moment later as Arlo stumbled behind me. His hands never left my skin, but I could feel the way his body quaked in pain. I lost control of the power, letting my consciousness slip out of the Void as I turned my head to look at him over my shoulder.

"Arlo, what's wrong?"

"Nothing, Hazel, just keep going."

I tried to turn around and look at him, but he held me firm, refusing to let me break my concentration. I could hear the screams and clashing of weapons just outside the wards and knew I needed to hurry if I was going to get us out of here in enough time to save everyone.

I rolled my shoulders as I turned back to the Rift and retreated back into the Void, but the moment my magic began to flow again, Arlo stumbled and could barely manage to keep one hand on me.

"Arlo," I pleaded, trying to understand what was happening.

Had a Daeomi made it through the wards? Was he injured?

He leaned into me, wrapping an arm around my waist and bringing his lips to my ear. "Don't stop, Hazel, no matter what. You have to keep going, you have to finish this. Don't break your concentration again or you'll be too late."

I felt a tear slip through my lashes as I squeezed my eyes shut and focused on keeping my magic at the surface.

"Arlo, tell me what's going on."

"You're strong, Hazel, you are so strong. I'm sorry I didn't see it before—didn't respect it. But you can do this." His voice sounded torn, like he was talking about more than just the Rift. "You have to promise me that you'll keep going, no matter what."

"What's going to happen if I do?" My voice cracked, my eyes still squeezed shut, isolating me into a world of complete darkness. His grip around my waist tightened as he pressed his lips against my temple. I could feel the tears streaming down his face as he kissed me, knew why they were there, what he'd known would happen if I closed the Rift. He paused there for a moment, breathing me in, before I felt his body slide out from behind me and step in between me and the Rift.

"No," I whispered, my own tears falling in streams now.

"Let me do this for you, Hazel. One last valiant effort to protect you, to help you."

"I can't lose you."

Those had been his words to me when we'd been back in our world, when I challenged him about finding answers to what had happened to me. I understood them now for all they were worth. He'd known then. Maybe not fully, but on some level he'd known that it was the single decision that would set all of this in motion. It was the moment that would bring us to the here and now, where I had to decide between saving myself and the family I'd found, or saving him.

I grabbed onto his hand just in front of me, desperate for any part of him I could feel. I couldn't say goodbye, I couldn't do this. I shook my head again as I moved to lower my other hand. He forced it back up, holding it in place.

"Hazel, you have to let me do this. I won't be the reason you lose yourself. I'm not supposed to exist. I'm an anomaly that needs correcting, just like the Rift, just like the Void in your mind. It's all connected, and you will not walk away from this unless we fix it. I won't be your downfall, Hazel."

His grip on my hand softened a little as he repeated, "Let me do this for you."

Tremors ravaged my body, threatening to take me out at the knees. I nodded, understanding what he was saying, the connections he had made. He was right; there was nothing to be done. They were all connected: the Void in my mind, the Rift and the world beyond it, and him. Vander might have split his soul, but it was *my* magic that brought Arlo to life as we traveled through the Rift, as I created whatever world lay beyond it. No matter how much I loved him, I couldn't ask him to change his mind. It would tear him apart to be the cause of my pain, just as it was killing me to admit I had to let him go.

I raised my hands with what little strength I had left and disappeared entirely into the Void, pushing through deeper than I had ever gone before. I would finish this, here and now.

"My darling divine."

His whispered words laced around my ear as he let his hand slip from my fingers and into the Rift. It penetrated the Void and anchored me as every other part of the world around me fell away.

CHAPTER 56
HAZLENN

I opened my eyes, not entirely sure what I was expecting to find. A female stood before me, the only other thing around as an inky black consumed us. She was the female from my vision, the one I'd watched die over and over again each time I'd visited the Void before. Only this time, she was whole, healed, healthy.

"Hazlenn," she purred, pride and love radiating from her as she looked upon me.

"Mother?" The word felt funny on my lips. I couldn't remember the last time I'd used it. Her eyes shone with fresh tears as she opened her arms to embrace me. I ran to her without a moment of hesitation. Her body was everything opposite of the Void. Where the Void had ice and hatred, she had warmth and acceptance. She squeezed me as I cried into her shoulder, for more things than I could count.

"We don't have much time, Hazlenn. I'm so sorry." She stroked my hair as I cried harder.

"For what?" I asked through shuddering breaths.

"For keeping things from you, for not explaining better what was expected of you. For the things I told you with my last breaths that spurred all of this into motion, that caused you to run away in the first place. There's so much I didn't have time to explain, but I was just trying to protect you."

"What did you tell me? I can't remember what happened, any of it. It's like this haunting presence that's just out of my reach, and I'm so confused and frustrated by it all."

She pulled back, fixing me with a sympathetic stare.

"You'll find out again in time, when you're ready." Her lips pressed into a line, an offer of a small smile as sadness clouded her features. "I never meant for any of this to happen."

She gestured to the cold darkness around us. "This isn't the life I wanted for you, Hazlenn, this pain and self-doubt. You are so much stronger than you even know."

I shook my head.

"No, I'm not. I can't even control my own mind, this darkness within me. This crippling fear and worry that snakes its way into every aspect of my life. I can't even go a day without feeling like I'm unraveling at my very seams, without feeling like I'm a breath away from falling apart and never being able to piece myself back together. How is that strength?"

She let go of me just long enough to shift her grasp on my shoulders and lowered her forehead to mine. "You are capable and strong, Hazlenn. Not despite your internal battles but because of them. You have more empathy, more mental stamina than most people could ever hope for. You are strong because of the battle you're forced to fight every day. Because you know what it's like to live with that struggle inside you, you have a strength that only comes from being forged in the fire. The strength of a warrior that chooses every day to continue fighting the battle, even when that battle wages war inside your mind."

Her chin quivered as desperation flooded her face. "You're so strong, baby. And I am so proud of you. For not giving up, for choosing to keep going despite how hard it has been for you. Do not ever forget that, and don't let that light go out in the midst of the battle. As long as you choose to keep fighting, keep putting one foot in front of the other, you're going to be okay."

I didn't know what to say, so instead I buried my head against her chest as I embraced her again.

"I wish I could remember you. I wish you were here with me again so we could build another life together."

I felt her smile crease against my forehead as she let out a small laugh.

"If only, little one. But I'm afraid it's time for you to return. Your world needs you. It would be selfish for me to keep you here any longer."

"But what do I do? How do I fix everything?"

She tapped my chest, a knowing gleam in her eye. "Listen here. It's been inside you all along, Hazlenn. You just have to accept it, believe you are exactly who you were meant to be—darkness and all. It's your destiny, baby. Stop fighting it."

I didn't fully understand, but I nodded in agreement as she squeezed my hands one last time and backed away. My body shook in the absence of her warmth, the creeping cold of the Void closing in around me. I didn't take my eyes off her, drank in every detail for as long as I could as she faded into vapors. Her voice echoed throughout every corner of my mind as she left.

"I'll be with you. Through it all, Hazlenn, I'll be with you."

CHAPTER 57
VANDER

I buried my hand within the chest of the closest Daeomi, grabbing its heart—or whatever organ gave life to the filth—and ripped it out in one swift motion. I hadn't shifted yet; I was trying to save that as a last resort. It was easier to handle weapons in my mortal form, and I had the power of the mark to spur me on. I'd noticed at some point that Bastian had shifted, though, a chill running through me for a moment as I remembered just how large his primal form was. He barely ever used it, and the image of him towering in front of Kahlis was a sight to behold.

More Daeomi and their deapthhounds crept out of the woods, their movements an oily black phantom before they were on top of us. They must have been lower in Kahlis' ranks for him to sacrifice them like this. He seemed to have left his most elite creatures at home, aside from the one we'd kidnapped and killed. Thank the Fates for that small mercy.

"For fuck's sake, how many of these assholes are there?"

Nox's words brought a coarse laugh to my throat.

"Not enough to stop us," I spit back as another one charged at me, only to be impaled by the blade I'd pulled from behind my back.

As if in answer, four more charged from the tree line.

"Truly Vander, we could do without your arrogant-ass commentary right now," Kirwan said, pivoting and slicing into one that had snuck its way up behind me while I disemboweled its friend.

Another one pounced on Kirwan, his sword buried in the Daeomi he'd just killed and otherwise preoccupied. I turned to grab it by the wings, my hands slipping over its skin before slamming it to the ground and smashing its face with my boot.

"I believe it's my arrogant ass that's saving yours right now," I said with a smirk.

Nox shot an arrow through another Daeomi as it dropped from the sky, almost taking both me and Kirwan out.

"Likewise, brother," he said as he nocked another arrow. I looked up at him briefly, expecting to see that sarcastic grin that seemed to be permanently plastered to his face. Instead, I found the fierce look of a warrior who'd been wronged and was fighting to chase a revenge he well deserved.

"Fucking Fates, they're everywhere." Kirwan's breath was ragged as we took several steps back and collected ourselves. The hoard had begun to concentrate on where Kahlis stood at the border of the wards. Most of them didn't even notice us anymore, simply existing to obey the command of their master.

I knew the moment we slowed, the moment we broke concentration long enough, the twins' focus would falter and they'd be too consumed by grief to keep going. They had reached Mirren's body first, or what was left of it. I'd never seen that kind of rage from either of them, pure molten anger as they tore into the filthy creatures that stood between them and their sister. The first thing I'd done was wrap her frail body in my shadows and carry her to the cover of the woods as her brothers sought revenge on every being outside the glowing wards. There she remained, still cloaked in shadows until we dealt with the threat at hand.

"They're like fucking cockroaches." Nox shuddered. "I hate cockroaches."

I suppressed the urge to tease him for the comment, realizing the gravity of the situation didn't lend itself to a joking mood. I let my shadows stretch out, wrapping around the first layer of oily black creatures and ripping them apart. It didn't matter; a new round of them rushed from the woods, replacing the ones that lay shredded and bleeding on the ground.

"We need a new plan," I said firmly, "something to buy them time to close the Rift, or whatever the fuck they're trying to do in there."

The wards were too far off, too much commotion with the writhing, slithering creatures trying to break through to communicate with Bastian. I could see the Rift shrinking in size, the very air it clung to stitching itself back together at a painfully slow speed. I didn't dare test the tether and risk pulling Hazel's concentration from whatever help she was offering Aerie. I didn't know how they were doing it, but it appeared to be working.

"Let's spread out," I called over the heavy din of the battle. "We each take a side of the dome and attack full force. Maybe we can get an advantage—at the very least, distract the Daeomi long enough from the wards to let them finish with the Rift."

Before we'd even had time to act on our new plan, Kahlis turned his attention our way; and with it, the full weight of his hoard came down on us. It was a storm of blood and chaos as we fought desperately to break free. Showers of the thick, black blood rained on me, sticking to my tongue and flooding my vision. I couldn't see, couldn't fight. Within mere minutes, they had us pinned and restrained. Kirwan and Nox went down first, cursing and stabbing until the last possible moment. I went down soon after, the mark on my skin fighting with an unprecedented amount of strength to keep me from getting captured. It was no use, though. Kahlis was too powerful. He would just keep creating more of them, just keep altering every aspect of our reality to maintain the upper hand.

It took four Daeomi each to hold us down, to force us to our knees and hold our faces in place as Kahlis made us watch as he brought down the wards around Hazel. Everything up to this point had just been for show, his sick and twisted way of having fun. He didn't need to fight us, didn't even need the Daeomi to help him. He just enjoyed the torment.

Within seconds the golden dome shattered. Bastian stepped forward, their last line of defense. Behind him, Aerie had taken one of Bastian's battle axes and stood where he'd been. I could barely make out Hazel beyond them, Arlo nowhere to be seen. *She* was closing the Rift.

Not Aerie. Hazel.

Pride beamed from me as I looked to her, the power that she'd finally discovered within herself.

"You're too late, Kahlis." I needed to distract him, needed to do anything I could to buy her more time. I tested my shadows, trying to let them stretch out, but whatever the Daeomi had snapped around my wrists to bind me was rendering them useless. I did the same with my primal form, failing to shift. All that I had left to use were my words. Luckily, I had plenty to say to the vile creature in front of me.

His laughter pierced the air as he stalked in front of us. "I love how much you want to believe that. It's adorable that you still think you can beat me, despite my Daeomi pinning you beneath my boot. One word from me and you'll be nothing more than the same shredded corpse as your little fawn."

Nox and Kirwan growled their curses at Kahlis as they fought to break free from their restraints. He was right, though; we were entirely at his mercy. The thought of that had the magic of the mark crawling against my skin in defiance. It didn't like to feel cornered.

He knelt before me, letting his dark red fingers trail over my cheek before grabbing my jaw and lifting to inspect me. "You know, I think I may start with you. Do you think that would get her attention?"

He forced my face to look at where Hazel stood, focusing solely on the Rift and the effort it took to close it. "I'm well aware of the connection you bear to her. You've made it quite... grating to accomplish all the plans I've had for her. Perhaps getting rid of you first would make things that much easier for me."

He leaned in close, his breath hot and rancid on my face. "Tell me, can she feel your pain through this special connection of yours? Do you think she will feel each ripple of agony as my power twists your mind and reduces you to mere pulp?"

My body tried to shift at the threat, my canines lengthening as I snarled at him for even thinking of harming her again. The restraints held, though, and my body sighed in frustration as it was forced back into its mortal form. He hummed in approval before standing back up and watching as Hazel finished mending the last of the Rift.

"Truthfully," he admitted with a casual hum, "I don't care much about this Rift, although I would have loved to feel the dark magic between my fingers. It's most tempting, but it's not why I'm here. It's her I want."

He turned on his heels, taking a singular step toward where Bastian guarded the girls, before the world around us erupted in a flash of blinding white light.

When I opened my eyes, the Daeomi had all fallen. Their bodies lay in wet, sticky puddles of black gore. My hands were still bound, but no one held me down anymore. I noted that Kirwan and Nox were in similar positions before I swiveled my gaze to where Hazel had been, trying to make sure she was okay. It was from where she stood that the blinding light had erupted. I'd thought it had been the Rift, perhaps growing too unstable to manage. Instead, I saw a being step out of the bright white light, its face shrouded in light, its blaze acting as its own sort of shadows. But I would have recognized that deep red hair anywhere.

She stepped toward Kahlis, her feet not entirely touching the ground as she moved like water through the air. When she spoke, it was a chorus of voices, none of them entirely her own:

"Your time here is limited, Kahlis. Crawl back to your hole before I finish you now."

Kahlis chuckled, but the uncertainty in his movements was impossible to miss – the way his steps faltered slightly as he approached with caution to examine whatever being now stood before him.

"You expect me to retreat? From you? You are *nothing*, Hazlenn. You are a weak, pathetic creature. I'll devour you in the blink of an eye, and enjoy every moment of your agony."

As if in show of his power, the red markings on his arms slithered from his skin like snakes as they tasted the air with their tongues. The world around him fell away and darkness itself enveloped him and grew into a ferocious beast, ready to strike. The ground around them crumbled, isolating the two of them, and I squirmed beneath the restraints in an effort to get to her. To protect her.

"I bend time and reality itself, little one," Kahlis said with a snarl. "I capture minds and do with them as I please. I've lived and ruled for centuries before you were even a mere concept to the Fates. What power do you hold that could be enough to challenge *me?*"

Hazel cocked her head to the side, as if Kahlis' show of magic was nothing but a mere parlor trick. She looked at him with total indifference.

"You see, Kahlis: there's a difference between you and me. I've been told many things about you. The Fates whisper of your ways. You are learned in your magic. You take and take until there's nothing left for you to steal. You claim ownership of power that is not yours to own and you wield it carelessly, taking from this world without so much as a drop of remorse." She stepped forward, the light around her growing to snuff out the darkness radiating from Kahlis. "I am Hazlenn, daughter of the earth and the cosmos. I am the land and the sky, the fire and the water, the sun and the moon. And I am everything that they are not. I am everything that existed before and will exist long after they are gone."

It was a prophecy from the Fates themselves, a divine intervention. She lifted her hands as she walked, uncurling her fists to reveal her palms at her sides. Deep black ink ebbed on her skin, depicting a celestial sun in one palm and a matching moon on the other. Kahlis recoiled at her movements.

His voice was little more than a whisper.

"Cailleach."

The Divine. It couldn't be. I looked to where Hazel stood in all her power, power that none of us could have even imagined she'd had. A broad smile split across my face, reaching from ear to ear as I looked at the female I loved more than life itself. The Divine, indeed.

There's my Hazlenn.

Her eyes found mine, the thought echoing down the tether and growing to an immeasurable joy. I didn't know how she did it, but there she was—everything she used to be and everything I could never have imagined she'd become. She was herself at last, finally and totally accepted within and throughout.

A ripple of shadow dragged my attention away from her as Kahlis disappeared in a wave of black smoke, utterly shaken at the new knowledge of who it was he was fighting against. Perhaps he'd known all along, and that was why he was so set on taking her down. The Divine was quite possibly the only power large enough to single-handedly threaten his own. She had to have been if the Fates decided it was time to bring her back.

I didn't care that he ran, didn't care that he got away as I stood, finally free of the Dark One's restraints, and took her in—Hazel, Hazlenn, the Divine in all her glory before I fell at her feet in a silent tribute to the goddess that stood before me.

CHAPTER 58
HAZEL

I stood in the silence of the library, cherishing every minute of the reprieve it offered. After Kahlis had disappeared from the Dark Woods, I'd collapsed in exhaustion. Channeling that much power for that long wiped me out, and whatever otherworldly being had possessed me left just as fast as Kahlis did. Closing the Rift might have unearthed my power, but I didn't fully understand what that meant.

Everything that had happened was a blur. I vaguely knew what I'd done, how I'd closed the Rift; I caught bits and pieces of the words I said to Kahlis, but none of it made sense to me. I spoke with a voice that wasn't entirely my own, and words that I hadn't even thought of, let alone believed.

Bastian had helped both Aerie and me back to our horses and insisted on riding straight through, back to the estate. We rode hard and long, only deepening the exhaustion I felt in my bones. Vander, Kirwan, and Nox stayed behind to ensure all of the Daeomi were indeed dealt with and to collect Mirren's body.

They would be back by now, though I hadn't seen any of them yet. They were all busy preparing for a ceremony to honor Mirren—Arlo too, I supposed. Though, there was no body for me to mourn over. He'd disappeared into the Rift itself, sacrificing himself so I could close it, so I could find my power. Aerie had tried to explain it to me—*for closure,* she'd said. Apparently, she'd known, or at least suspected, all along what he'd have to do. She made the spell in hopes that there would be a way around it, but in the end, it had to be me... and it had to be Arlo.

He was gone and that he'd saved me in the process. One last valiant effort, indeed.

I let another round of tears fall from my eyes as I breathed in the quiet of the library. A small cup of tea appeared on the edge of the table closest to me, just above the letters carved into the wood that I'd discovered on my first day here, along with a small leatherbound book that had a familiarity to it I couldn't place. I huffed out a laugh through the tears and thanked the library for its gesture. I didn't know what to do now, what was next. I traced the letters absent-mindedly, their grooves already becoming a familiar comfort as the pad of my finger moved over them.

How was I just supposed to move on from the hole Arlo left behind?

He might have saved me, but he broke something within me too.

I sat down in the chair, taking a sip from the warm tea as I tried to pull back the tears that wouldn't stop spilling over my cheeks.

A soft knock rapped on the library door, as Vander emerged from the dark hallway beyond.

"I thought I might find you here." He lingered, unsure whether to disturb me or not.

I wiped my eyes in a self-conscious attempt to hide my crying. He, no doubt, had already assessed as much. It was becoming increasingly impossible to keep things from him.

"I just wanted to check on you," he continued in a low, uncertain voice, "and let you know we're back. Aerie's prepared a ceremony down by the meadow for this evening."

"The one with the crystal spring?"

He gave me a curt nod.

"Good," I said, copying the nod in acknowledgment, "Mirren would want it done there."

Her joy had been contagious when we'd visited it together, and I remembered how Aerie spoke of the countless days they spent playing and napping in the tall grass or splashing in the water of the spring. She deserved a sacred resting place such as that: a young and wild spirit, laid to rest amongst the wildflowers and free to forever play there. It was the perfect spot for her young, innocent soul.

New tears pricked the back of my eyes as I fought the guilt gripping my chest for the loss of her life.

"How do I face them?" I said, my voice breaking.

Vander's head cocked to the side as he tried to understand my meaning.

"Face who?"

"Lennox and Kirwan. How do I face them after causing Mirren's death? They must hate me. I don't know how to see them after the mess that this became. After Mirren..." My words trailed off, being replaced by sobs that I could no longer suppress.

Vander was kneeling in front of me within moments, too fast to have moved at any natural speed. There was still so much I didn't know about his power, about any of their powers.

"Hey," he breathed softly as he took my face in his hands and brought his eyes to mine. "No one blames you for what happened. This is not your fault. Mirren's death is not your fault. That's on Kahlis. And trust me, he will pay. I'll make sure of it. Nox and Kirwan will too. But don't for a second put this on yourself, Hazel."

I let silence fall between us, unsure if I could agree with his sentiment. It did make me feel better to hear the twins weren't angry with me, though. I raised my gaze to his, finally making eye contact with him as his fingers brushed soft, sweet strokes across my wet cheeks.

"You called me Hazel." It wasn't a question, just an observation.

"Would you prefer I call you the Divine?"

He lifted my hands out of my lap and ran his fingers over the new markings there, as if to remind me of the power now coursing through my veins. A power, I realized, that might not be all that different from his, given how similar our markings were.

A small laugh passed through my lips, rolling my eyes at his audacity, even in the midst of everything going on.

"No, asshole."

"That mouth isn't very becoming for a goddess. I think I've been a bad influence on you." The corner of his lips tilted up. His fingers never slowed as they continued to wipe my tears away.

"Earlier, through the tether... you called me Hazlenn. That's what my mother called me, too, when I saw her."

He raised an eyebrow.

"When I was closing the Rift," I explained slowly, the memory still fresh, "I had to go back into the Void. She was there, actually there this time. She spoke to me, she called me Hazlenn."

He nodded, understanding. He didn't push for more details, didn't ask me to tell him the rest of what happened. There'd be time for that, later. For now, he just pressed his lips to my forehead, lingering there.

"I will call you whatever your heart desires, little spitfire, so long as you keep me around to hear it."

He pulled me out of my seat and wrapped his arms around me, the muscles flexing in a primal way as he did so. He could never replace Arlo—I didn't want him to. But perhaps he was my fate all along, my destiny. Perhaps Arlo was more so a guide to bring me to this exact moment rather than a choice I had to make.

"Do you remember what I told you about the Shadow of the Grimm?" he asked suddenly. "How shadow cannot exist without both light and dark?"

He pulled back only far enough to find my hands once again. His fingers continued to trace the new markings on my palms.

Vander's words echoed in my mind as he sent a thought down the tether:

I think our destiny was to go through everything we did, to become the people we have become, so that we could be everything the other needed.

He pulled away, looking not just into my eyes, but deep within me to the parts that I was sure only he would ever see.

"Two fractured souls finding their way back to each other," he said with a gentle confidence. "Not entirely fixed, but healed enough to complete the other."

He was right. Mending the Rift hadn't entirely fixed me. I was still missing my memories, still felt that darkness burrowing deep within. He was still marked by the curse, still missing that piece of his soul that had been Arlo. We didn't need those pieces, though. We were new people now, different beings entirely, and I wasn't so sure if those pieces of us would even fit back into whoever we were now. Maybe that was why the tether hadn't fully clicked in place before, because we were still on the path to becoming who the other needed.

"Come, Aerie's made us some food, and I'm sure the others would appreciate having eyes on you, after... everything."

I grabbed the small leather book the library had offered me from the table as he slid his hand down my arm and twined his fingers around mine.

It was time to return to the rest of the family. Our family.

CHAPTER 59
VANDER

Mirren's ceremony had been just as hard as I'd expected it to be, if not harder. We made the journey out there at dusk, burning what was left of her body on the pyre just as the sun dipped below the horizon. The glow of the sunset lit the whole meadow ablaze, echoing the burning flames as if the earth itself mourned her loss.

Aerie cried in agony, losing the closest thing she had to a daughter. The twins stood, stoic and hardened as they watched their sister's remains go up in a blaze of fire. The embers and ashes floated through the air before landing across the wildflowers of the meadow. Hazel buried her face in my chest as the fire grew, disintegrating the last pieces of her earthly tether to this world.

Kirwan and Nox each lifted a hand, letting out a tendril of their magic as they said goodbye to their sister. Inky black night and golden sunlight danced through the air to represent their tribal magic, joining Mirren's ashes as they blew through the summer night's breeze. Aerie followed suit, letting her warm fae light ebb from her and dance across the meadow. Bastian and I joined last, allowing tendrils of our earth magic to spread throughout the ground, making the wildflowers sway and grow as they reached up to accept the ashes that now floated down to them.

Bastian's voice broke out over the field, loud and binding as he recited an old blessing to guide Mirren's spirit beyond the Veil:

"May you always have clear skies

And stars that shine at night.

May you find peace beyond understanding

And the warmth of the sun burning bright.

Until we meet again,

May the Earth hold you close, Mirren."

He repeated it again, in our ancient tongue, Nox and Kirwan joining in to sing the haunting words.

Hazel watched in awe, not remembering what our traditions for burial entailed.

"It's so beautiful," she whispered to me. "In the most heartbreaking way."

I squeezed her tighter against my side, releasing an extra wave of magic.

She gasped as the earth around us sprouted yarrow.

"For Arlo," I whispered back to her.

Hazel disappeared to her room as soon as we returned to the estate. She promised she was okay, just needed a minute. I let her go, but not without sending a shadow down the hall after her.

Kirwan and Nox had shown up to the ceremony in full battle gear, armed to the teeth. I'd thought at the time it was perhaps another show of respect, but the way they lingered in the living room, I knew what their plans entailed.

"Leaving so soon?" I offered, trying to lighten the mood that sat heavy in the air.

Kirwan gave me a solemn nod as Nox pushed forward and clasped a hand down on my shoulder.

"We have to." Nox's voice had lost any remnant of his usual humor. "We can't let this go unpunished."

I understood. Mirren had been completely innocent in all of this—still just a child. It was an unmeasurable cruelty for Kahlis to have done what he did. The image of her bruised and bleeding still echoed in my mind, the look of horror on her face beneath Kahlis' power. It was a pain unfathomable to die the way she had, not to mention the torment Kahlis and his creatures had inflicted on her beforehand. It was unforgivable. I was a moment away from packing my things and joining their crusade.

"I know." I returned his gesture, clamping my hand down on his arm before pulling him into a hug.

"We'll send word when we can," added Kirwan, "let you know what we find. We're going to bring his entire kingdom to its knees, Vander. He will pay for this."

I didn't doubt his words. Thirst for revenge was a powerful tool and Kahlis had just hand-delivered a heaping pile of it for them.

"Let us know how we can help. You aren't alone in this, brother." I pulled Kirwan into mine and Nox's embrace. "Neither of you are."

When we let go, there was a smattering of grumbles and cleared throats as we all worked to cover up the tears that burned the back of our throats. There'd been enough of those shed today. Now was the time for work.

When I turned away from them, Hazel stood just within the hall-way. Her face was white as a sheet, one hand grasped to the wall for support. In the other dangled a black leatherbound book.

"Hazel, what's wrong?" I was beside her in an instant, pulling her hand off the wall and over my shoulder for support.

"I—it's this book." Her body was going into shock, her skin cold to the touch as tremors began to swell inside her. "It showed up in the library. I thought I'd seen it before, but—couldn't place it."

Every word was like gravel as it came out, her voice rough and ragged as she tried to form words to explain to us what was going on. Kirwan and Nox were at her other side and they helped me guide her to the sofa. Nox grabbed the bottle of amber alcohol, not even bothering with a glass as he handed it to her and insisted she take a sip.

"It was in the cottage, that day you took me there." Her eyes shot to mine, causing heat to rise in my ears as I remembered the feel of her mouth on mine, her skin in my teeth. The smallest bit of color rose in her cheeks, as if she could sense where my thoughts had gone. "I don't know how it got in the library. It just showed up while I was there."

"Yeah, the library has a tendency to do things like that," Nox said as he eyed the book still dangling between her fingers.

"What is it?" I pushed. She was avoiding the question, not wanting to admit to whatever she'd discovered within its pages.

"It's a journal, from my mom. I guess she left it behind for me, after she died. I hadn't known, or hadn't remembered."

"Okay," I offered, gently easing the book out of her fingers. "And that's bad because…"

She didn't answer, couldn't answer. She just gestured for me to read the page she'd been holding open.

I watched her for a moment longer before turning my attention to the book. I was vaguely aware of Bastian and Aerie emerging from the kitchen as I let my eyes pore over the scribbled text on the old pages. It took a minute to decipher the handwriting, a minute longer to figure out which part she was referring to.

"Holy fuck." The curse rippled through the air as I looked back to Hazel. I understood why she was so visibly shaken, so rattled by the words on this page.

"What in the Depths is it?" Nox's tone was as impatient and sarcastic as ever as he tried to grab for the book. I let him have it, dragging my eyes back to where Hazel shook on the sofa. She looked as scared and confused as she had been the day I found her in the Dark Woods beneath the Daeomi's depthhound.

"Holy fuck is right," Nox breathed, letting the book fumble into Kirwan's grasp. I squeezed Hazel's hand tightly as I waited for Nox to say the words out loud, to breathe life to the secret that had been kept on the page for Fates knew how long.

"Kahlis is Hazel's father."

EPILOGUE
KIRWAN

The night air of the Dark Woods was still and heavy. The heat of summer was growing with each passing day and droplets of sweat beaded my skin thanks to the thickness of the air. I could still see the dim glow of our campsite as I slunk through the trees, moving from shadow to shadow and watching carefully to ensure Nox was not following me. He'd been asleep for some time now. If our exhausting day of travel hadn't been enough to ensure that, then the sleeping drought I spiked his drink with tonight would be.

We'd left the estate with our sights set on revenge, promising to return in two week's time for the summer solstice celebration, and Hazel's birthday. Although, I wasn't sure any of us felt like celebrating. Vander talked of joining us in the Dark Woods soon, to try and hunt down answers about the truth that the journal had claimed. Kahlis being Hazel's father was almost too bizarre to wrap our minds around, although there were several similarities in their magic that made it a little easier to believe the longer I thought on it. I gave one last look back toward camp before slipping beneath a particularly large hemlock and closing my eyes long enough to verify my mental blocks were up, denying Nox access to anything I might see or hear tonight.

"You can come out now." My words drifted into the canopy above me, feeling uneven and awkward as I waited for the creature to appear. Moments passed, long enough to make me wonder if the shadow I'd sensed following us the last half of the day hadn't just been my imagination. My gut clenched in apprehension as a black mist finally crawled through the air, twining in tendrils of obsidian before coming together and taking shape. Within an instant, a slender male with silver hair and midnight eyes was standing before me. Adonis. Head advisor to the Dark One, Kahlis' number two. I didn't give him time to talk before pulling my dagger and pushing him up against the bark of the oversized tree, the silver metal of my blade glinting in the moonlight as I pressed it against his throat.

His chuckle was a deep rumble through the leaves above us. "What exactly is your plan, Kirwan? You kill me, it's only going to further anger the Dark One. And he's already quite agitated with you."

"I don't care." The words vibrated through my clenched teeth, anger boiling my blood as I looked at the calculated calm in the eyes of the male beneath my blade. As if I wasn't a threat—as if I wasn't poised to rip him limb from limb. "You said she'd be safe. You promised she wouldn't be harmed."

"Ah, ah, ah," Adonis scolded. "You were assured that every effort would be given to keep her out of it. It's not our fault you couldn't follow instructions and keep her at the estate."

I pressed the blade against his skin, small droplets of blood beading onto the metal. He didn't so much as flinch as he lowered his gaze to mine.

"Come now, Kirwan." Adonis snapped his fingers and the dagger in my hand disappeared. He raised his other hand to the side, something catching the moonlight in my peripheral vision as he waved the dagger for me to see.

"Let's not forget who's in charge here, shall we?" he said with a sickening grin.

"She's dead," I argued, somewhere between a plea and an accusation. I held firm, refusing to let the male go. "I said I'd help you if you spared her, and now she's dead."

Adonis clicked his tongue. "Yes, and what a shame that is."

The corner of his lip curled up with amusement. Something snapped within me, my fist landing hard against his smug face before I even realized I'd hit him. I didn't give myself time to stop as I landed another blow, then another.

"She's dead!" I shouted at him. At the trees, at anything that would listen.

Dead. Dead. Dead.

Beautiful, young, wonderful, innocent Mirren. My baby sister, the one I raised with Lennox by my side. The one I was meant to protect no matter the cost. She was dead and it was all because of me. What was I supposed to do now? How was I to move on from that? I reeled back for another punch when Adonis' form dispersed into a thick black mist. My fist skimmed through the dark cloud and straight into the rough bark of the tree. I barely stifled the cry of pain, suddenly aware how loud my voice had to be, and sent up a silent prayer to the Fates that Nox hadn't heard.

I let out a muffled groan, staggering backward and rippling curses as Adonis came back together from the mist and stalked toward me.

"Need I remind you that you are not the one who made this deal." Vines from the forest floor slithered through the fallen leaves and up around my legs, pulling me down to my knees in front of him. More reached up to snake around my wrists, holding me firm beneath him. He leaned over, grabbing me by the hair and forcing my gaze up to his dark, lifeless eyes.

"You were nothing but a blubbering pile of rot and flesh when I came to you with this deal. You should be *thanking* me for this opportunity, not cursing me." His finger trailed over my temple, forcing memories of the darkest days of torment into my mind.

I had been Talamh's spy, infiltrating the Dark One's territory and gathering any information to help the tribe that had become my home. But eventually, their contact grew less frequent and my restlessness reached new heights. I got too bold—too brazen—and ended up at the mercy of Adonis, and subsequently Kahlis. I spent months locked in the deepest inner workings of his palace, enduring the excruciating cruelty of Adonis, and on occasion, Kahlis himself.

That is, until they came to me with their offer. Turn on my tribe, return as a spy *against* them, and feed Kahlis any information that would prove useful in aiding their attempt to take back control of Tir Nadaar. I'd said no. Fuck, I lost count of how many times I said no. Each time I was met with another beating, another punishment—each one more cruel than the last. It didn't matter. I'd planned to keep saying no forever, till they ripped my last breath from my lungs. I had come to terms with my cell becoming my tomb, understanding that I'd never feel the warm sunlight on my skin or bask in the glow of a full moon. The tribal magic in my veins begged for it, called out to once again be reunited with the source from which my magic flowed, but I'd do anything before I turned traitor against my tribe.

That was when they brought me a new ultimatum: turn traitor and spy for them, or they'd go after Mirren and Lennox.

I gritted my teeth against the visions of endless pain and torment, willing my mental blocks to push him out of my mind.

"Enough," I seethed, spitting on his boots for good measure. He might have me pinned, but there wasn't enough magic in the world to keep me from showing him the wrath that filled my veins, one way or another.

"Why are you here?" I hated myself for even asking, feeling like some sort of collared pet, reporting back to its master.

Adonis pulled a piece of cloth from the pocket of his too-perfect tunic, backing up several steps to wipe the spittle from his boots. "Like I said, the Dark One is agitated. His encounter with your friends didn't go as planned."

"It's not my fault the Dark One couldn't get the job done," I bit back.

He hummed, pursing his lips together and watching me. "We'll see if you still have that kind of confidence when you're back in a cell watching the life drain out of your brother's eyes."

I writhed against my restraints, flinging curses and threats at him. He would not touch Lennox. Kahlis had already taken Mirren from me. These vile creatures would take nothing else. "I don't know how, but I will find a way to end each and every one of you, starting with Kahlis."

It was a promise to Adonis, to Kahlis, to the night and the moon, and the earth itself.

"Whatever you say, Kirwan. Just be there when we summon you next. The Dark One will expect your cooperation, regardless of whatever casualties may have occurred."

Before I could respond, before I could scream at him for mentioning Mirren's death in such an incidental way, he disappeared on a breeze, his mortal form retreating into a mist of black shadow. The vines holding me in place went lax as the mist disappeared into the canopy above. I rubbed at my wrists absent-mindedly as I stayed kneeling on the forest floor.

He might not have heeded my threats, but they weren't empty. I meant what I said. I may not know how just yet, but I *would* find a way. I would stop their bloodshed. I was weak before. I had too much to live for, too much to lose—they knew that and they used it against me. Not anymore. I would burn myself whole as long as it meant seeing them burn with me.

That was the danger of taking things from those who had something to live for. Eventually, they had nothing left. And that was a reckless place to be.

ACKNOWLEDGMENTS

Oh boy, where do I even start? Writing this page is kind of a bucket list item for me because it means that we made it. My debut novel is done. The book is written and edited and published, ergo why it needs an acknowledgments page. And that just seems too good to be true.

I have to start this off by thanking my best friend and partner in crime for the past fourteen years, my wonderful husband, Tim. Thank you so much for constantly supporting me, believing in me, and pushing me to keep going. Thank you for pretending like you knew what I was talking about every time I went on a two-hour plotting tangent. It was always utter, nonsensical chaos—but you were never even phased. Most importantly, thank you for stepping up and taking over all the bedtime routines, diaper changes, and parenting moments I missed so I could actually write this book. Literally none of this would have been possible without you. You are my biggest supporter—my biggest cheerleader—and I can't even put into words how much I love you.

To my IRL author bestie, Thea Claire. Thank you for walking this journey with me. We've been through so many seasons of life together. We've drifted and reconnected, supported each other from afar and been there for each other through some crazy moments (I'm looking at you UNT icepocalypse of 2013). And now here we are, both published authors with stories to tell and I couldn't be more proud of you and grateful for our friendship.

To my booksta besties, Rina and Julia. The bookstagram community has offered me a lot of amazing things, but y'all may in fact be the pieces I'm most grateful for. There's nothing quite like total strangers on the internet being some of the biggest cheerleaders in your life. I am forever grateful for not only y'alls support, but also for the friendships we've built along the way. I love y'all.

And to the bookstagram and writing community as a whole, thank you for being my safe place to land, for encouraging fellow readers and authors to pursue what makes them happy and for being the wonderful, amazing, found family that you are. Y'all have created, posted, shared, brainstormed, liked, and commented all in the name of helping promote this book. Y'all have kept me going these past few months and I'm eternally grateful for the encouragement y'all have poured into me throughout this process. There's too many of you to list, but you know who you are and I love you all so much.

To my IRL bookish best friends, Alexandra and Marie. Thank you for taking the chance on my book, even though it would have been incredibly awkward for our friendship if y'all hated it. I promise there is more to come, even though I'm sure you'll be there, looking over my shoulder as I write it. I apologize in advance for the emotional trauma.

To all of my amazing beta readers, there are not enough words in the world to tell y'all how grateful I am for your help. This book wouldn't be even a fraction of the story it is without y'alls critiques and words of encouragement. Y'all helped take my book baby and mold it into the wonderful creation it is today. Thank you for taking a chance on it, and caring about this story as much as I do.

To Myanna, thank you for loving these characters so much that you created beautiful pieces of art for them. Seeing your vision of my book come to life through your art was just the coolest thing ever. You are so talented and I feel honored that you used those talents to bring my characters to life.

To my editor, Sophie. Girl. You took the parts of this book that were just okay and helped me make them *great*. I don't know how you do it but I am so thankful for your attention to detail and for not being afraid to push me to dig deeper. Without your guidance, this book wouldn't shine as brightly as it does. You are amazing. And to my proofreader, E.F. Watson, thank you thank you thank you for polishing this book and giving me all sorts of juicy ideas for marketing. You are one amazing proofreader and I am so grateful for you.

To my ARC team, thank you for all of your hard work and spreading the word about my debut novel. I know the work you put in as an ARC reader and I am forever grateful that y'all took a chance on this book. Your role is so important and so deeply appreciated.

To the other indie authors who have inspired me on this journey, thank you for believing in yourself and writing your story. You paved the way before me and I am forever grateful for your hard work, your advice, and your stories. If you'd like to check out some other indie authors that have inspired me please look up these amazing names:

Rebecca Quinn, Alexis L. Menard, R. V. Wilbur, Thea Claire, Elle Mitchell, Kara Douglas.

To the family that I've lost, Ann, Missy, Bee, and Kellie. I made sure to sprinkle little pieces of you throughout this book. I know they will go unnoticed by most, but I couldn't publish this book without putting a little part of y'all in there too. I love you all so much and I miss y'all every day.

To my Kickstarter backers. Thank you for being the first group to invest in this story. Y'all bought this book before it even hit shelves, and that is the ultimate flex. Y'all are amazing.

And finally—to you, the reader. Thank you for picking this book up. And hats off to you if you've made it this far! Thank you for taking time out of your busy schedule and choosing to spend it in this little world I created. I hope something in this story resonated with you and you fell in love with the characters as much as I did while writing them. Thank you for your love of books and fantasy. And most importantly, don't ever stop reading.

About The Author

Lindsey N. Rhoden is a mom to four crazy kiddos, full-time home-schooler, devoted wife, and a (sometimes more than) part-time writer. Located in the North Texas region, she has spent the last few years as a birth and postpartum doula and photographer, specializing in the art of Ayurvedic and herbal care. She enjoys nature, herbalism, and obviously lots and lots of reading. You can often find her cuddled up at home with a fantasy book, a cup of coffee, and either her German Shepherd (Stella) or her cat (Benji) by her side. And probably one of her four kids crawling on her.

Her journey through motherhood and her struggle with anxiety and depression helped rekindle her love for the written word after a long reprieve through college and early adulthood. After a particularly rough season in 2022, she decided to dive back into writing—and found out that she apparently has a lot to say.

To stay up to date on upcoming work from Lindsey N. Rhoden, be sure to follow her on social media @bootrovertbynature or check out her website at www.lindseynrhoden.com

www.ingramcontent.com/pod-product-compliance
Lightning Source LLC
Chambersburg PA
CBHW061854310726
48972CB00004B/1023